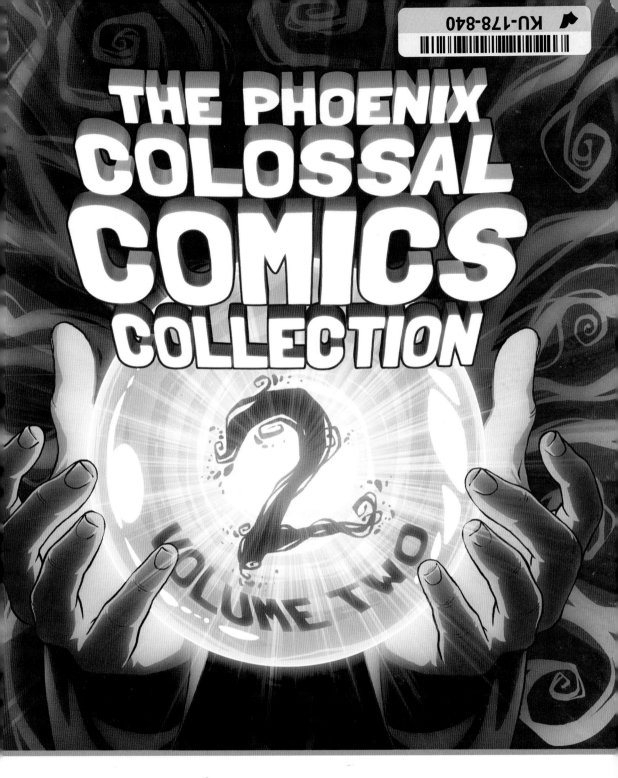

THE PHOENIX COLOSSAL COMICS COLLECTION

2

VOLUME TWO

FICKLING

d|b

David Fickling Books

the PHOENIX

SCHOLASTIC

First published in the United Kingdom as comic book issues by
The Phoenix Comic, 29 Beaumont Street, Oxford OX1 2NP.

Library of Congress Cataloging-in-Publication Data available

ISBN 978-1-338-20680-7

10 9 8 7 6 5 4 3 2 1   18 19 20 21 22

Printed in China 38
First edition, September 2018

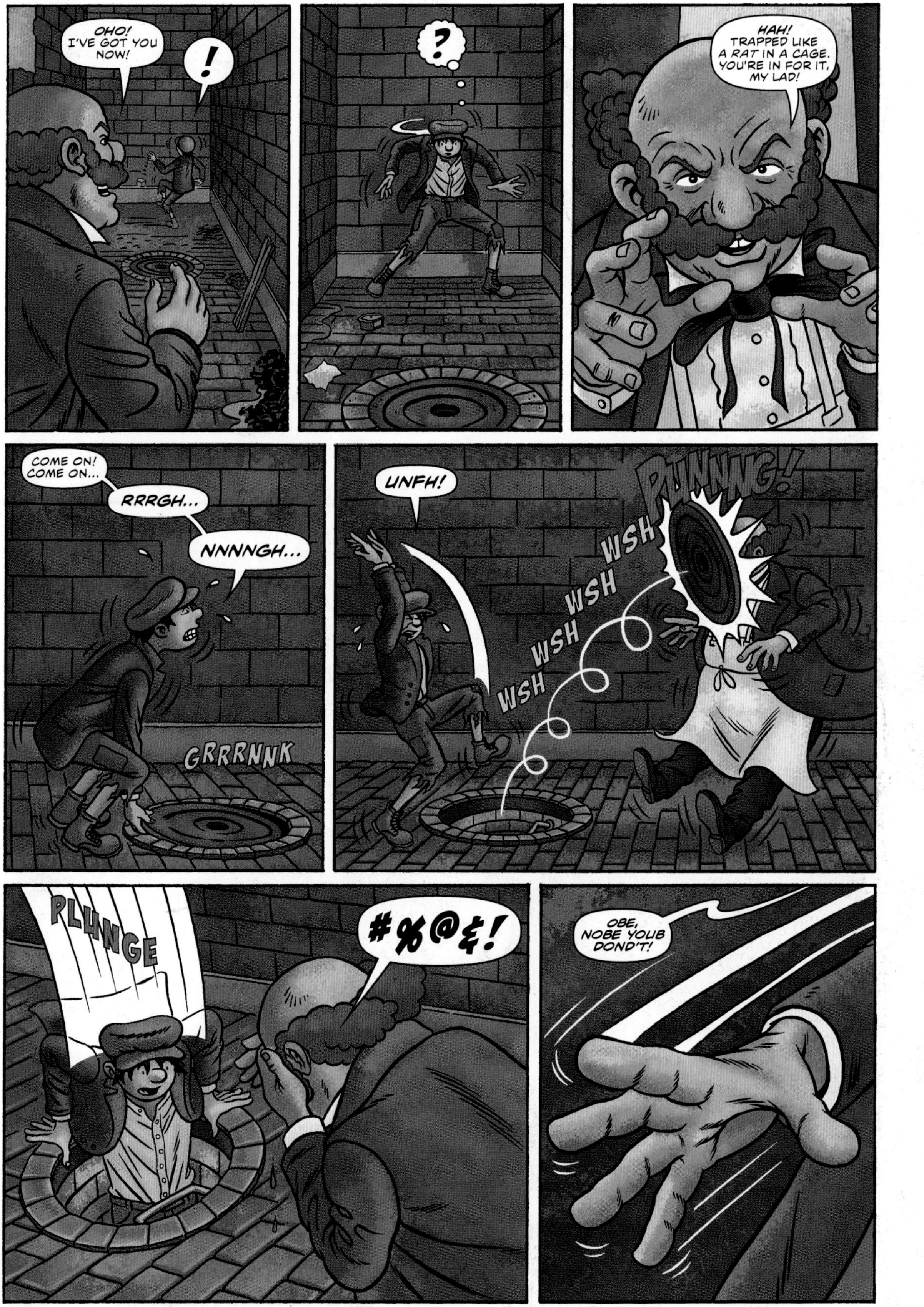
OHO! I'VE GOT YOU NOW!
!
?
HAH! TRAPPED LIKE A RAT IN A CAGE. YOU'RE IN FOR IT, MY LAD!
COME ON! COME ON...
RRRGH...
NNNNGH...
GRRRNNK
UNFH!
BUNNNG!
WSH
WSH
WSH
WSH
WSH
PLUNGE
#%@&!
OBE, NOBE YOUB DOND'T!

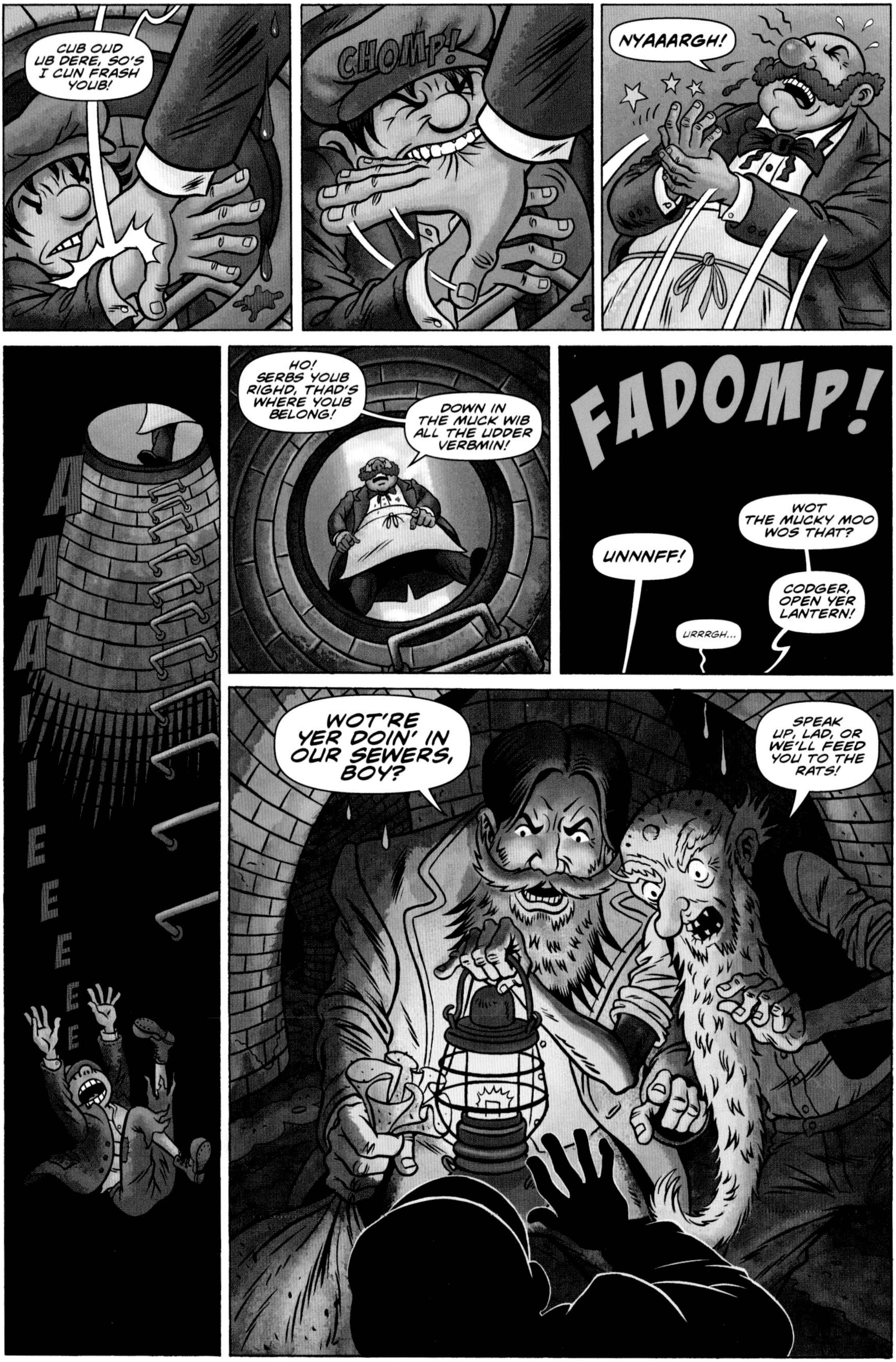
CUB OUD UB DERE, SO'S I CUN FRASH YOUB!
CHOMP!
NYAAARGH!
AAAAAIIEEEEEE
HO! SERBS YOUB RIGHD, THAD'S WHERE YOUB BELONG!
DOWN IN THE MUCK WIB ALL THE UDDER VERBMIN!
FADOMP!
UNNNFF!
WOT THE MUCKY MOO WOS THAT?
CODGER, OPEN YER LANTERN!
URRRGH...
WOT'RE YER DOIN' IN OUR SEWERS, BOY?
SPEAK UP, LAD, OR WE'LL FEED YOU TO THE RATS!

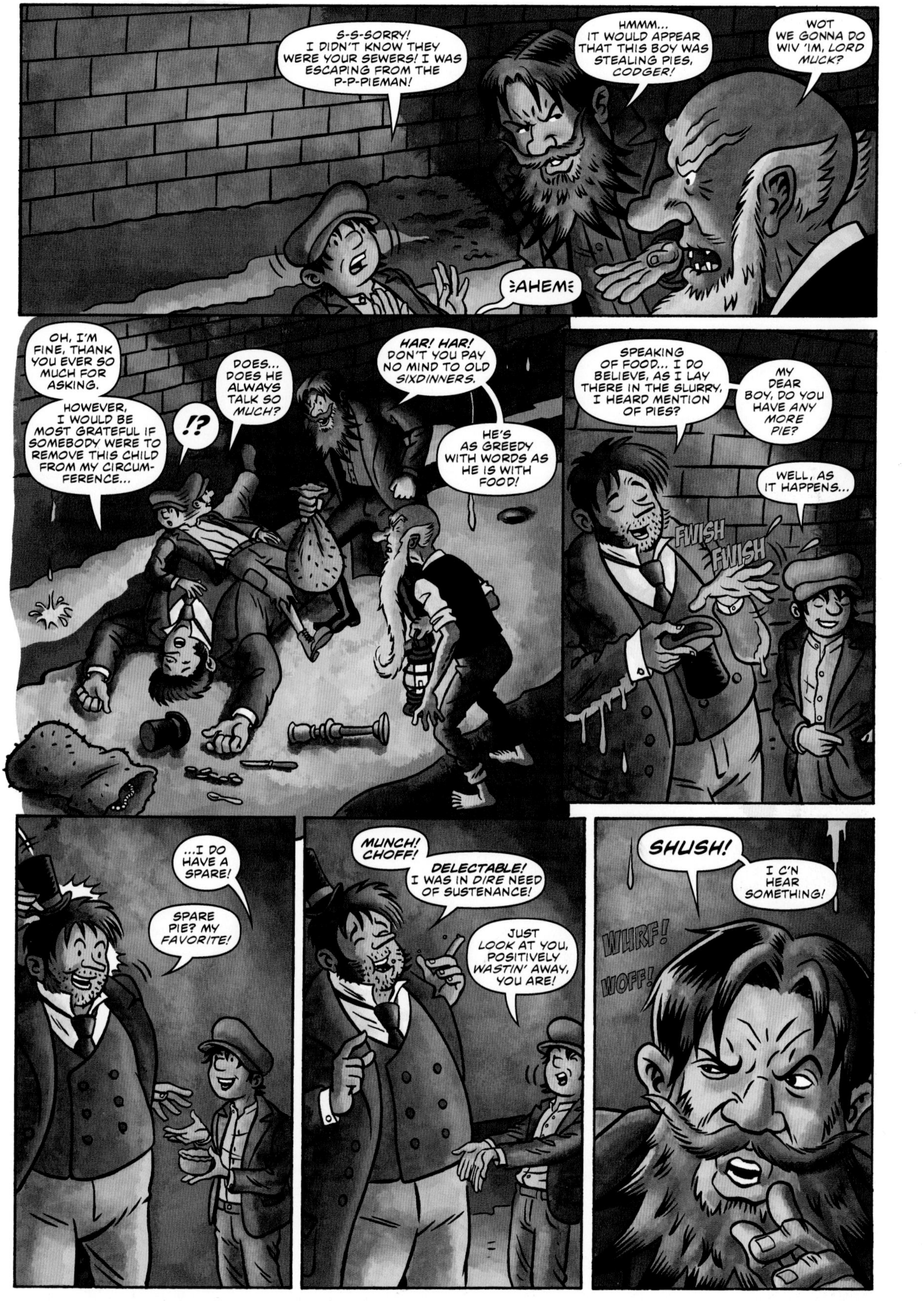
S-S-SORRY! I DIDN'T KNOW THEY WERE YOUR SEWERS! I WAS ESCAPING FROM THE P-P-PIEMAN!
HMMM... IT WOULD APPEAR THAT THIS BOY WAS STEALING PIES, CODGER!
WOT WE GONNA DO WIV 'IM, LORD MUCK?
AHEM
OH, I'M FINE, THANK YOU EVER SO MUCH FOR ASKING.
HOWEVER, I WOULD BE MOST GRATEFUL IF SOMEBODY WERE TO REMOVE THIS CHILD FROM MY CIRCUMFERENCE...
!?
DOES... DOES HE ALWAYS TALK SO MUCH?
HAR! HAR! DON'T YOU PAY NO MIND TO OLD SIXDINNERS.
HE'S AS GREEDY WITH WORDS AS HE IS WITH FOOD!
SPEAKING OF FOOD... I DO BELIEVE, AS I LAY THERE IN THE SLURRY, I HEARD MENTION OF PIES?
MY DEAR BOY, DO YOU HAVE ANY MORE PIE?
WELL, AS IT HAPPENS...
FWISH FWISH
...I DO HAVE A SPARE!
SPARE PIE? MY FAVORITE!
MUNCH! CHOFF!
DELECTABLE! I WAS IN DIRE NEED OF SUSTENANCE!
JUST LOOK AT YOU, POSITIVELY WASTIN' AWAY, YOU ARE!
SHUSH!
I C'N HEAR SOMETHING!
WURF!
WOFF!

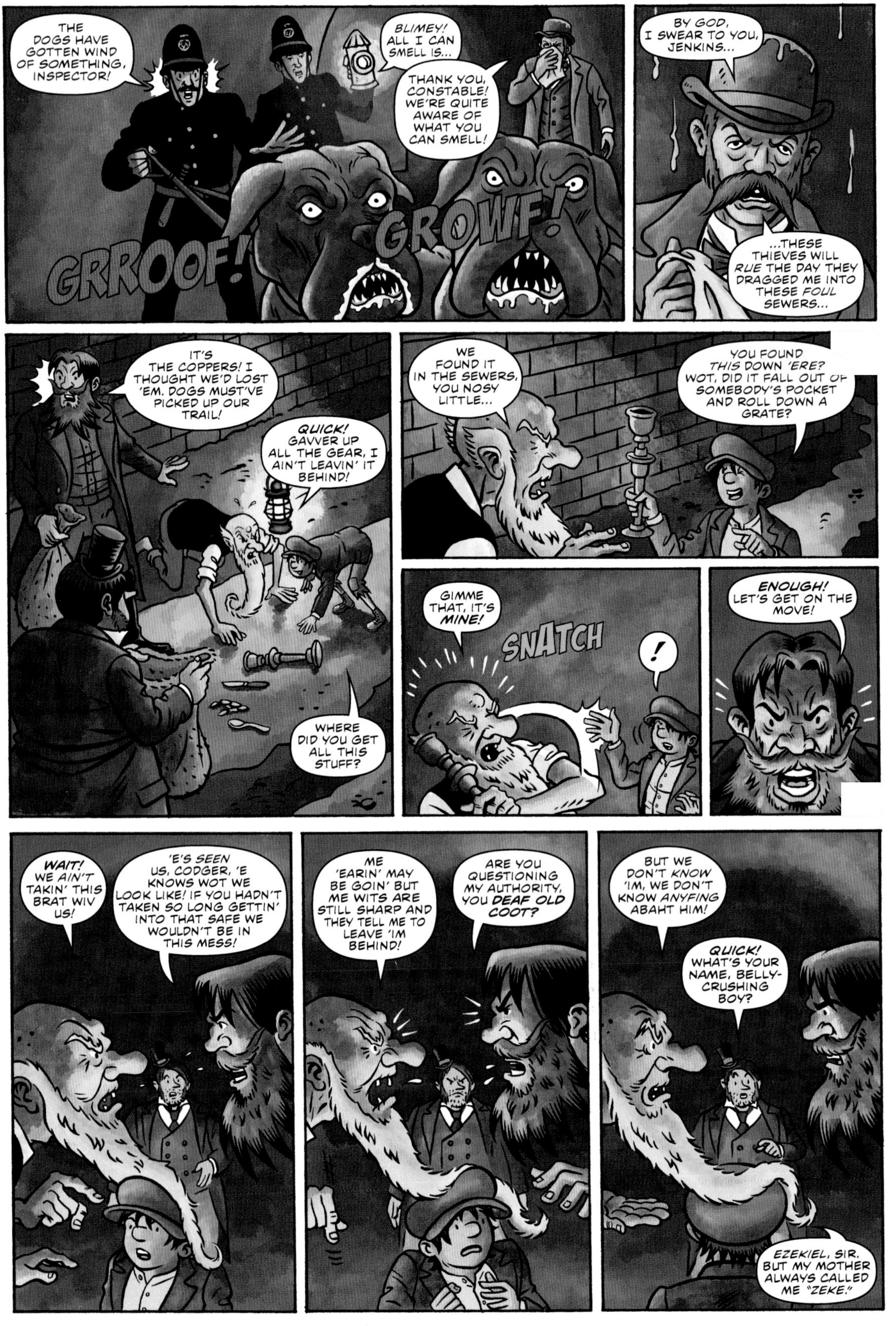
THE DOGS HAVE GOTTEN WIND OF SOMETHING, INSPECTOR!
BLIMEY! ALL I CAN SMELL IS...
THANK YOU, CONSTABLE! WE'RE QUITE AWARE OF WHAT YOU CAN SMELL!
GRROOF!
GROWF!
BY GOD, I SWEAR TO YOU, JENKINS...
...THESE THIEVES WILL *RUE* THE DAY THEY DRAGGED ME INTO THESE *FOUL* SEWERS...
IT'S THE COPPERS! I THOUGHT WE'D LOST 'EM. DOGS MUST'VE PICKED UP OUR TRAIL!
QUICK! GAVVER UP ALL THE GEAR, I AIN'T LEAVIN' IT BEHIND!
WHERE DID YOU GET ALL THIS STUFF?
WE FOUND IT IN THE SEWERS, YOU NOSY LITTLE...
YOU FOUND *THIS DOWN 'ERE?* WOT, DID IT FALL OUT OF SOMEBODY'S POCKET AND ROLL DOWN A GRATE?
GIMME THAT, IT'S ***MINE!***
SNATCH
!
ENOUGH! LET'S GET ON THE MOVE!
WAIT! WE *AIN'T* TAKIN' THIS BRAT WIV US!
'E'S *SEEN* US, CODGER, 'E KNOWS WOT WE LOOK LIKE! IF YOU HADN'T TAKEN SO LONG GETTIN' INTO THAT SAFE WE WOULDN'T BE IN THIS MESS!
ME 'EARIN' MAY BE GOIN' BUT ME WITS ARE STILL SHARP AND THEY TELL ME TO LEAVE 'IM BEHIND!
ARE YOU QUESTIONING MY AUTHORITY, YOU ***DEAF OLD COOT?***
BUT WE DON'T *KNOW* 'IM, WE DON'T KNOW *ANYFING* ABAHT HIM!
QUICK! WHAT'S YOUR NAME, BELLY-CRUSHING BOY?
EZEKIEL, SIR. BUT MY MOTHER ALWAYS CALLED ME "ZEKE."

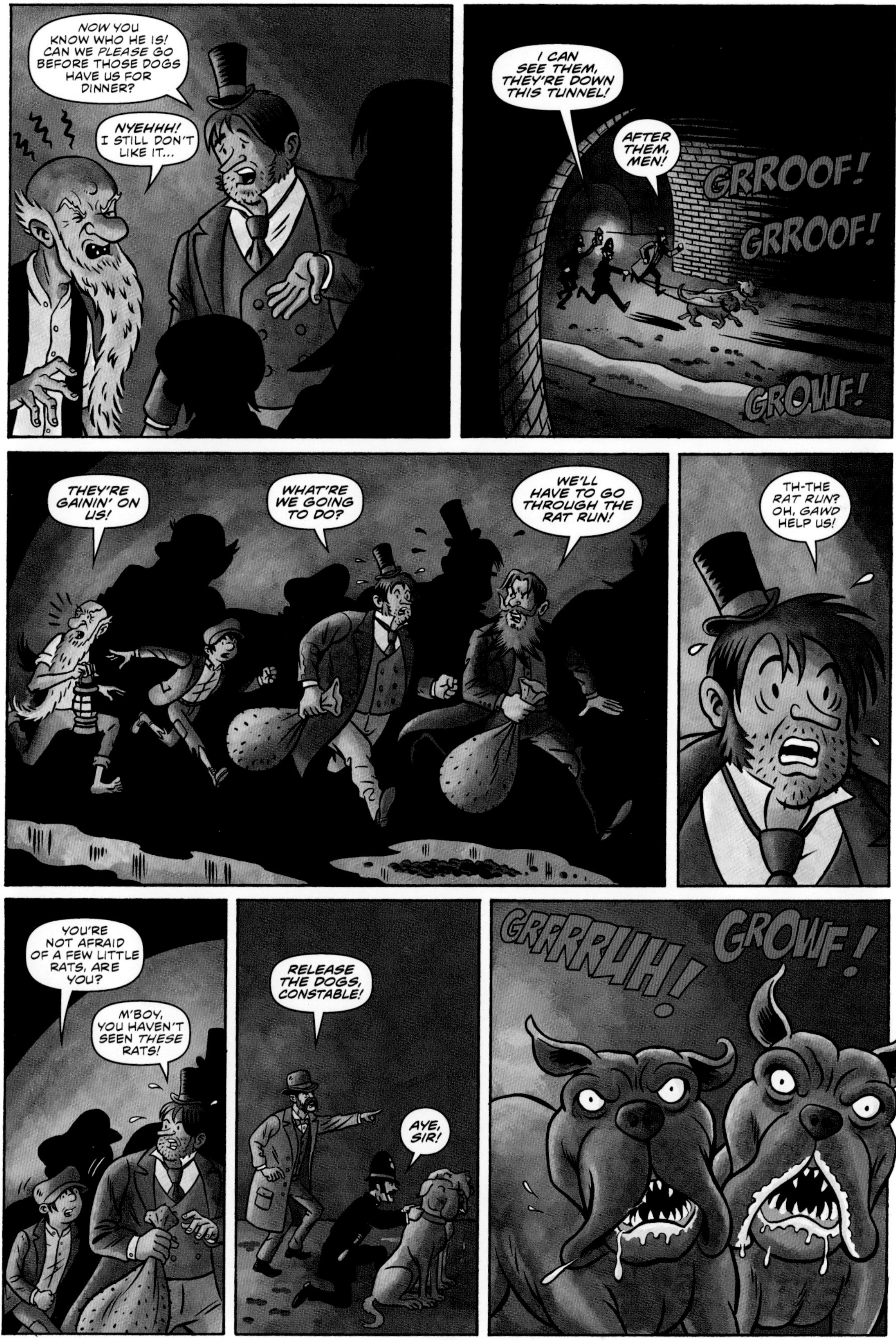
NOW YOU KNOW WHO HE IS! CAN WE PLEASE GO BEFORE THOSE DOGS HAVE US FOR DINNER?
NYEHHH! I STILL DON'T LIKE IT...
I CAN SEE THEM, THEY'RE DOWN THIS TUNNEL!
AFTER THEM, MEN!
GRROOF!
GRROOF!
GROWF!
THEY'RE GAININ' ON US!
WHAT'RE WE GOING TO DO?
WE'LL HAVE TO GO THROUGH THE RAT RUN!
TH-THE RAT RUN? OH, GAWD HELP US!
YOU'RE NOT AFRAID OF A FEW LITTLE RATS, ARE YOU?
M'BOY, YOU HAVEN'T SEEN THESE RATS!
RELEASE THE DOGS, CONSTABLE!
AYE, SIR!
GRRRRUH!
GROWF!

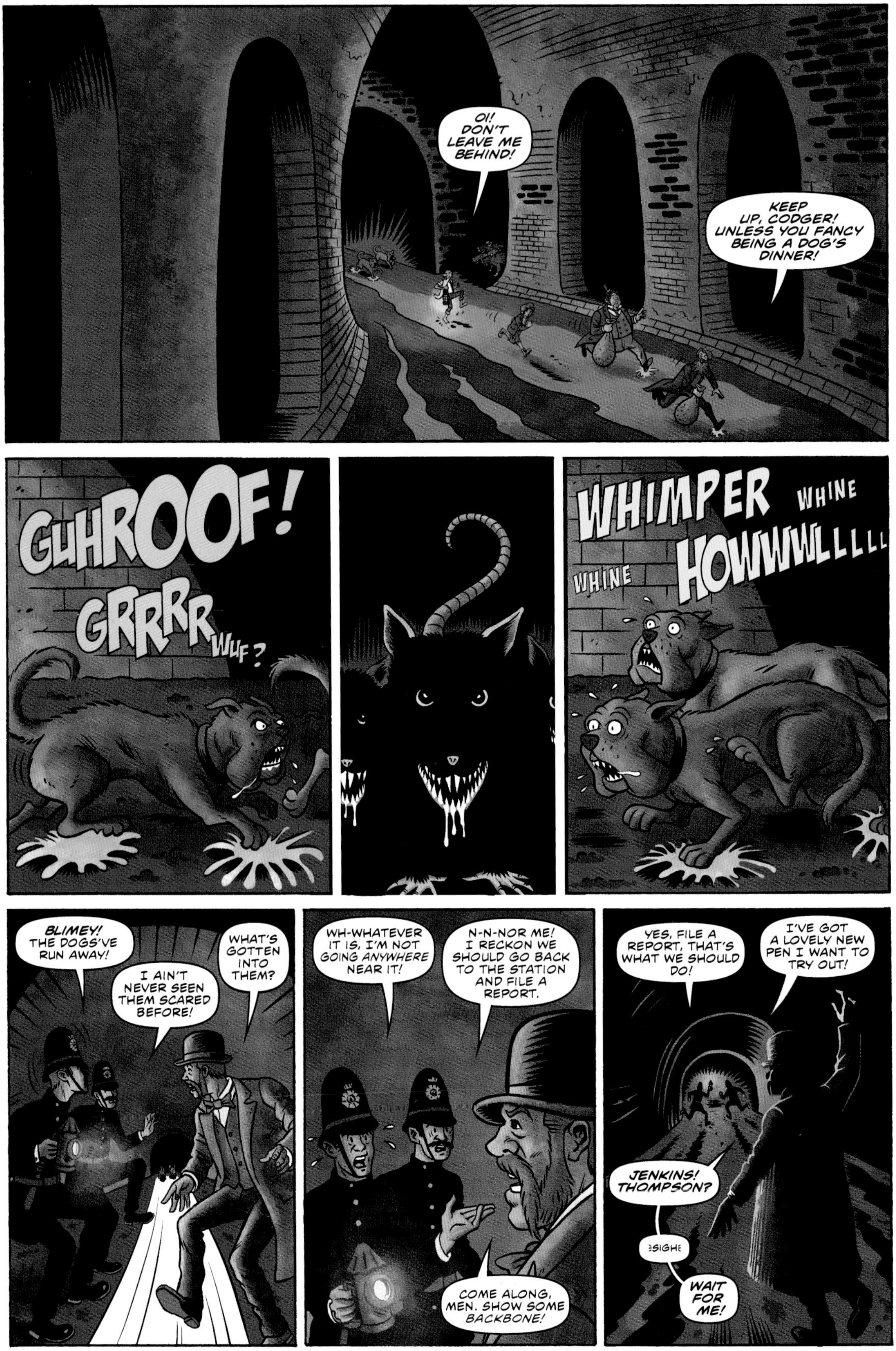
OI! DON'T LEAVE ME BEHIND!
KEEP UP, CODGER! UNLESS YOU FANCY BEING A DOG'S DINNER!
GUHROOF!
GRRRR
WUF?
WHIMPER
WHINE
WHINE
HOWWWLLLLL
BLIMEY! THE DOGS'VE RUN AWAY!
I AIN'T NEVER SEEN THEM SCARED BEFORE!
WHAT'S GOTTEN INTO THEM?
WH-WHATEVER IT IS, I'M NOT GOING ANYWHERE NEAR IT!
N-N-NOR ME! I RECKON WE SHOULD GO BACK TO THE STATION AND FILE A REPORT.
COME ALONG, MEN. SHOW SOME BACKBONE!
YES, FILE A REPORT, THAT'S WHAT WE SHOULD DO!
I'VE GOT A LOVELY NEW PEN I WANT TO TRY OUT!
JENKINS! THOMPSON?
SIGH
WAIT FOR ME!

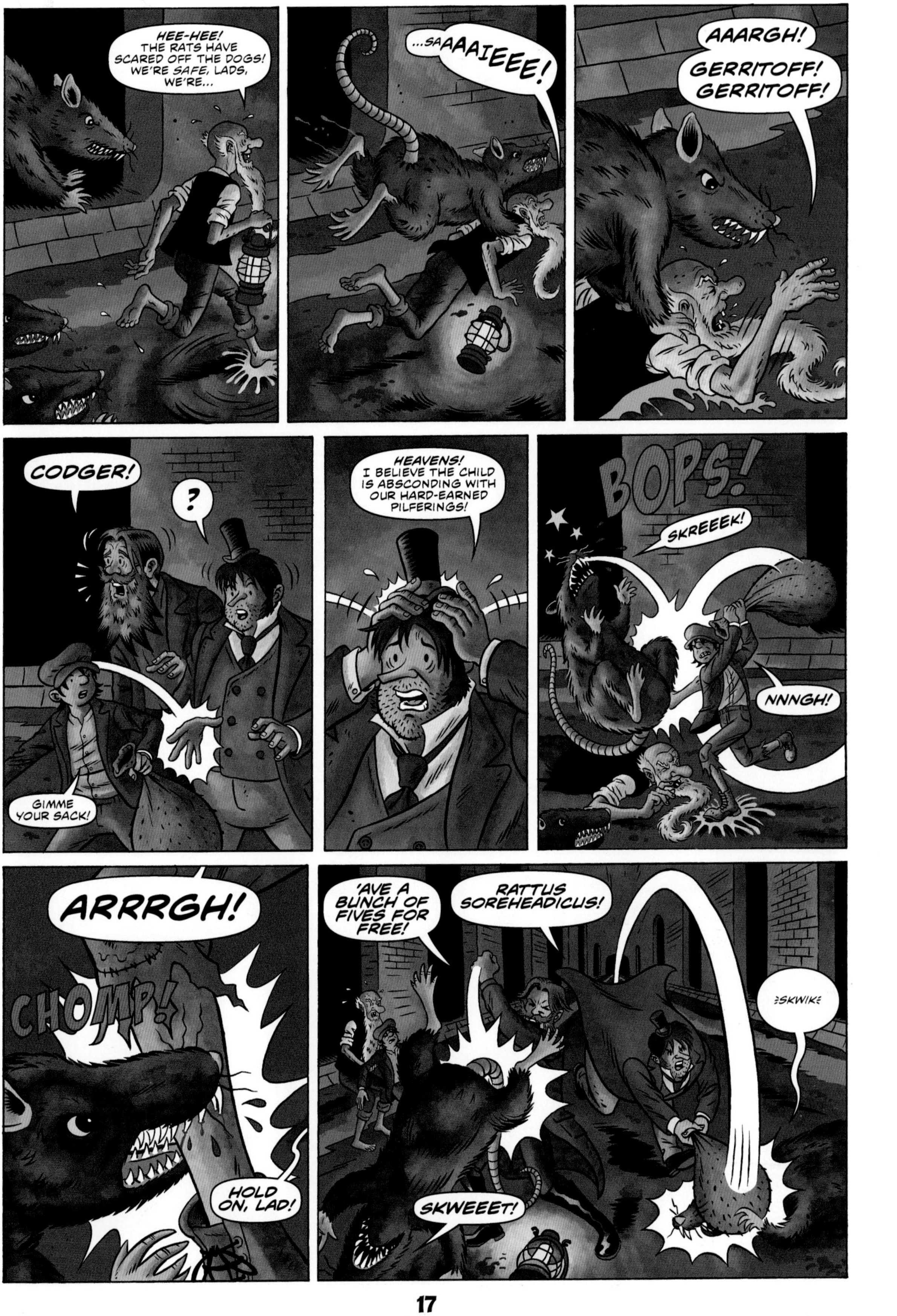
HEE-HEE! THE RATS HAVE SCARED OFF THE DOGS! WE'RE SAFE, LADS, WE'RE...
...SAAAAAIEEE!
AAARGH! GERRITOFF! GERRITOFF!
CODGER!
?
GIMME YOUR SACK!
HEAVENS! I BELIEVE THE CHILD IS ABSCONDING WITH OUR HARD-EARNED PILFERINGS!
BOPS!
SKREEEK!
NNNGH!
ARRRGH!
CHOMP!
HOLD ON, LAD!
'AVE A BUNCH OF FIVES FOR FREE!
RATTUS SOREHEADICUS!
SKWIK
SKWEEET!

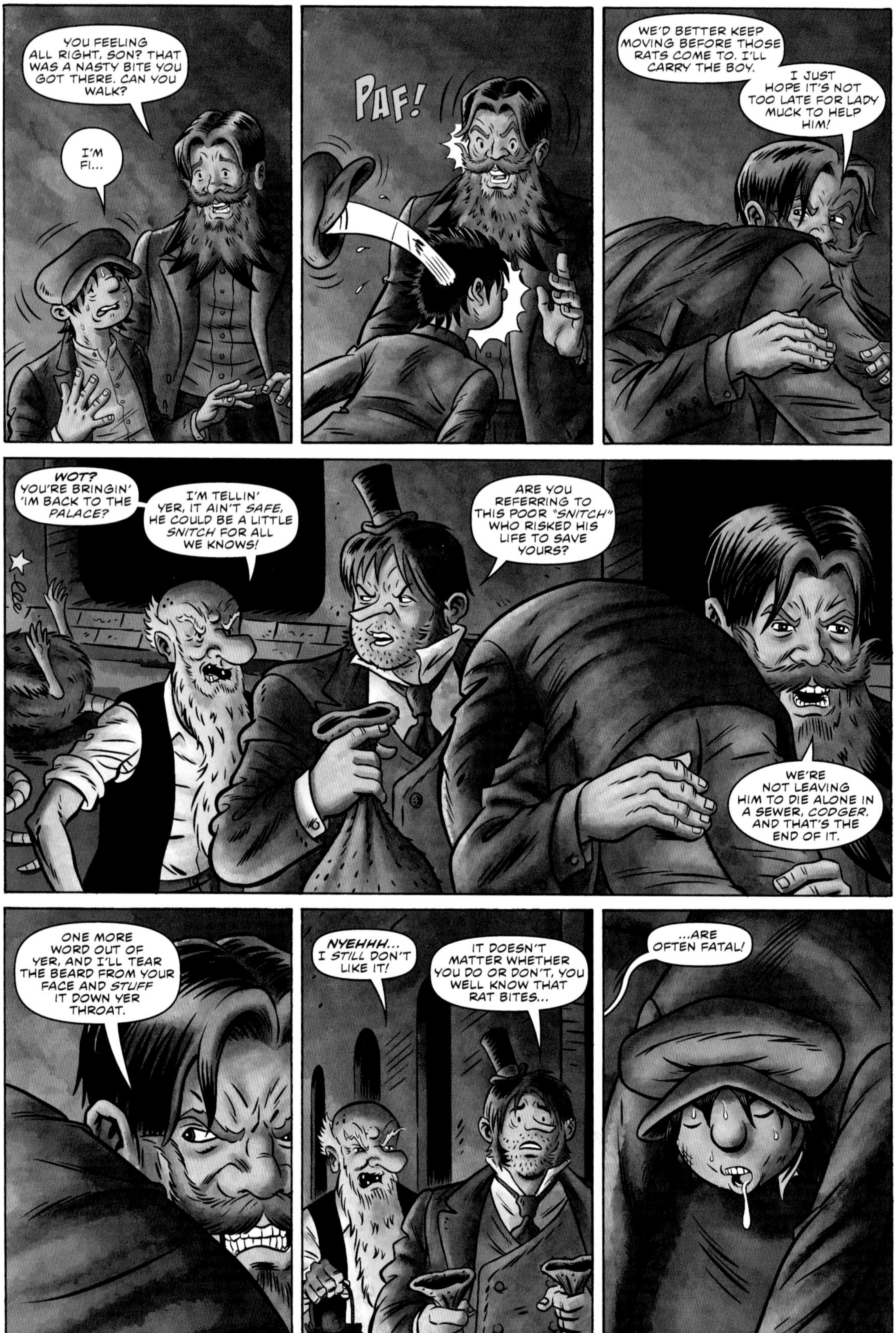
YOU FEELING ALL RIGHT, SON? THAT WAS A NASTY BITE YOU GOT THERE. CAN YOU WALK?
I'M FI...
PAF!
WE'D BETTER KEEP MOVING BEFORE THOSE RATS COME TO. I'LL CARRY THE BOY.
I JUST HOPE IT'S NOT TOO LATE FOR LADY MUCK TO HELP HIM!
WOT? YOU'RE BRINGIN' 'IM BACK TO THE PALACE?
I'M TELLIN' YER, IT AIN'T SAFE, HE COULD BE A LITTLE SNITCH FOR ALL WE KNOWS!
ARE YOU REFERRING TO THIS POOR "SNITCH" WHO RISKED HIS LIFE TO SAVE YOURS?
WE'RE NOT LEAVING HIM TO DIE ALONE IN A SEWER, CODGER. AND THAT'S THE END OF IT.
ONE MORE WORD OUT OF YER, AND I'LL TEAR THE BEARD FROM YOUR FACE AND STUFF IT DOWN YER THROAT.
NYEHHH... I STILL DON'T LIKE IT!
IT DOESN'T MATTER WHETHER YOU DO OR DON'T, YOU WELL KNOW THAT RAT BITES...
...ARE OFTEN FATAL!

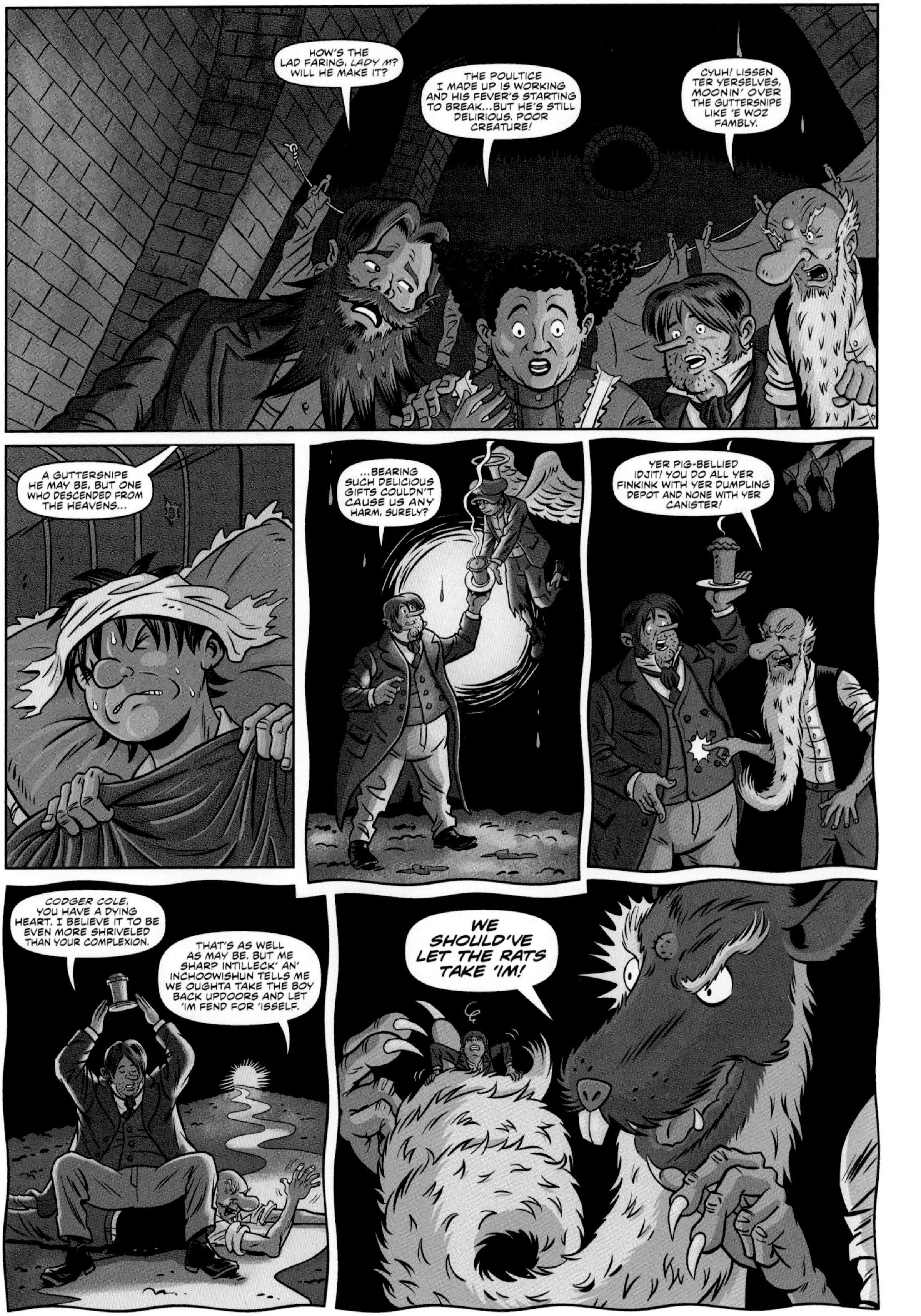
HOW'S THE LAD FARING, LADY M? WILL HE MAKE IT?
THE POULTICE I MADE UP IS WORKING AND HIS FEVER'S STARTING TO BREAK...BUT HE'S STILL DELIRIOUS. POOR CREATURE!
CYUH! LISSEN TER YERSELVES, MOONIN' OVER THE GUTTERSNIPE LIKE 'E WOZ FAMBLY.
A GUTTERSNIPE HE MAY BE, BUT ONE WHO DESCENDED FROM THE HEAVENS...
...BEARING SUCH DELICIOUS GIFTS COULDN'T CAUSE US ANY HARM, SURELY?
YER PIG-BELLIED IDJIT! YOU DO ALL YER FINKINK WITH YER DUMPLING DEPOT AND NONE WITH YER CANISTER!
CODGER COLE, YOU HAVE A DYING HEART. I BELIEVE IT TO BE EVEN MORE SHRIVELED THAN YOUR COMPLEXION.
THAT'S AS WELL AS MAY BE. BUT ME SHARP INTILLECK' AN' INCHOOWISHUN TELLS ME WE OUGHTA TAKE THE BOY BACK UPDOORS AND LET 'IM FEND FOR 'ISSELF.
WE SHOULD'VE LET THE RATS TAKE 'IM!

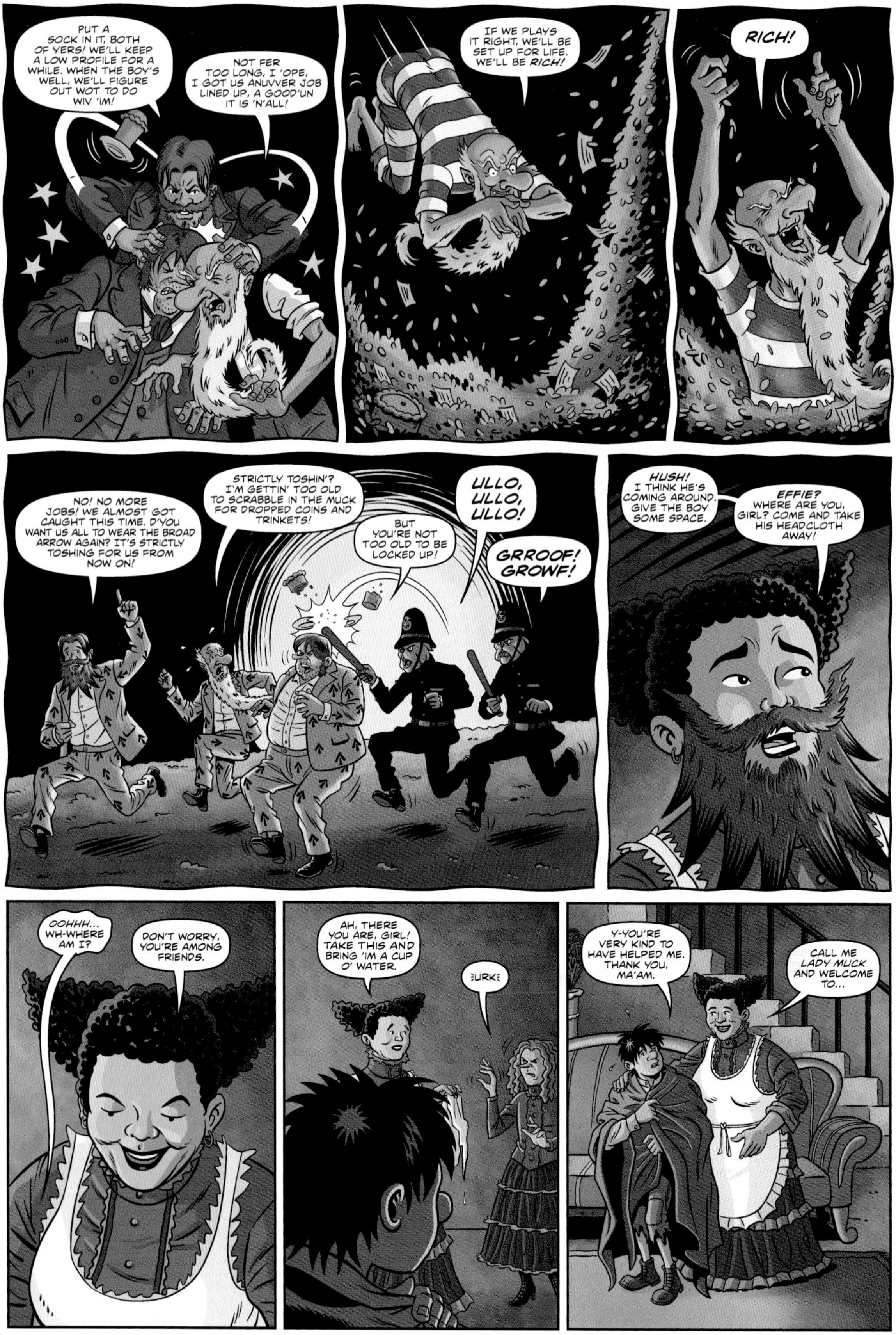
PUT A SOCK IN IT, BOTH OF YERS! WE'LL KEEP A LOW PROFILE FOR A WHILE. WHEN THE BOY'S WELL, WE'LL FIGURE OUT WOT TO DO WIV 'IM!
NOT FER TOO LONG, I 'OPE, I GOT US ANUVVER JOB LINED UP, A GOOD'UN IT IS 'N'ALL!
IF WE PLAYS IT RIGHT, WE'LL BE SET UP FOR LIFE. WE'LL BE RICH!
RICH!
NO! NO MORE JOBS! WE ALMOST GOT CAUGHT THIS TIME. D'YOU WANT US ALL TO WEAR THE BROAD ARROW AGAIN? IT'S STRICTLY TOSHING FOR US FROM NOW ON!
STRICTLY TOSHIN'? I'M GETTIN' TOO OLD TO SCRABBLE IN THE MUCK FOR DROPPED COINS AND TRINKETS!
BUT YOU'RE NOT TOO OLD TO BE LOCKED UP!
ULLO, ULLO, ULLO!
GRROOF! GROWF!
HUSH! I THINK HE'S COMING AROUND. GIVE THE BOY SOME SPACE.
EFFIE? WHERE ARE YOU, GIRL? COME AND TAKE HIS HEADCLOTH AWAY!
OOHHH... WH-WHERE AM I?
DON'T WORRY, YOU'RE AMONG FRIENDS.
AH, THERE YOU ARE, GIRL! TAKE THIS AND BRING 'IM A CUP O' WATER.
URK
Y-YOU'RE VERY KIND TO HAVE HELPED ME. THANK YOU, MA'AM.
CALL ME LADY MUCK AND WELCOME TO...

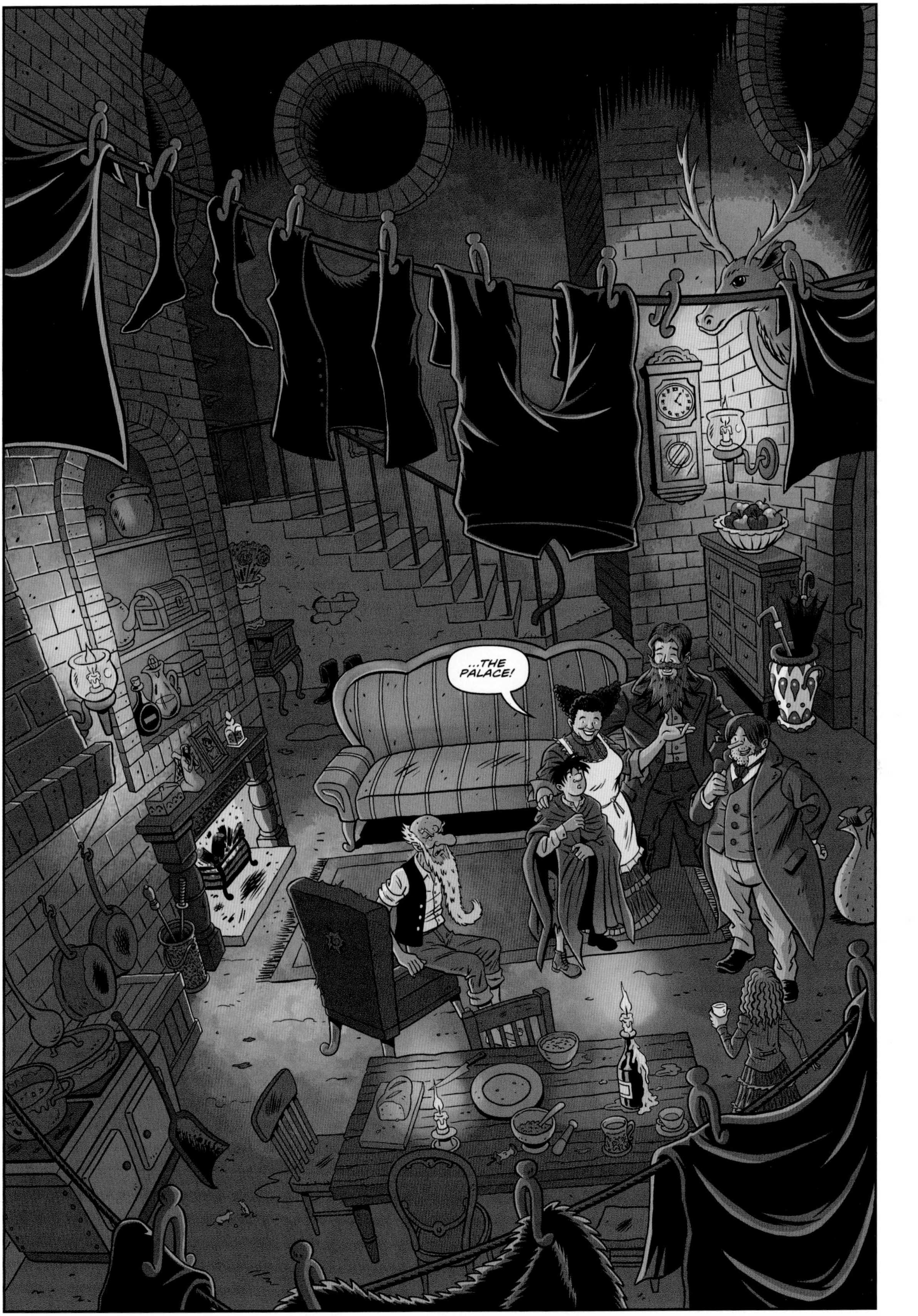
...THE PALACE!

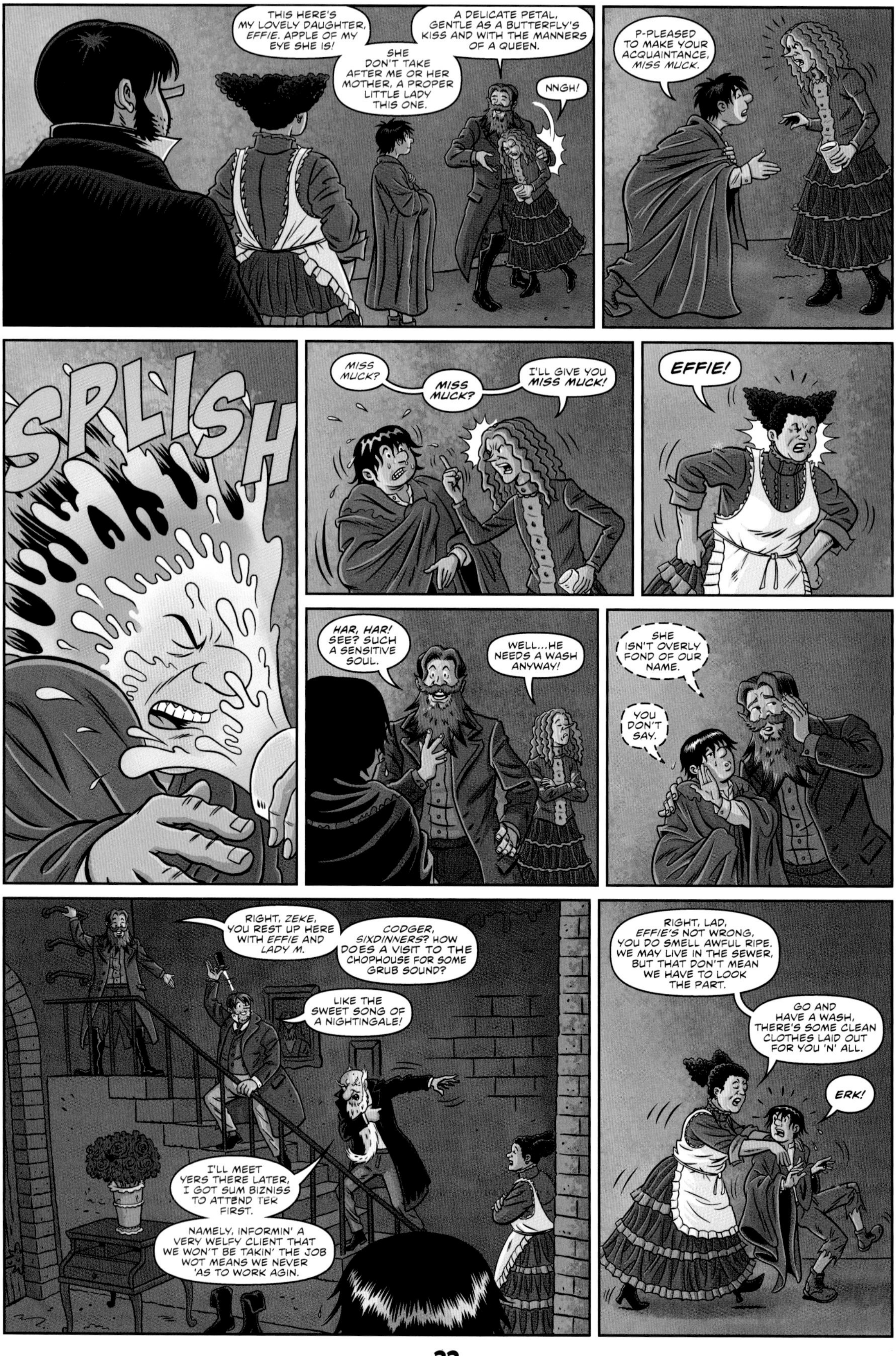
THIS HERE'S MY LOVELY DAUGHTER, EFFIE. APPLE OF MY EYE SHE IS!
SHE DON'T TAKE AFTER ME OR HER MOTHER, A PROPER LITTLE LADY THIS ONE.
A DELICATE PETAL, GENTLE AS A BUTTERFLY'S KISS AND WITH THE MANNERS OF A QUEEN.
NNGH!
P-PLEASED TO MAKE YOUR ACQUAINTANCE, MISS MUCK.
SPLISH
MISS MUCK?
MISS MUCK?
I'LL GIVE YOU MISS MUCK!
EFFIE!
HAR, HAR! SEE? SUCH A SENSITIVE SOUL.
WELL...HE NEEDS A WASH ANYWAY!
SHE ISN'T OVERLY FOND OF OUR NAME.
YOU DON'T SAY.
RIGHT, ZEKE, YOU REST UP HERE WITH EFFIE AND LADY M.
CODGER, SIXDINNERS? HOW DOES A VISIT TO THE CHOPHOUSE FOR SOME GRUB SOUND?
LIKE THE SWEET SONG OF A NIGHTINGALE!
I'LL MEET YERS THERE LATER, I GOT SUM BIZNISS TO ATTEND TER FIRST.
NAMELY, INFORMIN' A VERY WELFY CLIENT THAT WE WON'T BE TAKIN' THE JOB WOT MEANS WE NEVER 'AS TO WORK AGIN.
RIGHT, LAD, EFFIE'S NOT WRONG, YOU DO SMELL AWFUL RIPE. WE MAY LIVE IN THE SEWER, BUT THAT DON'T MEAN WE HAVE TO LOOK THE PART.
GO AND HAVE A WASH, THERE'S SOME CLEAN CLOTHES LAID OUT FOR YOU 'N' ALL.
ERK!

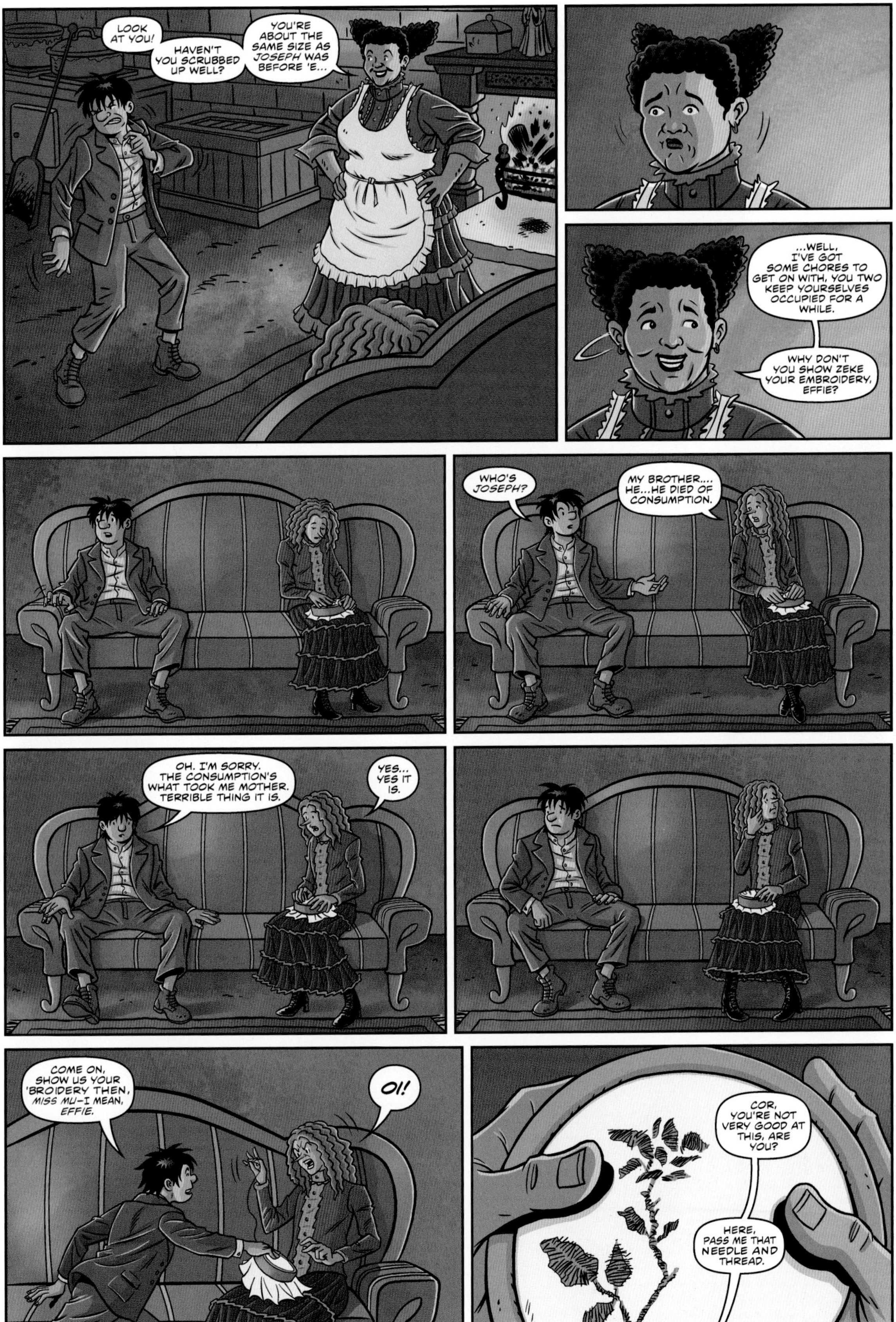
LOOK AT YOU!
HAVEN'T YOU SCRUBBED UP WELL?
YOU'RE ABOUT THE SAME SIZE AS JOSEPH WAS BEFORE 'E...
...WELL, I'VE GOT SOME CHORES TO GET ON WITH, YOU TWO KEEP YOURSELVES OCCUPIED FOR A WHILE.
WHY DON'T YOU SHOW ZEKE YOUR EMBROIDERY, EFFIE?
WHO'S JOSEPH?
MY BROTHER.... HE...HE DIED OF CONSUMPTION.
OH. I'M SORRY. THE CONSUMPTION'S WHAT TOOK ME MOTHER. TERRIBLE THING IT IS.
YES... YES IT IS.
COME ON, SHOW US YOUR 'BROIDERY THEN, MISS MU–I MEAN, EFFIE.
OI!
COR, YOU'RE NOT VERY GOOD AT THIS, ARE YOU?
HERE, PASS ME THAT NEEDLE AND THREAD.

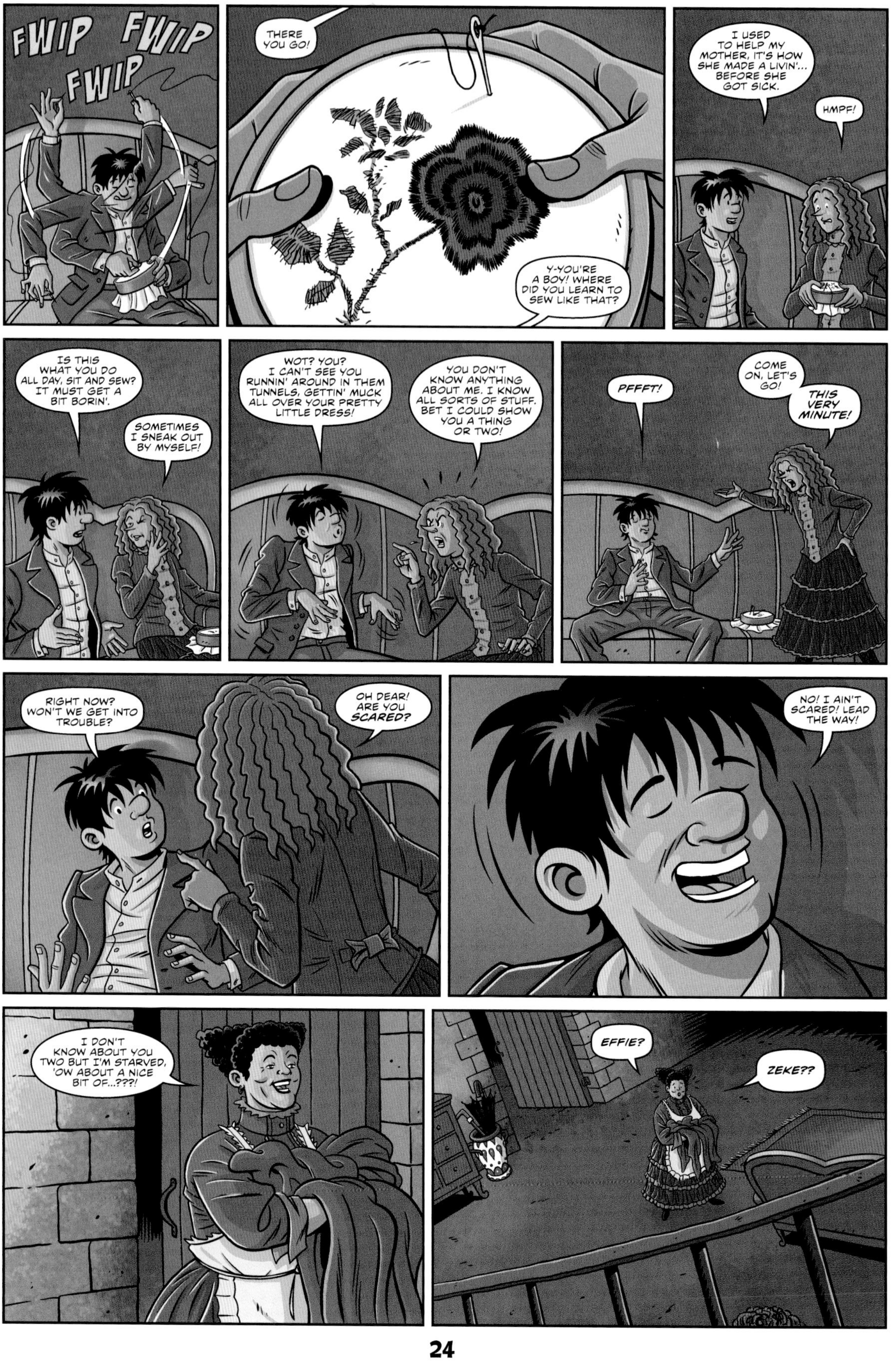
FWIP FWIP
FWIP
THERE YOU GO!
Y-YOU'RE A BOY! WHERE DID YOU LEARN TO SEW LIKE THAT?
I USED TO HELP MY MOTHER, IT'S HOW SHE MADE A LIVIN'... BEFORE SHE GOT SICK.
HMPF!
IS THIS WHAT YOU DO ALL DAY, SIT AND SEW? IT MUST GET A BIT BORIN'.
SOMETIMES I SNEAK OUT BY MYSELF!
WOT? YOU? I CAN'T SEE YOU RUNNIN' AROUND IN THEM TUNNELS, GETTIN' MUCK ALL OVER YOUR PRETTY LITTLE DRESS!
YOU DON'T KNOW ANYTHING ABOUT ME. I KNOW ALL SORTS OF STUFF. BET I COULD SHOW YOU A THING OR TWO!
PFFFT!
COME ON, LET'S GO!
THIS VERY MINUTE!
RIGHT NOW? WON'T WE GET INTO TROUBLE?
OH DEAR! ARE YOU SCARED?
NO! I AIN'T SCARED! LEAD THE WAY!
I DON'T KNOW ABOUT YOU TWO BUT I'M STARVED, 'OW ABOUT A NICE BIT OF...???!
EFFIE?
ZEKE??

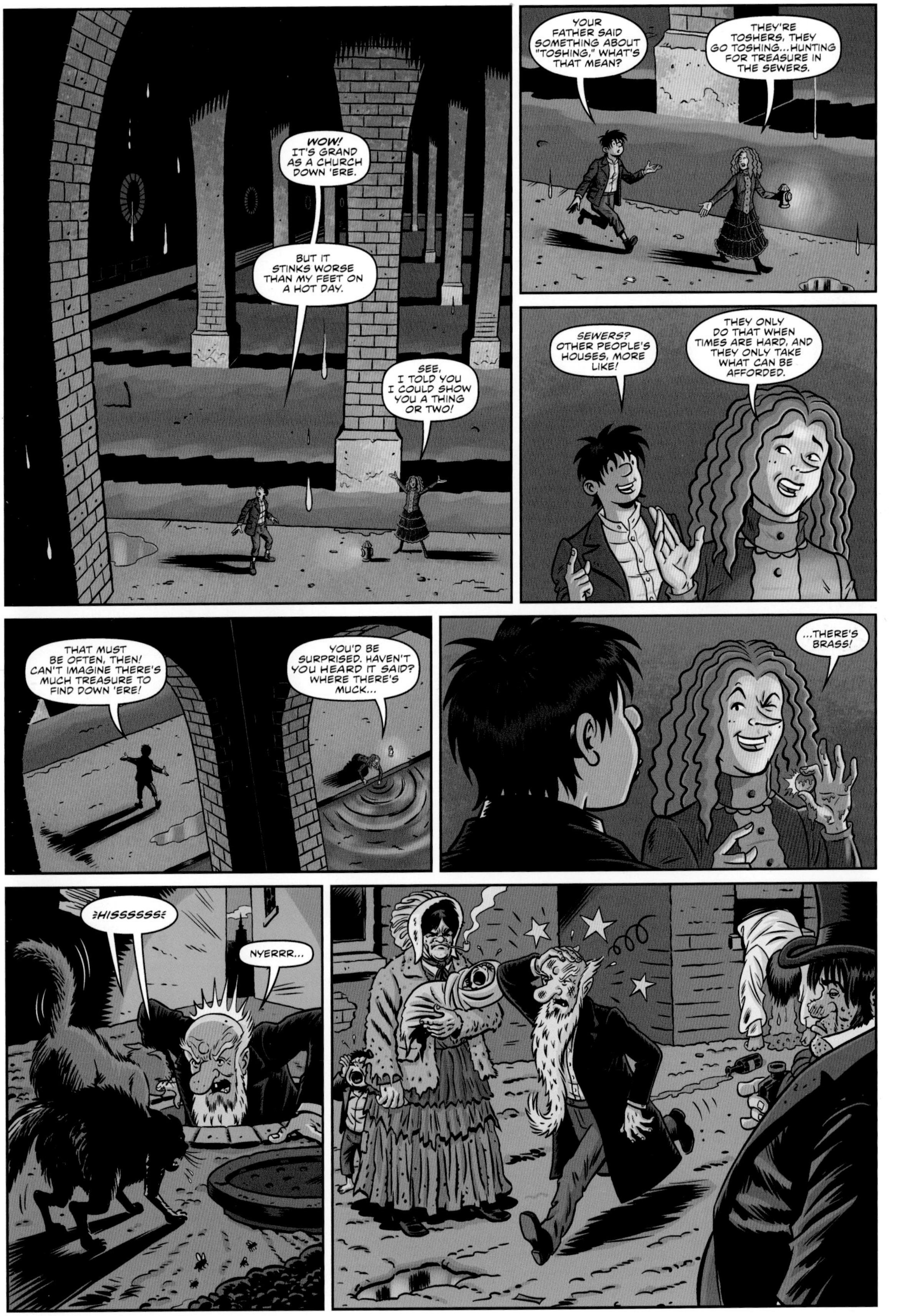
WOW! IT'S GRAND AS A CHURCH DOWN 'ERE.
BUT IT STINKS WORSE THAN MY FEET ON A HOT DAY.
SEE, I TOLD YOU I COULD SHOW YOU A THING OR TWO!
YOUR FATHER SAID SOMETHING ABOUT "TOSHING," WHAT'S THAT MEAN?
THEY'RE TOSHERS, THEY GO TOSHING...HUNTING FOR TREASURE IN THE SEWERS.
SEWERS? OTHER PEOPLE'S HOUSES, MORE LIKE!
THEY ONLY DO THAT WHEN TIMES ARE HARD, AND THEY ONLY TAKE WHAT CAN BE AFFORDED.
THAT MUST BE OFTEN, THEN! CAN'T IMAGINE THERE'S MUCH TREASURE TO FIND DOWN 'ERE!
YOU'D BE SURPRISED. HAVEN'T YOU HEARD IT SAID? WHERE THERE'S MUCK...
...THERE'S BRASS!
HISSSSSS
NYERRR...

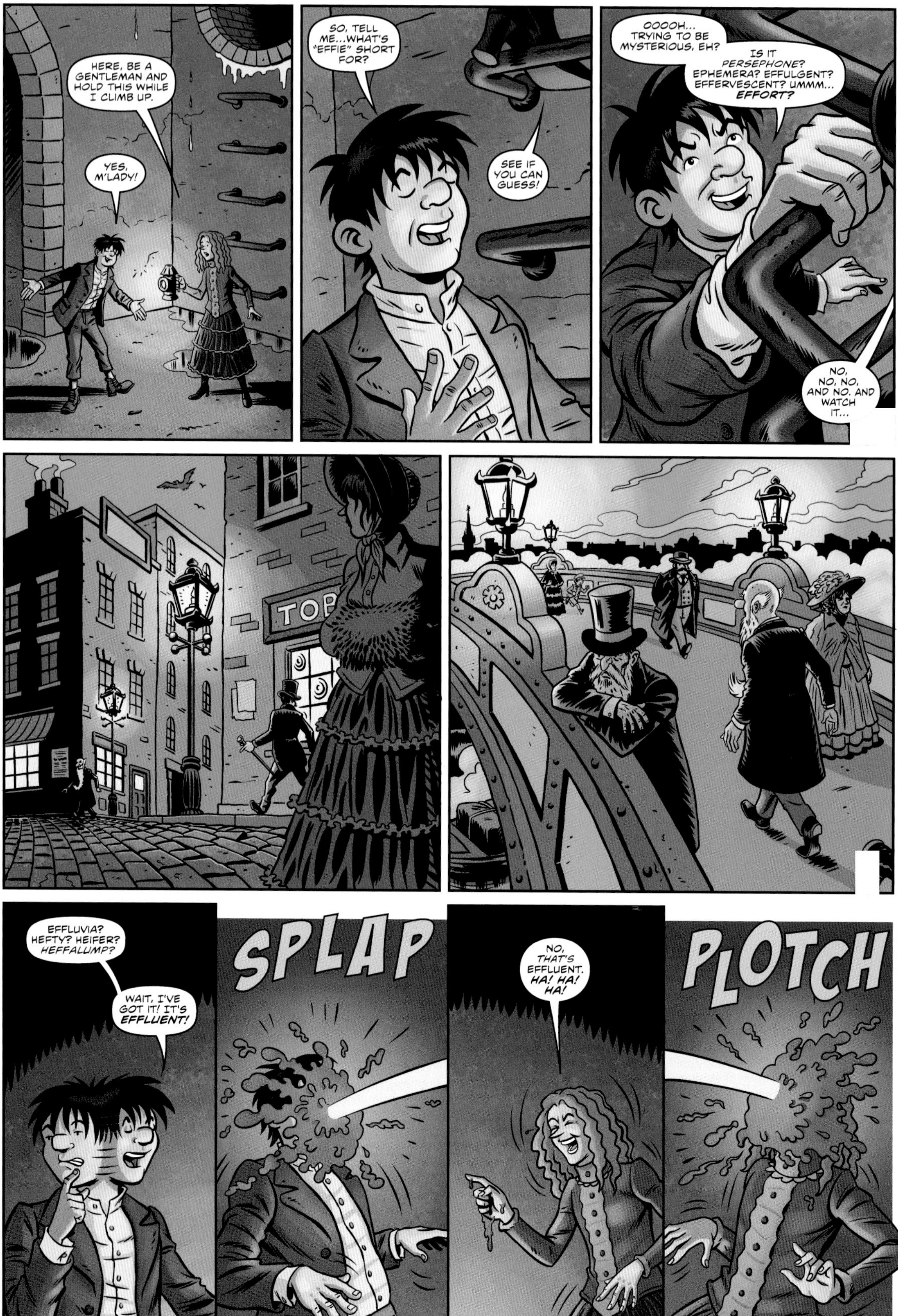
HERE, BE A GENTLEMAN AND HOLD THIS WHILE I CLIMB UP.
YES, M'LADY!
SO, TELL ME...WHAT'S "EFFIE" SHORT FOR?
SEE IF YOU CAN GUESS!
OOOOH... TRYING TO BE MYSTERIOUS, EH?
IS IT *PERSEPHONE?* EPHEMERA? EFFULGENT? EFFERVESCENT? UMMM... ***EFFORT?***
NO, NO, NO, AND NO. AND WATCH IT...
TOP
EFFLUVIA? HEFTY? HEIFER? *HEFFALUMP?*
WAIT, I'VE GOT IT! IT'S ***EFFLUENT!***
SPLAP
NO, THAT'S EFFLUENT. ***HA! HA! HA!***
PLOTCH

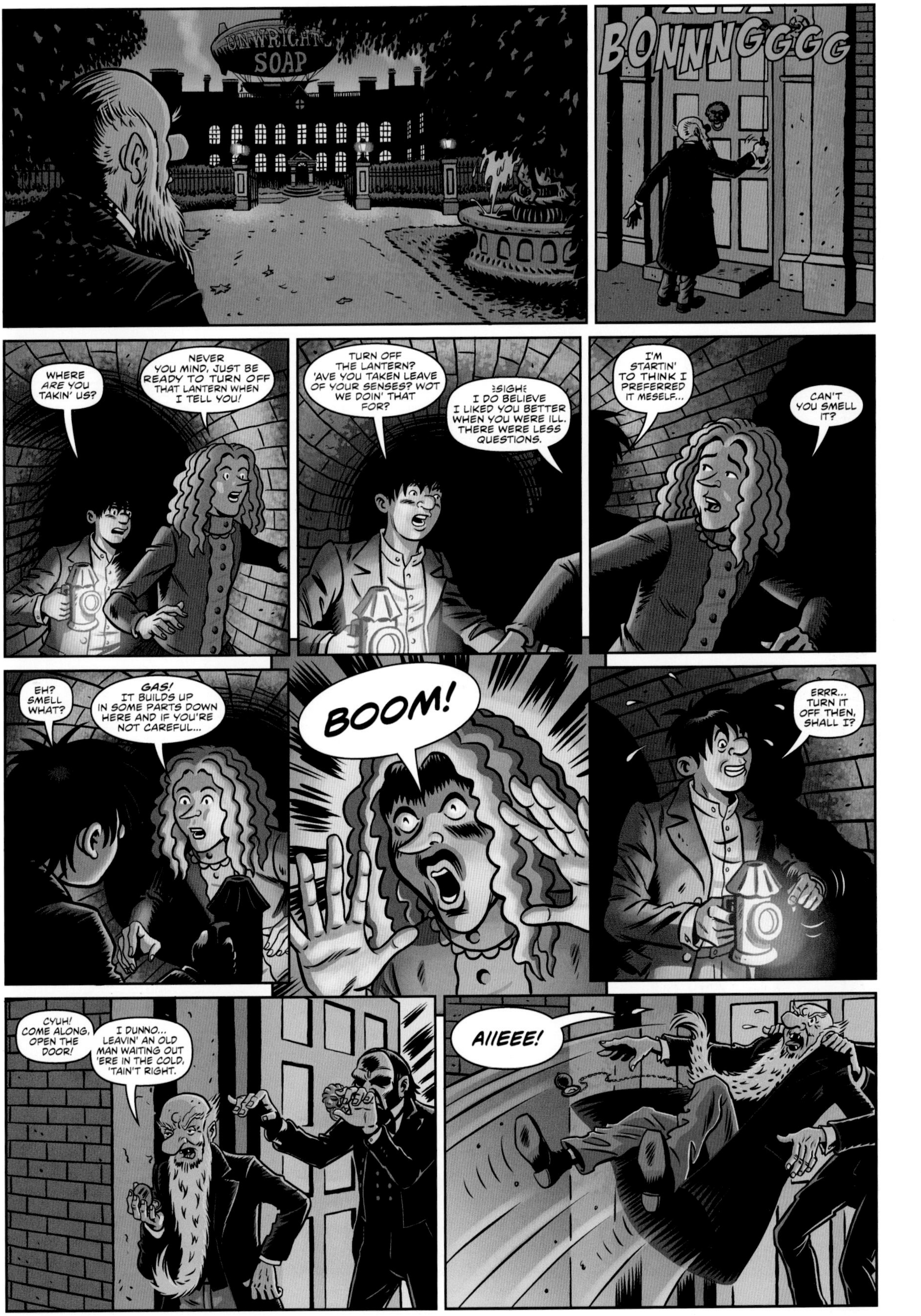

UNWRIGHT SOAP
BONNNGGGG
WHERE ARE YOU TAKIN' US?
NEVER YOU MIND, JUST BE READY TO TURN OFF THAT LANTERN WHEN I TELL YOU!
TURN OFF THE LANTERN? 'AVE YOU TAKEN LEAVE OF YOUR SENSES? WOT WE DOIN' THAT FOR?
SIGH I DO BELIEVE I LIKED YOU BETTER WHEN YOU WERE ILL. THERE WERE LESS QUESTIONS.
I'M STARTIN' TO THINK I PREFERRED IT MESELF...
CAN'T YOU SMELL IT?
EH? SMELL WHAT?
GAS! IT BUILDS UP IN SOME PARTS DOWN HERE AND IF YOU'RE NOT CAREFUL...
BOOM!
ERRR... TURN IT OFF THEN, SHALL I?
CYUH! COME ALONG, OPEN THE DOOR!
I DUNNO... LEAVIN' AN OLD MAN WAITING OUT 'ERE IN THE COLD, 'TAIN'T RIGHT.
AIIEEE!

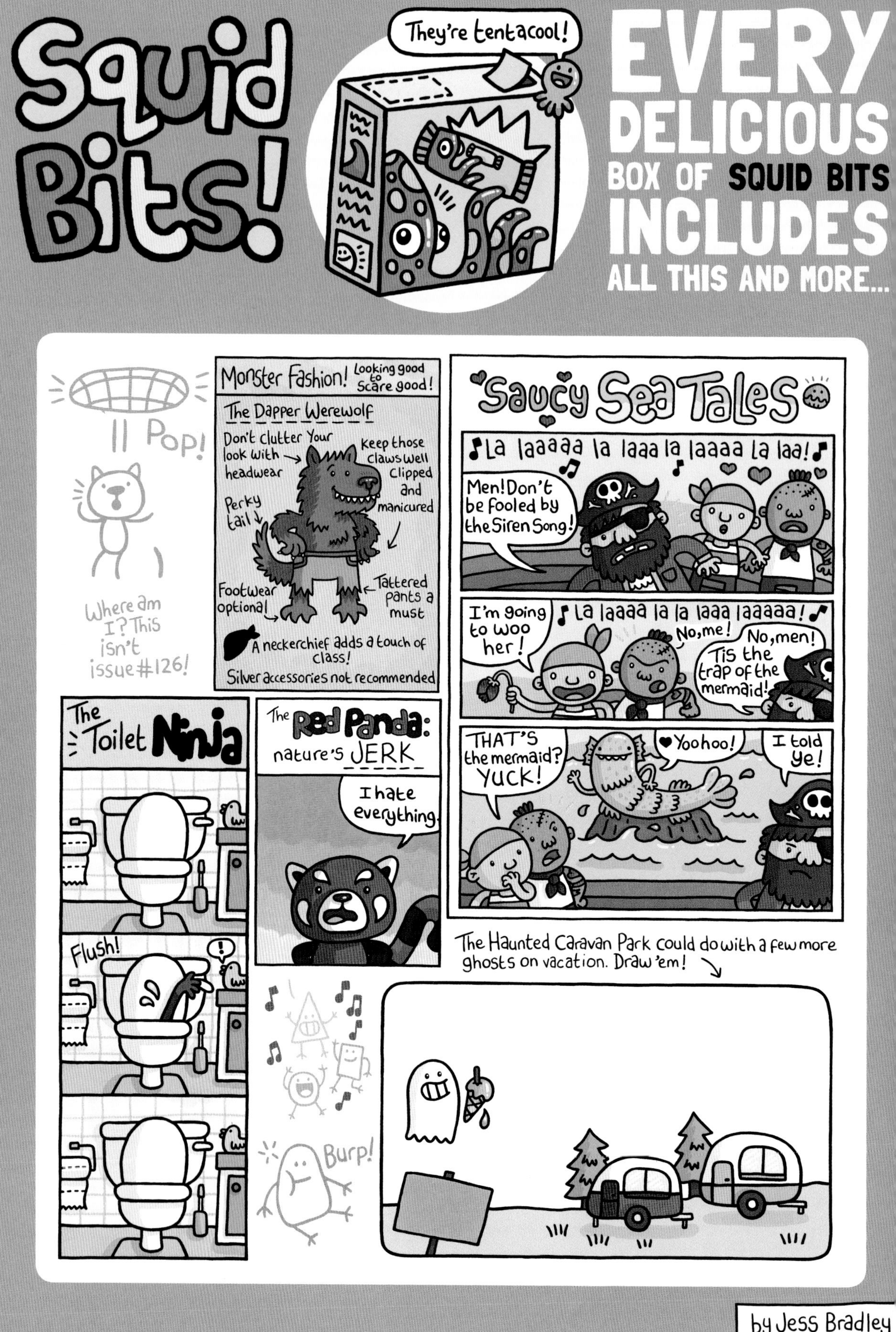
Squid Bits!
They're tentacool!
EVERY DELICIOUS BOX OF SQUID BITS INCLUDES ALL THIS AND MORE...
Pop!
Where am I? This isn't issue #126!
Monster Fashion! Looking good to scare good!
The Dapper Werewolf
Don't clutter your look with headwear
Keep those claws well clipped and manicured
Perky tail
Footwear optional!
Tattered pants a must
A neckerchief adds a touch of class!
Silver accessories not recommended
Saucy Sea Tales
La laaaaa la laaa la laaaa la laa!
Men! Don't be fooled by the Siren Song!
I'm going to woo her!
La laaaa la la laaa laaaaa!
No, me!
No, men! Tis the trap of the mermaid!
THAT'S the mermaid? YUCK!
Yoohoo!
I told ye!
The Toilet Ninja
Flush!
!
The Red Panda: nature's JERK
I hate everything.
The Haunted Caravan Park could do with a few more ghosts on vacation. Draw 'em!
Burp!

by Jess Bradley

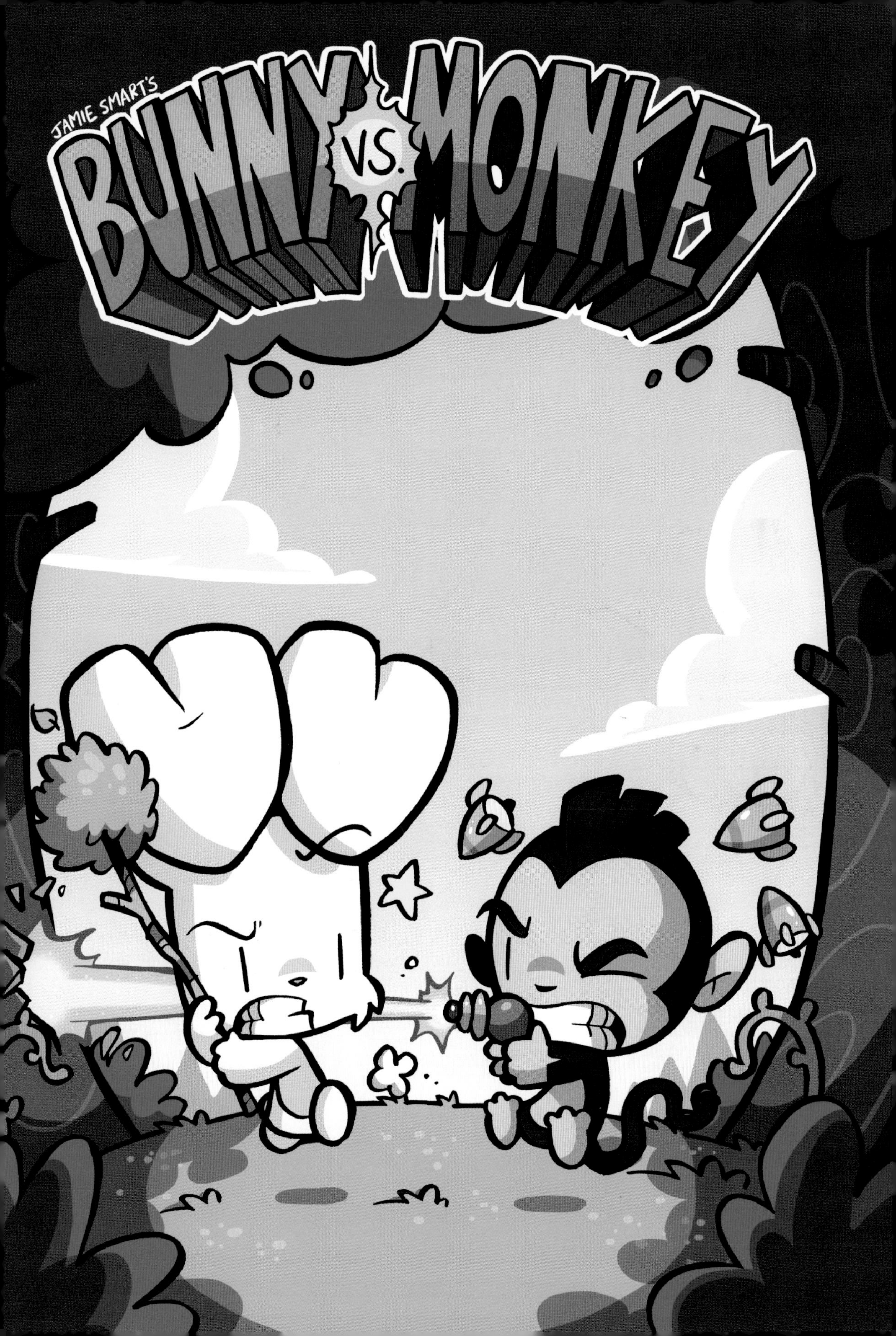
JAMIE SMART'S
BUNNY VS. MONKEY

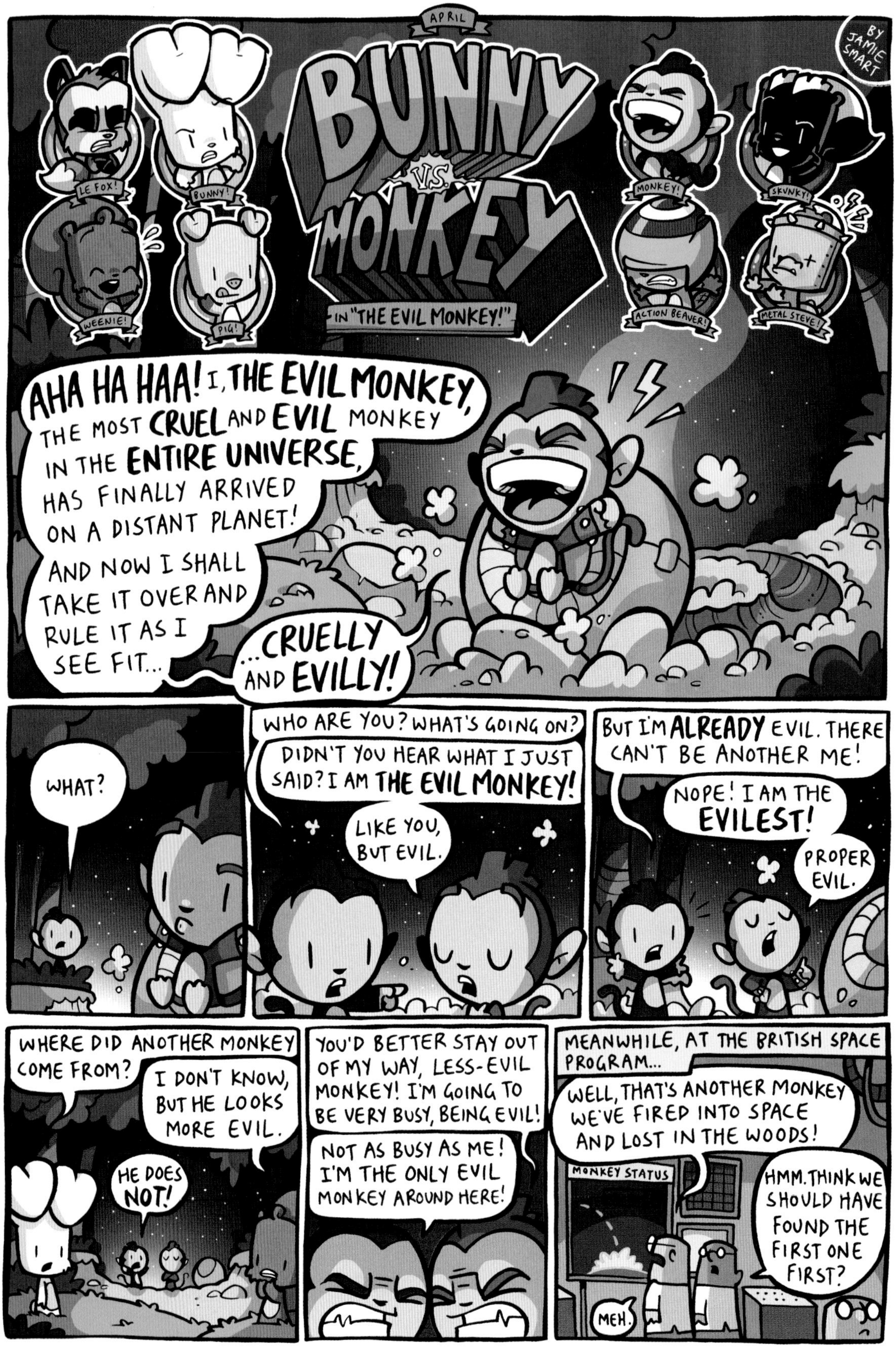
APRIL
BUNNY VS. MONKEY
BY JAMIE SMART
LE FOX!
BUNNY!
WEENIE!
PIG!
IN "THE EVIL MONKEY!"
MONKEY!
SKUNKY!
ACTION BEAVER!
METAL STEVE!
AHA HA HAA! I, THE EVIL MONKEY, THE MOST CRUEL AND EVIL MONKEY IN THE ENTIRE UNIVERSE, HAS FINALLY ARRIVED ON A DISTANT PLANET!
AND NOW I SHALL TAKE IT OVER AND RULE IT AS I SEE FIT...
...CRUELLY AND EVILLY!
WHAT?
WHO ARE YOU? WHAT'S GOING ON?
DIDN'T YOU HEAR WHAT I JUST SAID? I AM THE EVIL MONKEY!
LIKE YOU, BUT EVIL.
BUT I'M ALREADY EVIL. THERE CAN'T BE ANOTHER ME!
NOPE! I AM THE EVILEST!
PROPER EVIL.
WHERE DID ANOTHER MONKEY COME FROM?
I DON'T KNOW, BUT HE LOOKS MORE EVIL.
HE DOES NOT!
YOU'D BETTER STAY OUT OF MY WAY, LESS-EVIL MONKEY! I'M GOING TO BE VERY BUSY, BEING EVIL!
NOT AS BUSY AS ME! I'M THE ONLY EVIL MONKEY AROUND HERE!
MEANWHILE, AT THE BRITISH SPACE PROGRAM...
WELL, THAT'S ANOTHER MONKEY WE'VE FIRED INTO SPACE AND LOST IN THE WOODS!
MONKEY STATUS
HMM. THINK WE SHOULD HAVE FOUND THE FIRST ONE FIRST?
MEH.

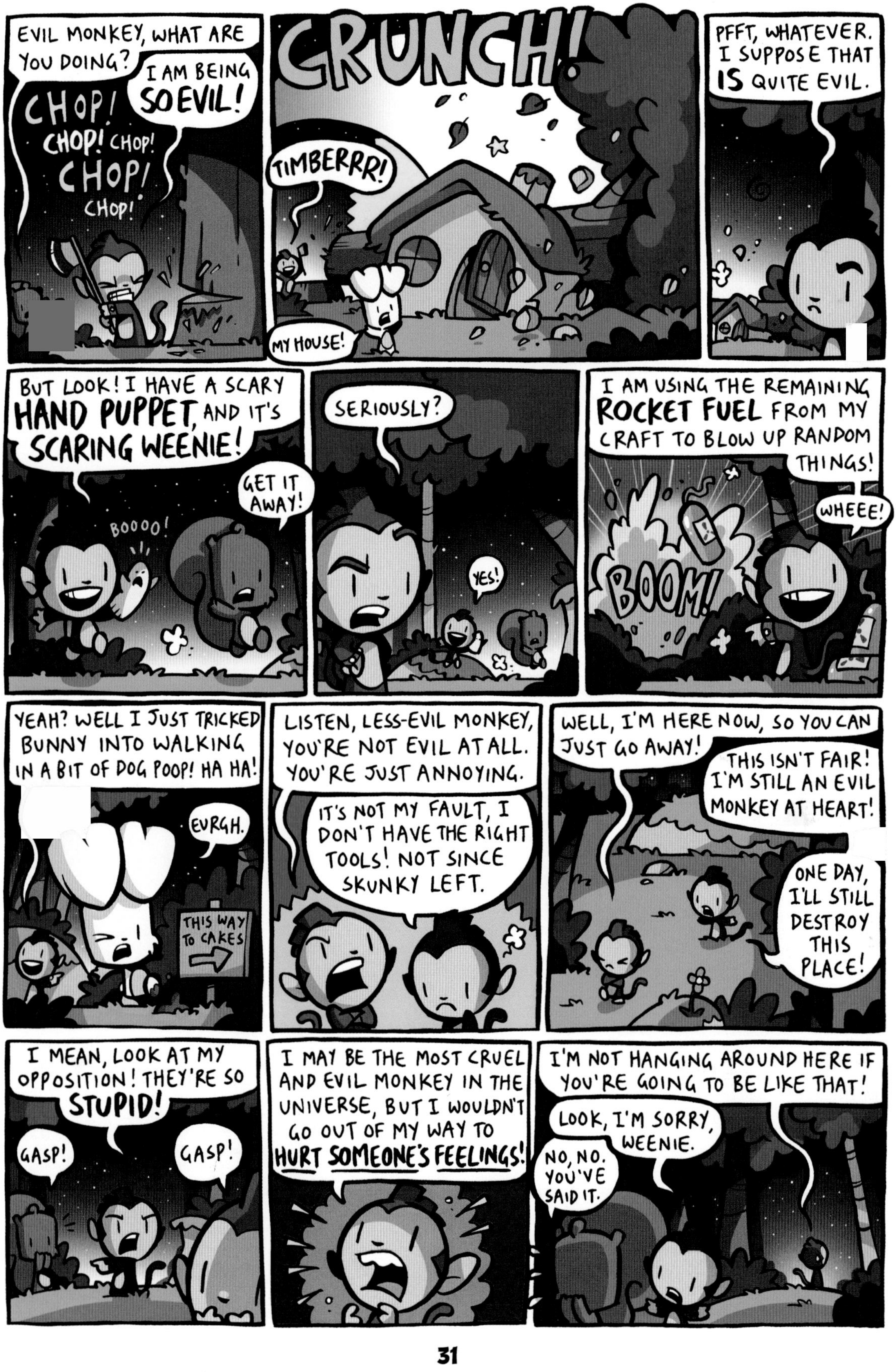
EVIL MONKEY, WHAT ARE YOU DOING?
I AM BEING SO EVIL!
CHOP! CHOP! CHOP! CHOP! CHOP!
CRUNCH!
TIMBERRR!
MY HOUSE!
PFFT, WHATEVER. I SUPPOSE THAT IS QUITE EVIL.
BUT LOOK! I HAVE A SCARY HAND PUPPET, AND IT'S SCARING WEENIE!
BOOOO!
GET IT AWAY!
SERIOUSLY?
YES!
I AM USING THE REMAINING ROCKET FUEL FROM MY CRAFT TO BLOW UP RANDOM THINGS!
BOOM!
WHEEE!
YEAH? WELL I JUST TRICKED BUNNY INTO WALKING IN A BIT OF DOG POOP! HA HA!
EVRGH.
THIS WAY TO CAKES
LISTEN, LESS-EVIL MONKEY, YOU'RE NOT EVIL AT ALL. YOU'RE JUST ANNOYING.
IT'S NOT MY FAULT, I DON'T HAVE THE RIGHT TOOLS! NOT SINCE SKUNKY LEFT.
WELL, I'M HERE NOW, SO YOU CAN JUST GO AWAY!
THIS ISN'T FAIR! I'M STILL AN EVIL MONKEY AT HEART!
ONE DAY, I'LL STILL DESTROY THIS PLACE!
I MEAN, LOOK AT MY OPPOSITION! THEY'RE SO STUPID!
GASP!
GASP!
I MAY BE THE MOST CRUEL AND EVIL MONKEY IN THE UNIVERSE, BUT I WOULDN'T GO OUT OF MY WAY TO HURT SOMEONE'S FEELINGS!
I'M NOT HANGING AROUND HERE IF YOU'RE GOING TO BE LIKE THAT!
LOOK, I'M SORRY, WEENIE.
NO, NO. YOU'VE SAID IT.

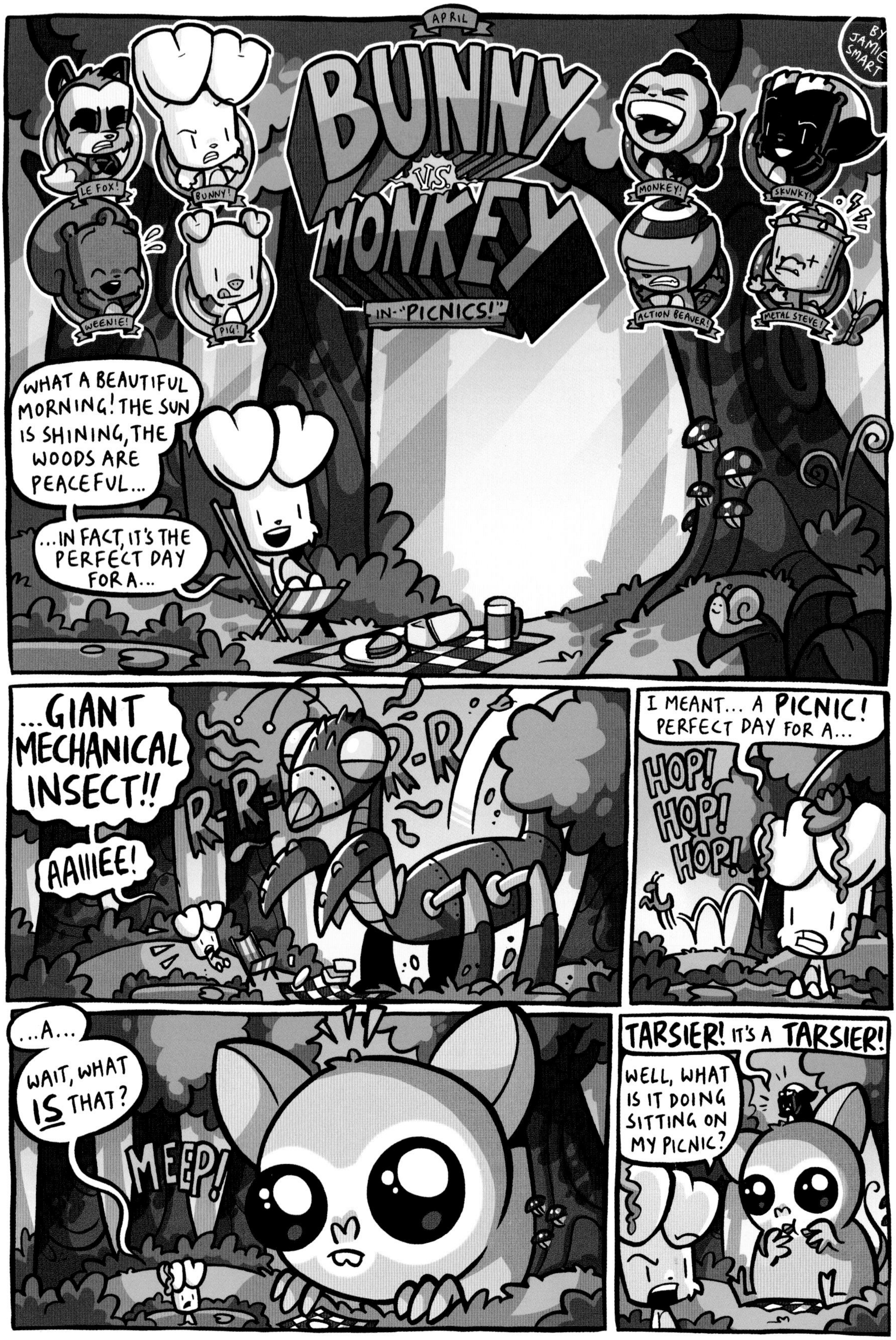
APRIL
BUNNY VS. MONKEY
IN "PICNICS!"
BY JAMIE SMART
LE FOX!
BUNNY!
WEENIE!
PIG!
MONKEY!
SKUNKY!
ACTION BEAVER!
METAL STEVE!
WHAT A BEAUTIFUL MORNING! THE SUN IS SHINING, THE WOODS ARE PEACEFUL...
...IN FACT, IT'S THE PERFECT DAY FOR A...
...GIANT MECHANICAL INSECT!!
AAIIIEE!
R-R-R-R
I MEANT... A PICNIC! PERFECT DAY FOR A...
HOP! HOP! HOP!
...A...
WAIT, WHAT IS THAT?
MEEP!
TARSIER! IT'S A TARSIER!
WELL, WHAT IS IT DOING SITTING ON MY PICNIC?

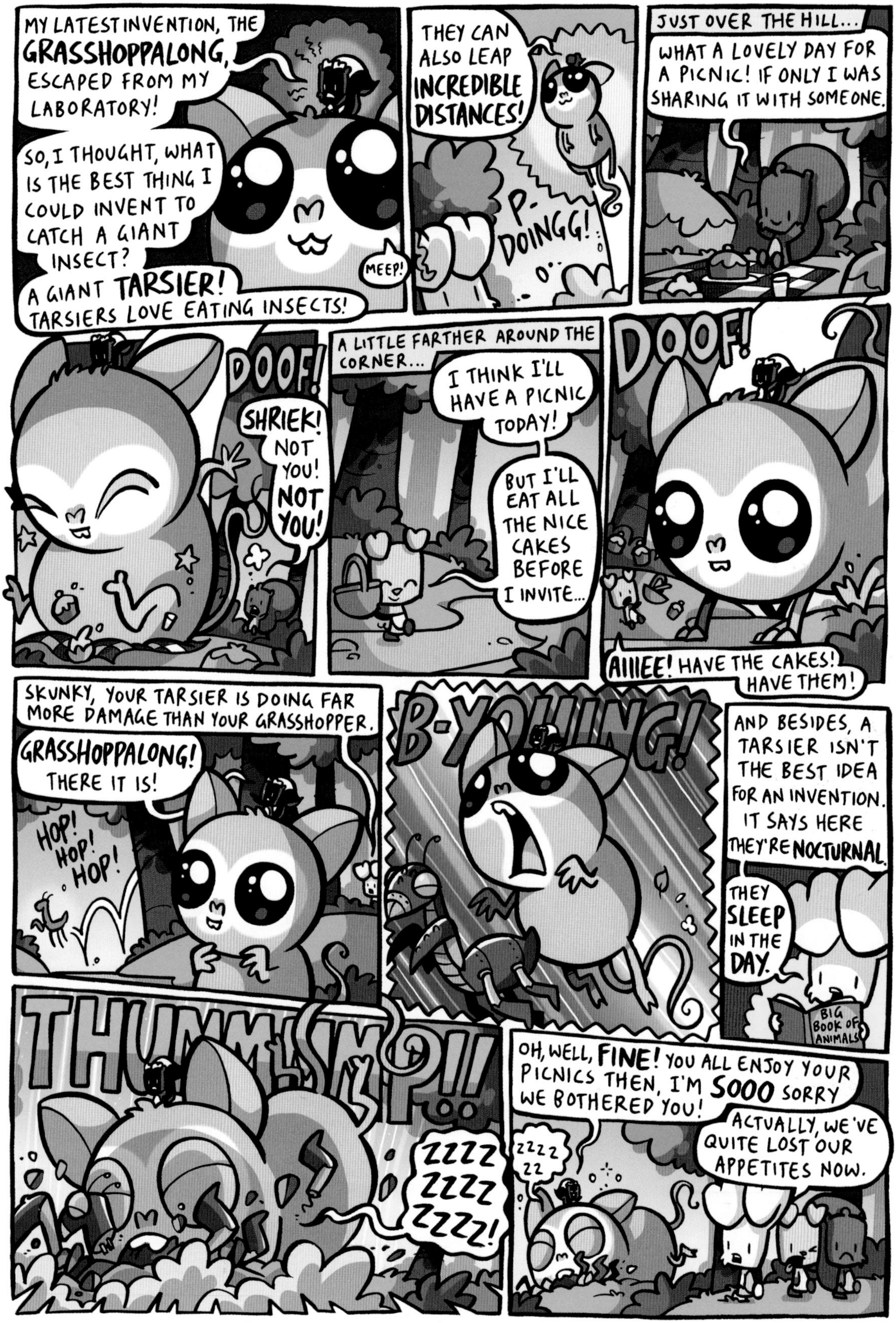
MY LATEST INVENTION, THE GRASSHOPPALONG, ESCAPED FROM MY LABORATORY!
SO, I THOUGHT, WHAT IS THE BEST THING I COULD INVENT TO CATCH A GIANT INSECT?
A GIANT TARSIER! TARSIERS LOVE EATING INSECTS!
MEEP!
THEY CAN ALSO LEAP INCREDIBLE DISTANCES!
P-DOINGG!
JUST OVER THE HILL...
WHAT A LOVELY DAY FOR A PICNIC! IF ONLY I WAS SHARING IT WITH SOMEONE.
DOOF!
SHRIEK! NOT YOU! NOT YOU!
A LITTLE FARTHER AROUND THE CORNER...
I THINK I'LL HAVE A PICNIC TODAY!
BUT I'LL EAT ALL THE NICE CAKES BEFORE I INVITE...
DOOF!
AIIIEE! HAVE THE CAKES! HAVE THEM!
SKUNKY, YOUR TARSIER IS DOING FAR MORE DAMAGE THAN YOUR GRASSHOPPER.
GRASSHOPPALONG! THERE IT IS!
HOP! HOP! HOP!
B-YOING!
AND BESIDES, A TARSIER ISN'T THE BEST IDEA FOR AN INVENTION. IT SAYS HERE THEY'RE NOCTURNAL.
THEY SLEEP IN THE DAY.
BIG BOOK OF ANIMALS
THUMMSMP!!
ZZZZ ZZZZ ZZZZ!
OH, WELL, FINE! YOU ALL ENJOY YOUR PICNICS THEN, I'M SOOO SORRY WE BOTHERED YOU!
ACTUALLY, WE'VE QUITE LOST OUR APPETITES NOW.
ZZZZ ZZ

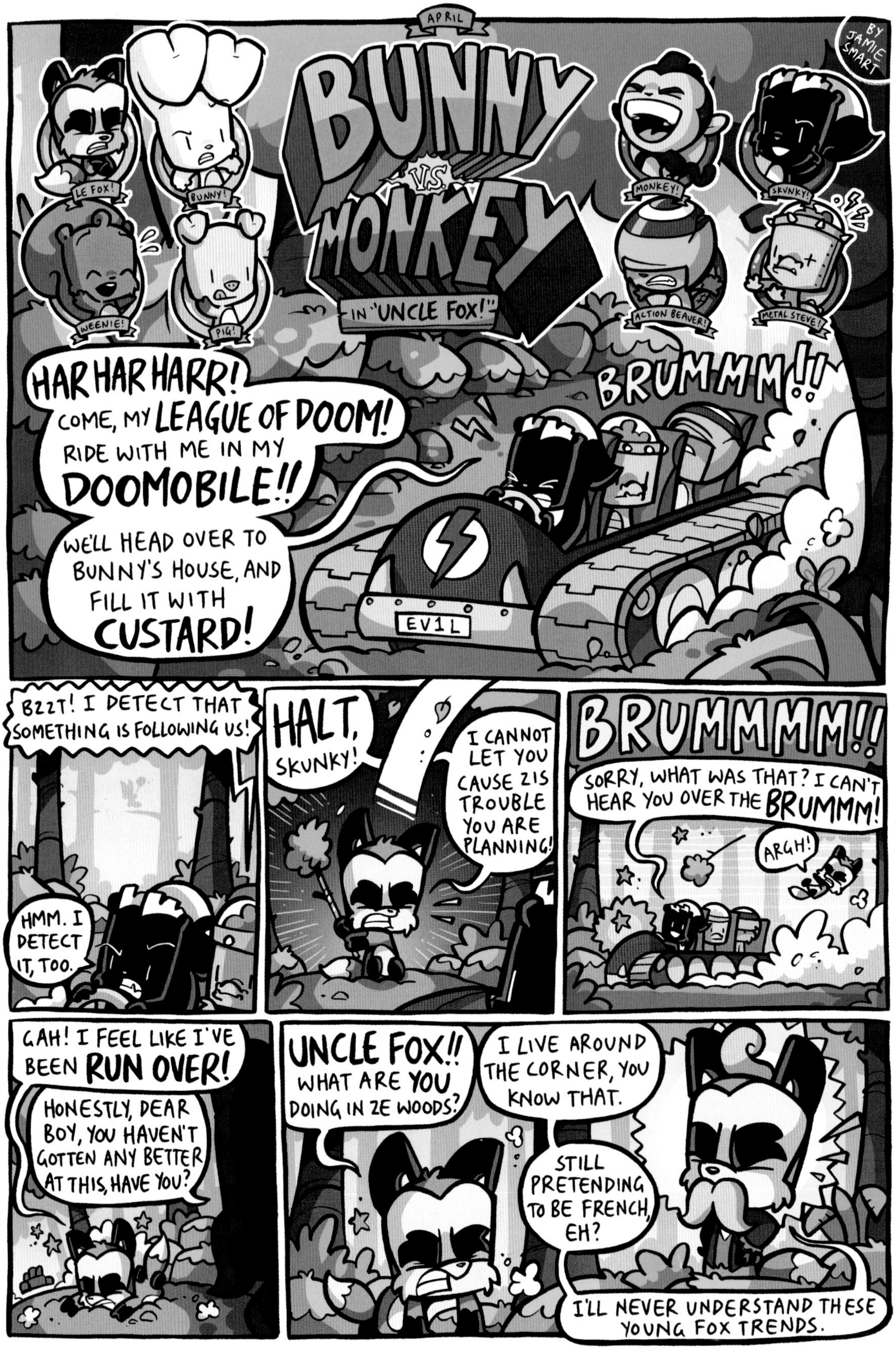
APRIL
BUNNY VS. MONKEY
IN "UNCLE FOX!"
BY JAMIE SMART
LE FOX!
BUNNY!
WEENIE!
PIG!
MONKEY!
SKUNKY!
ACTION BEAVER!
METAL STEVE!
HAR HAR HARR! COME, MY LEAGUE OF DOOM! RIDE WITH ME IN MY DOOMOBILE!!
WE'LL HEAD OVER TO BUNNY'S HOUSE, AND FILL IT WITH CUSTARD!
BRUMMM!!
EV1L
BZZT! I DETECT THAT SOMETHING IS FOLLOWING US!
HMM. I DETECT IT, TOO.
HALT, SKUNKY!
I CANNOT LET YOU CAUSE ZIS TROUBLE YOU ARE PLANNING!
BRUMMMM!!
SORRY, WHAT WAS THAT? I CAN'T HEAR YOU OVER THE BRUMMM!
ARGH!
GAH! I FEEL LIKE I'VE BEEN RUN OVER!
HONESTLY, DEAR BOY, YOU HAVEN'T GOTTEN ANY BETTER AT THIS, HAVE YOU?
UNCLE FOX!! WHAT ARE YOU DOING IN ZE WOODS?
I LIVE AROUND THE CORNER, YOU KNOW THAT.
STILL PRETENDING TO BE FRENCH, EH?
I'LL NEVER UNDERSTAND THESE YOUNG FOX TRENDS.

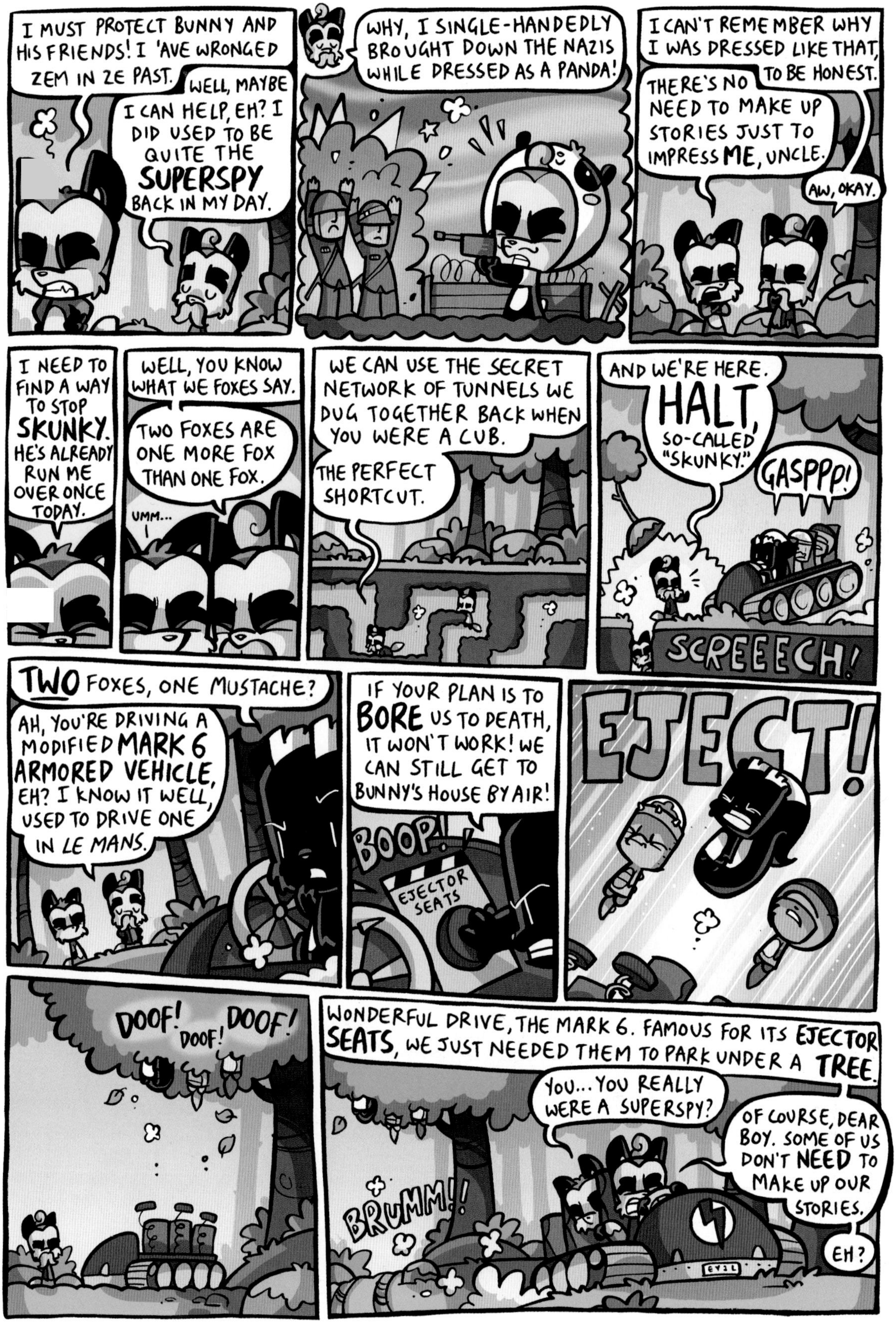
I MUST PROTECT BUNNY AND HIS FRIENDS! I 'AVE WRONGED ZEM IN ZE PAST.
WELL, MAYBE I CAN HELP, EH? I DID USED TO BE QUITE THE SUPERSPY BACK IN MY DAY.
WHY, I SINGLE-HANDEDLY BROUGHT DOWN THE NAZIS WHILE DRESSED AS A PANDA!
I CAN'T REMEMBER WHY I WAS DRESSED LIKE THAT, TO BE HONEST.
THERE'S NO NEED TO MAKE UP STORIES JUST TO IMPRESS ME, UNCLE.
AW, OKAY.
I NEED TO FIND A WAY TO STOP SKUNKY. HE'S ALREADY RUN ME OVER ONCE TODAY.
WELL, YOU KNOW WHAT WE FOXES SAY.
TWO FOXES ARE ONE MORE FOX THAN ONE FOX.
UMM...
WE CAN USE THE SECRET NETWORK OF TUNNELS WE DUG TOGETHER BACK WHEN YOU WERE A CUB.
THE PERFECT SHORTCUT.
AND WE'RE HERE.
HALT, SO-CALLED "SKUNKY."
GASPPP!
SCREEECH!
TWO FOXES, ONE MUSTACHE?
AH, YOU'RE DRIVING A MODIFIED MARK 6 ARMORED VEHICLE, EH? I KNOW IT WELL, USED TO DRIVE ONE IN LE MANS.
IF YOUR PLAN IS TO BORE US TO DEATH, IT WON'T WORK! WE CAN STILL GET TO BUNNY'S HOUSE BY AIR!
BOOP!
EJECTOR SEATS
EJECT!
DOOF! DOOF! DOOF!
WONDERFUL DRIVE, THE MARK 6. FAMOUS FOR ITS EJECTOR SEATS, WE JUST NEEDED THEM TO PARK UNDER A TREE.
YOU... YOU REALLY WERE A SUPERSPY?
OF COURSE, DEAR BOY. SOME OF US DON'T NEED TO MAKE UP OUR STORIES.
BRUMM!
EVIL
EH?

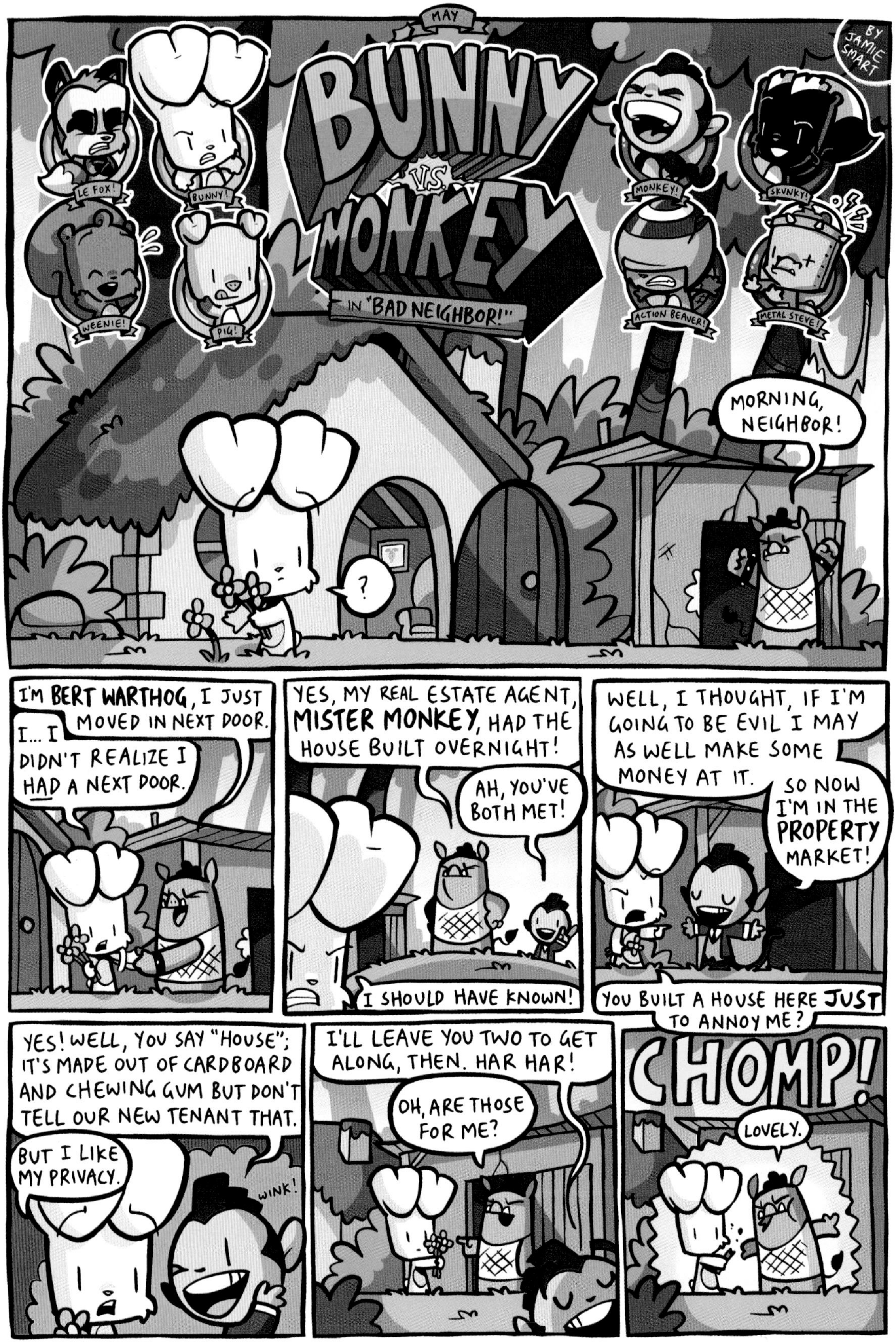
MAY
BUNNY VS. MONKEY
IN "BAD NEIGHBOR!"
BY JAMIE SMART
LE FOX!
BUNNY!
WEENIE!
PIG!
MONKEY!
SKUNKY!
ACTION BEAVER!
METAL STEVE!
MORNING, NEIGHBOR!
?
I'M BERT WARTHOG, I JUST MOVED IN NEXT DOOR.
I... I DIDN'T REALIZE I HAD A NEXT DOOR.
YES, MY REAL ESTATE AGENT, MISTER MONKEY, HAD THE HOUSE BUILT OVERNIGHT!
AH, YOU'VE BOTH MET!
I SHOULD HAVE KNOWN!
WELL, I THOUGHT, IF I'M GOING TO BE EVIL I MAY AS WELL MAKE SOME MONEY AT IT.
SO NOW I'M IN THE PROPERTY MARKET!
YOU BUILT A HOUSE HERE JUST TO ANNOY ME?
YES! WELL, YOU SAY "HOUSE"; IT'S MADE OUT OF CARDBOARD AND CHEWING GUM BUT DON'T TELL OUR NEW TENANT THAT.
BUT I LIKE MY PRIVACY.
WINK!
I'LL LEAVE YOU TWO TO GET ALONG, THEN. HAR HAR!
OH, ARE THOSE FOR ME?
CHOMP!
LOVELY.

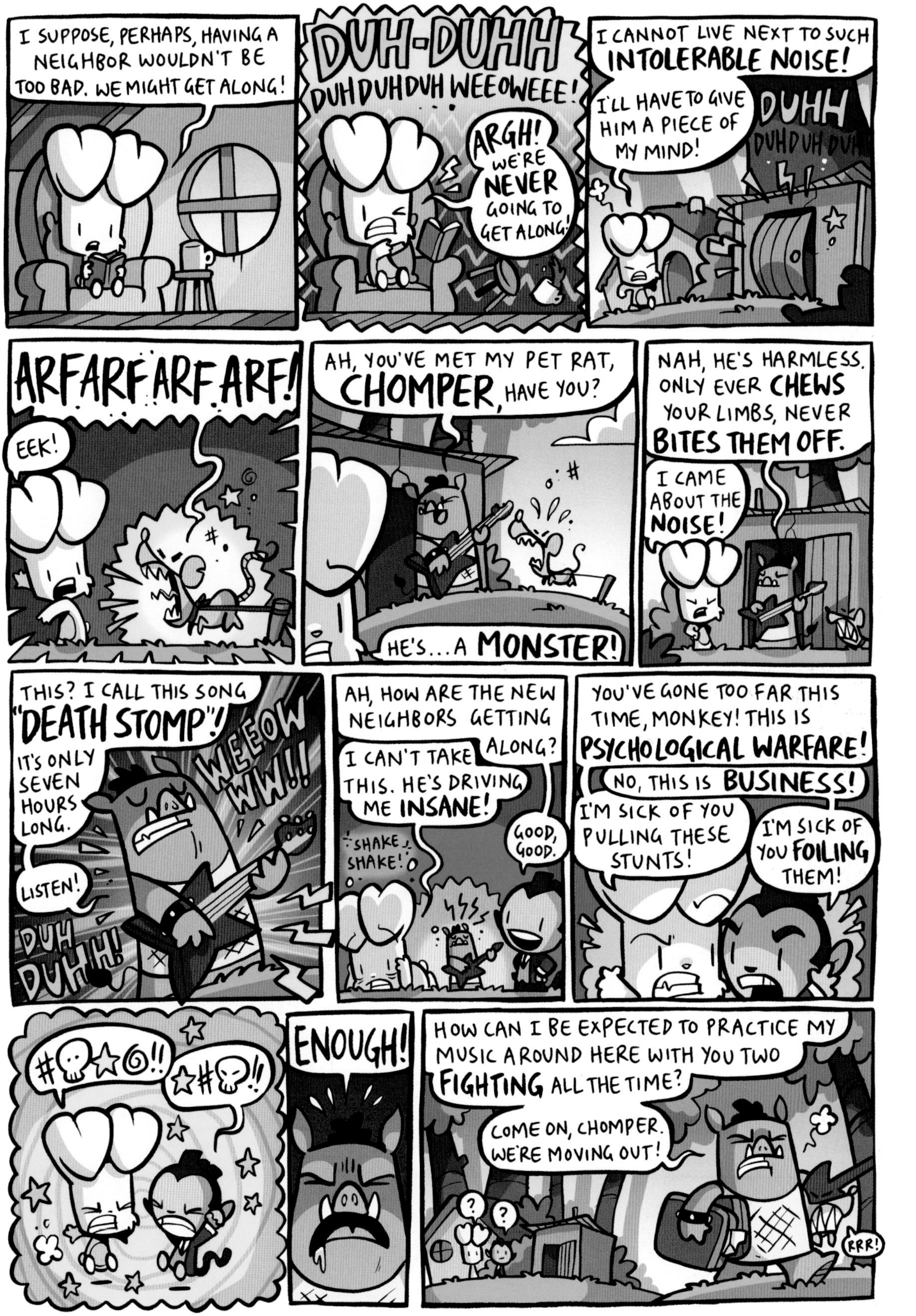
I SUPPOSE, PERHAPS, HAVING A NEIGHBOR WOULDN'T BE TOO BAD. WE MIGHT GET ALONG!
DUH-DUHH
DUH DUH DUH WEEOWEEE!
ARGH! WE'RE NEVER GOING TO GET ALONG!
I CANNOT LIVE NEXT TO SUCH INTOLERABLE NOISE!
I'LL HAVE TO GIVE HIM A PIECE OF MY MIND!
DUHH
DUH DUH DUH
ARFARFARFARFARF!
EEK!
AH, YOU'VE MET MY PET RAT, CHOMPER, HAVE YOU?
HE'S... A MONSTER!
NAH, HE'S HARMLESS. ONLY EVER CHEWS YOUR LIMBS, NEVER BITES THEM OFF.
I CAME ABOUT THE NOISE!
THIS? I CALL THIS SONG "DEATH STOMP"!
IT'S ONLY SEVEN HOURS LONG.
WEEOW WW!!
LISTEN!
DUH DUHH!
AH, HOW ARE THE NEW NEIGHBORS GETTING ALONG?
I CAN'T TAKE THIS. HE'S DRIVING ME INSANE!
SHAKE SHAKE!
GOOD, GOOD.
YOU'VE GONE TOO FAR THIS TIME, MONKEY! THIS IS PSYCHOLOGICAL WARFARE!
NO, THIS IS BUSINESS!
I'M SICK OF YOU PULLING THESE STUNTS!
I'M SICK OF YOU FOILING THEM!
ENOUGH!
HOW CAN I BE EXPECTED TO PRACTICE MY MUSIC AROUND HERE WITH YOU TWO FIGHTING ALL THE TIME?
COME ON, CHOMPER. WE'RE MOVING OUT!
RRR!

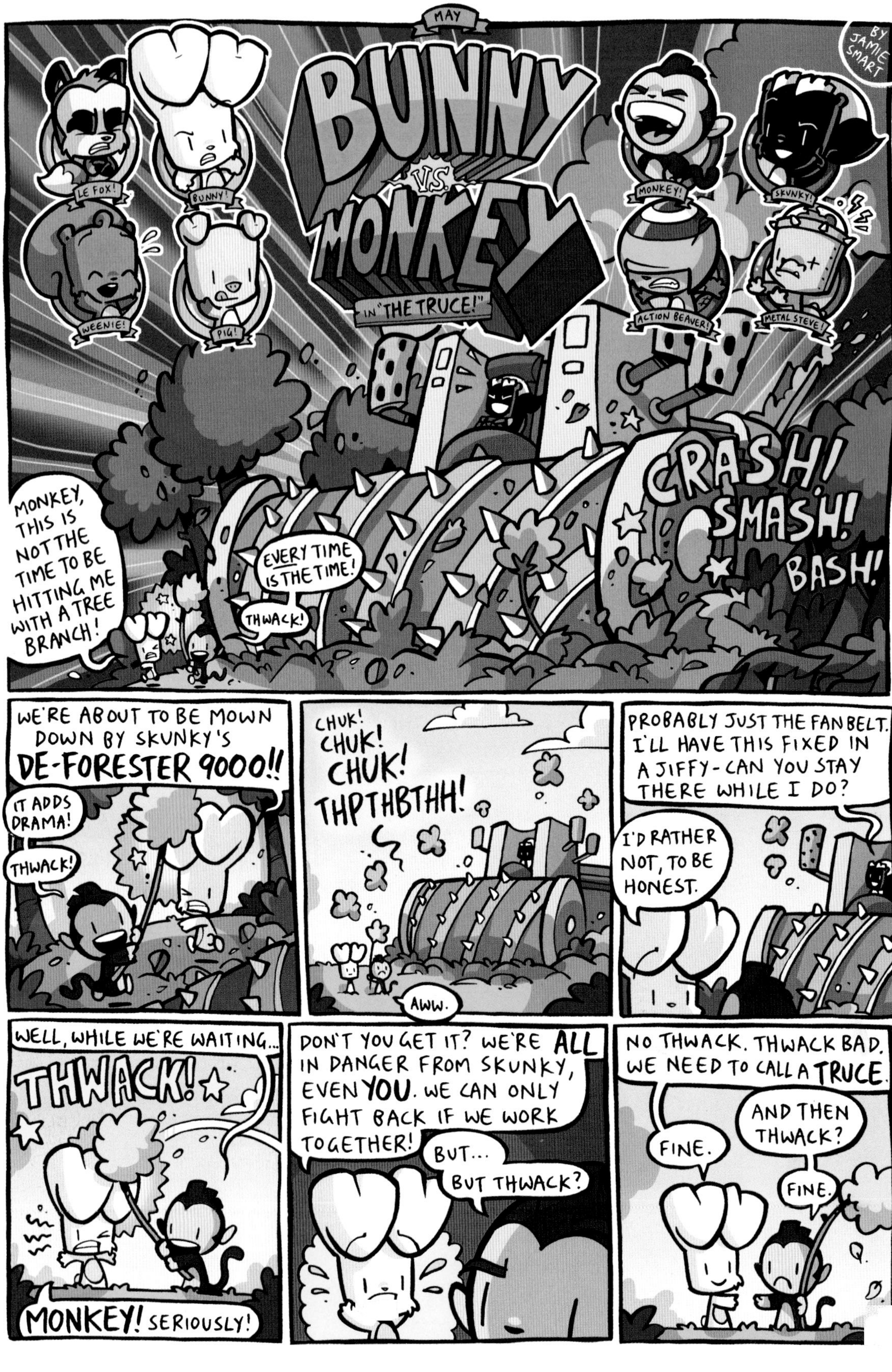
MAY
BUNNY VS. MONKEY
IN "THE TRUCE!"
BY JAMIE SMART
LE FOX!
BUNNY!
WEENIE!
PIG!
MONKEY!
SKUNKY!
ACTION BEAVER!
METAL STEVE!
MONKEY, THIS IS NOT THE TIME TO BE HITTING ME WITH A TREE BRANCH!
EVERY TIME IS THE TIME!
THWACK!
CRASH! SMASH! BASH!
WE'RE ABOUT TO BE MOWN DOWN BY SKUNKY'S DE-FORESTER 9000!!
IT ADDS DRAMA!
THWACK!
CHUK! CHUK! CHUK! THPTHBTHH!
AWW.
PROBABLY JUST THE FAN BELT. I'LL HAVE THIS FIXED IN A JIFFY - CAN YOU STAY THERE WHILE I DO?
I'D RATHER NOT, TO BE HONEST.
WELL, WHILE WE'RE WAITING...
THWACK!
MONKEY! SERIOUSLY!
DON'T YOU GET IT? WE'RE ALL IN DANGER FROM SKUNKY, EVEN YOU. WE CAN ONLY FIGHT BACK IF WE WORK TOGETHER!
BUT... BUT THWACK?
NO THWACK. THWACK BAD. WE NEED TO CALL A TRUCE.
FINE.
AND THEN THWACK?
FINE.

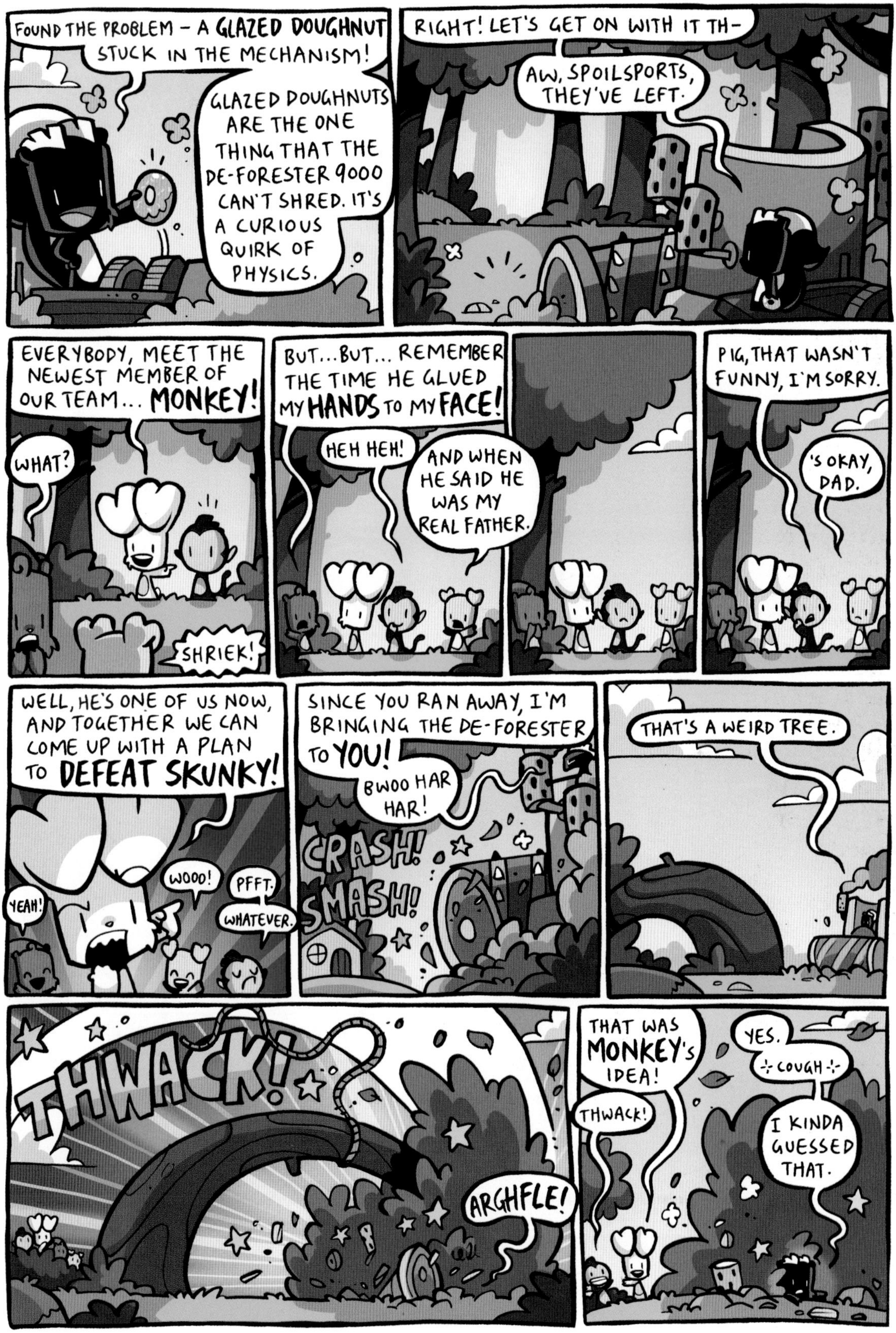
FOUND THE PROBLEM – A GLAZED DOUGHNUT STUCK IN THE MECHANISM!
GLAZED DOUGHNUTS ARE THE ONE THING THAT THE DE-FORESTER 9000 CAN'T SHRED. IT'S A CURIOUS QUIRK OF PHYSICS.
RIGHT! LET'S GET ON WITH IT TH–
AW, SPOILSPORTS, THEY'VE LEFT.
EVERYBODY, MEET THE NEWEST MEMBER OF OUR TEAM... MONKEY!
WHAT?
SHRIEK!
BUT...BUT... REMEMBER THE TIME HE GLUED MY HANDS TO MY FACE!
HEH HEH!
AND WHEN HE SAID HE WAS MY REAL FATHER.
PIG, THAT WASN'T FUNNY, I'M SORRY.
'S OKAY, DAD.
WELL, HE'S ONE OF US NOW, AND TOGETHER WE CAN COME UP WITH A PLAN TO DEFEAT SKUNKY!
YEAH!
WOOO!
PFFT.
WHATEVER.
SINCE YOU RAN AWAY, I'M BRINGING THE DE-FORESTER TO YOU!
BWOO HAR HAR!
CRASH!
SMASH!
THAT'S A WEIRD TREE.
THWACK!
ARGHFLE!
THAT WAS MONKEY'S IDEA!
THWACK!
YES.
COUGH
I KINDA GUESSED THAT.

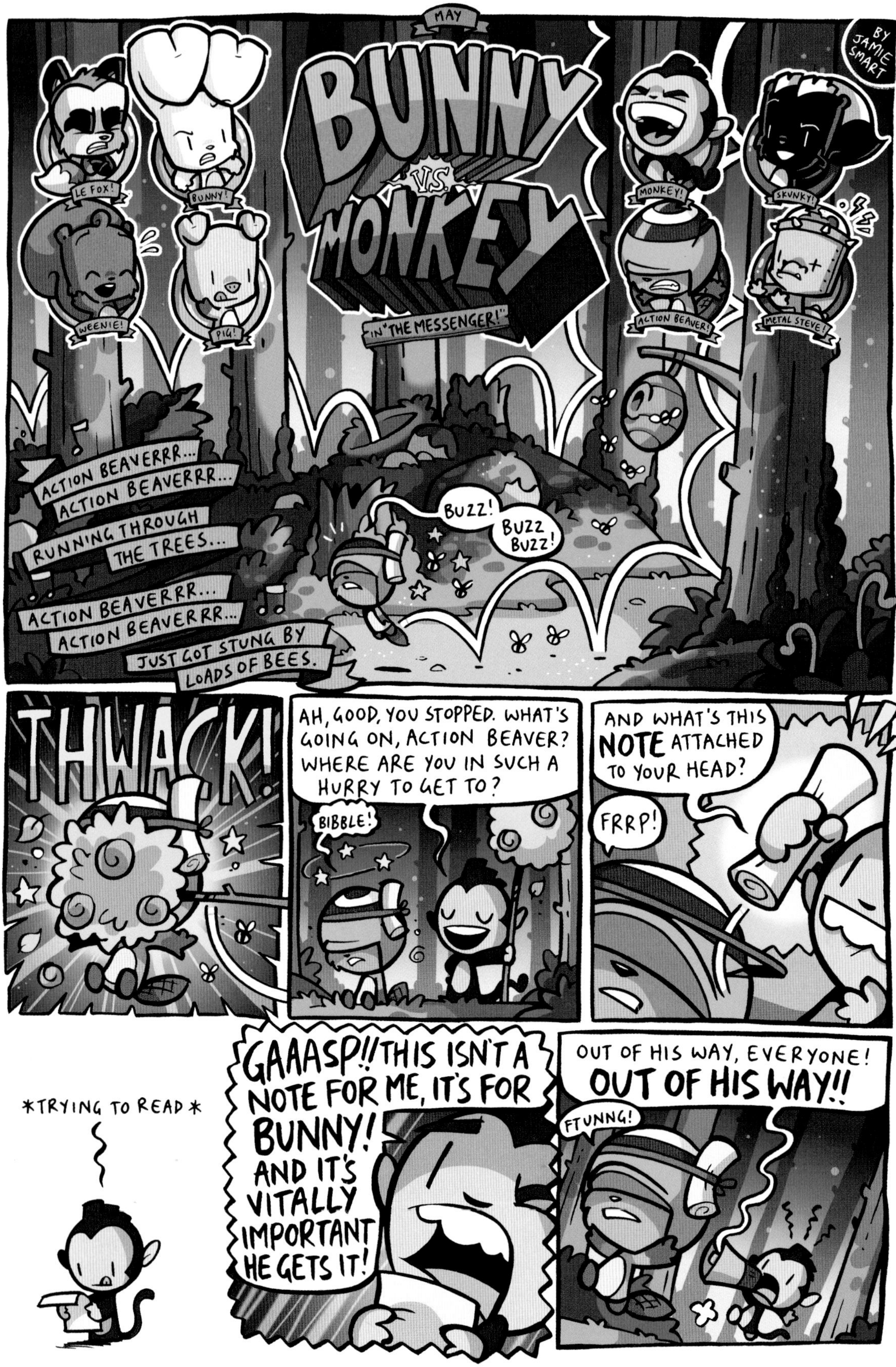
MAY
BUNNY VS. MONKEY
IN "THE MESSENGER!"
BY JAMIE SMART
LE FOX!
BUNNY!
MONKEY!
SKUNKY!
WEENIE!
PIG!
ACTION BEAVER!
METAL STEVE!
ACTION BEAVERRR... ACTION BEAVERRR... ACTION BEAVERRR RUNNING THROUGH THE TREES...
ACTION BEAVERRR... ACTION BEAVERRR... ACTION BEAVERRR JUST GOT STUNG BY LOADS OF BEES.
BUZZ!
BUZZ BUZZ!
THWACK!
AH, GOOD, YOU STOPPED. WHAT'S GOING ON, ACTION BEAVER? WHERE ARE YOU IN SUCH A HURRY TO GET TO?
BIBBLE!
AND WHAT'S THIS NOTE ATTACHED TO YOUR HEAD?
FRRP!
TRYING TO READ
GAAASP!! THIS ISN'T A NOTE FOR ME, IT'S FOR BUNNY! AND IT'S VITALLY IMPORTANT HE GETS IT!
OUT OF HIS WAY, EVERYONE! OUT OF HIS WAY!!
FTUNNG!

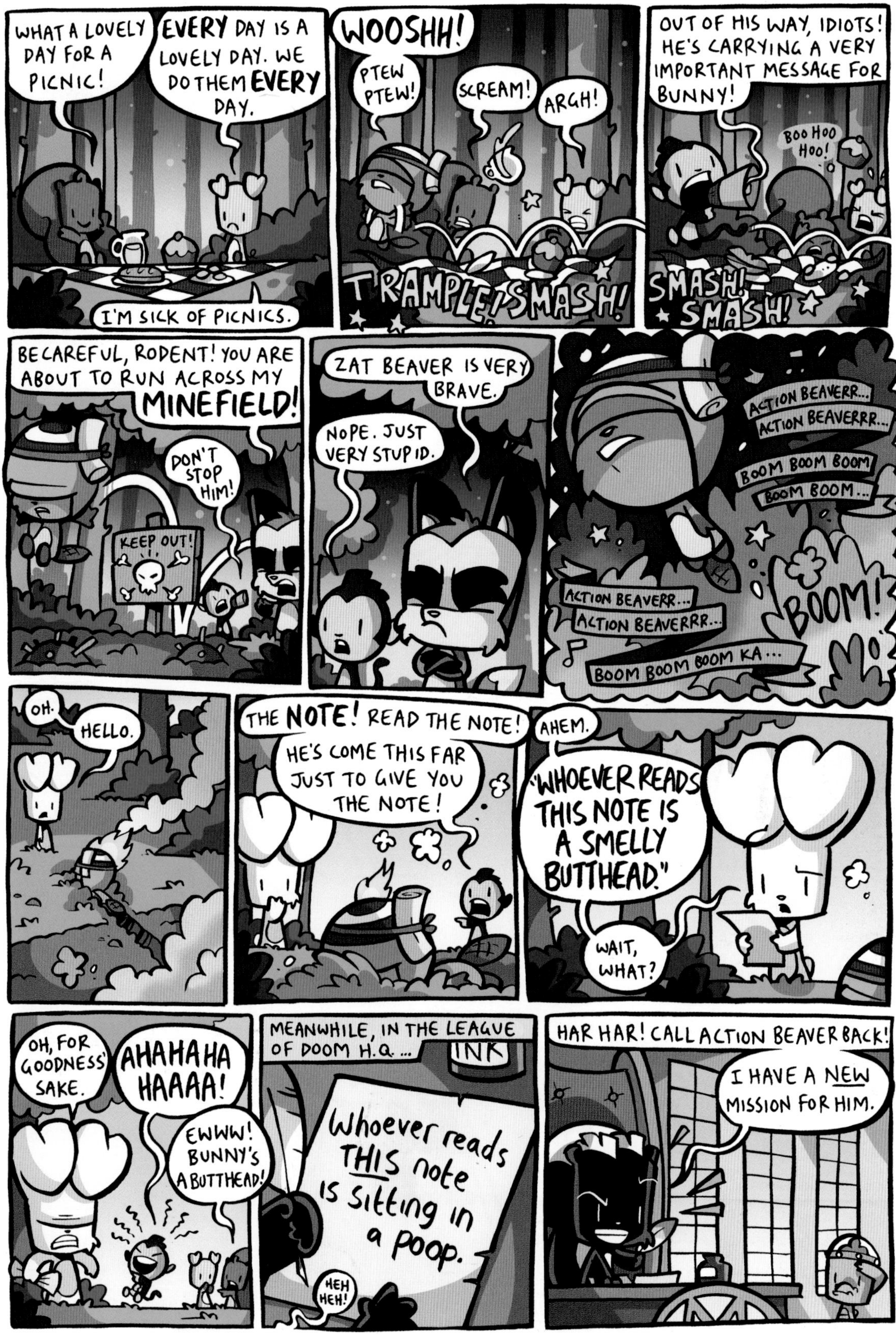

WHAT A LOVELY DAY FOR A PICNIC!
EVERY DAY IS A LOVELY DAY. WE DO THEM EVERY DAY.
I'M SICK OF PICNICS.
WOOSHH!
PTEW PTEW!
SCREAM!
ARGH!
TRAMPLE! SMASH!
OUT OF HIS WAY, IDIOTS! HE'S CARRYING A VERY IMPORTANT MESSAGE FOR BUNNY!
BOO HOO HOO!
SMASH! SMASH!
BE CAREFUL, RODENT! YOU ARE ABOUT TO RUN ACROSS MY MINEFIELD!
DON'T STOP HIM!
KEEP OUT!
ZAT BEAVER IS VERY BRAVE.
NOPE. JUST VERY STUPID.
ACTION BEAVERR...
ACTION BEAVERRR...
BOOM BOOM BOOM
BOOM BOOM...
ACTION BEAVERR...
ACTION BEAVERRR...
BOOM BOOM BOOM KA...
BOOM!
OH.
HELLO.
THE NOTE! READ THE NOTE!
HE'S COME THIS FAR JUST TO GIVE YOU THE NOTE!
AHEM.
"WHOEVER READS THIS NOTE IS A SMELLY BUTTHEAD."
WAIT, WHAT?
OH, FOR GOODNESS' SAKE.
AHAHAHA HAAAA!
EWWW! BUNNY'S A BUTTHEAD!
MEANWHILE, IN THE LEAGUE OF DOOM H.Q. ...
INK
Whoever reads THIS note is sitting in a poop.
HEH HEH!
HAR HAR! CALL ACTION BEAVER BACK!
I HAVE A NEW MISSION FOR HIM.

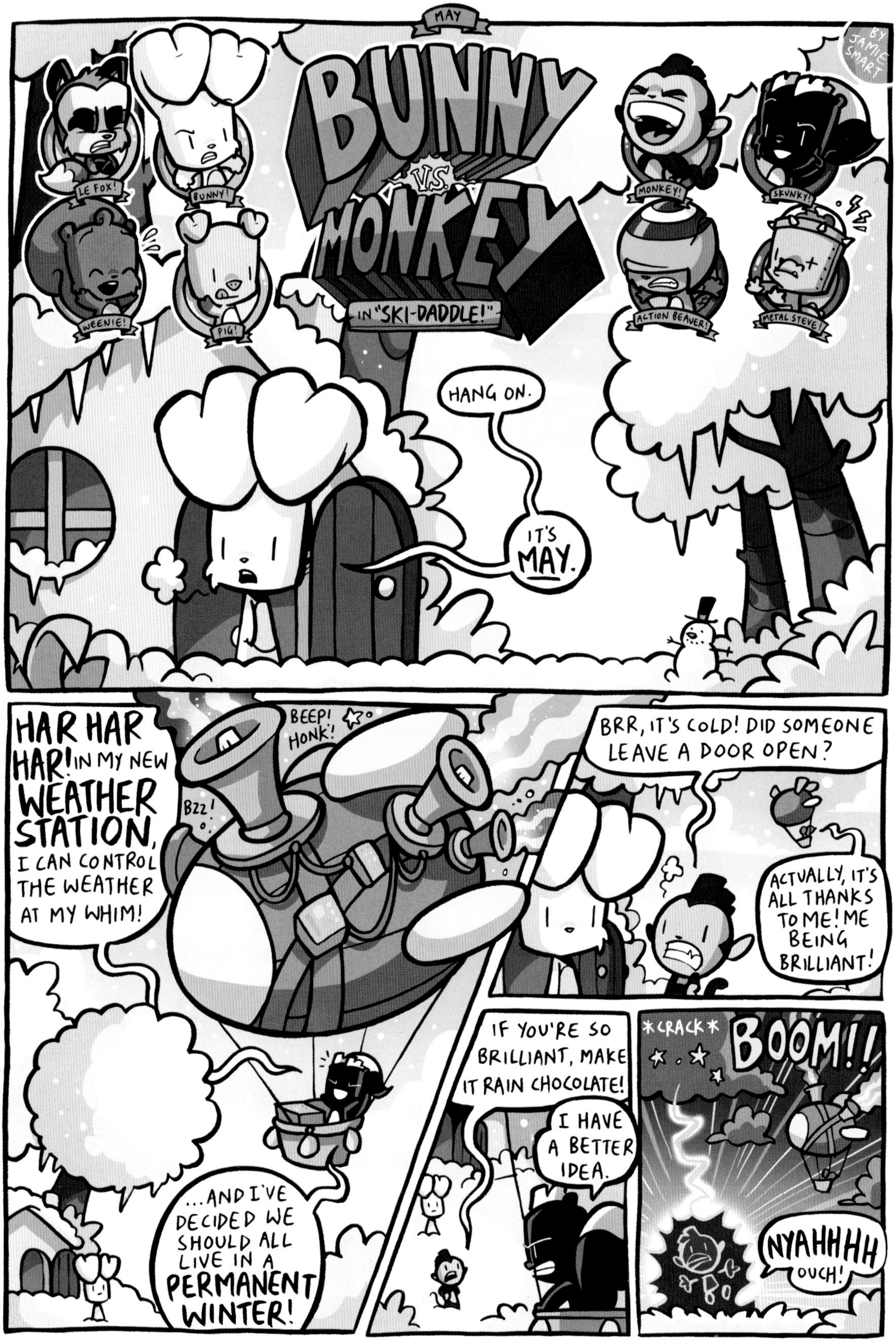
MAY
BUNNY VS. MONKEY
IN "SKI-DADDLE!"
BY JAMIE SMART
LE FOX!
BUNNY!
WEENIE!
PIG!
MONKEY!
SKUNKY!
ACTION BEAVER!
METAL STEVE!
HANG ON.
IT'S MAY.
HAR HAR HAR! IN MY NEW WEATHER STATION, I CAN CONTROL THE WEATHER AT MY WHIM!
BEEP! HONK!
BZZ!
...AND I'VE DECIDED WE SHOULD ALL LIVE IN A PERMANENT WINTER!
BRR, IT'S COLD! DID SOMEONE LEAVE A DOOR OPEN?
ACTUALLY, IT'S ALL THANKS TO ME! ME BEING BRILLIANT!
IF YOU'RE SO BRILLIANT, MAKE IT RAIN CHOCOLATE!
I HAVE A BETTER IDEA.
CRACK
BOOM!!
NYAHHHH
OUCH!

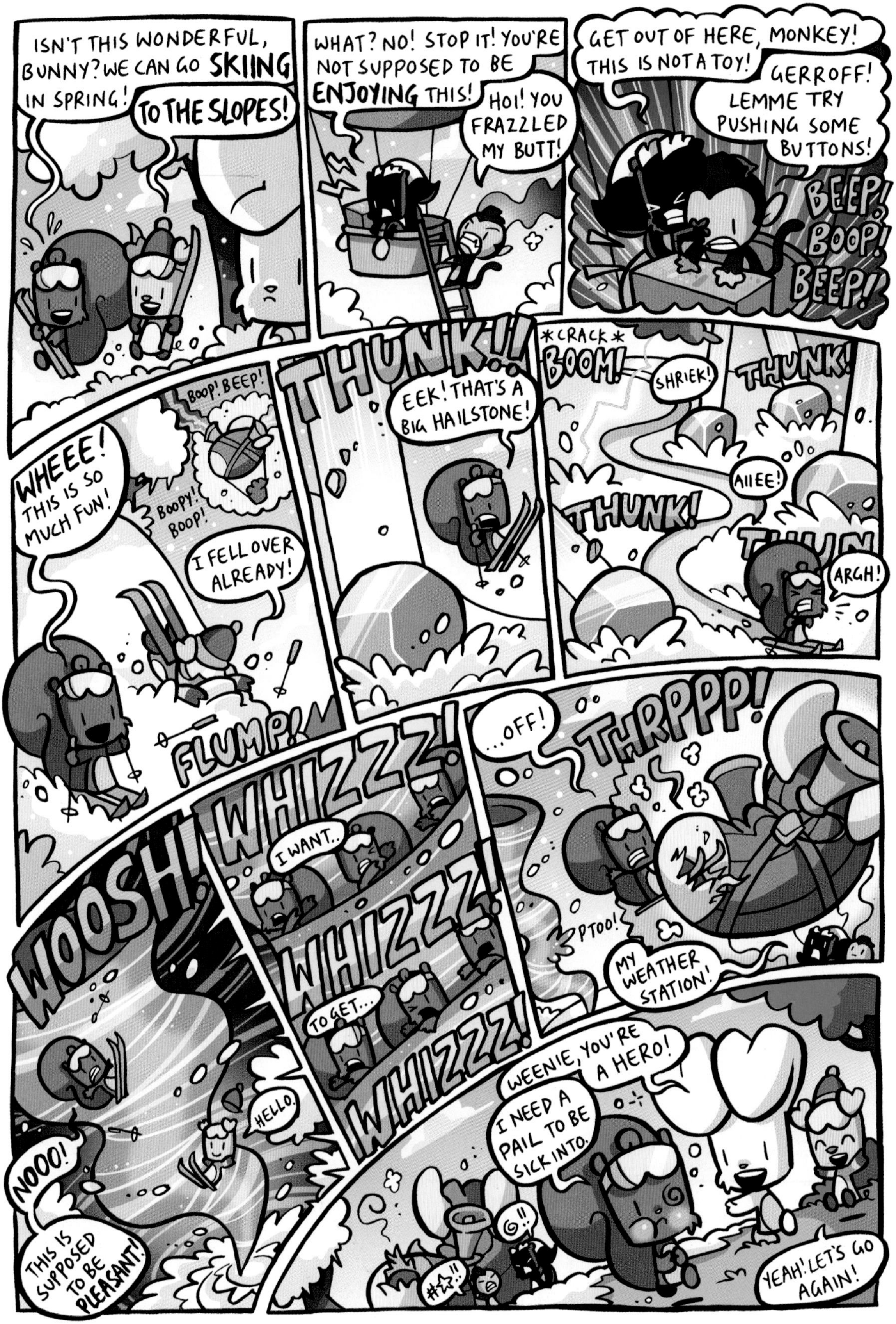
ISN'T THIS WONDERFUL, BUNNY? WE CAN GO SKIING IN SPRING!
TO THE SLOPES!
WHAT? NO! STOP IT! YOU'RE NOT SUPPOSED TO BE ENJOYING THIS!
HOI! YOU FRAZZLED MY BUTT!
GET OUT OF HERE, MONKEY! THIS IS NOT A TOY!
GERROFF! LEMME TRY PUSHING SOME BUTTONS!
BEEP! BOOP! BEEP!
WHEEE! THIS IS SO MUCH FUN!
BOOP! BEEP!
BOOPY! BOOP!
I FELL OVER ALREADY!
FLUMP!
THUNK!!!
EEK! THAT'S A BIG HAILSTONE!
CRACK BOOM!
SHRIEK!
THUNK!
AIIEE!
THUNK!
ARGH!
WOOSH!
WHIZZZ!
I WANT..
WHIZZZ!
TO GET...
WHIZZZ!
...OFF!
THRPPP!
PTOO!
MY WEATHER STATION!
NOOO!
THIS IS SUPPOSED TO BE PLEASANT!
HELLO.
WEENIE, YOU'RE A HERO!
I NEED A PAIL TO BE SICK INTO.
YEAH! LET'S GO AGAIN!

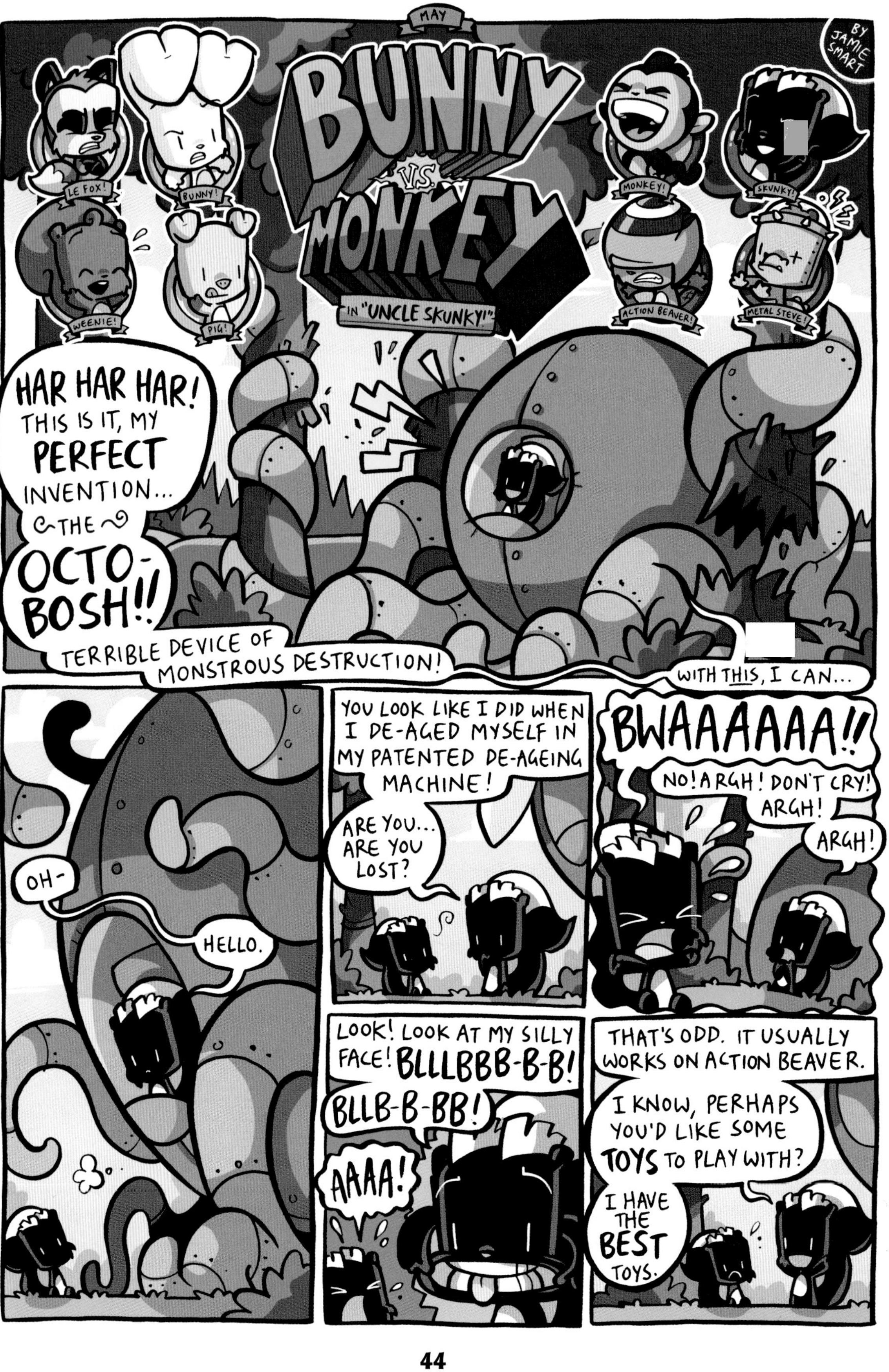

MAY
BY JAMIE SMART
BUNNY V.S. MONKEY
IN "UNCLE SKUNKY!"
LE FOX!
BUNNY!
WEENIE!
PIG!
MONKEY!
SKUNKY!
ACTION BEAVER!
METAL STEVE!
HAR HAR HAR! THIS IS IT, MY PERFECT INVENTION... THE OCTO-BOSH!!
TERRIBLE DEVICE OF MONSTROUS DESTRUCTION!
WITH THIS, I CAN...
OH-
HELLO.
YOU LOOK LIKE I DID WHEN I DE-AGED MYSELF IN MY PATENTED DE-AGEING MACHINE!
ARE YOU... ARE YOU LOST?
BWAAAAAA!!
NO! ARGH! DON'T CRY! ARGH!
ARGH!
LOOK! LOOK AT MY SILLY FACE! BLLLBBB-B-B!
BLLB-B-BB!
AAAA!
THAT'S ODD. IT USUALLY WORKS ON ACTION BEAVER.
I KNOW, PERHAPS YOU'D LIKE SOME TOYS TO PLAY WITH?
I HAVE THE BEST TOYS.

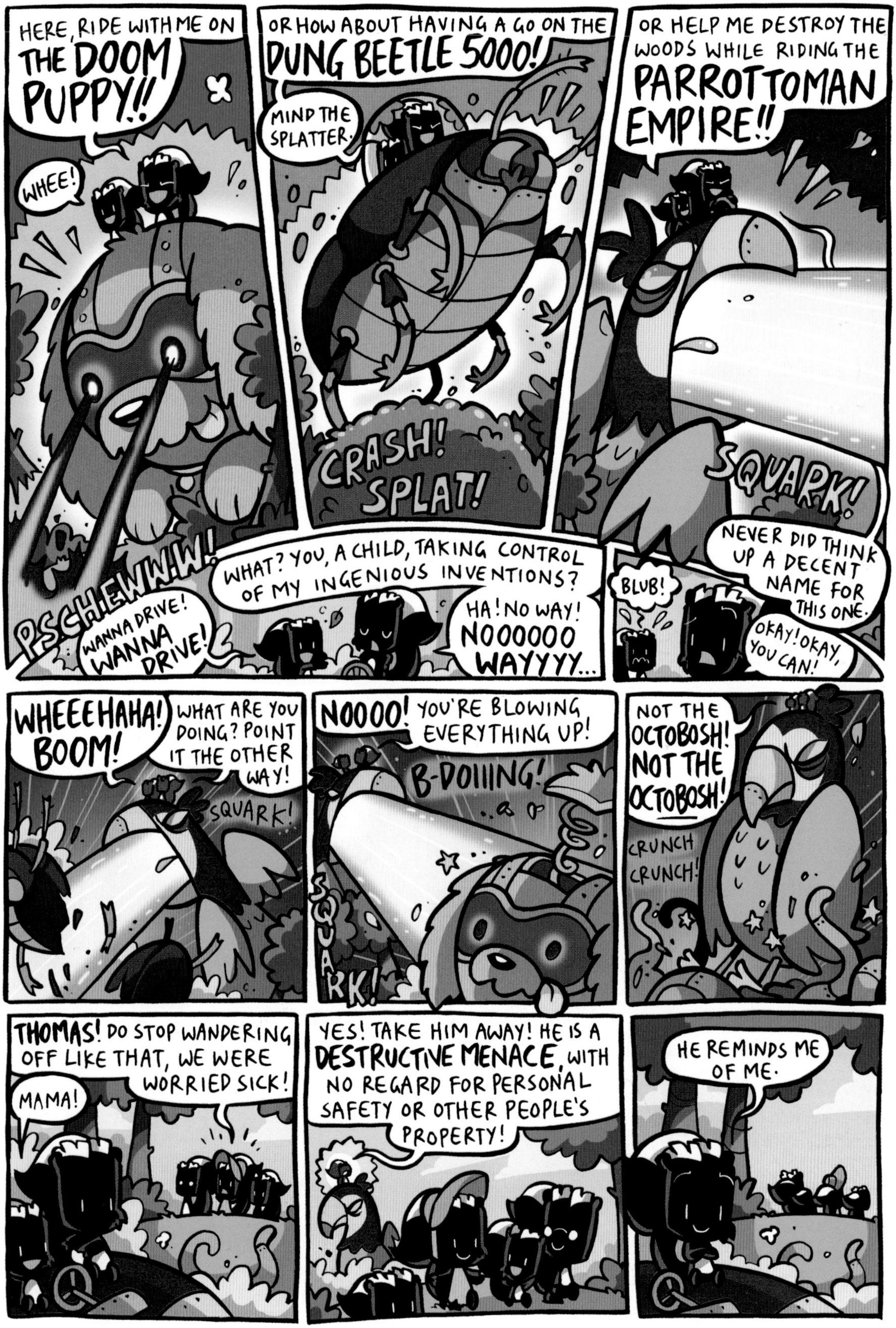
HERE, RIDE WITH ME ON THE DOOM PUPPY!!
WHEE!
PSCHEWWWW!
OR HOW ABOUT HAVING A GO ON THE DUNG BEETLE 5000!
MIND THE SPLATTER.
CRASH! SPLAT!
OR HELP ME DESTROY THE WOODS WHILE RIDING THE PARROTTOMAN EMPIRE!!
SQUARK!
WANNA DRIVE! WANNA DRIVE!
WHAT? YOU, A CHILD, TAKING CONTROL OF MY INGENIOUS INVENTIONS?
HA! NO WAY! NOOOOOO WAYYYY...
BLUB!
NEVER DID THINK UP A DECENT NAME FOR THIS ONE.
OKAY! OKAY, YOU CAN!
WHEEEHAHA! BOOM!
WHAT ARE YOU DOING? POINT IT THE OTHER WAY!
SQUARK!
NOOOO! YOU'RE BLOWING EVERYTHING UP!
B-DOIIING!
SQUARK!
NOT THE OCTOBOSH! NOT THE OCTOBOSH!
CRUNCH CRUNCH!
THOMAS! DO STOP WANDERING OFF LIKE THAT, WE WERE WORRIED SICK!
MAMA!
YES! TAKE HIM AWAY! HE IS A DESTRUCTIVE MENACE, WITH NO REGARD FOR PERSONAL SAFETY OR OTHER PEOPLE'S PROPERTY!
HE REMINDS ME OF ME.

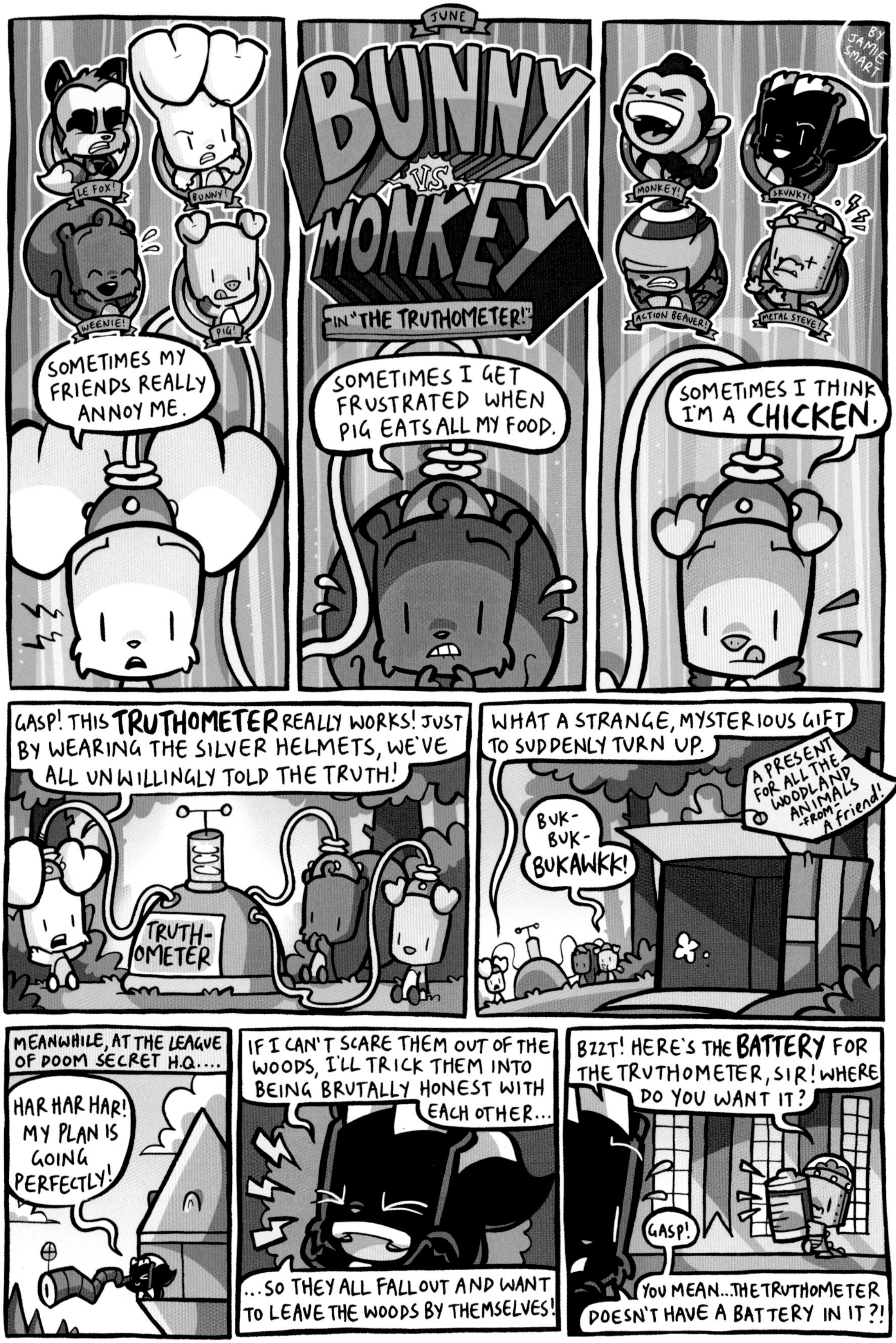
JUNE
BUNNY VS MONKEY
IN "THE TRUTHOMETER!"
BY JAMIE SMART
LE FOX!
BUNNY!
WEENIE!
PIG!
MONKEY!
SKUNKY!
ACTION BEAVER!
METAL STEVE!
SOMETIMES MY FRIENDS REALLY ANNOY ME.
SOMETIMES I GET FRUSTRATED WHEN PIG EATS ALL MY FOOD.
SOMETIMES I THINK I'M A CHICKEN.
GASP! THIS TRUTHOMETER REALLY WORKS! JUST BY WEARING THE SILVER HELMETS, WE'VE ALL UNWILLINGLY TOLD THE TRUTH!
TRUTH-OMETER
WHAT A STRANGE, MYSTERIOUS GIFT TO SUDDENLY TURN UP.
A PRESENT FOR ALL THE WOODLAND ANIMALS -FROM- A friend!
BUK-BUK-BUKAWKK!
MEANWHILE, AT THE LEAGUE OF DOOM SECRET H.Q....
HAR HAR HAR! MY PLAN IS GOING PERFECTLY!
IF I CAN'T SCARE THEM OUT OF THE WOODS, I'LL TRICK THEM INTO BEING BRUTALLY HONEST WITH EACH OTHER...
...SO THEY ALL FALL OUT AND WANT TO LEAVE THE WOODS BY THEMSELVES!
BZZT! HERE'S THE BATTERY FOR THE TRUTHOMETER, SIR! WHERE DO YOU WANT IT?
GASP!
YOU MEAN... THE TRUTHOMETER DOESN'T HAVE A BATTERY IN IT?!

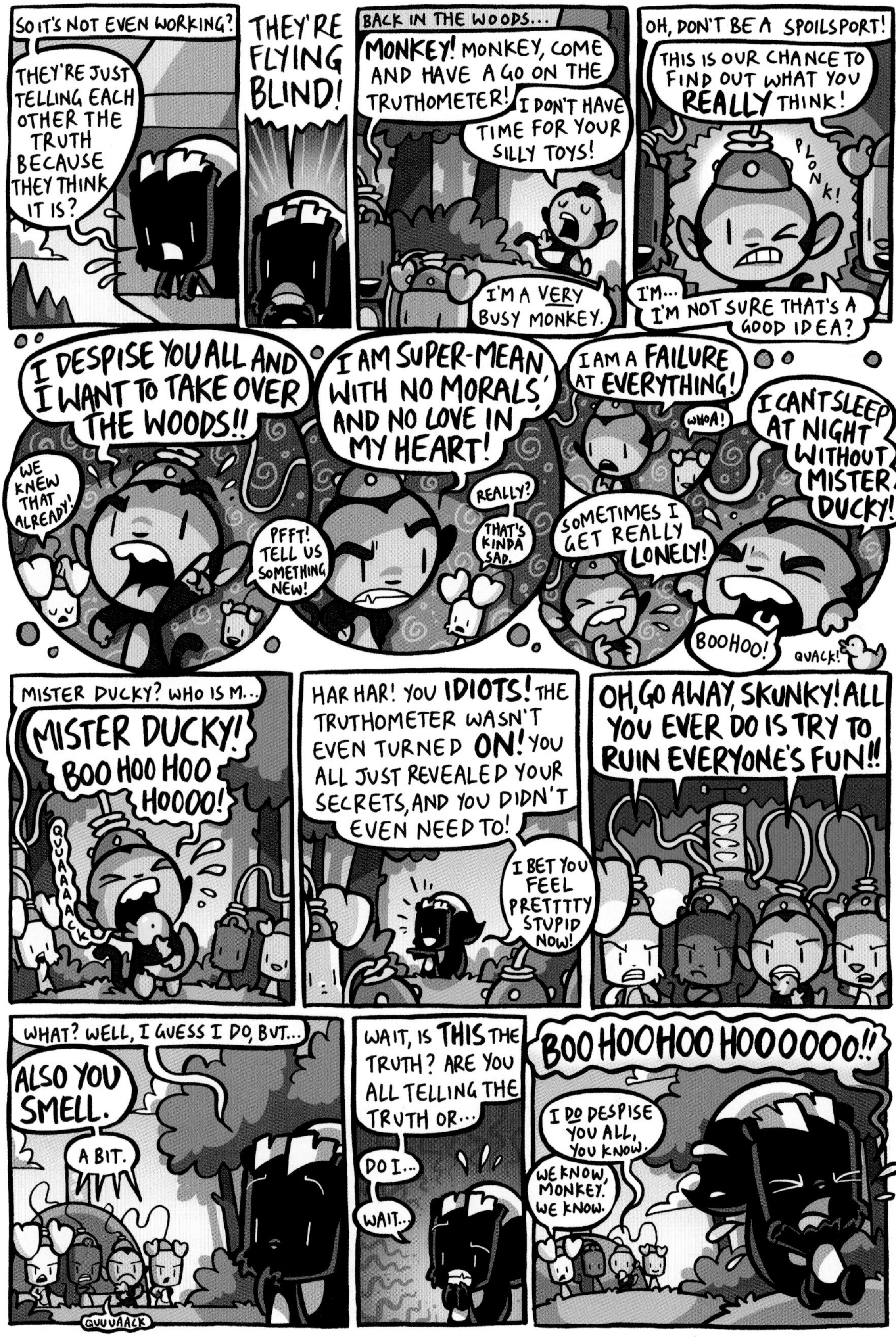
SO IT'S NOT EVEN WORKING?
THEY'RE JUST TELLING EACH OTHER THE TRUTH BECAUSE THEY THINK IT IS?
THEY'RE FLYING BLIND!
BACK IN THE WOODS...
MONKEY! MONKEY, COME AND HAVE A GO ON THE TRUTHOMETER!
I DON'T HAVE TIME FOR YOUR SILLY TOYS!
I'M A VERY BUSY MONKEY.
OH, DON'T BE A SPOILSPORT!
THIS IS OUR CHANCE TO FIND OUT WHAT YOU REALLY THINK!
PLONK!
I'M... I'M NOT SURE THAT'S A GOOD IDEA?
I DESPISE YOU ALL AND I WANT TO TAKE OVER THE WOODS!!
WE KNEW THAT ALREADY!
I AM SUPER-MEAN WITH NO MORALS, AND NO LOVE IN MY HEART!
PFFT! TELL US SOMETHING NEW!
REALLY?
THAT'S KINDA SAD.
I AM A FAILURE AT EVERYTHING!
WHOA!
SOMETIMES I GET REALLY LONELY!
I CAN'T SLEEP AT NIGHT WITHOUT MISTER DUCKY!
BOOHOO!
QUACK!
MISTER DUCKY? WHO IS M...
MISTER DUCKY! BOO HOO HOO HOOOO!
QUUAAAACK
HAR HAR! YOU IDIOTS! THE TRUTHOMETER WASN'T EVEN TURNED ON! YOU ALL JUST REVEALED YOUR SECRETS, AND YOU DIDN'T EVEN NEED TO!
I BET YOU FEEL PRETTTTY STUPID NOW!
OH, GO AWAY, SKUNKY! ALL YOU EVER DO IS TRY TO RUIN EVERYONE'S FUN!!
WHAT? WELL, I GUESS I DO, BUT...
ALSO YOU SMELL.
A BIT.
QUUVAACK
WAIT, IS THIS THE TRUTH? ARE YOU ALL TELLING THE TRUTH OR...
DO I...
WAIT...
BOO HOOHOO HOOOOOO!!
I DO DESPISE YOU ALL, YOU KNOW.
WE KNOW, MONKEY. WE KNOW.

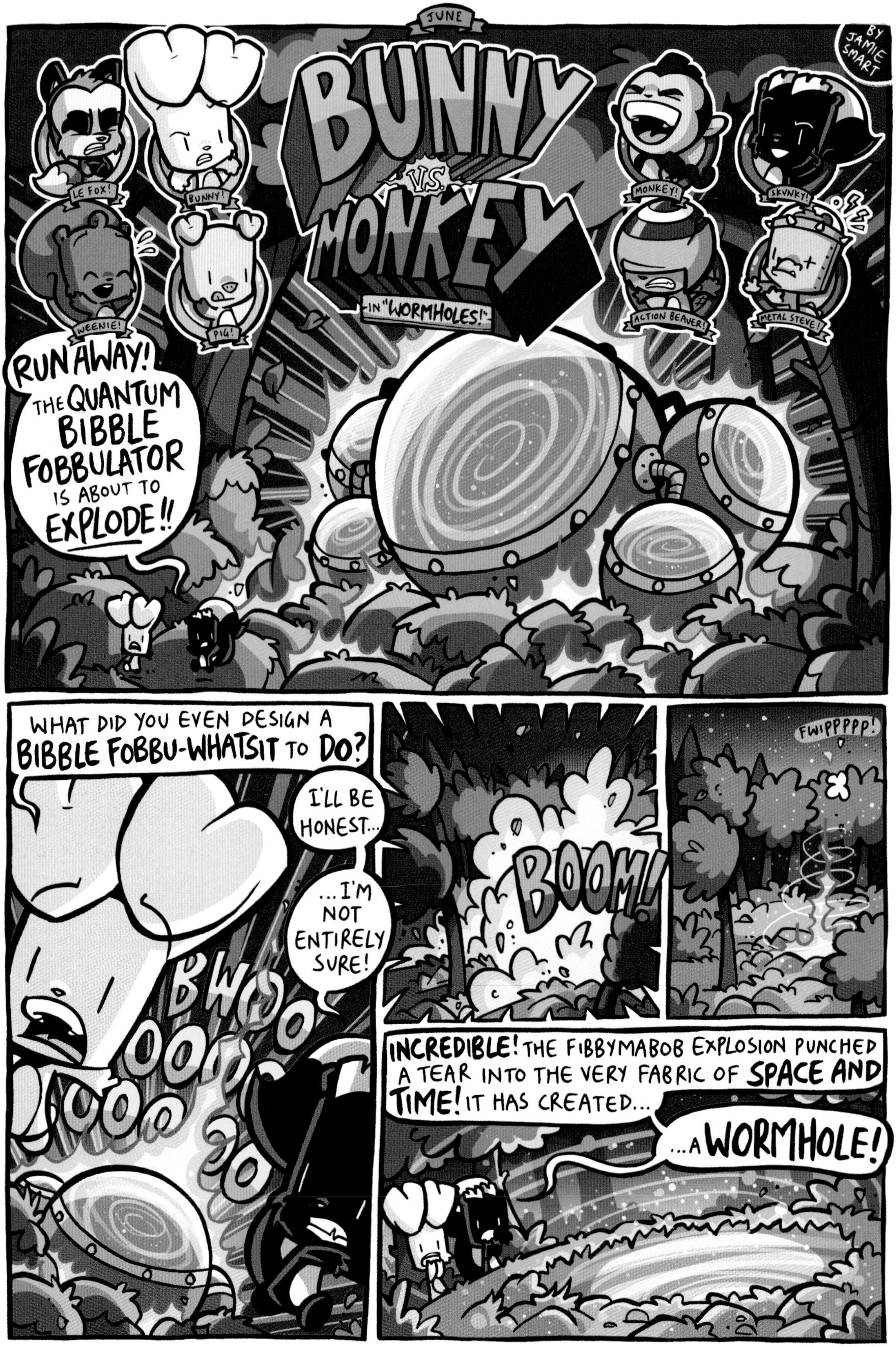

JUNE
BUNNY V.S. MONKEY
IN "WORMHOLES!"
BY JAMIE SMART
LE FOX!
BUNNY!
WEENIE!
PIG!
MONKEY!
SKUNKY!
ACTION BEAVER!
METAL STEVE!
RUN AWAY! THE QUANTUM BIBBLE FOBBULATOR IS ABOUT TO EXPLODE!!
WHAT DID YOU EVEN DESIGN A BIBBLE FOBBU-WHATSIT TO DO?
I'LL BE HONEST...
...I'M NOT ENTIRELY SURE!
BWOOOOOOOOOOO
BOOM!!
FWIPPPPP!
INCREDIBLE! THE FIBBYMABOB EXPLOSION PUNCHED A TEAR INTO THE VERY FABRIC OF SPACE AND TIME! IT HAS CREATED...
...A WORMHOLE!

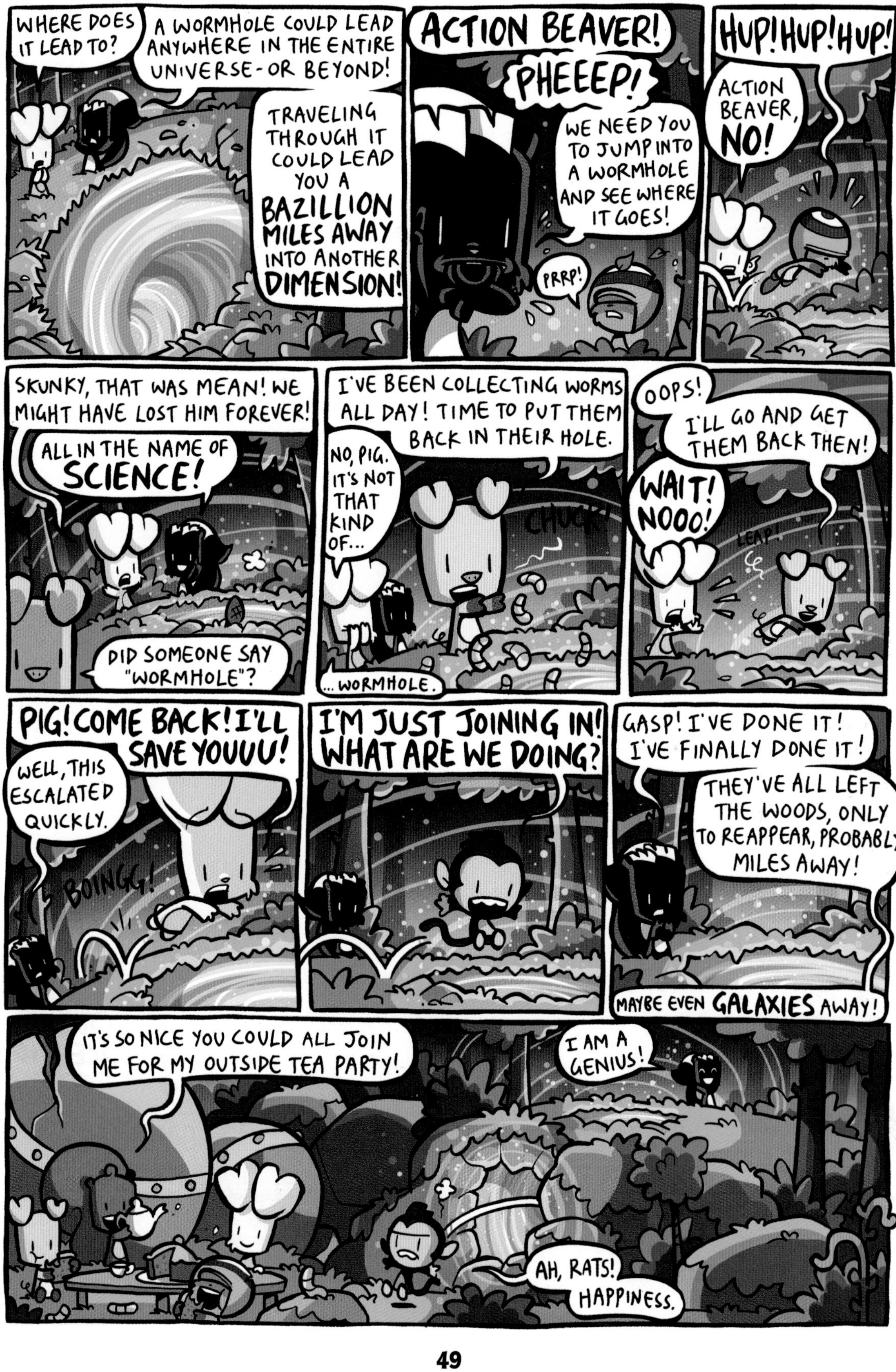
WHERE DOES IT LEAD TO?
A WORMHOLE COULD LEAD ANYWHERE IN THE ENTIRE UNIVERSE - OR BEYOND!
TRAVELING THROUGH IT COULD LEAD YOU A BAZILLION MILES AWAY INTO ANOTHER DIMENSION!
ACTION BEAVER!
PHEEEP!
WE NEED YOU TO JUMP INTO A WORMHOLE AND SEE WHERE IT GOES!
PRRP!
HUP! HUP! HUP!
ACTION BEAVER, NO!
SKUNKY, THAT WAS MEAN! WE MIGHT HAVE LOST HIM FOREVER!
ALL IN THE NAME OF SCIENCE!
DID SOMEONE SAY "WORMHOLE"?
I'VE BEEN COLLECTING WORMS ALL DAY! TIME TO PUT THEM BACK IN THEIR HOLE.
NO, PIG. IT'S NOT THAT KIND OF...
CHUCK!
...WORMHOLE.
OOPS!
I'LL GO AND GET THEM BACK THEN!
WAIT! NOOO!
LEAP!
PIG! COME BACK! I'LL SAVE YOUUU!
WELL, THIS ESCALATED QUICKLY.
BOINGG!
I'M JUST JOINING IN! WHAT ARE WE DOING?
GASP! I'VE DONE IT! I'VE FINALLY DONE IT!
THEY'VE ALL LEFT THE WOODS, ONLY TO REAPPEAR, PROBABLY MILES AWAY!
MAYBE EVEN GALAXIES AWAY!
IT'S SO NICE YOU COULD ALL JOIN ME FOR MY OUTSIDE TEA PARTY!
I AM A GENIUS!
AH, RATS! HAPPINESS.

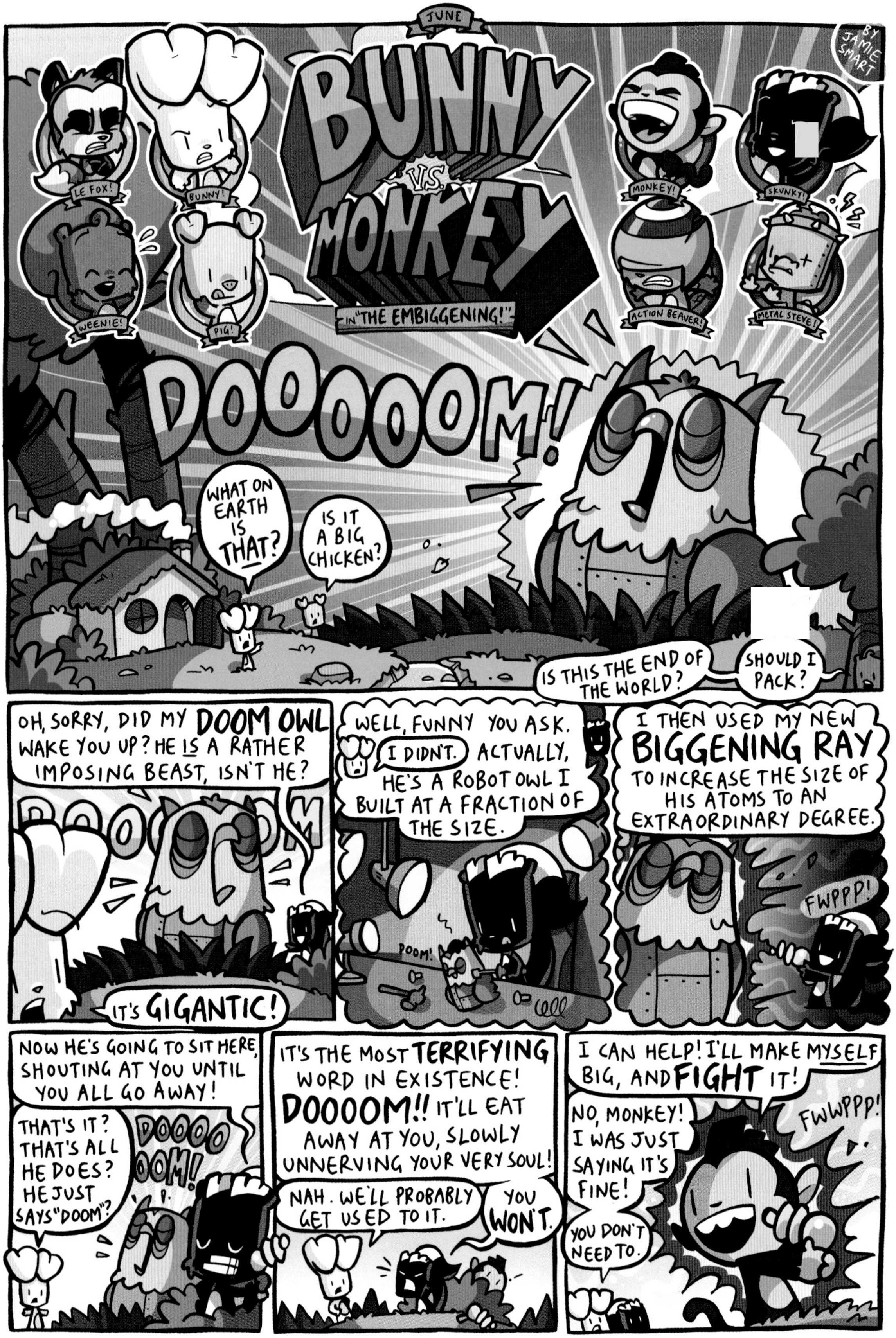
JUNE
BUNNY VS. MONKEY
IN "THE EMBIGGENING!"
BY JAMIE SMART
LE FOX!
BUNNY!
MONKEY!
SKUNKY!
WEENIE!
PIG!
ACTION BEAVER!
METAL STEVE!
DOOOOOM!
WHAT ON EARTH IS THAT?
IS IT A BIG CHICKEN?
IS THIS THE END OF THE WORLD?
SHOULD I PACK?
OH, SORRY, DID MY DOOM OWL WAKE YOU UP? HE IS A RATHER IMPOSING BEAST, ISN'T HE?
IT'S GIGANTIC!
WELL, FUNNY YOU ASK.
I DIDN'T.
ACTUALLY, HE'S A ROBOT OWL I BUILT AT A FRACTION OF THE SIZE.
DOOM!
I THEN USED MY NEW BIGGENING RAY TO INCREASE THE SIZE OF HIS ATOMS TO AN EXTRAORDINARY DEGREE.
FWPPP!
NOW HE'S GOING TO SIT HERE, SHOUTING AT YOU UNTIL YOU ALL GO AWAY!
THAT'S IT? THAT'S ALL HE DOES? HE JUST SAYS "DOOM"?
DOOOOOOM!
IT'S THE MOST TERRIFYING WORD IN EXISTENCE! DOOOOM!! IT'LL EAT AWAY AT YOU, SLOWLY UNNERVING YOUR VERY SOUL!
NAH. WE'LL PROBABLY GET USED TO IT.
YOU WON'T.
I CAN HELP! I'LL MAKE MYSELF BIG, AND FIGHT IT!
FWWPPP!
NO, MONKEY! I WAS JUST SAYING IT'S FINE!
YOU DON'T NEED TO.

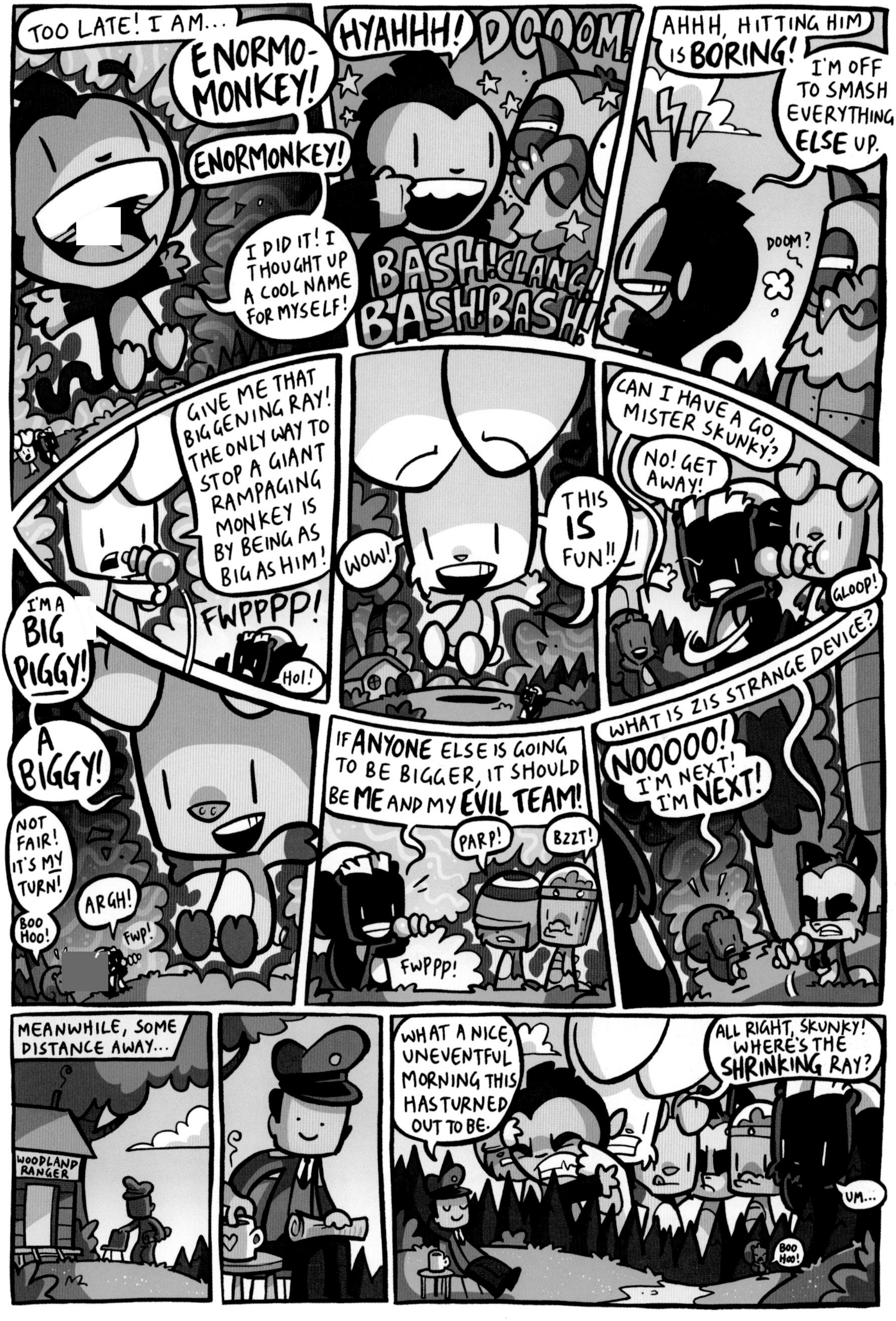
TOO LATE! I AM...
ENORMO-MONKEY!
ENORMONKEY!
I DID IT! I THOUGHT UP A COOL NAME FOR MYSELF!
HYAHHH!
DOOOM!
BASH! CLANG! BASH! BASH!
AHHH, HITTING HIM IS BORING!
I'M OFF TO SMASH EVERYTHING ELSE UP.
DOOM?
GIVE ME THAT BIGGENING RAY! THE ONLY WAY TO STOP A GIANT RAMPAGING MONKEY IS BY BEING AS BIG AS HIM!
FWPPPP!
HO!
WOW!
THIS IS FUN!!
CAN I HAVE A GO, MISTER SKUNKY?
NO! GET AWAY!
GLOOP!
I'M A BIG PIGGY!
A BIGGY!
NOT FAIR! IT'S MY TURN!
ARGH!
BOO HOO!
FWP!
IF ANYONE ELSE IS GOING TO BE BIGGER, IT SHOULD BE ME AND MY EVIL TEAM!
PARP!
BZZT!
FWPPP!
WHAT IS ZIS STRANGE DEVICE?
NOOOOO! I'M NEXT! I'M NEXT!
MEANWHILE, SOME DISTANCE AWAY...
WOODLAND RANGER
WHAT A NICE, UNEVENTFUL MORNING THIS HAS TURNED OUT TO BE.
ALL RIGHT, SKUNKY! WHERE'S THE SHRINKING RAY?
UM...
BOO HOO!

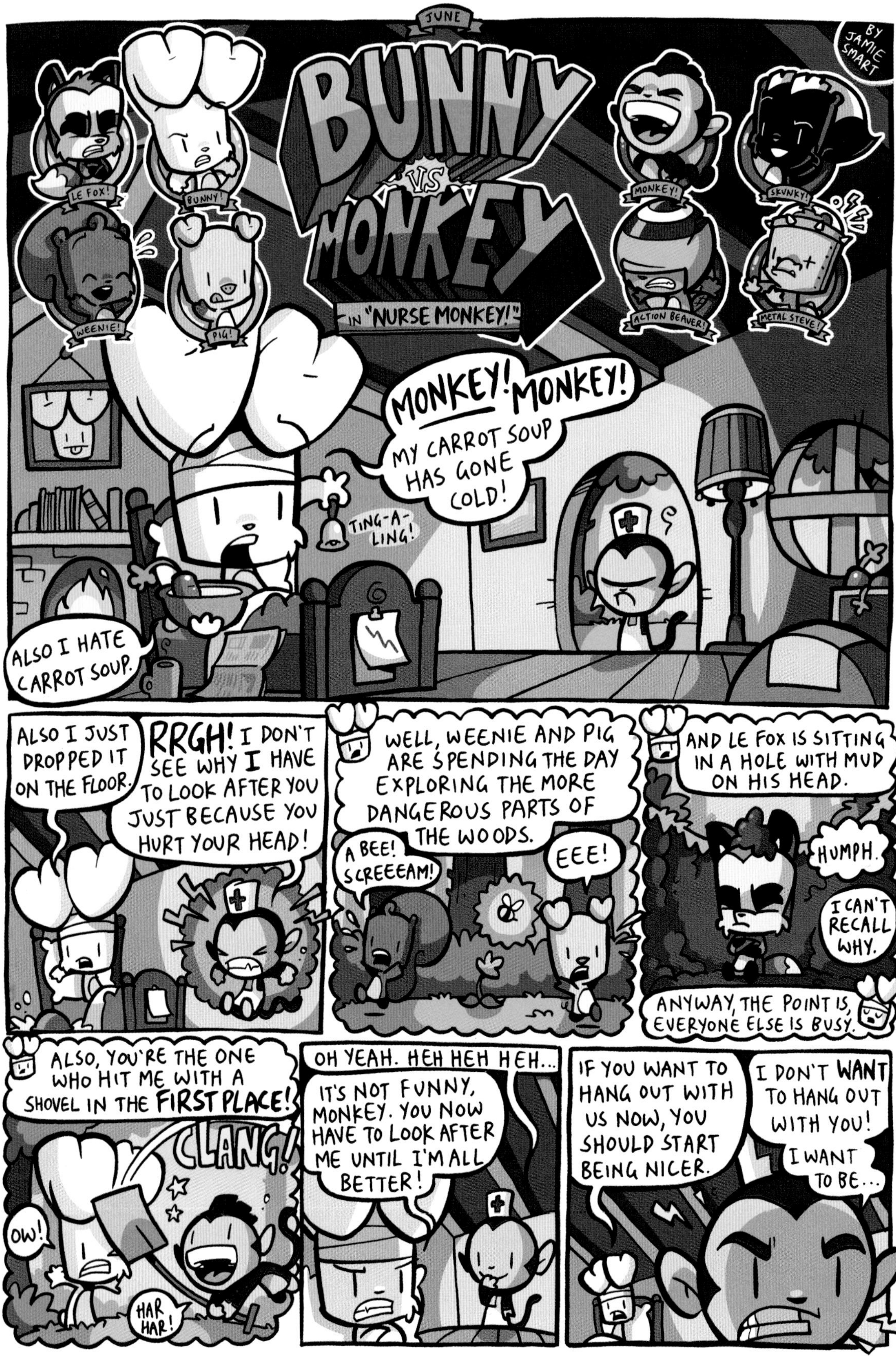
JUNE
BY JAMIE SMART
BUNNY VS MONKEY
IN "NURSE MONKEY!"
LE FOX!
BUNNY!
WEENIE!
PIG!
MONKEY!
SKUNKY!
ACTION BEAVER!
METAL STEVE!
MONKEY! MONKEY! MY CARROT SOUP HAS GONE COLD!
TING-A-LING!
ALSO I HATE CARROT SOUP.
ALSO I JUST DROPPED IT ON THE FLOOR.
RRGH! I DON'T SEE WHY I HAVE TO LOOK AFTER YOU JUST BECAUSE YOU HURT YOUR HEAD!
WELL, WEENIE AND PIG ARE SPENDING THE DAY EXPLORING THE MORE DANGEROUS PARTS OF THE WOODS.
A BEE! SCREEEAM!
EEE!
AND LE FOX IS SITTING IN A HOLE WITH MUD ON HIS HEAD.
HUMPH.
I CAN'T RECALL WHY.
ANYWAY, THE POINT IS, EVERYONE ELSE IS BUSY.
ALSO, YOU'RE THE ONE WHO HIT ME WITH A SHOVEL IN THE FIRST PLACE!
CLANG!
OW!
HAR HAR!
OH YEAH. HEH HEH HEH...
IT'S NOT FUNNY, MONKEY. YOU NOW HAVE TO LOOK AFTER ME UNTIL I'M ALL BETTER!
IF YOU WANT TO HANG OUT WITH US NOW, YOU SHOULD START BEING NICER.
I DON'T WANT TO HANG OUT WITH YOU!
I WANT TO BE...

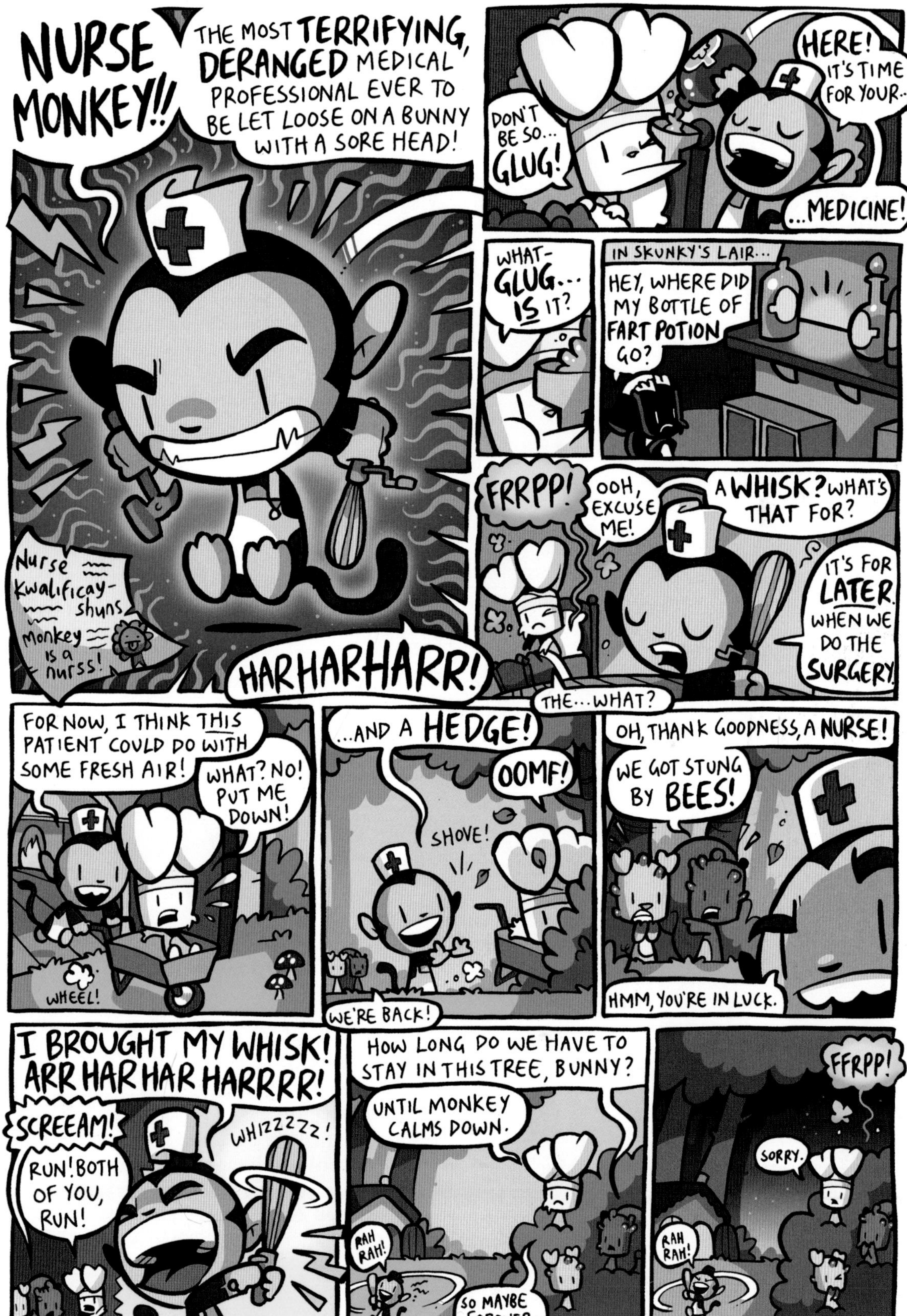
NURSE MONKEY!!
THE MOST TERRIFYING, DERANGED MEDICAL PROFESSIONAL EVER TO BE LET LOOSE ON A BUNNY WITH A SORE HEAD!
Nurse Kwalificayshuns
Monkey is a nurss!
HARHARHARR!
HERE! IT'S TIME FOR YOUR...
DON'T BE SO... GLUG!
...MEDICINE!
WHAT-GLUG... IS IT?
IN SKUNKY'S LAIR...
HEY, WHERE DID MY BOTTLE OF FART POTION GO?
FRRPP!
OOH, EXCUSE ME!
A WHISK? WHAT'S THAT FOR?
IT'S FOR LATER. WHEN WE DO THE SURGERY.
THE...WHAT?
FOR NOW, I THINK THIS PATIENT COULD DO WITH SOME FRESH AIR!
WHAT? NO! PUT ME DOWN!
WHEEL!
...AND A HEDGE!
OOMF!
SHOVE!
WE'RE BACK!
OH, THANK GOODNESS, A NURSE!
WE GOT STUNG BY BEES!
HMM, YOU'RE IN LUCK.
I BROUGHT MY WHISK! ARR HAR HAR HARRRR!
SCREEAM!
RUN! BOTH OF YOU, RUN!
WHIZZZZZ!
HOW LONG DO WE HAVE TO STAY IN THIS TREE, BUNNY?
UNTIL MONKEY CALMS DOWN.
RAH RAH!
SO MAYBE FOREVER.
FFRPP!
SORRY.
RAH RAH!

PLEASE DO NOT IMITATE ANYTHING MONKEY DOES. HE IS A TRAINED IDIOT!

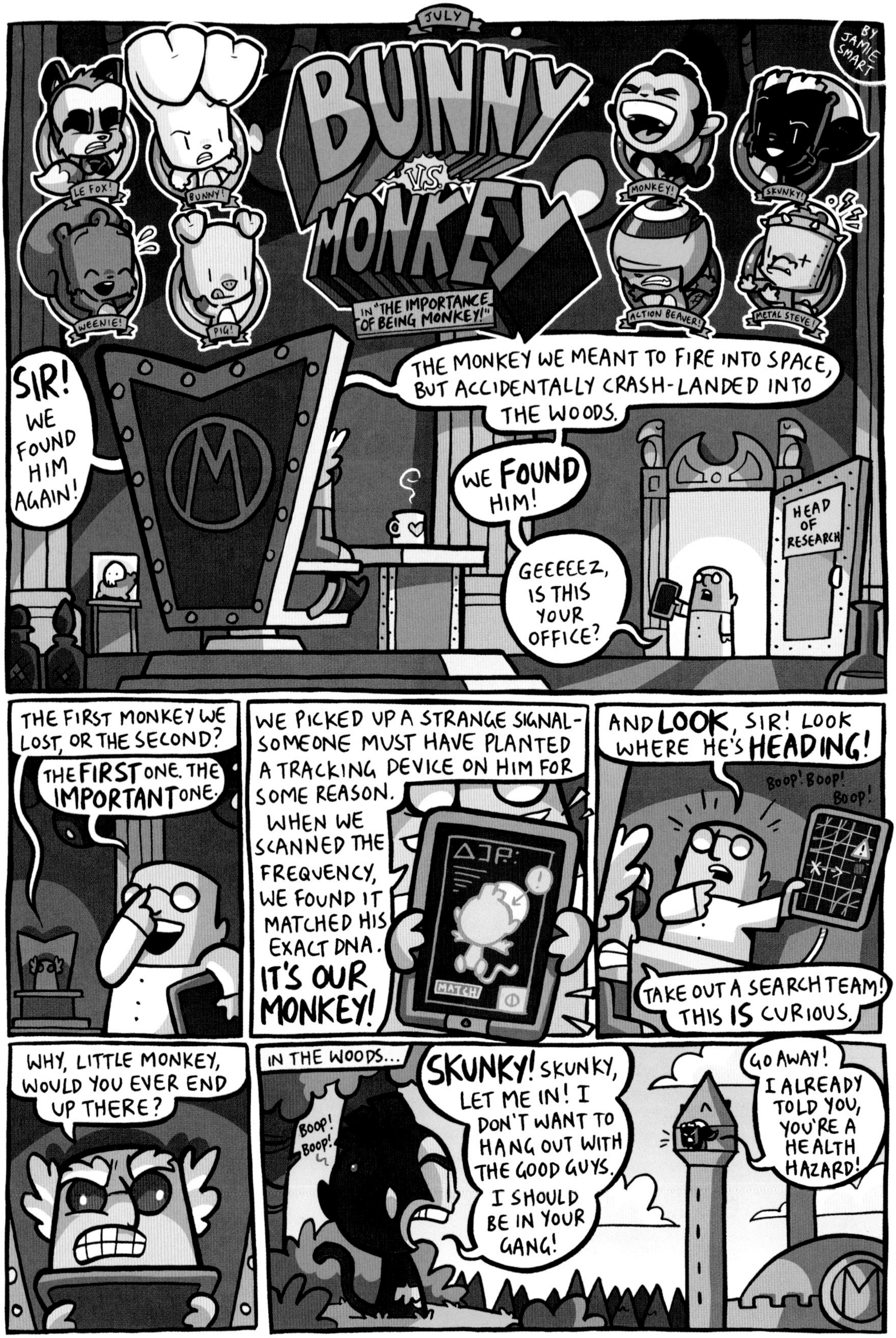
JULY
BUNNY VS. MONKEY
IN "THE IMPORTANCE OF BEING MONKEY!"
BY JAMIE SMART
LE FOX!
BUNNY!
MONKEY!
SKUNKY!
WEENIE!
PIG!
ACTION BEAVER!
METAL STEVE!
SIR! WE FOUND HIM AGAIN!
THE MONKEY WE MEANT TO FIRE INTO SPACE, BUT ACCIDENTALLY CRASH-LANDED INTO THE WOODS.
WE FOUND HIM!
GEEEEEZ, IS THIS YOUR OFFICE?
HEAD OF RESEARCH
THE FIRST MONKEY WE LOST, OR THE SECOND?
THE FIRST ONE. THE IMPORTANT ONE.
WE PICKED UP A STRANGE SIGNAL- SOMEONE MUST HAVE PLANTED A TRACKING DEVICE ON HIM FOR SOME REASON.
WHEN WE SCANNED THE FREQUENCY, WE FOUND IT MATCHED HIS EXACT DNA.
IT'S OUR MONKEY!
MATCH
AND LOOK, SIR! LOOK WHERE HE'S HEADING!
BOOP! BOOP! BOOP!
TAKE OUT A SEARCH TEAM! THIS IS CURIOUS.
WHY, LITTLE MONKEY, WOULD YOU EVER END UP THERE?
IN THE WOODS...
BOOP! BOOP!
SKUNKY! SKUNKY, LET ME IN! I DON'T WANT TO HANG OUT WITH THE GOOD GUYS.
I SHOULD BE IN YOUR GANG!
GO AWAY! I ALREADY TOLD YOU, YOU'RE A HEALTH HAZARD!

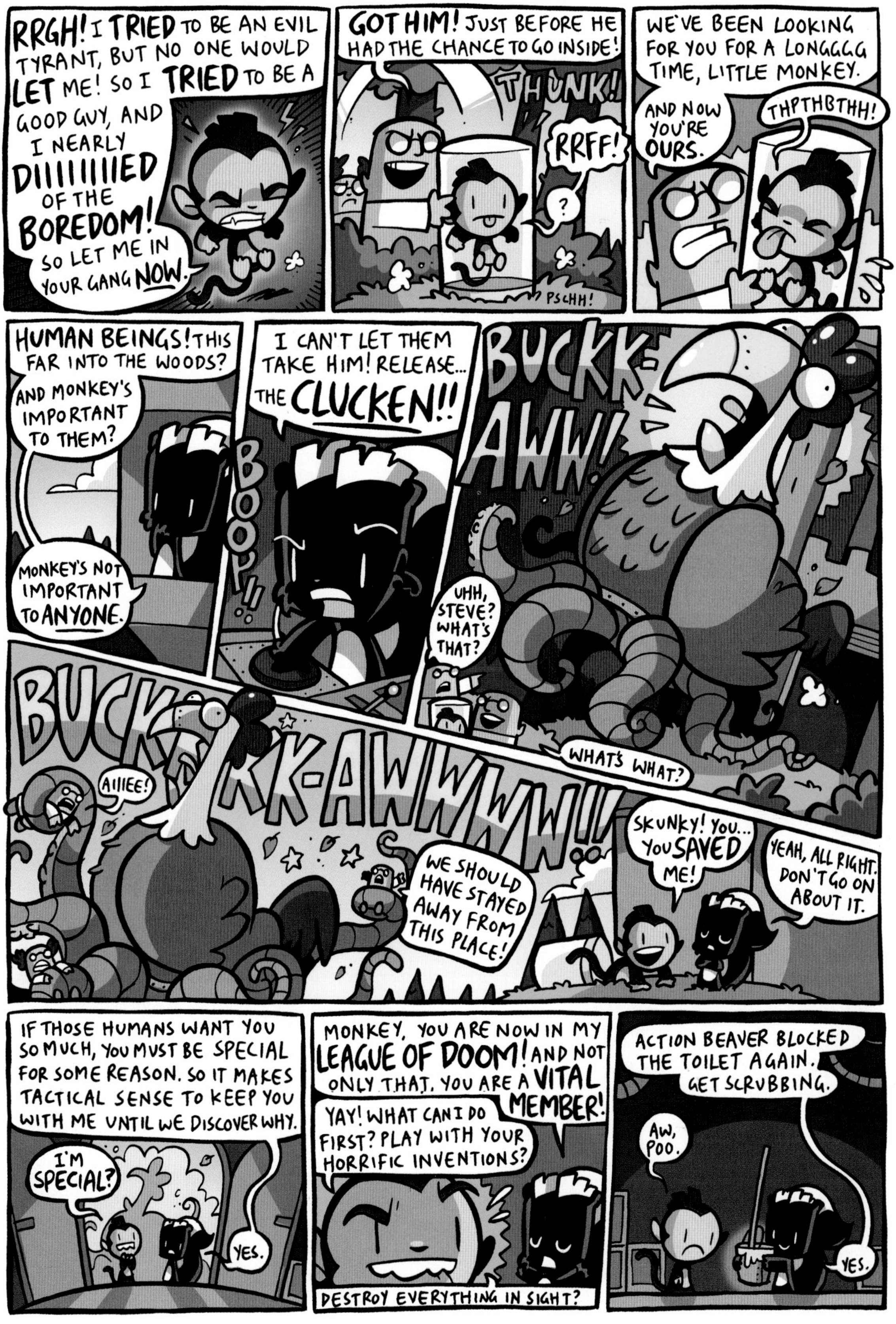
RRGH! I TRIED TO BE AN EVIL TYRANT, BUT NO ONE WOULD LET ME! SO I TRIED TO BE A GOOD GUY, AND I NEARLY DIIIIIIIIED OF THE BOREDOM! SO LET ME IN YOUR GANG NOW.
GOT HIM! JUST BEFORE HE HAD THE CHANCE TO GO INSIDE!
THUNK!
RRFF!
?
PSCHH!
WE'VE BEEN LOOKING FOR YOU FOR A LONGGGG TIME, LITTLE MONKEY.
AND NOW YOU'RE OURS.
THPTHBTHH!
HUMAN BEINGS! THIS FAR INTO THE WOODS?
AND MONKEY'S IMPORTANT TO THEM?
MONKEY'S NOT IMPORTANT TO ANYONE.
I CAN'T LET THEM TAKE HIM! RELEASE... THE CLUCKEN!!
BOOP!!
BUCKK-AWW!
UHH, STEVE? WHAT'S THAT?
WHAT'S WHAT?
BUCKKKK-AWWWWW!!
AIIIEE!
WE SHOULD HAVE STAYED AWAY FROM THIS PLACE!
SKUNKY! YOU... YOU SAVED ME!
YEAH, ALL RIGHT. DON'T GO ON ABOUT IT.
IF THOSE HUMANS WANT YOU SO MUCH, YOU MUST BE SPECIAL FOR SOME REASON. SO IT MAKES TACTICAL SENSE TO KEEP YOU WITH ME UNTIL WE DISCOVER WHY.
I'M SPECIAL?
YES.
MONKEY, YOU ARE NOW IN MY LEAGUE OF DOOM! AND NOT ONLY THAT. YOU ARE A VITAL MEMBER!
YAY! WHAT CAN I DO FIRST? PLAY WITH YOUR HORRIFIC INVENTIONS?
DESTROY EVERYTHING IN SIGHT?
ACTION BEAVER BLOCKED THE TOILET AGAIN. GET SCRUBBING.
AW, POO.
YES.

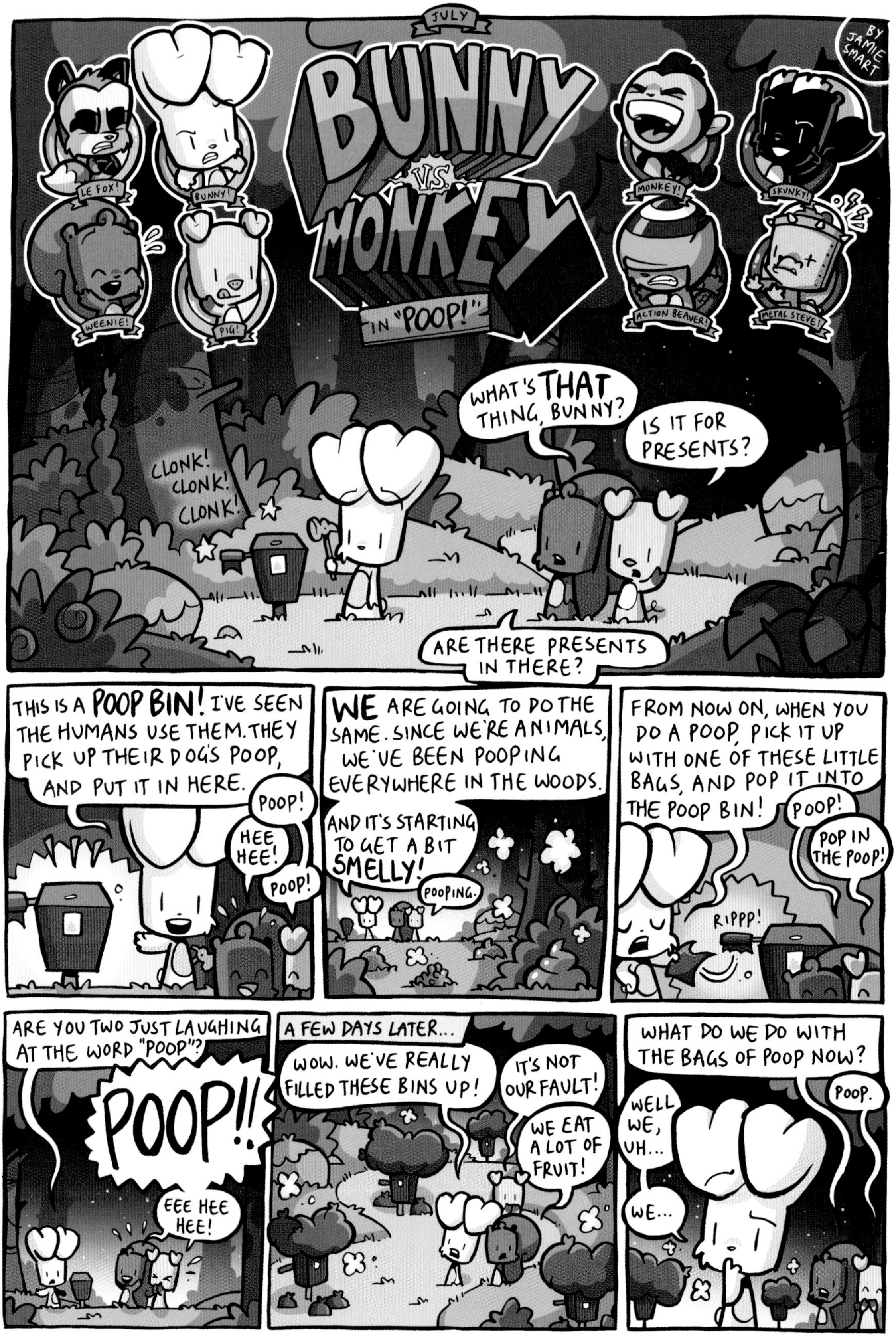
JULY
BUNNY VS. MONKEY
IN "POOP!"
BY JAMIE SMART
LE FOX!
BUNNY!
WEENIE!
PIG!
MONKEY!
SKUNKY!
ACTION BEAVER!
METAL STEVE!
CLONK! CLONK! CLONK!
WHAT'S THAT THING, BUNNY?
IS IT FOR PRESENTS?
ARE THERE PRESENTS IN THERE?
THIS IS A POOP BIN! I'VE SEEN THE HUMANS USE THEM. THEY PICK UP THEIR DOG'S POOP, AND PUT IT IN HERE.
POOP!
HEE HEE!
POOP!
WE ARE GOING TO DO THE SAME. SINCE WE'RE ANIMALS, WE'VE BEEN POOPING EVERYWHERE IN THE WOODS.
AND IT'S STARTING TO GET A BIT SMELLY!
POOPING.
FROM NOW ON, WHEN YOU DO A POOP, PICK IT UP WITH ONE OF THESE LITTLE BAGS, AND POP IT INTO THE POOP BIN!
POOP!
POP IN THE POOP!
RIPPP!
ARE YOU TWO JUST LAUGHING AT THE WORD "POOP"?
POOP!!
EEE HEE HEE!
A FEW DAYS LATER...
WOW. WE'VE REALLY FILLED THESE BINS UP!
IT'S NOT OUR FAULT!
WE EAT A LOT OF FRUIT!
WHAT DO WE DO WITH THE BAGS OF POOP NOW?
POOP.
WELL WE, UH...
WE...

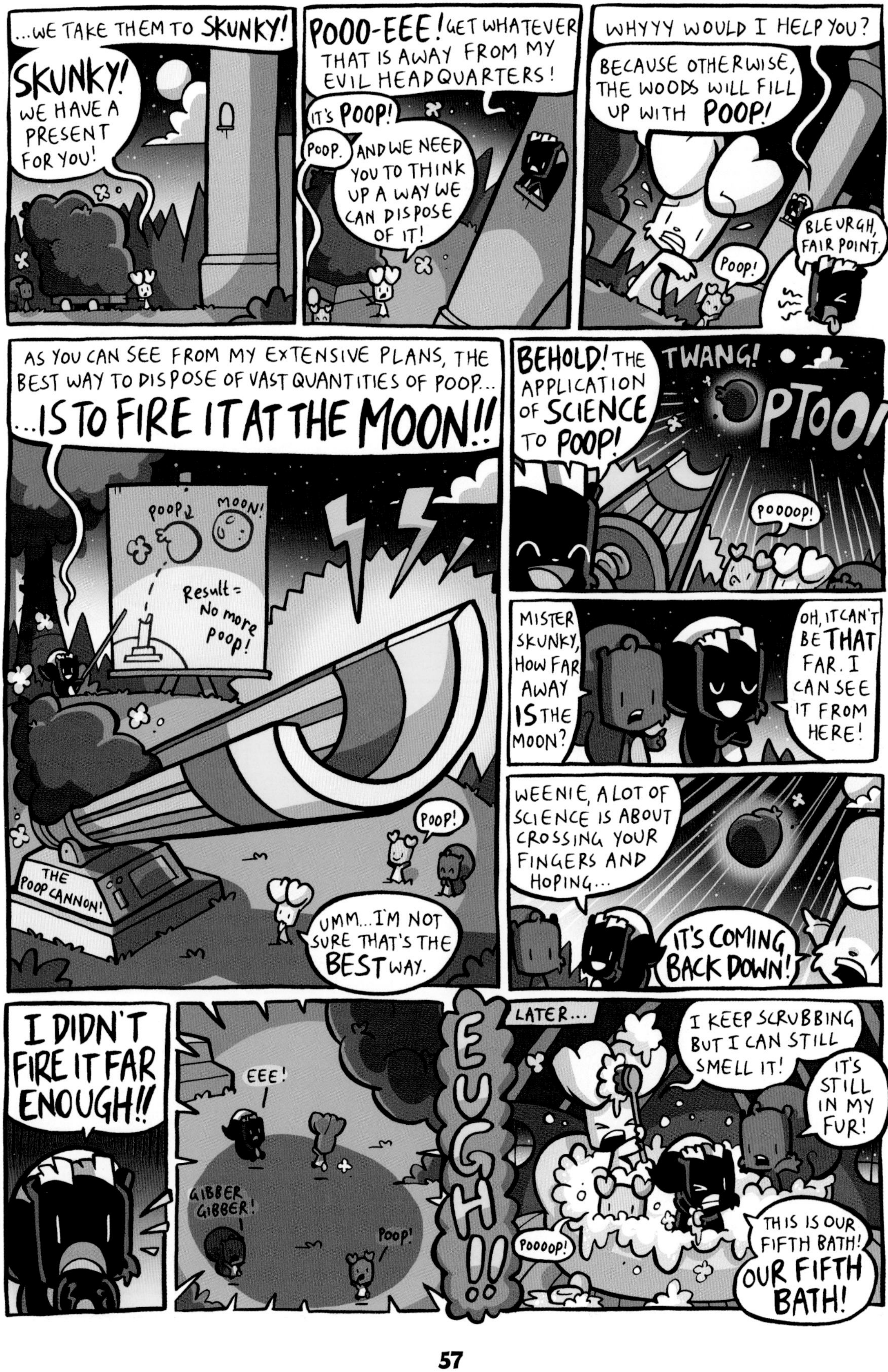
...WE TAKE THEM TO SKUNKY!
SKUNKY! WE HAVE A PRESENT FOR YOU!
POOO-EEE! GET WHATEVER THAT IS AWAY FROM MY EVIL HEADQUARTERS!
IT'S POOP!
POOP.
AND WE NEED YOU TO THINK UP A WAY WE CAN DISPOSE OF IT!
WHYYY WOULD I HELP YOU?
BECAUSE OTHERWISE, THE WOODS WILL FILL UP WITH POOP!
BLEURGH, FAIR POINT.
POOP!
AS YOU CAN SEE FROM MY EXTENSIVE PLANS, THE BEST WAY TO DISPOSE OF VAST QUANTITIES OF POOP...
...IS TO FIRE IT AT THE MOON!!
POOP
MOON!
Result = No more poop!
THE POOP CANNON!
POOP!
UMM...I'M NOT SURE THAT'S THE BEST WAY.
BEHOLD! THE APPLICATION OF SCIENCE TO POOP!
TWANG!
PTOO!
POOOOP!
MISTER SKUNKY, HOW FAR AWAY IS THE MOON?
OH, IT CAN'T BE THAT FAR. I CAN SEE IT FROM HERE!
WEENIE, A LOT OF SCIENCE IS ABOUT CROSSING YOUR FINGERS AND HOPING...
IT'S COMING BACK DOWN!
I DIDN'T FIRE IT FAR ENOUGH!!
EEE!
GIBBER GIBBER!
POOP!
EUGH!!
LATER...
I KEEP SCRUBBING BUT I CAN STILL SMELL IT!
IT'S STILL IN MY FUR!
POOOOP!
THIS IS OUR FIFTH BATH! OUR FIFTH BATH!

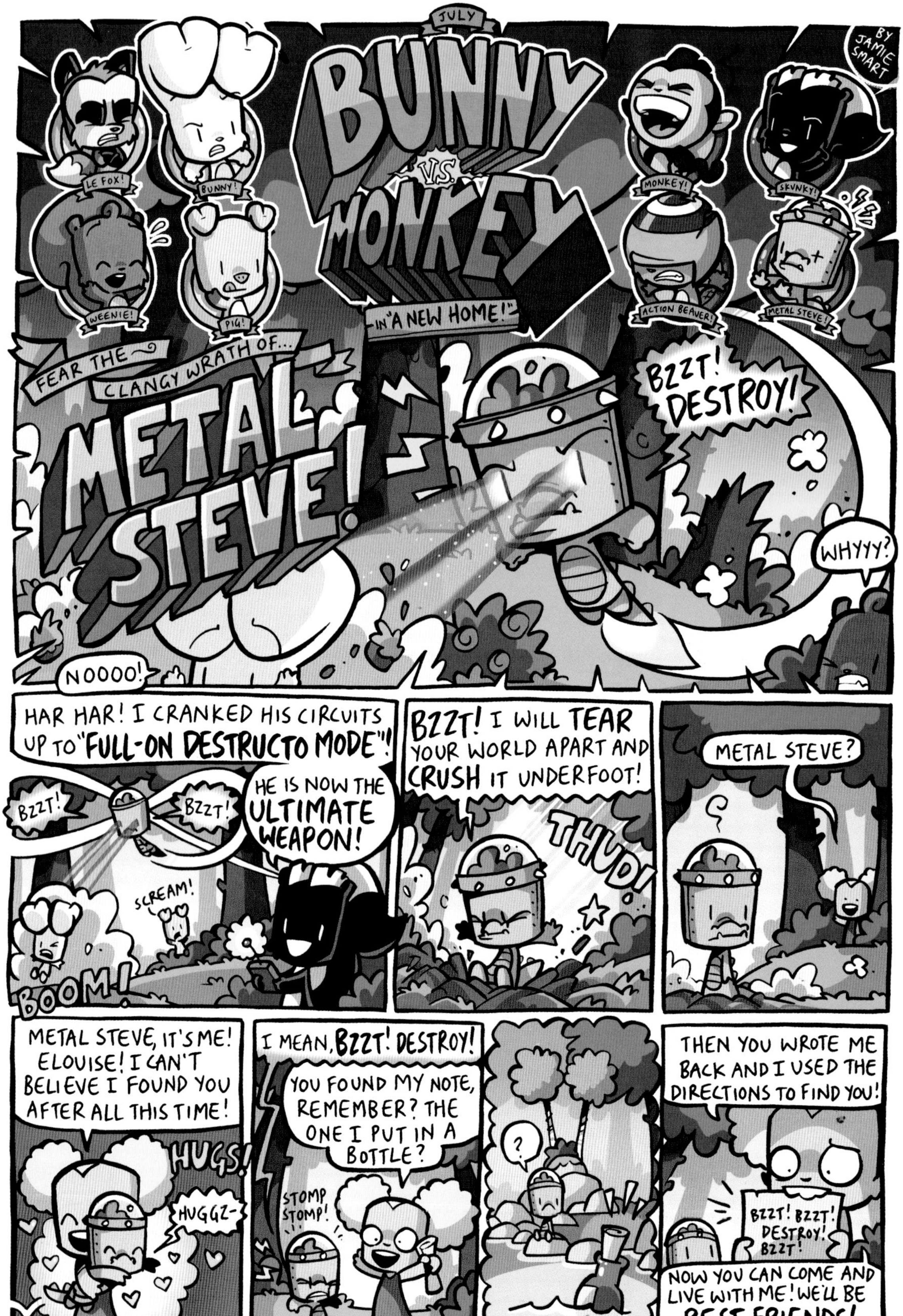

JULY
BUNNY VS. MONKEY
BY JAMIE SMART
LE FOX!
BUNNY!
MONKEY!
SKUNKY!
WEENIE!
PIG!
ACTION BEAVER!
METAL STEVE!
IN "A NEW HOME!"
FEAR THE CLANGY WRATH OF...
METAL STEVE!
BZZT! DESTROY!
WHYYY?
NOOOO!
HAR HAR! I CRANKED HIS CIRCUITS UP TO "FULL-ON DESTRUCTO MODE"!
BZZT!
BZZT!
HE IS NOW THE ULTIMATE WEAPON!
SCREAM!
BOOM!
BZZT! I WILL TEAR YOUR WORLD APART AND CRUSH IT UNDERFOOT!
THUD!
METAL STEVE?
METAL STEVE, IT'S ME! ELOUISE! I CAN'T BELIEVE I FOUND YOU AFTER ALL THIS TIME!
HUGS!
HUGGZ-
I MEAN, BZZT! DESTROY!
YOU FOUND MY NOTE, REMEMBER? THE ONE I PUT IN A BOTTLE?
STOMP STOMP!
?
THEN YOU WROTE ME BACK AND I USED THE DIRECTIONS TO FIND YOU!
BZZT! BZZT! DESTROY! BZZT!
NOW YOU CAN COME AND LIVE WITH ME! WE'LL BE BEST FRIENDS!

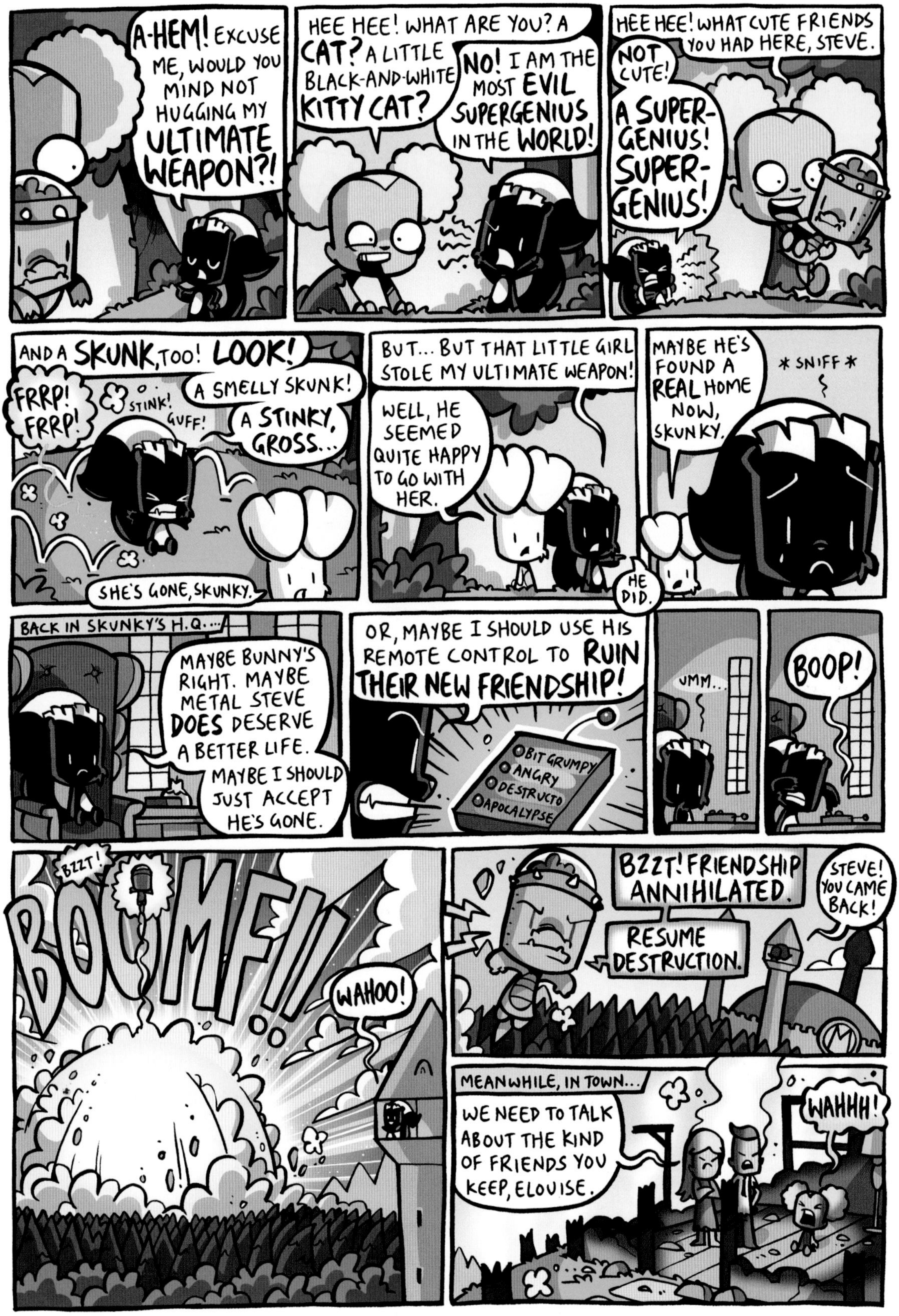
A-HEM! EXCUSE ME, WOULD YOU MIND NOT HUGGING MY ULTIMATE WEAPON?!
HEE HEE! WHAT ARE YOU? A CAT? A LITTLE BLACK-AND-WHITE KITTY CAT?
NO! I AM THE MOST EVIL SUPERGENIUS IN THE WORLD!
HEE HEE! WHAT CUTE FRIENDS YOU HAD HERE, STEVE.
NOT CUTE!
A SUPER-GENIUS! SUPER-GENIUS!
AND A SKUNK, TOO! LOOK!
FRRP! FRRP!
STINK!
GUFF!
A SMELLY SKUNK!
A STINKY, GROSS...
SHE'S GONE, SKUNKY.
BUT... BUT THAT LITTLE GIRL STOLE MY ULTIMATE WEAPON!
WELL, HE SEEMED QUITE HAPPY TO GO WITH HER.
MAYBE HE'S FOUND A REAL HOME NOW, SKUNKY.
* SNIFF *
HE DID.
BACK IN SKUNKY'S H.Q....
MAYBE BUNNY'S RIGHT. MAYBE METAL STEVE DOES DESERVE A BETTER LIFE.
MAYBE I SHOULD JUST ACCEPT HE'S GONE.
OR, MAYBE I SHOULD USE HIS REMOTE CONTROL TO RUIN THEIR NEW FRIENDSHIP!
BIT GRUMPY
ANGRY
DESTRUCTO
APOCALYPSE
UMM...
BOOP!
BZZT!
BOOMF!!!
WAHOO!
BZZT! FRIENDSHIP ANNIHILATED.
RESUME DESTRUCTION.
STEVE! YOU CAME BACK!
MEANWHILE, IN TOWN...
WE NEED TO TALK ABOUT THE KIND OF FRIENDS YOU KEEP, ELOUISE.
WAHHH!

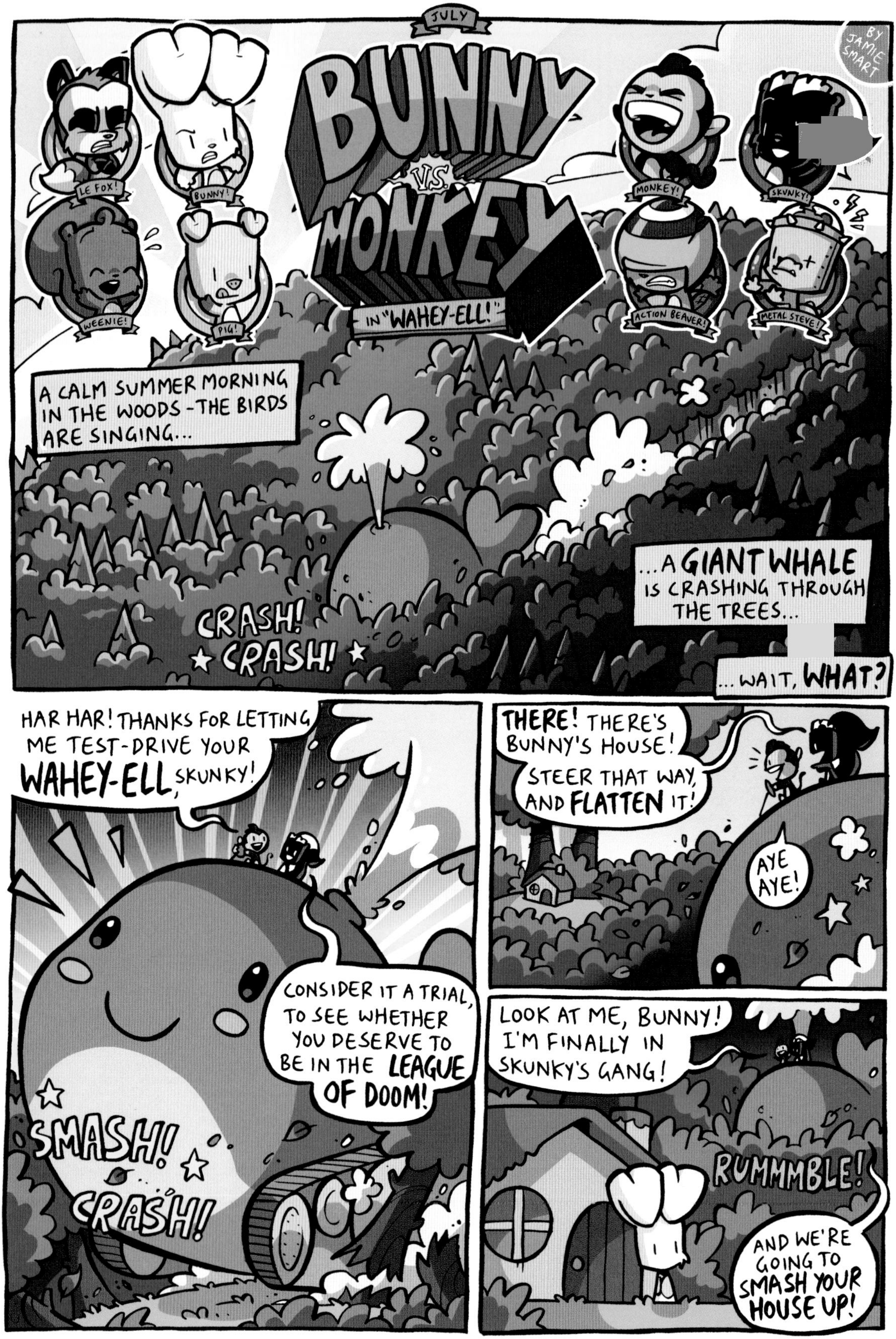
JULY
BUNNY VS. MONKEY
BY JAMIE SMART
LE FOX!
BUNNY!
WEENIE!
PIG!
MONKEY!
SKUNKY!
ACTION BEAVER!
METAL STEVE!
IN "WAHEY-ELL!"
A CALM SUMMER MORNING IN THE WOODS - THE BIRDS ARE SINGING...
CRASH! CRASH!
...A GIANT WHALE IS CRASHING THROUGH THE TREES...
...WAIT, WHAT?
HAR HAR! THANKS FOR LETTING ME TEST-DRIVE YOUR WAHEY-ELL, SKUNKY!
CONSIDER IT A TRIAL, TO SEE WHETHER YOU DESERVE TO BE IN THE LEAGUE OF DOOM!
SMASH!
CRASH!
THERE! THERE'S BUNNY'S HOUSE!
STEER THAT WAY, AND FLATTEN IT!
AYE AYE!
LOOK AT ME, BUNNY! I'M FINALLY IN SKUNKY'S GANG!
RUMMMBLE!
AND WE'RE GOING TO SMASH YOUR HOUSE UP!

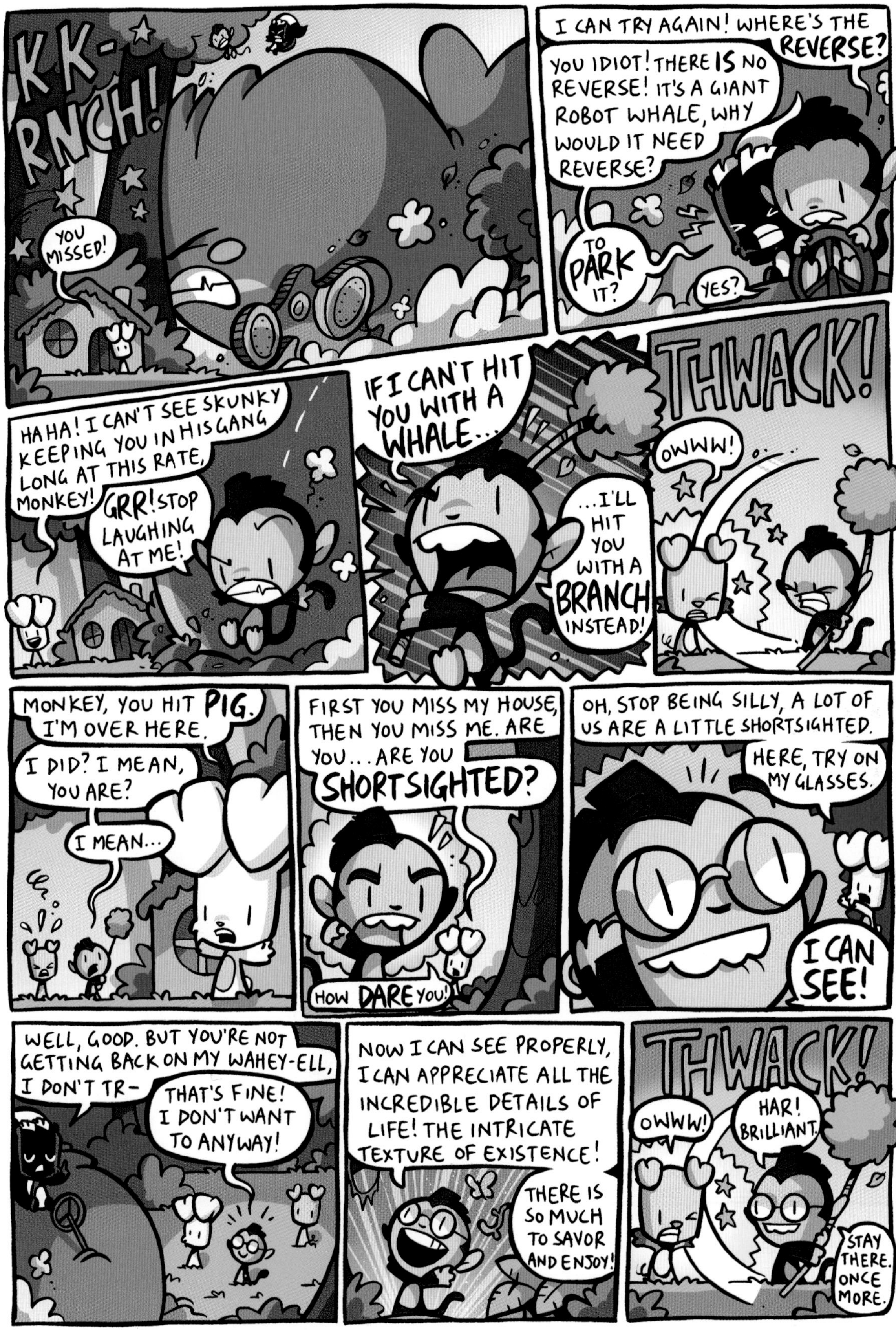
K K-RNCH!
YOU MISSED!
I CAN TRY AGAIN! WHERE'S THE REVERSE?
YOU IDIOT! THERE IS NO REVERSE! IT'S A GIANT ROBOT WHALE, WHY WOULD IT NEED REVERSE?
TO PARK IT?
YES?
HA HA! I CAN'T SEE SKUNKY KEEPING YOU IN HIS GANG LONG AT THIS RATE, MONKEY!
GRR! STOP LAUGHING AT ME!
IF I CAN'T HIT YOU WITH A WHALE...
...I'LL HIT YOU WITH A BRANCH INSTEAD!
THWACK!
OWWW!
MONKEY, YOU HIT PIG. I'M OVER HERE.
I DID? I MEAN, YOU ARE?
I MEAN...
FIRST YOU MISS MY HOUSE, THEN YOU MISS ME. ARE YOU... ARE YOU SHORTSIGHTED?
HOW DARE YOU!
OH, STOP BEING SILLY, A LOT OF US ARE A LITTLE SHORTSIGHTED.
HERE, TRY ON MY GLASSES.
I CAN SEE!
WELL, GOOD. BUT YOU'RE NOT GETTING BACK ON MY WAHEY-ELL, I DON'T TR-
THAT'S FINE! I DON'T WANT TO ANYWAY!
NOW I CAN SEE PROPERLY, I CAN APPRECIATE ALL THE INCREDIBLE DETAILS OF LIFE! THE INTRICATE TEXTURE OF EXISTENCE!
THERE IS SO MUCH TO SAVOR AND ENJOY!
THWACK!
OWWW!
HAR! BRILLIANT.
STAY THERE. ONCE MORE.

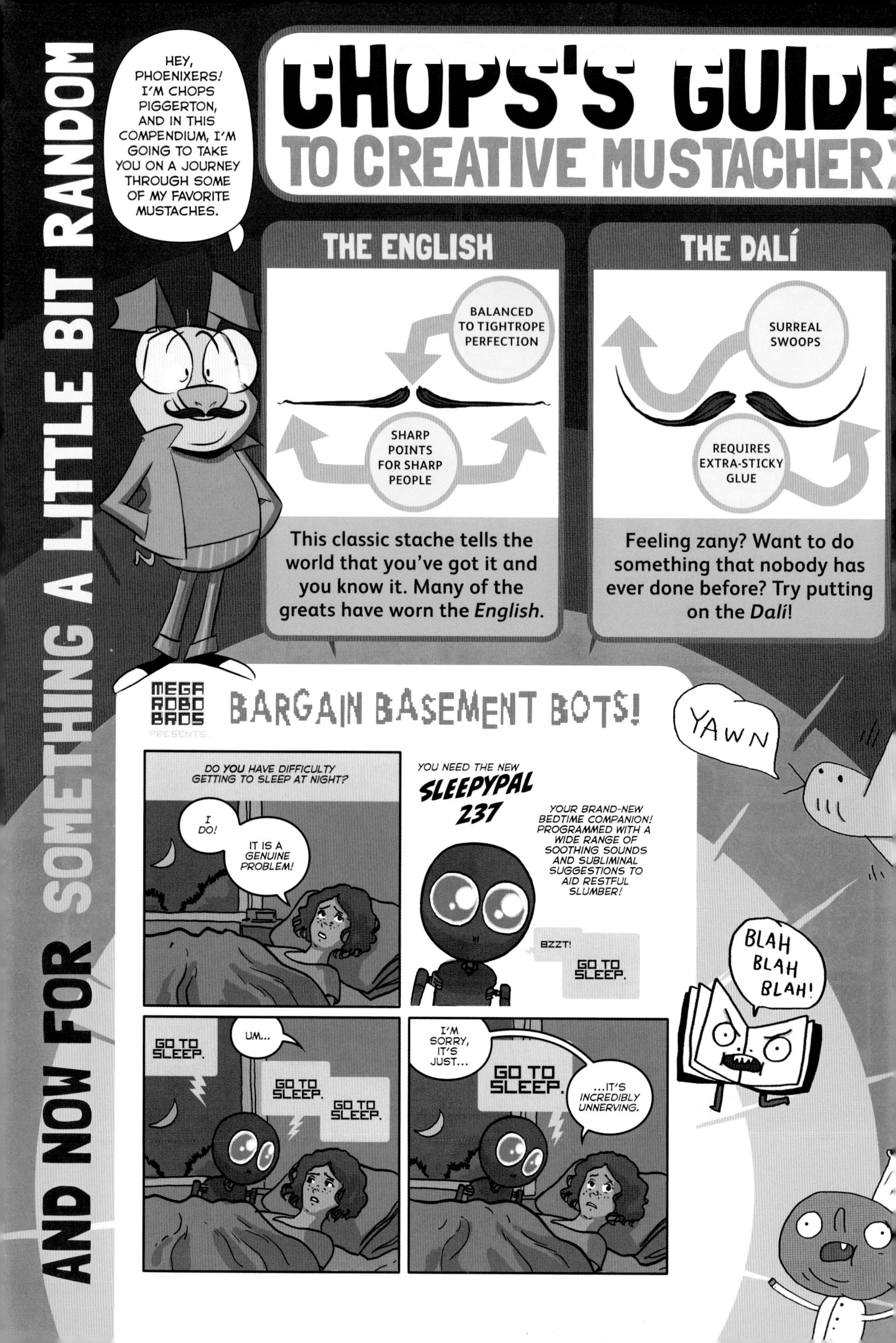
AND NOW FOR SOMETHING A LITTLE BIT RANDOM
HEY, PHOENIXERS! I'M CHOPS PIGGERTON, AND IN THIS COMPENDIUM, I'M GOING TO TAKE YOU ON A JOURNEY THROUGH SOME OF MY FAVORITE MUSTACHES.
CHOPS'S GUIDE
TO CREATIVE MUSTACHERY
THE ENGLISH
BALANCED TO TIGHTROPE PERFECTION
SHARP POINTS FOR SHARP PEOPLE
This classic stache tells the world that you've got it and you know it. Many of the greats have worn the English.
THE DALÍ
SURREAL SWOOPS
REQUIRES EXTRA-STICKY GLUE
Feeling zany? Want to do something that nobody has ever done before? Try putting on the Dalí!
MEGA ROBO BROS PRESENTS...
BARGAIN BASEMENT BOTS!
DO YOU HAVE DIFFICULTY GETTING TO SLEEP AT NIGHT?
I DO!
IT IS A GENUINE PROBLEM!
YOU NEED THE NEW
SLEEPYPAL 237
YOUR BRAND-NEW BEDTIME COMPANION! PROGRAMMED WITH A WIDE RANGE OF SOOTHING SOUNDS AND SUBLIMINAL SUGGESTIONS TO AID RESTFUL SLUMBER!
BZZT!
GO TO SLEEP.
GO TO SLEEP.
UM...
GO TO SLEEP.
GO TO SLEEP.
I'M SORRY, IT'S JUST...
GO TO SLEEP.
...IT'S INCREDIBLY UNNERVING.
YAWN
BLAH BLAH BLAH!

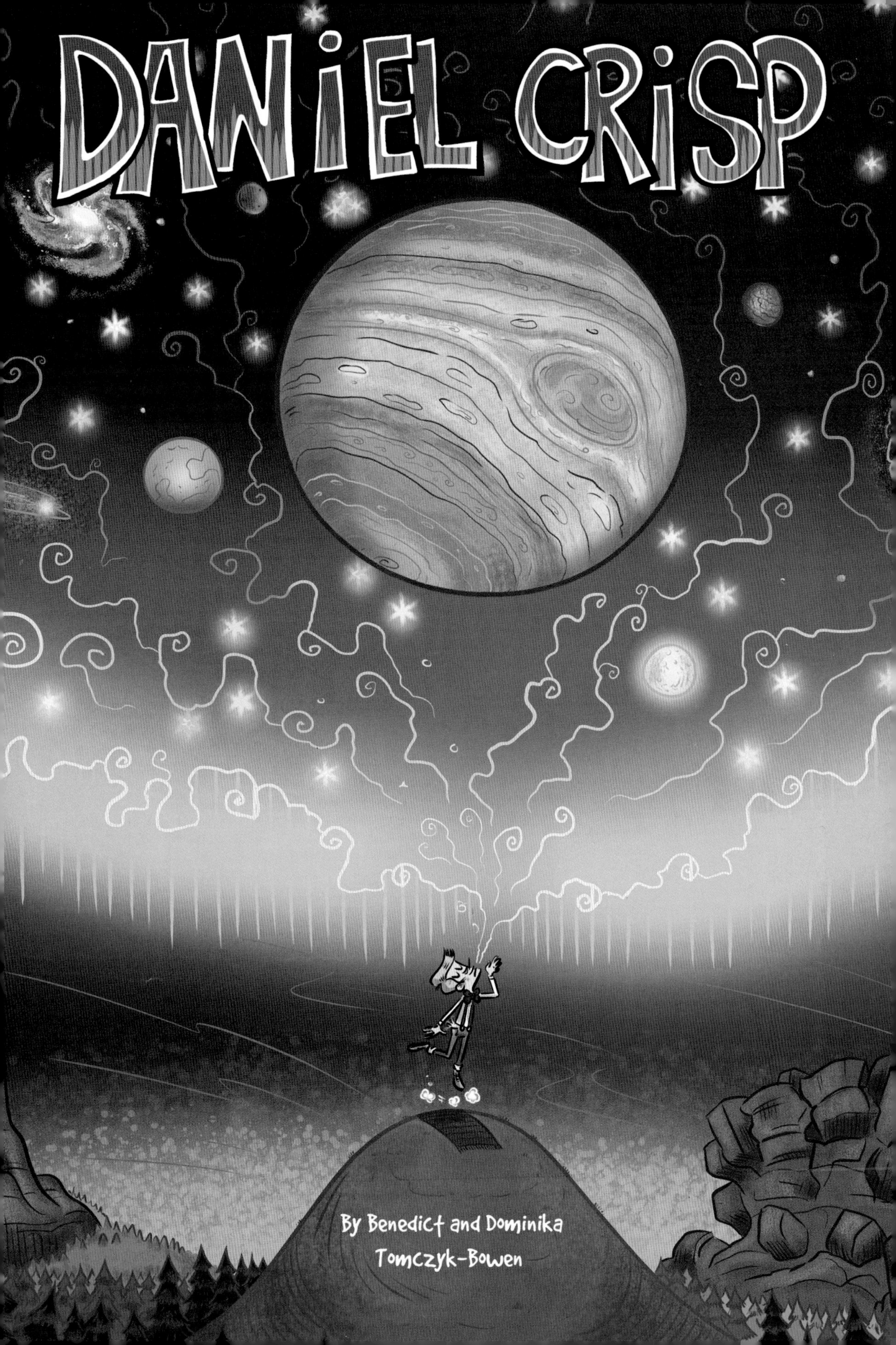
DANIEL CRISP
By Benedict and Dominika
Tomczyk-Bowen

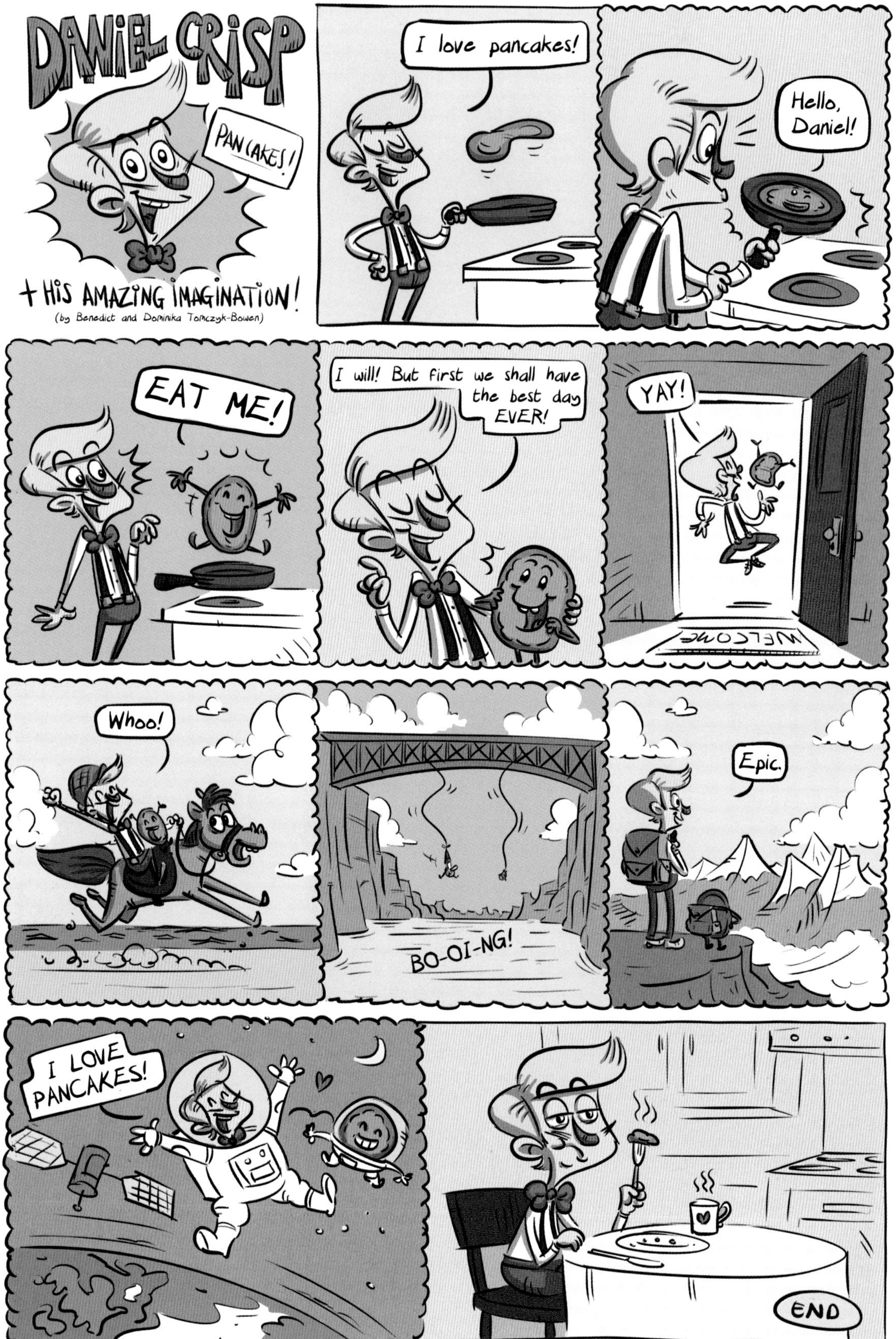
DANIEL CRISP
PANCAKES!
+ HIS AMAZING IMAGINATION!
(by Benedict and Dominika Tomczyk-Bowen)
I love pancakes!
Hello, Daniel!
EAT ME!
I will! But first we shall have the best day EVER!
YAY!
WELCOME
Whoo!
BO-OI-NG!
Epic.
I LOVE PANCAKES!
END

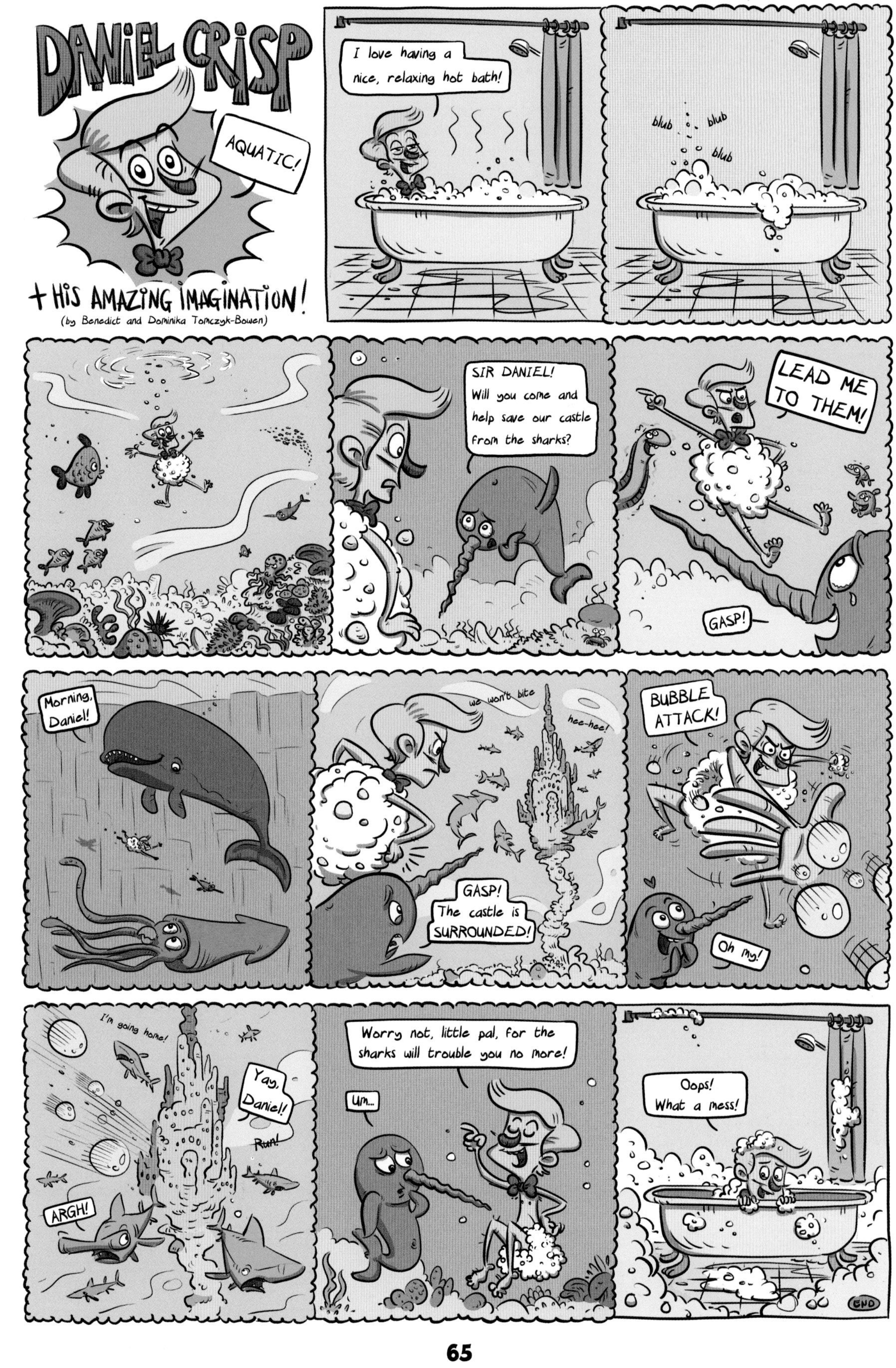
DANIEL CRISP
AQUATIC!
+ HIS AMAZING IMAGINATION!
(by Benedict and Dominika Tomczyk-Bowen)
I love having a nice, relaxing hot bath!
blub
blub
blub
SIR DANIEL! Will you come and help save our castle from the sharks?
LEAD ME TO THEM!
GASP!
Morning, Daniel!
we won't bite
hee-hee!
GASP! The castle is SURROUNDED!
BUBBLE ATTACK!
Oh my!
I'm going home!
Yay, Daniel!
Run!
ARGH!
Worry not, little pal, for the sharks will trouble you no more!
Um...
Oops! What a mess!
END

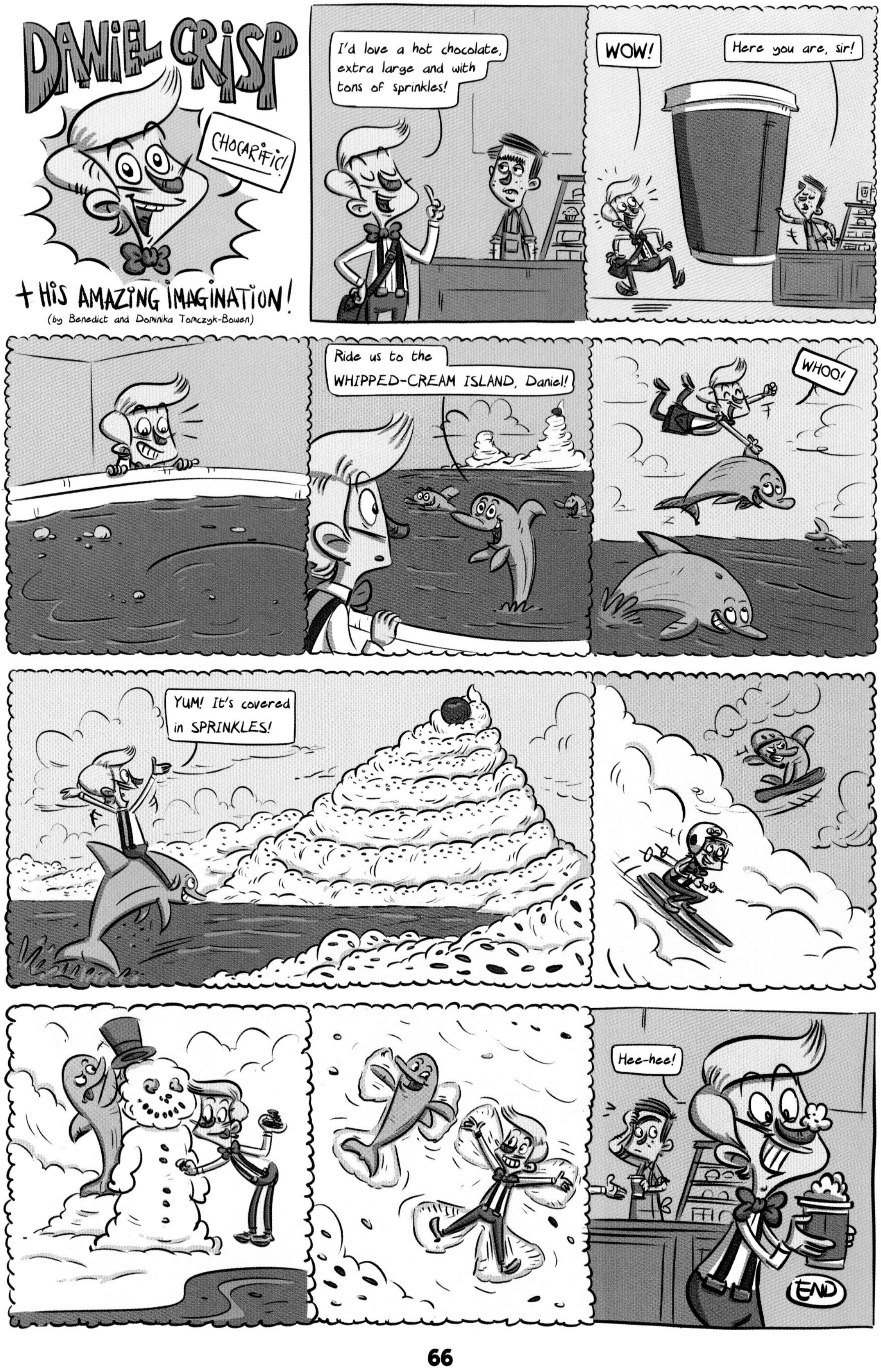
DANIEL CRISP
CHOCARIFIC!
+ HIS AMAZING IMAGINATION!
(by Benedict and Dominika Tomczyk-Bowen)
I'd love a hot chocolate, extra large and with tons of sprinkles!
WOW!
Here you are, sir!
Ride us to the WHIPPED-CREAM ISLAND, Daniel!
WHOO!
YUM! It's covered in SPRINKLES!
Hee-hee!
END

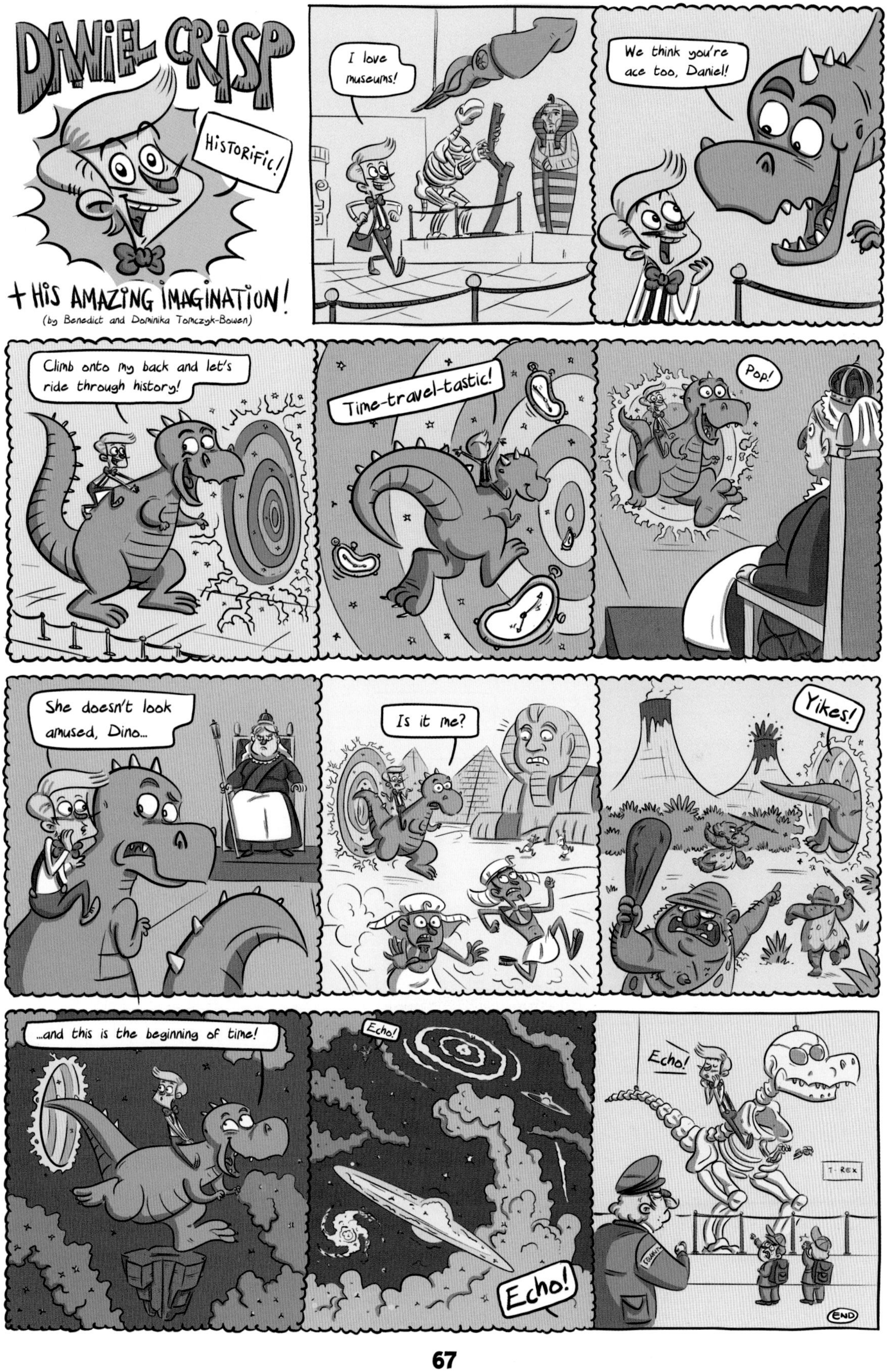
DANIEL CRISP
HISTORIFIC!
+ HIS AMAZING IMAGINATION!
(by Benedict and Dominika Tomczyk-Bowen)
I love museums!
We think you're ace too, Daniel!
Climb onto my back and let's ride through history!
Time-travel-tastic!
Pop!
She doesn't look amused, Dino...
Is it me?
Yikes!
...and this is the beginning of time!
Echo!
Echo!
Echo!
T-REX
SECURITY
END

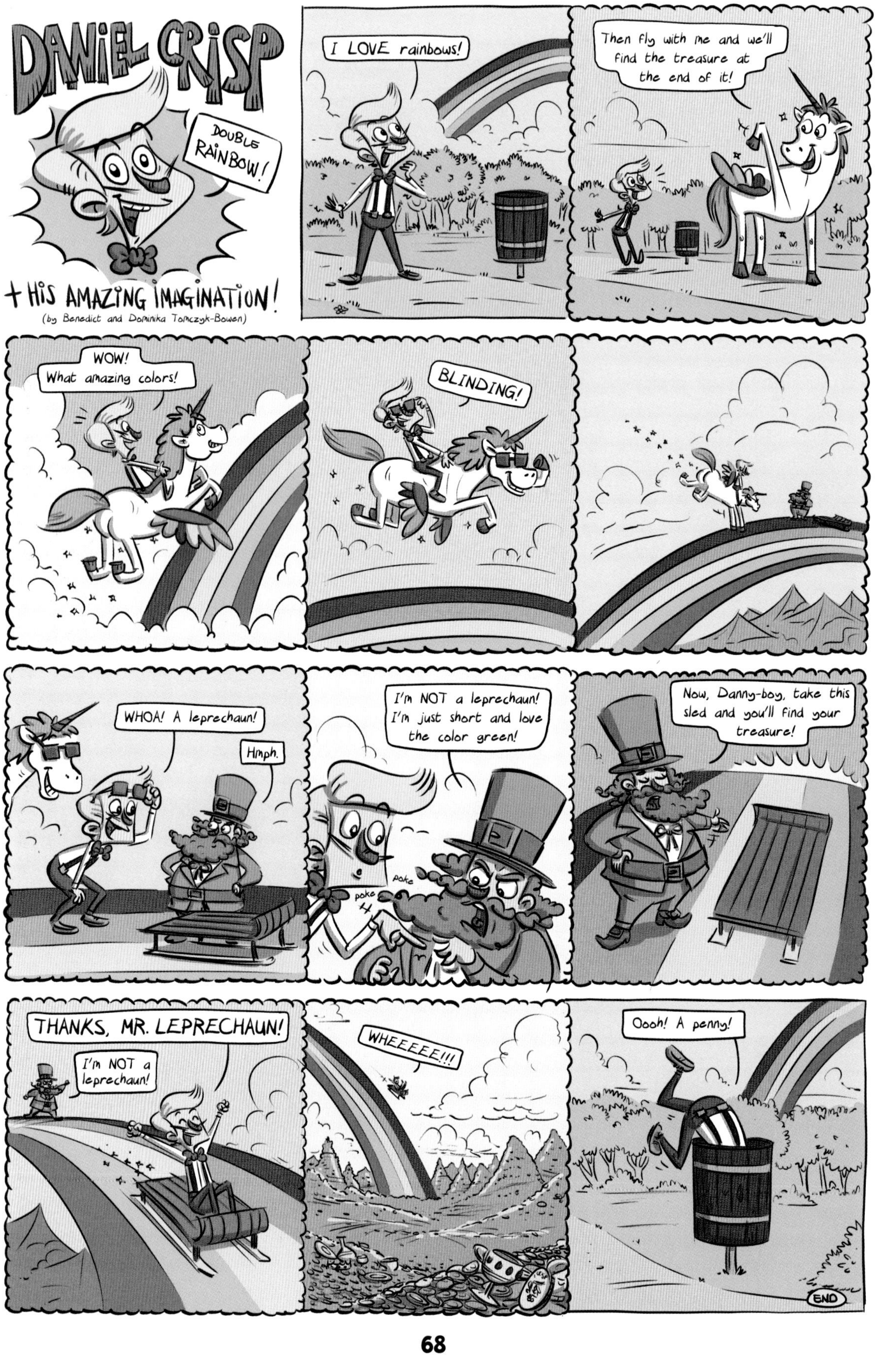
DANIEL CRISP
DOUBLE RAINBOW!
+ HIS AMAZING IMAGINATION!
(by Benedict and Dominika Tomczyk-Bowen)
I LOVE rainbows!
Then fly with me and we'll find the treasure at the end of it!
WOW! What amazing colors!
BLINDING!
WHOA! A leprechaun!
Hmph.
I'm NOT a leprechaun! I'm just short and love the color green!
poke
poke
Now, Danny-boy, take this sled and you'll find your treasure!
THANKS, MR. LEPRECHAUN!
I'm NOT a leprechaun!
WHEEEEE!!!
Oooh! A penny!
END

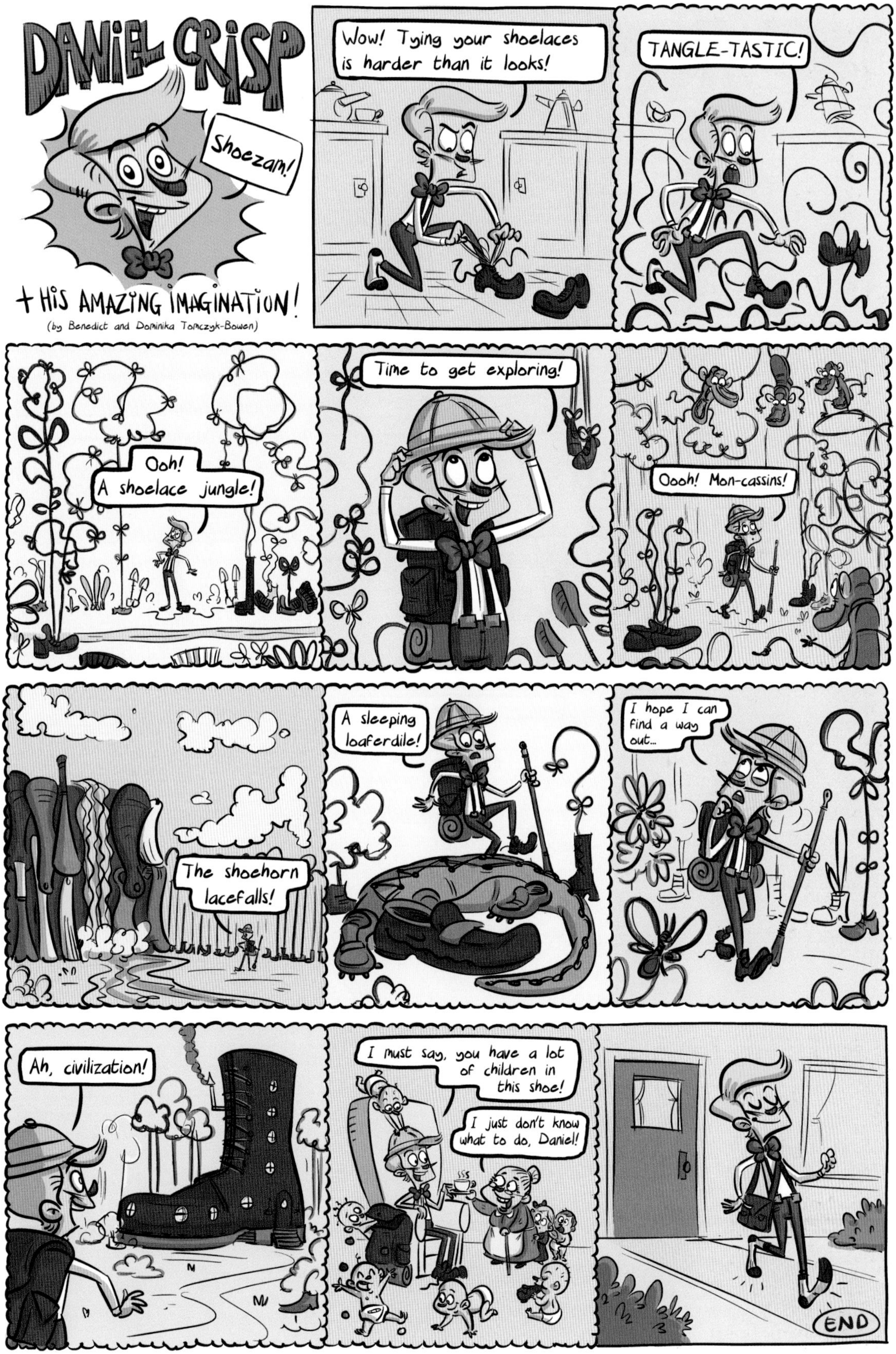
DANIEL CRISP
Shoezam!
+ HIS AMAZING IMAGINATION!
(by Benedict and Dominika Tomczyk-Bowen)
Wow! Tying your shoelaces is harder than it looks!
TANGLE-TASTIC!
Ooh! A shoelace jungle!
Time to get exploring!
Oooh! Mon-cassins!
The shoehorn lacefalls!
A sleeping loaferdile!
I hope I can find a way out...
Ah, civilization!
I must say, you have a lot of children in this shoe!
I just don't know what to do, Daniel!
END

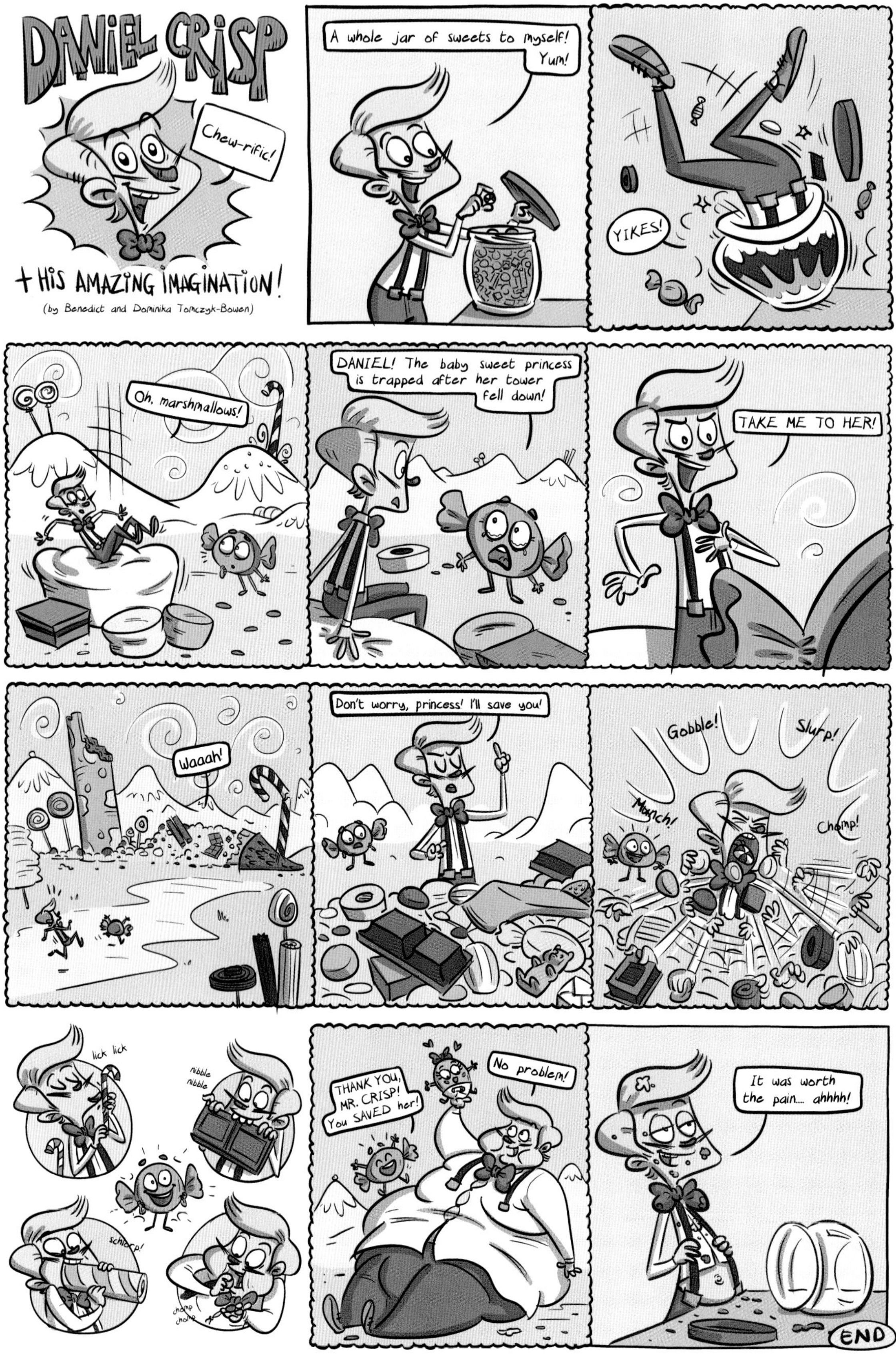
DANIEL CRISP
Chew-rific!
+ HIS AMAZING IMAGINATION!
(by Benedict and Dominika Tomczyk-Bowen)
A whole jar of sweets to myself!
Yum!
YIKES!
Oh, marshmallows!
DANIEL! The baby sweet princess is trapped after her tower fell down!
TAKE ME TO HER!
Waaah!
Don't worry, princess! I'll save you!
Gobble!
Slurp!
Munch!
Chomp!
lick lick
nibble nibble
schlorp!
chomp chomp
THANK YOU, MR. CRISP! You SAVED her!
No problem!
It was worth the pain.... ahhhh!
END

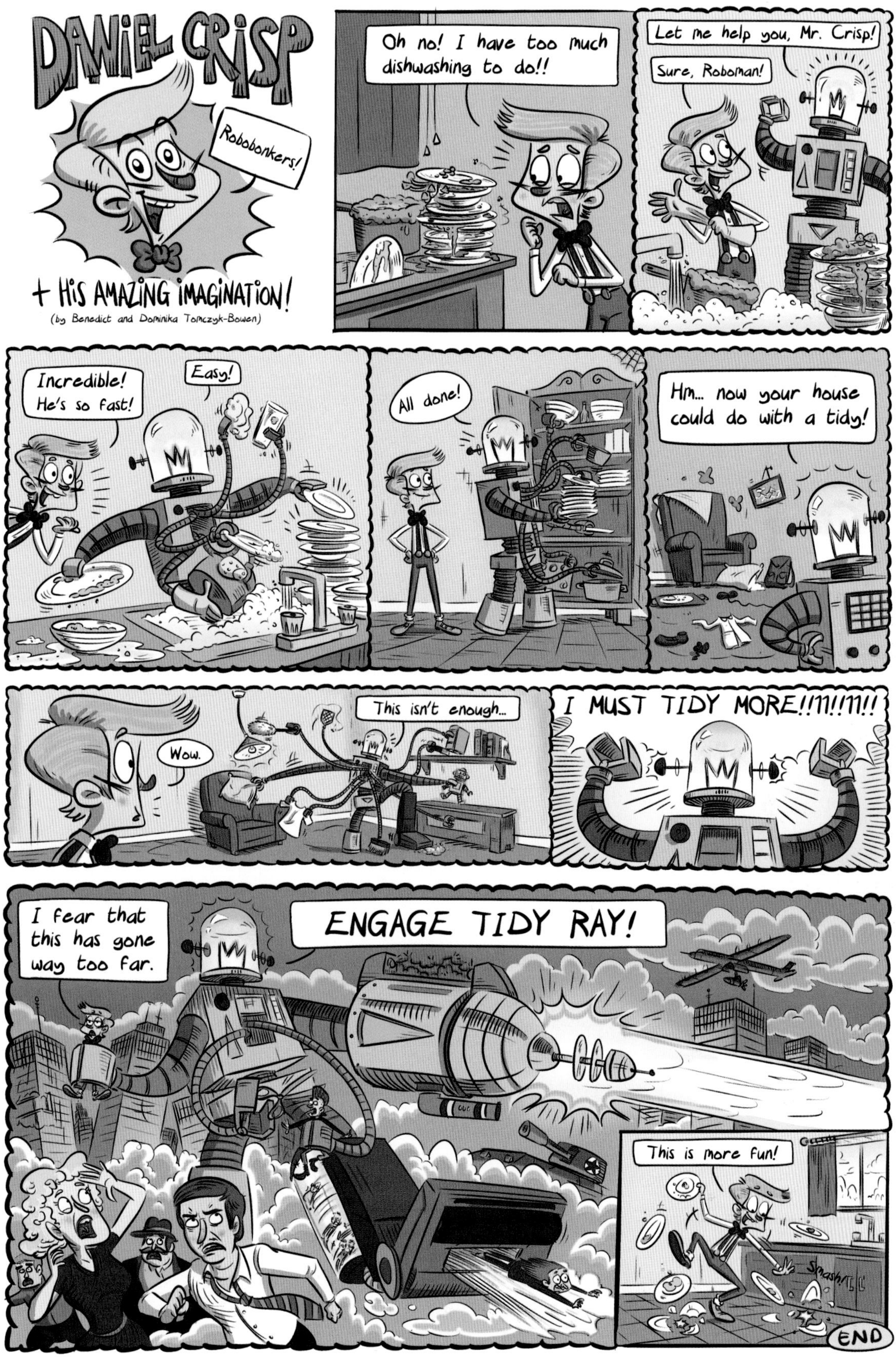
DANIEL CRISP
Robobonkers!
+ HIS AMAZING IMAGINATION!
(by Benedict and Dominika Tomczyk-Bowen)
Oh no! I have too much dishwashing to do!!
Let me help you, Mr. Crisp!
Sure, Roboman!
Incredible! He's so fast!
Easy!
All done!
Hm... now your house could do with a tidy!
Wow.
This isn't enough...
I MUST TIDY MORE!!11!!11!!
I fear that this has gone way too far.
ENGAGE TIDY RAY!
This is more fun!
Smash!
END

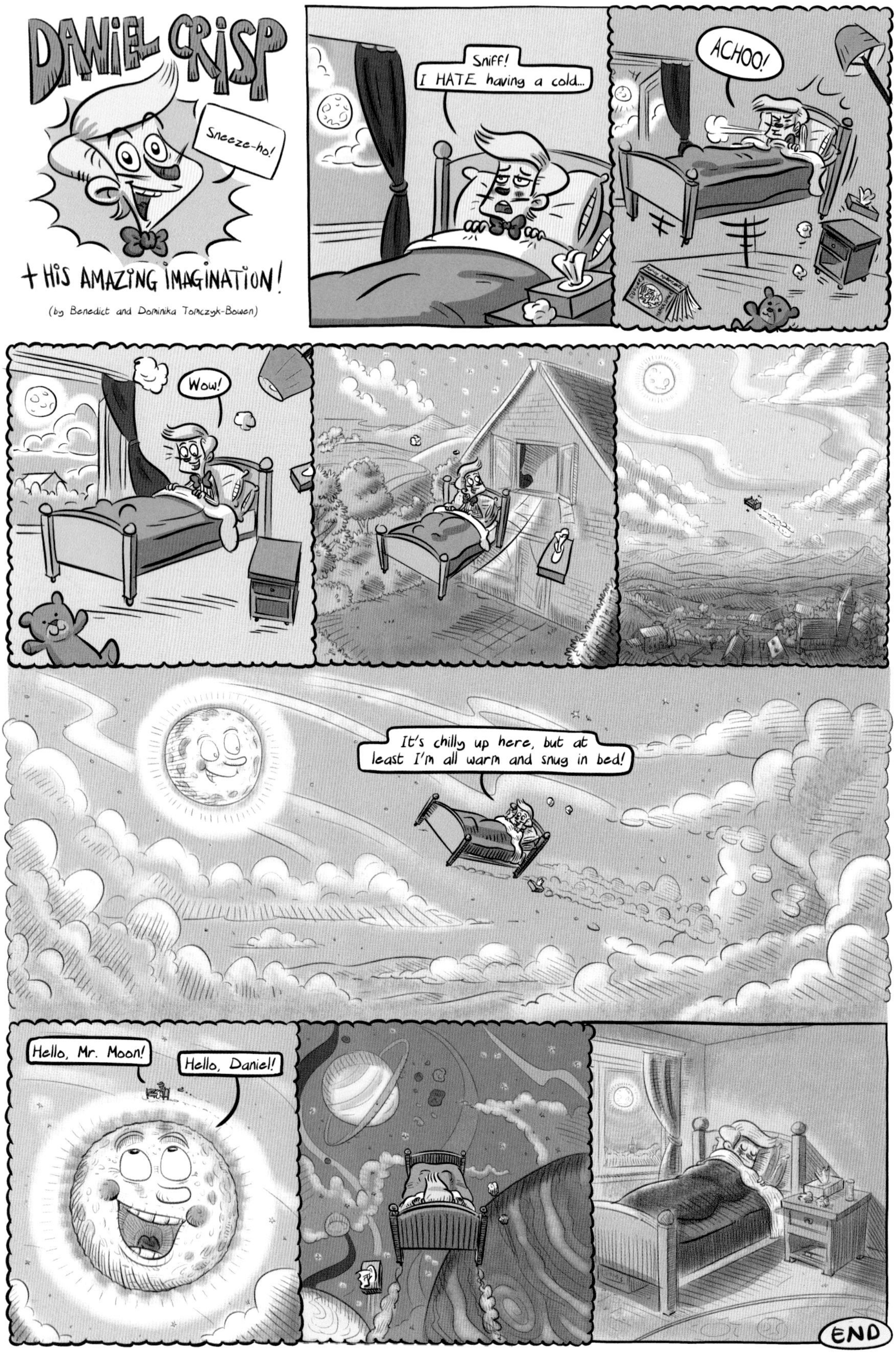
DANIEL CRISP
Sneeze-ho!
+ HIS AMAZING IMAGINATION!
(by Benedict and Dominika Tomczyk-Bowen)
Sniff! I HATE having a cold...
ACHOO!
Wow!
It's chilly up here, but at least I'm all warm and snug in bed!
Hello, Mr. Moon!
Hello, Daniel!
END

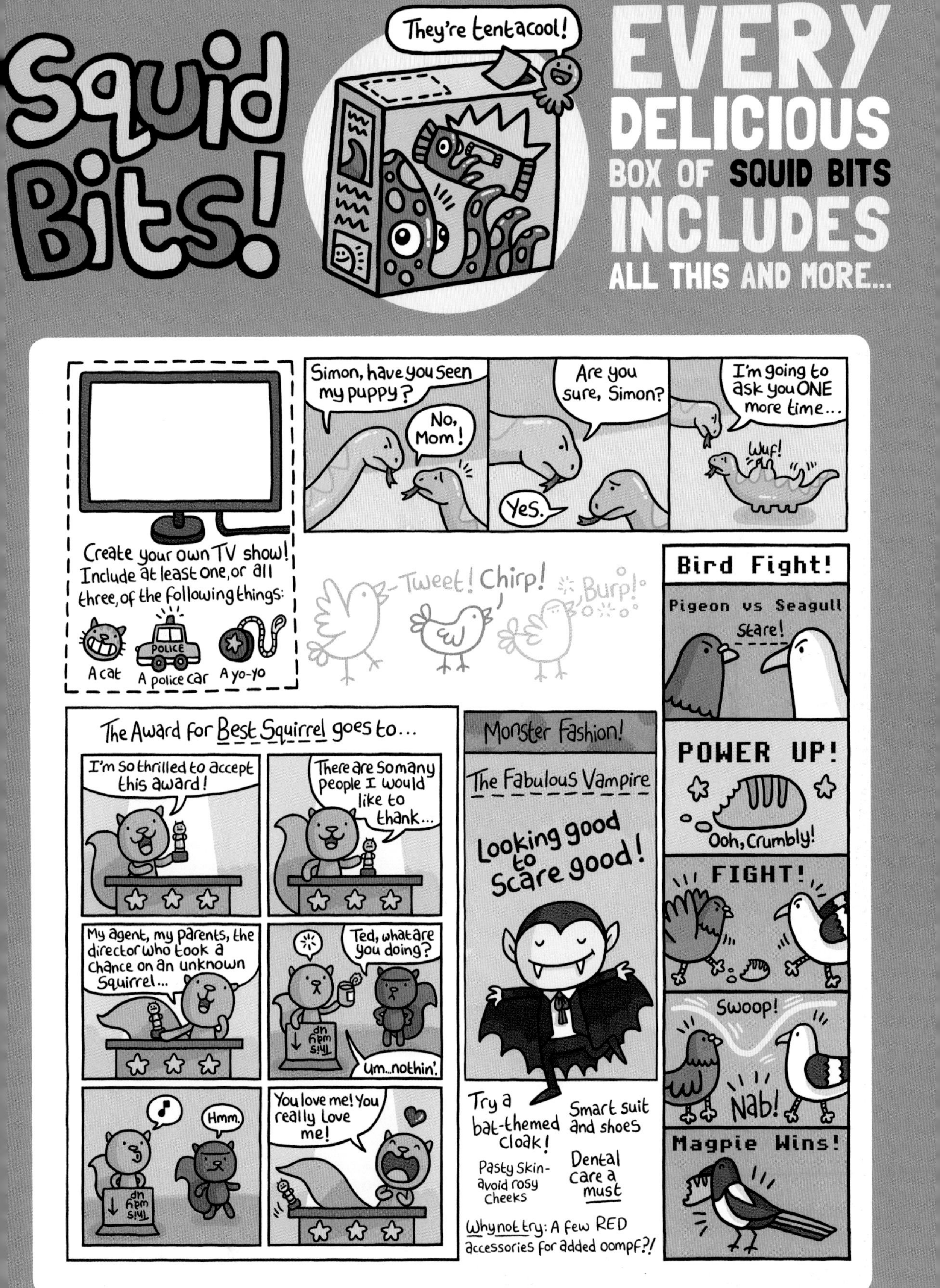
Squid Bits!
They're tentacool!
EVERY DELICIOUS BOX OF SQUID BITS INCLUDES ALL THIS AND MORE...
Create your own TV show! Include at least one, or all three, of the following things:
POLICE
A cat
A police car
A yo-yo
Simon, have you seen my puppy?
No, Mom!
Are you sure, Simon?
Yes.
I'm going to ask you ONE more time...
Wuf!
Tweet!
Chirp!
Burp!
Bird Fight!
Pigeon vs Seagull
Stare!
POWER UP!
Ooh, Crumbly!
FIGHT!
Swoop!
Nab!
Magpie Wins!
The Award for Best Squirrel goes to...
I'm so thrilled to accept this award!
There are so many people I would like to thank...
My agent, my parents, the director who took a chance on an unknown squirrel...
Ted, what are you doing?
This way up
Um...nothin'.
Hmm.
This way up
You love me! You really love me!
Monster Fashion!
The Fabulous Vampire
Looking good to scare good!
Try a bat-themed cloak!
Smart suit and shoes
Pasty skin-avoid rosy cheeks
Dental care a must
Why not try: A few RED accessories for added oompf?!

by Jess Bradley

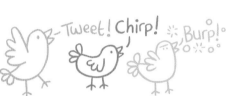

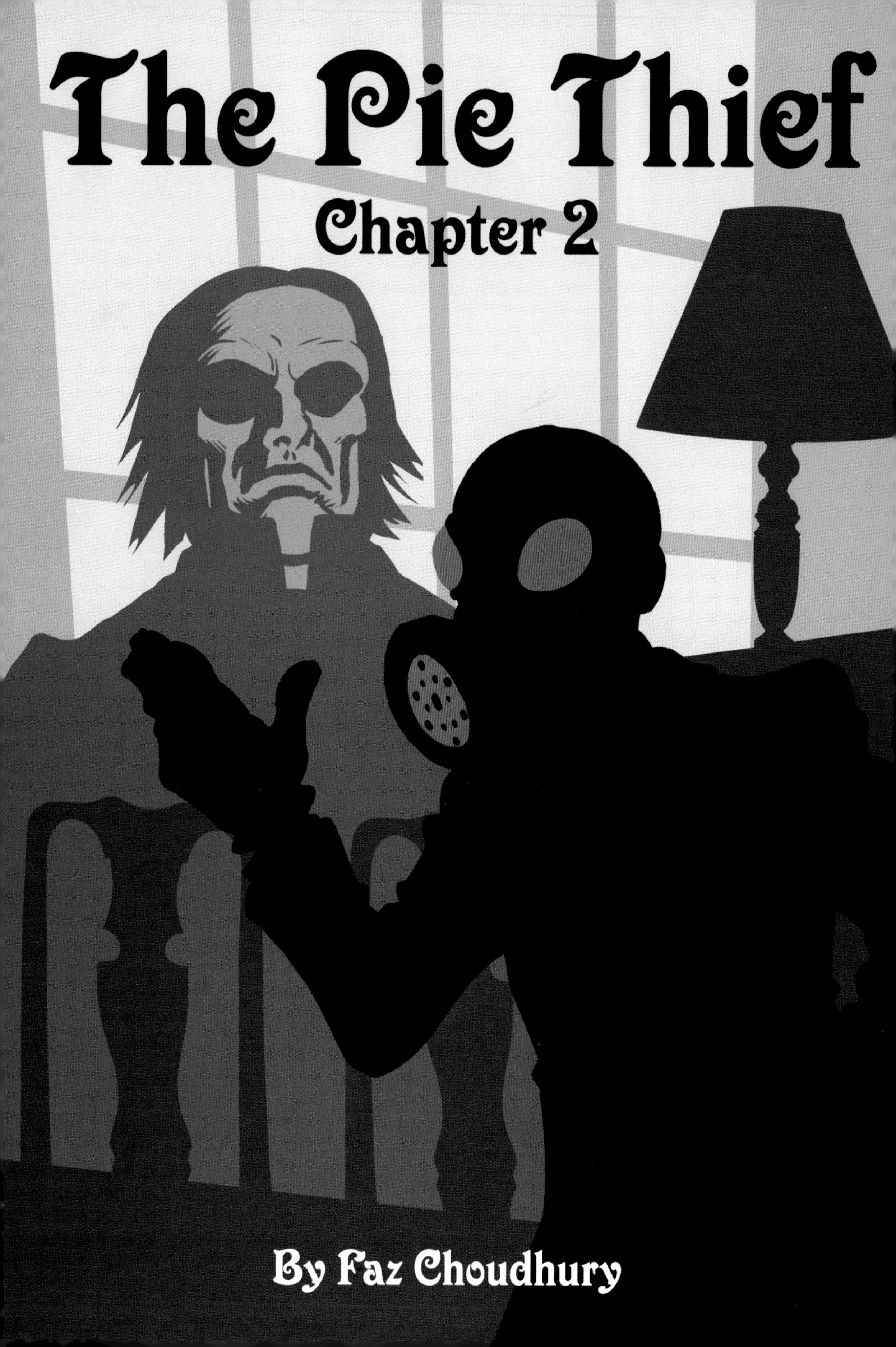
The Pie Thief
Chapter 2
By Faz Choudhury

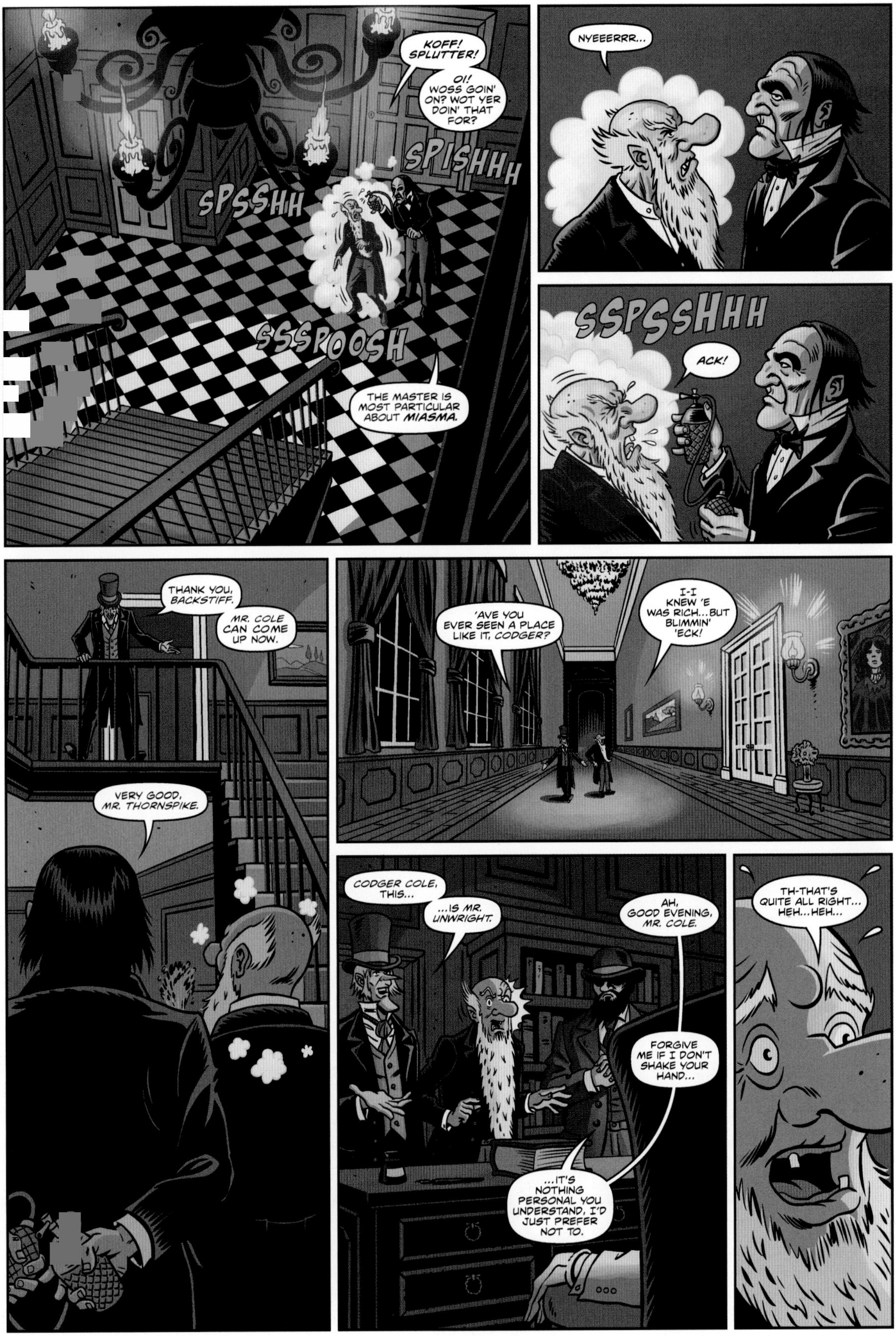

KOFF! SPLUTTER!
OI! WOSS GOIN' ON? WOT YER DOIN' THAT FOR?
SPISHHH
SPSSHH
SSSPOOSH
THE MASTER IS MOST PARTICULAR ABOUT *MIASMA.*
NYEEERRR...
SSPSSHHH
ACK!
THANK YOU, *BACKSTIFF.*
MR. COLE CAN COME UP NOW.
VERY GOOD, MR. THORNSPIKE.
'AVE YOU EVER SEEN A PLACE LIKE IT, CODGER?
I-I KNEW 'E WAS RICH...BUT BLIMMIN' 'ECK!
CODGER COLE, THIS...
...IS *MR. UNWRIGHT.*
AH, GOOD EVENING, MR. COLE.
FORGIVE ME IF I DON'T SHAKE YOUR HAND...
...IT'S NOTHING PERSONAL YOU UNDERSTAND, I'D JUST PREFER NOT TO.
TH-THAT'S QUITE ALL RIGHT... HEH...HEH...

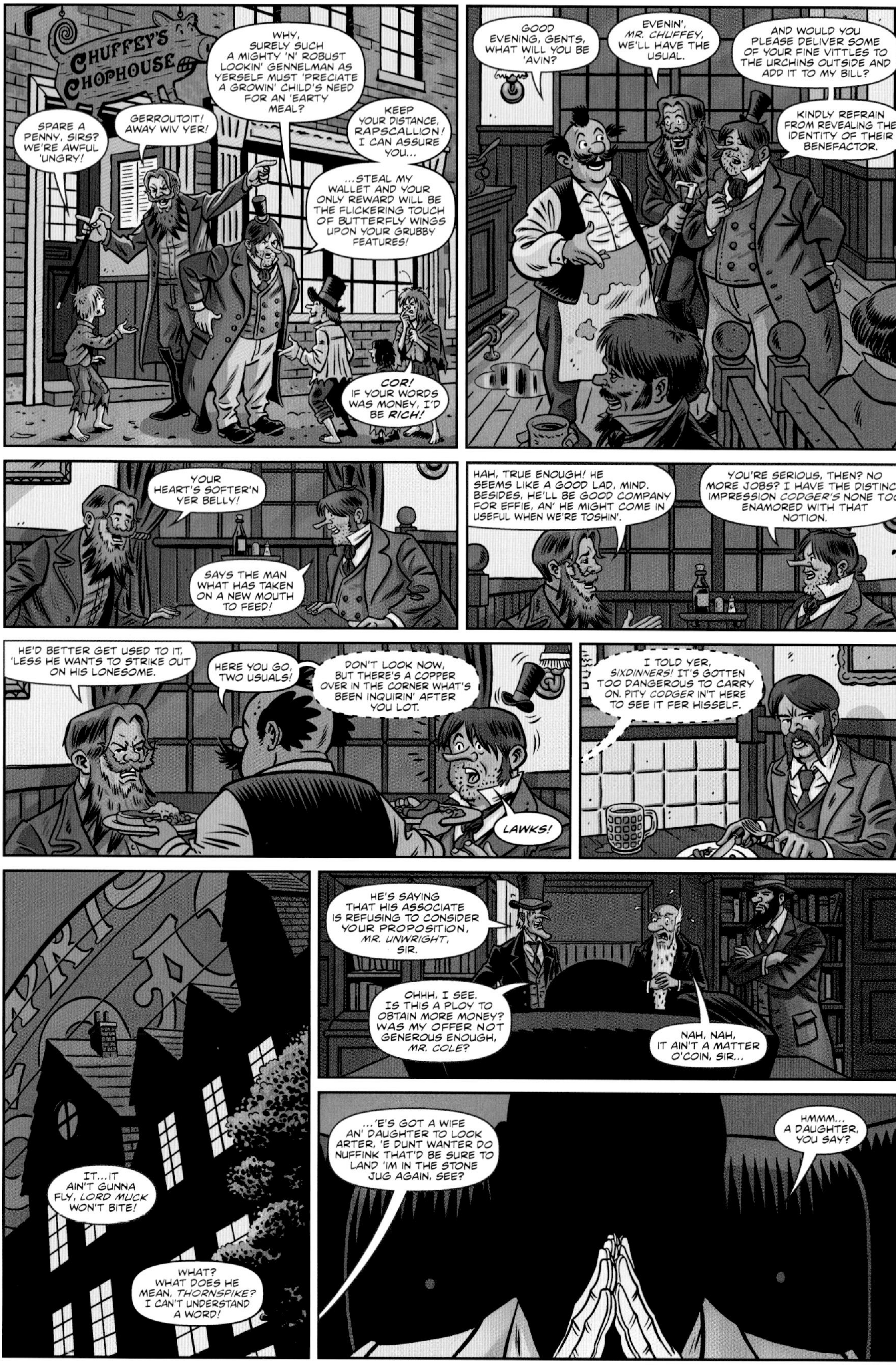
CHUFFEY'S CHOPHOUSE
SPARE A PENNY, SIRS? WE'RE AWFUL 'UNGRY!
GERROUTOIT! AWAY WIV YER!
WHY, SURELY SUCH A MIGHTY 'N' ROBUST LOOKIN' GENNELMAN AS YERSELF MUST 'PRECIATE A GROWIN' CHILD'S NEED FOR AN 'EARTY MEAL?
KEEP YOUR DISTANCE, RAPSCALLION! I CAN ASSURE YOU...
...STEAL MY WALLET AND YOUR ONLY REWARD WILL BE THE FLICKERING TOUCH OF BUTTERFLY WINGS UPON YOUR GRUBBY FEATURES!
COR! IF YOUR WORDS WAS MONEY, I'D BE RICH!
GOOD EVENING, GENTS, WHAT WILL YOU BE 'AVIN?
EVENIN', MR. CHUFFEY, WE'LL HAVE THE USUAL.
AND WOULD YOU PLEASE DELIVER SOME OF YOUR FINE VITTLES TO THE URCHINS OUTSIDE AND ADD IT TO MY BILL?
KINDLY REFRAIN FROM REVEALING THE IDENTITY OF THEIR BENEFACTOR.
YOUR HEART'S SOFTER'N YER BELLY!
SAYS THE MAN WHAT HAS TAKEN ON A NEW MOUTH TO FEED!
HAH, TRUE ENOUGH! HE SEEMS LIKE A GOOD LAD, MIND. BESIDES, HE'LL BE GOOD COMPANY FOR EFFIE, AN' HE MIGHT COME IN USEFUL WHEN WE'RE TOSHIN'.
YOU'RE SERIOUS, THEN? NO MORE JOBS? I HAVE THE DISTINCT IMPRESSION CODGER'S NONE TOO ENAMORED WITH THAT NOTION.
HE'D BETTER GET USED TO IT, 'LESS HE WANTS TO STRIKE OUT ON HIS LONESOME.
HERE YOU GO, TWO USUALS!
DON'T LOOK NOW, BUT THERE'S A COPPER OVER IN THE CORNER WHAT'S BEEN INQUIRIN' AFTER YOU LOT.
LAWKS!
I TOLD YER, SIXDINNERS! IT'S GOTTEN TOO DANGEROUS TO CARRY ON. PITY CODGER IN'T HERE TO SEE IT FER HISSELF.
IT...IT AIN'T GUNNA FLY, LORD MUCK WON'T BITE!
WHAT? WHAT DOES HE MEAN, THORNSPIKE? I CAN'T UNDERSTAND A WORD!
HE'S SAYING THAT HIS ASSOCIATE IS REFUSING TO CONSIDER YOUR PROPOSITION, MR. UNWRIGHT, SIR.
OHHH, I SEE. IS THIS A PLOY TO OBTAIN MORE MONEY? WAS MY OFFER NOT GENEROUS ENOUGH, MR. COLE?
NAH, NAH, IT AIN'T A MATTER O'COIN, SIR...
...'E'S GOT A WIFE AN' DAUGHTER TO LOOK ARTER, 'E DUNT WANTER DO NUFFINK THAT'D BE SURE TO LAND 'IM IN THE STONE JUG AGAIN, SEE?
HMMM... A DAUGHTER, YOU SAY?

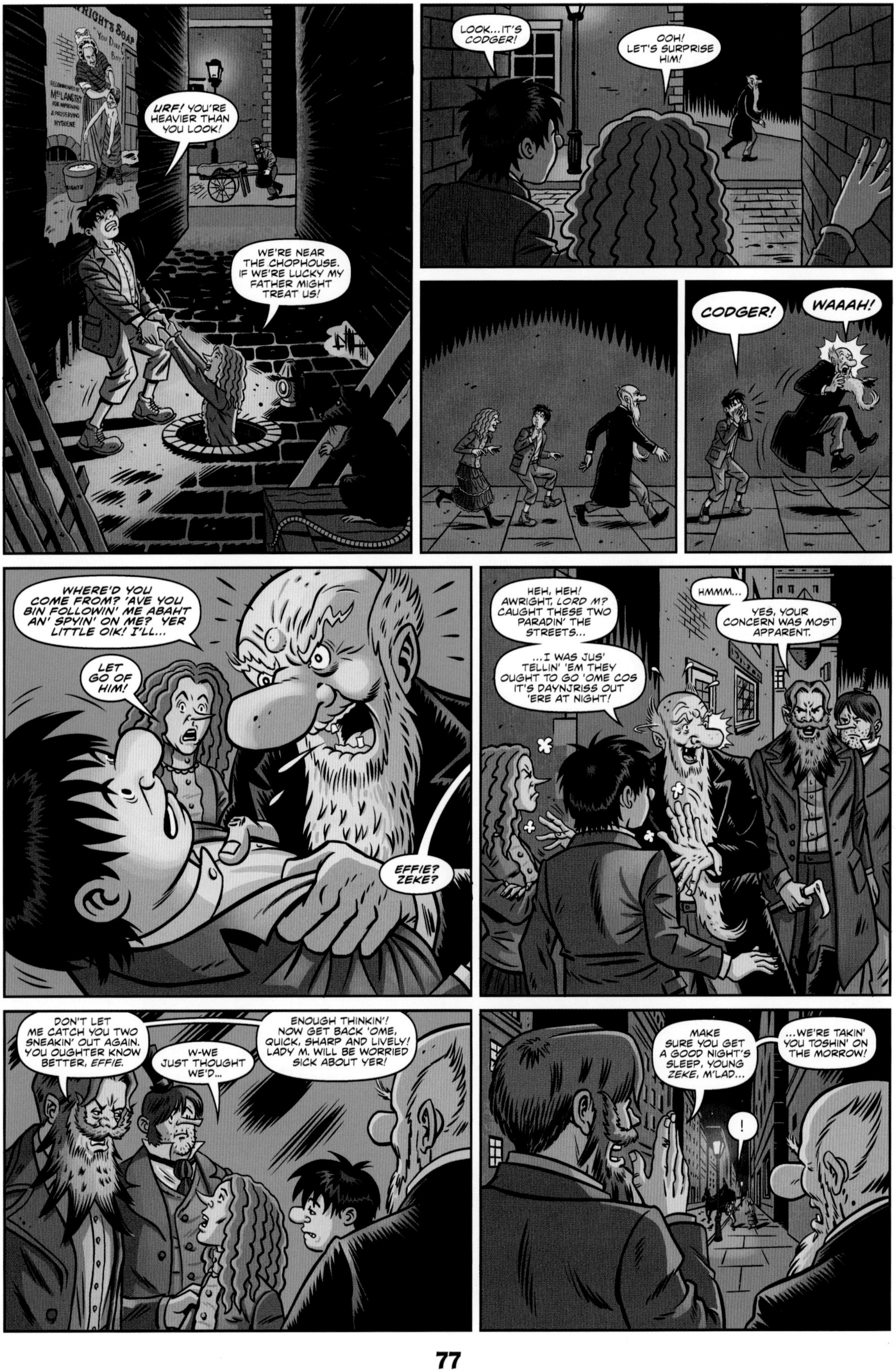
URF! YOU'RE HEAVIER THAN YOU LOOK!
WE'RE NEAR THE CHOPHOUSE. IF WE'RE LUCKY MY FATHER MIGHT TREAT US!
LOOK... IT'S CODGER!
OOH! LET'S SURPRISE HIM!
CODGER!
WAAAH!
WHERE'D YOU COME FROM? 'AVE YOU BIN FOLLOWIN' ME ABAHT AN' SPYIN' ON ME? YER LITTLE OIK! I'LL...
LET GO OF HIM!
EFFIE? ZEKE?
HEH, HEH! AWRIGHT, LORD M? CAUGHT THESE TWO PARADIN' THE STREETS...
...I WAS JUS' TELLIN' 'EM THEY OUGHT TO GO 'OME COS IT'S DAYNJRISS OUT 'ERE AT NIGHT!
HMMM...
YES, YOUR CONCERN WAS MOST APPARENT.
DON'T LET ME CATCH YOU TWO SNEAKIN' OUT AGAIN. YOU OUGHTER KNOW BETTER, EFFIE.
W-WE JUST THOUGHT WE'D...
ENOUGH THINKIN'! NOW GET BACK 'OME, QUICK, SHARP AND LIVELY! LADY M. WILL BE WORRIED SICK ABOUT YER!
MAKE SURE YOU GET A GOOD NIGHT'S SLEEP, YOUNG ZEKE, M'LAD...
...WE'RE TAKIN' YOU TOSHIN' ON THE MORROW!
!

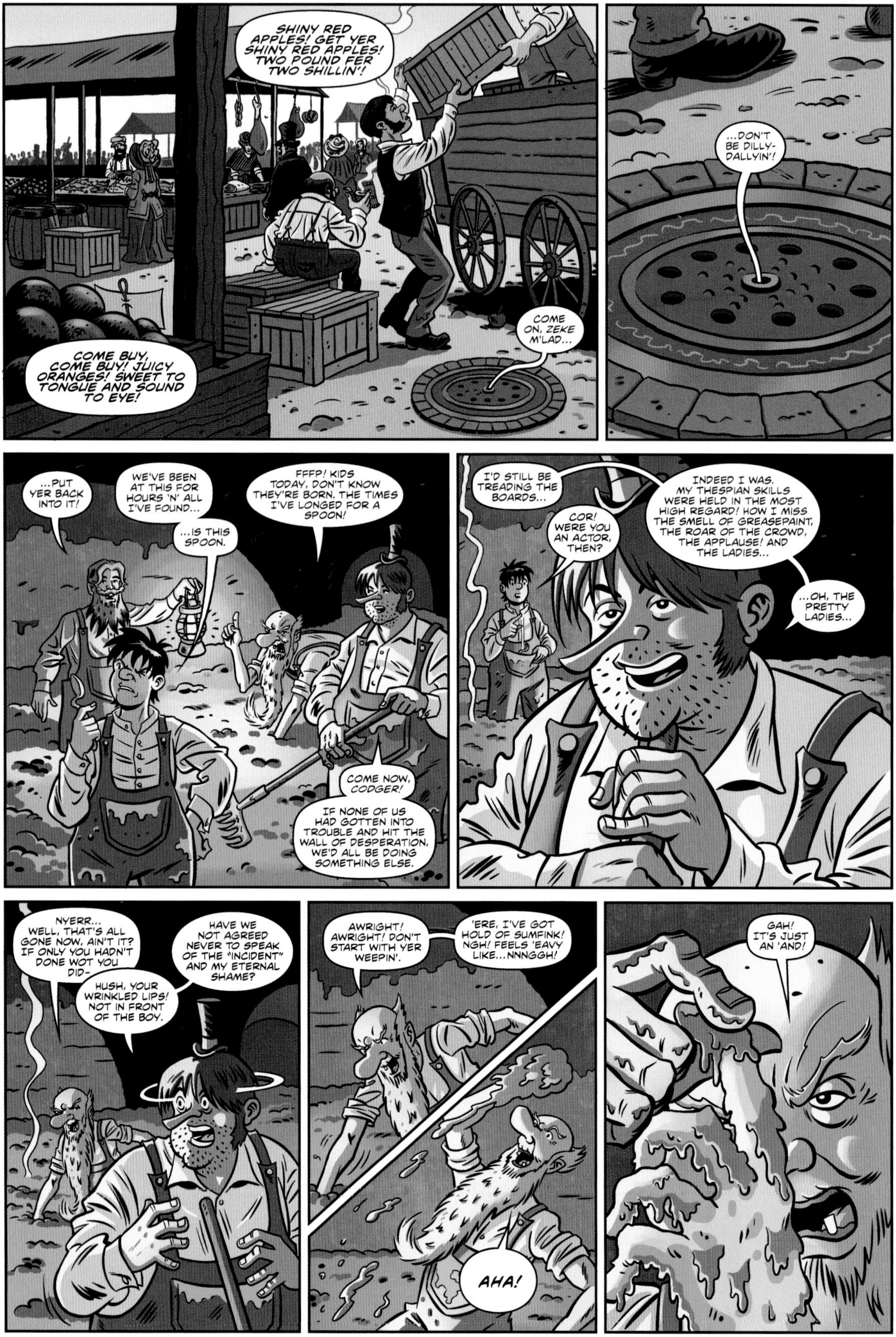
SHINY RED APPLES! GET YER SHINY RED APPLES! TWO POUND FER TWO SHILLIN'!
COME BUY, COME BUY! JUICY ORANGES! SWEET TO TONGUE AND SOUND TO EYE!
COME ON, ZEKE M'LAD...
...DON'T BE DILLY-DALLYIN'!
...PUT YER BACK INTO IT!
WE'VE BEEN AT THIS FOR HOURS 'N' ALL I'VE FOUND...
...IS THIS SPOON.
FFFP! KIDS TODAY, DON'T KNOW THEY'RE BORN. THE TIMES I'VE LONGED FOR A SPOON!
COME NOW, CODGER!
IF NONE OF US HAD GOTTEN INTO TROUBLE AND HIT THE WALL OF DESPERATION, WE'D ALL BE DOING SOMETHING ELSE.
I'D STILL BE TREADING THE BOARDS...
COR! WERE YOU AN ACTOR, THEN?
INDEED I WAS. MY THESPIAN SKILLS WERE HELD IN THE MOST HIGH REGARD! HOW I MISS THE SMELL OF GREASEPAINT, THE ROAR OF THE CROWD, THE APPLAUSE! AND THE LADIES...
...OH, THE PRETTY LADIES...
NYERR... WELL, THAT'S ALL GONE NOW, AIN'T IT? IF ONLY YOU HADN'T DONE WOT YOU DID-
HUSH, YOUR WRINKLED LIPS! NOT IN FRONT OF THE BOY.
HAVE WE NOT AGREED NEVER TO SPEAK OF THE "INCIDENT" AND MY ETERNAL SHAME?
AWRIGHT! AWRIGHT! DON'T START WITH YER WEEPIN'.
'ERE, I'VE GOT HOLD OF SUMFINK! NGH! FEELS 'EAVY LIKE... NNNGGH!
AHA!
GAH! IT'S JUST AN 'AND!

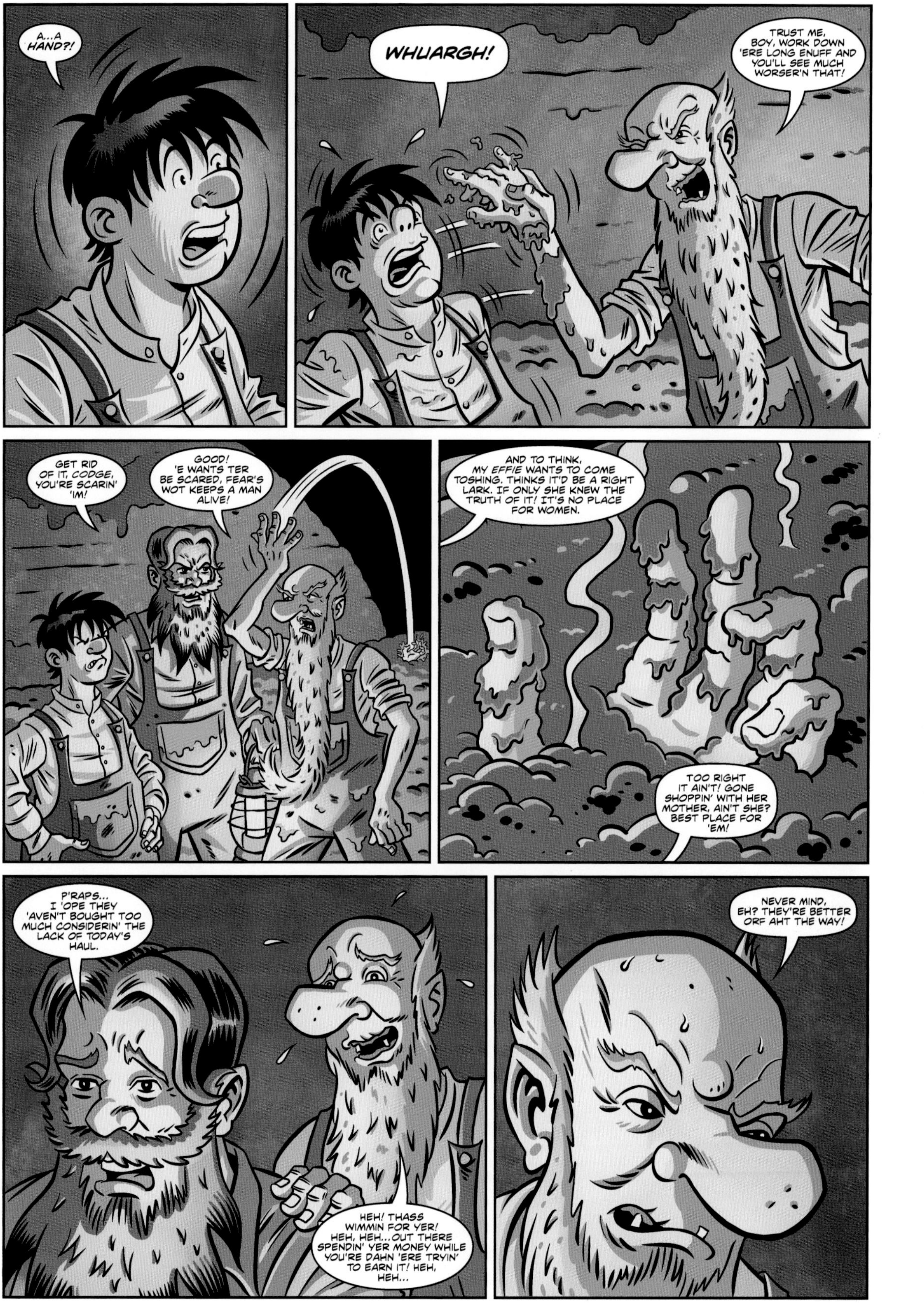
A...A HAND?!
WHUARGH!
TRUST ME, BOY, WORK DOWN 'ERE LONG ENUFF AND YOU'LL SEE MUCH WORSER'N THAT!
GET RID OF IT, CODGE, YOU'RE SCARIN' 'IM!
GOOD! 'E WANTS TER BE SCARED, FEAR'S WOT KEEPS A MAN ALIVE!
AND TO THINK, MY EFFIE WANTS TO COME TOSHING. THINKS IT'D BE A RIGHT LARK. IF ONLY SHE KNEW THE TRUTH OF IT! IT'S NO PLACE FOR WOMEN.
TOO RIGHT IT AIN'T! GONE SHOPPIN' WITH HER MOTHER, AIN'T SHE? BEST PLACE FOR 'EM!
P'RAPS... I 'OPE THEY 'AVEN'T BOUGHT TOO MUCH CONSIDERIN' THE LACK OF TODAY'S HAUL.
HEH! THASS WIMMIN FOR YER! HEH, HEH...OUT THERE SPENDIN' YER MONEY WHILE YOU'RE DAHN 'ERE TRYIN' TO EARN IT! HEH, HEH...
NEVER MIND, EH? THEY'RE BETTER ORF AHT THE WAY!

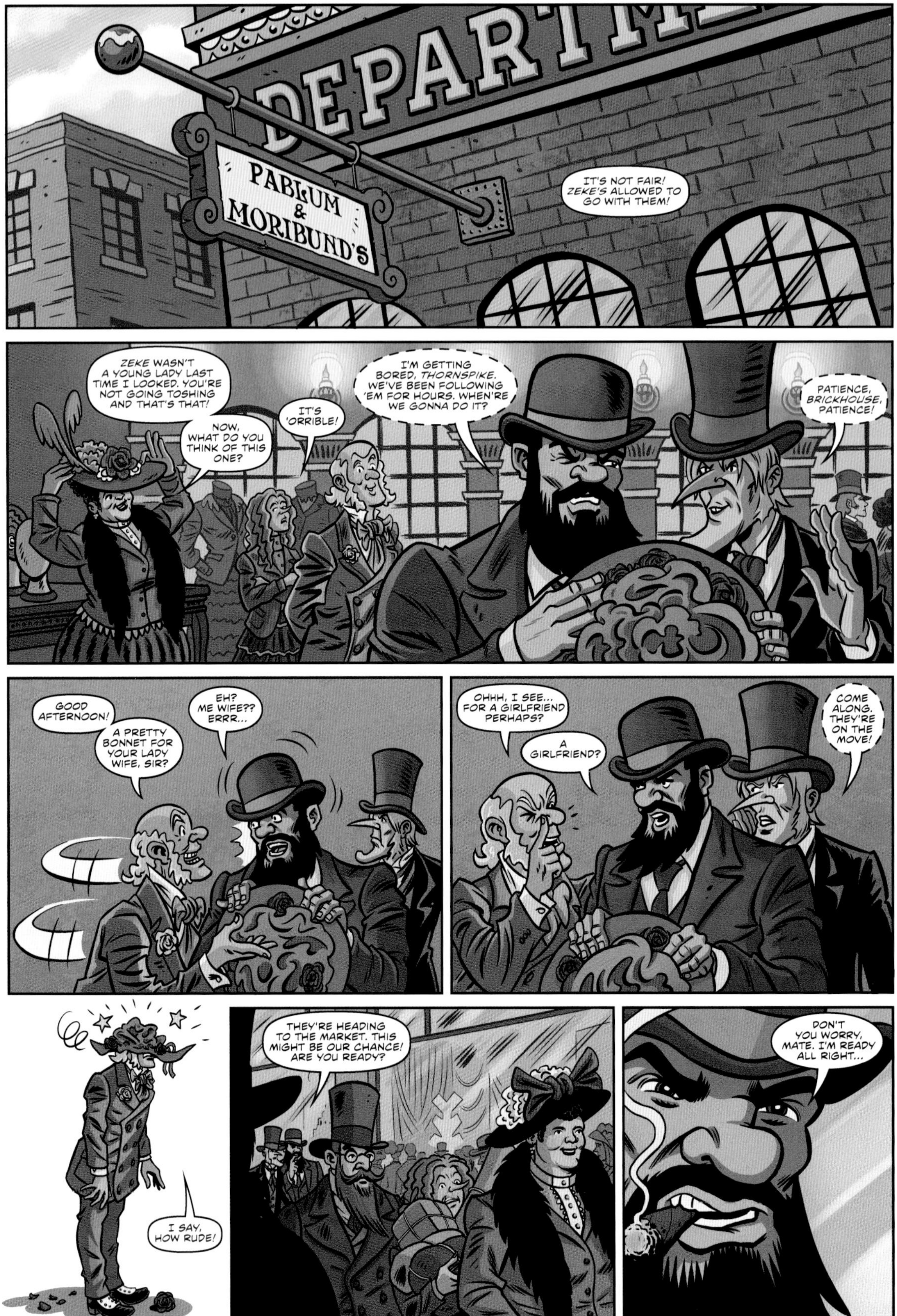
DEPARTM
PABLUM & MORIBUND'S
IT'S NOT FAIR! ZEKE'S ALLOWED TO GO WITH THEM!
ZEKE WASN'T A YOUNG LADY LAST TIME I LOOKED. YOU'RE NOT GOING TOSHING AND THAT'S THAT!
NOW, WHAT DO YOU THINK OF THIS ONE?
IT'S 'ORRIBLE!
I'M GETTING BORED, THORNSPIKE. WE'VE BEEN FOLLOWING 'EM FOR HOURS. WHEN'RE WE GONNA DO IT?
PATIENCE, BRICKHOUSE, PATIENCE!
GOOD AFTERNOON!
A PRETTY BONNET FOR YOUR LADY WIFE, SIR?
EH? ME WIFE?? ERRR...
OHHH, I SEE... FOR A GIRLFRIEND PERHAPS?
A GIRLFRIEND?
COME ALONG. THEY'RE ON THE MOVE!
I SAY, HOW RUDE!
THEY'RE HEADING TO THE MARKET. THIS MIGHT BE OUR CHANCE! ARE YOU READY?
DON'T YOU WORRY, MATE. I'M READY ALL RIGHT...

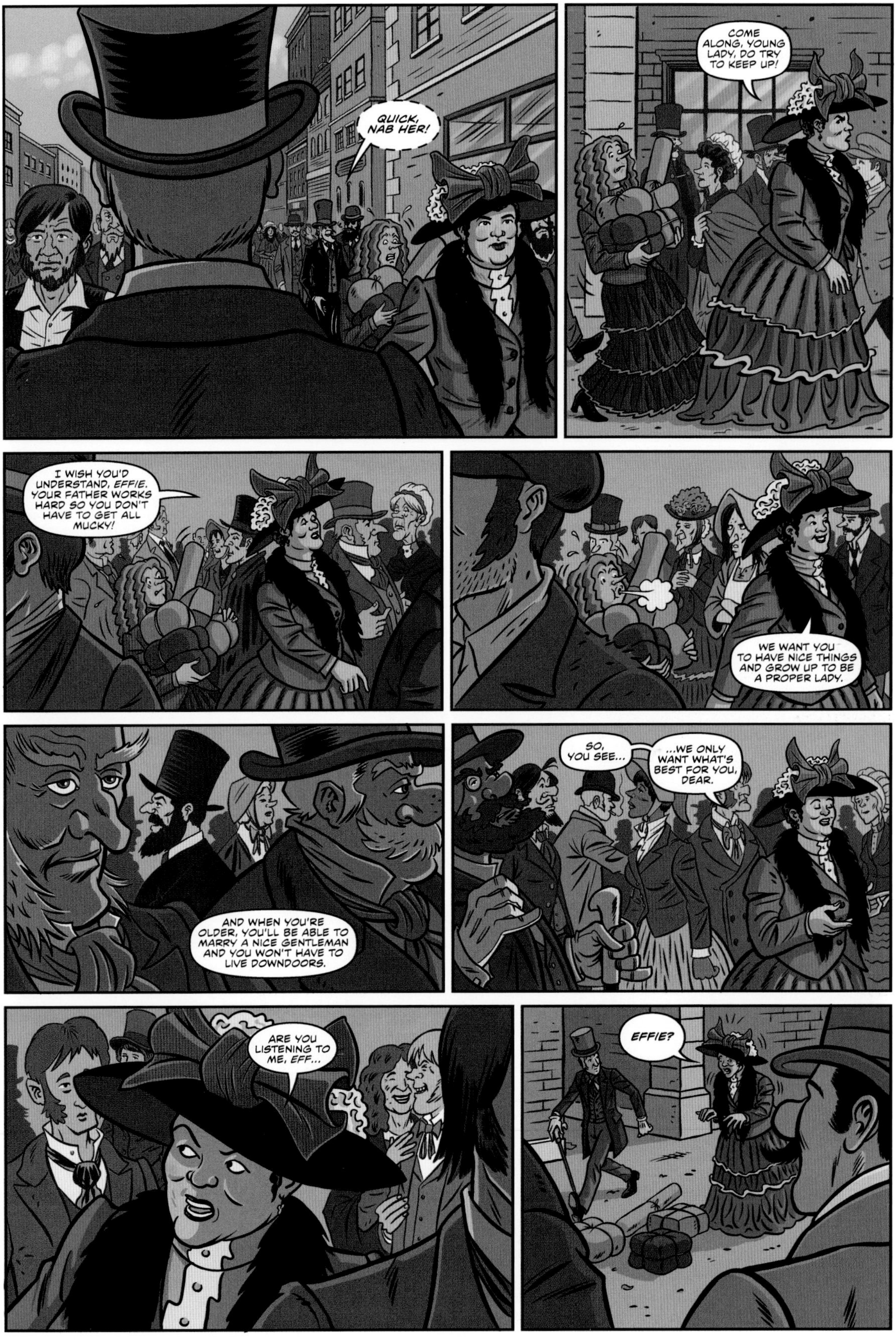
QUICK, NAB HER!
COME ALONG, YOUNG LADY, DO TRY TO KEEP UP!
I WISH YOU'D UNDERSTAND, EFFIE. YOUR FATHER WORKS HARD SO YOU DON'T HAVE TO GET ALL MUCKY!
WE WANT YOU TO HAVE NICE THINGS AND GROW UP TO BE A PROPER LADY.
AND WHEN YOU'RE OLDER, YOU'LL BE ABLE TO MARRY A NICE GENTLEMAN AND YOU WON'T HAVE TO LIVE DOWNDOORS.
SO, YOU SEE...
...WE ONLY WANT WHAT'S BEST FOR YOU, DEAR.
ARE YOU LISTENING TO ME, EFF...
EFFIE?

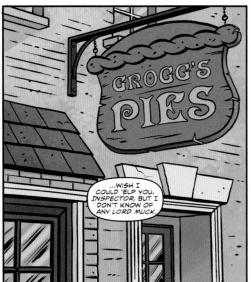

GROGG'S PIES

...WISH I COULD 'ELP YOU, INSPECTOR, BUT I DON'T KNOW OF ANY LORD MUCK.

WHAT I DO WANT TO KNOW IS...WHAT'S THE LAW GOING TO DO ABOUT THE BRAT WHAT'S BEEN STEALING MY PIES, EH? *EH?*

≋SIGH≋ IF YOU GIVE ME A DESCRIPTION, SIR, I'LL SEE WHAT I CAN DO.

WELL, HE'S A BOY, DARK HAIR, DIRTY FACE. SCRUFFY. OH, AND HE WEARS A CAP.

MHMM. BOY...HAIR... FACE. I SEE. SCRUFFY... A CAP.

MY, MY! THAT NARROWS IT DOWN, SIR.

WE SHOULDN'T HAVE ANY TROUBLE APPREHENDING HIM NOW.

EGGS
TEA
MILK

EFFIIIIEEEE!

LAWKS! WHAT'S THE COMMOTION?

I'D BETTER GO SEE WHAT THAT'S ALL ABOUT!

OI! COME BACK 'ERE AND PAY FOR THAT PIE!

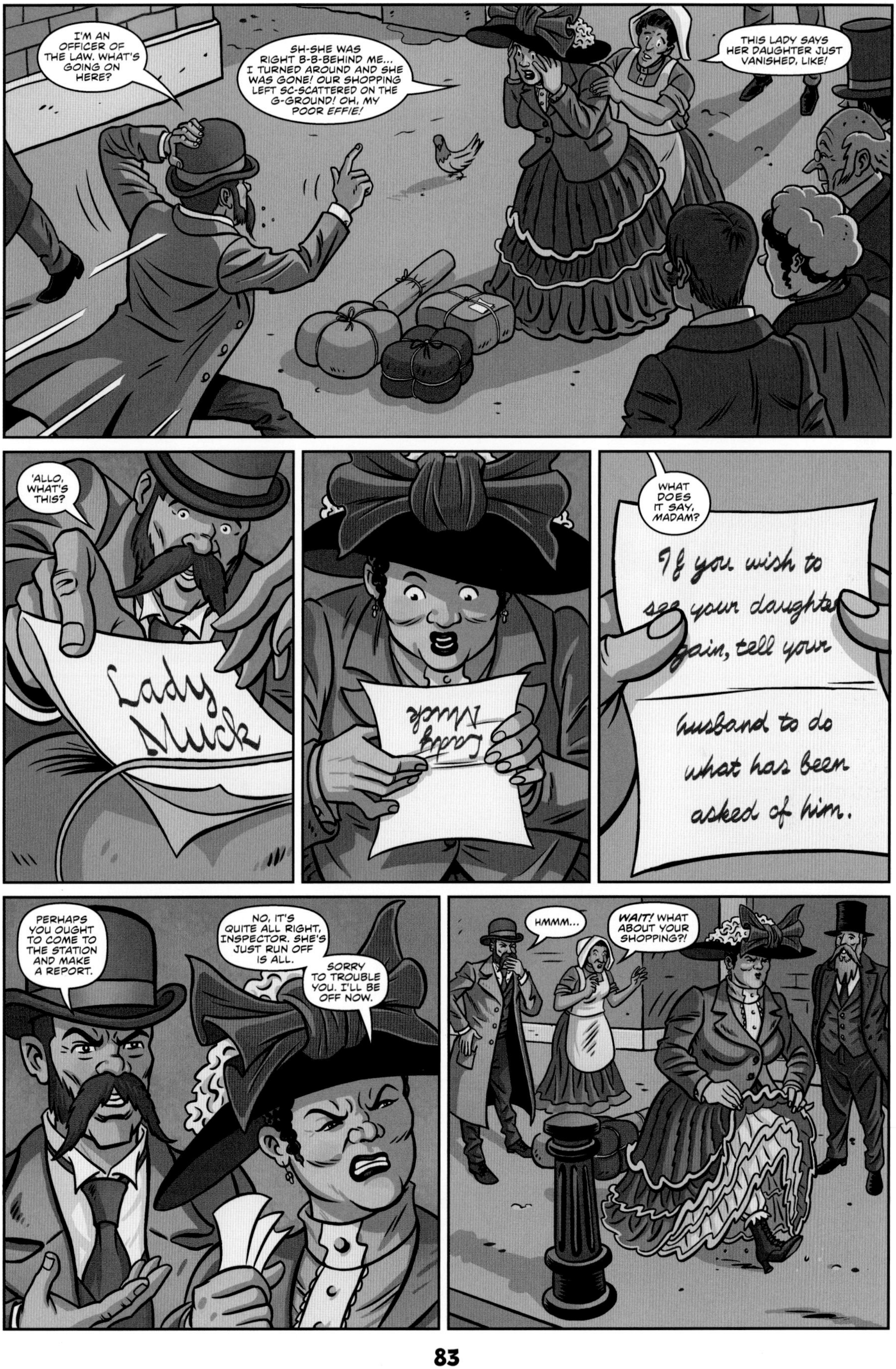
I'M AN OFFICER OF THE LAW. WHAT'S GOING ON HERE?
SH-SHE WAS RIGHT B-B-BEHIND ME... I TURNED AROUND AND SHE WAS GONE! OUR SHOPPING LEFT SC-SCATTERED ON THE G-GROUND! OH, MY POOR EFFIE!
THIS LADY SAYS HER DAUGHTER JUST VANISHED, LIKE!
'ALLO, WHAT'S THIS?
Lady Muck
WHAT DOES IT SAY, MADAM?
If you wish to see your daughter again, tell your husband to do what has been asked of him.
PERHAPS YOU OUGHT TO COME TO THE STATION AND MAKE A REPORT.
NO, IT'S QUITE ALL RIGHT, INSPECTOR. SHE'S JUST RUN OFF IS ALL.
SORRY TO TROUBLE YOU. I'LL BE OFF NOW.
HMMM...
WAIT! WHAT ABOUT YOUR SHOPPING?!

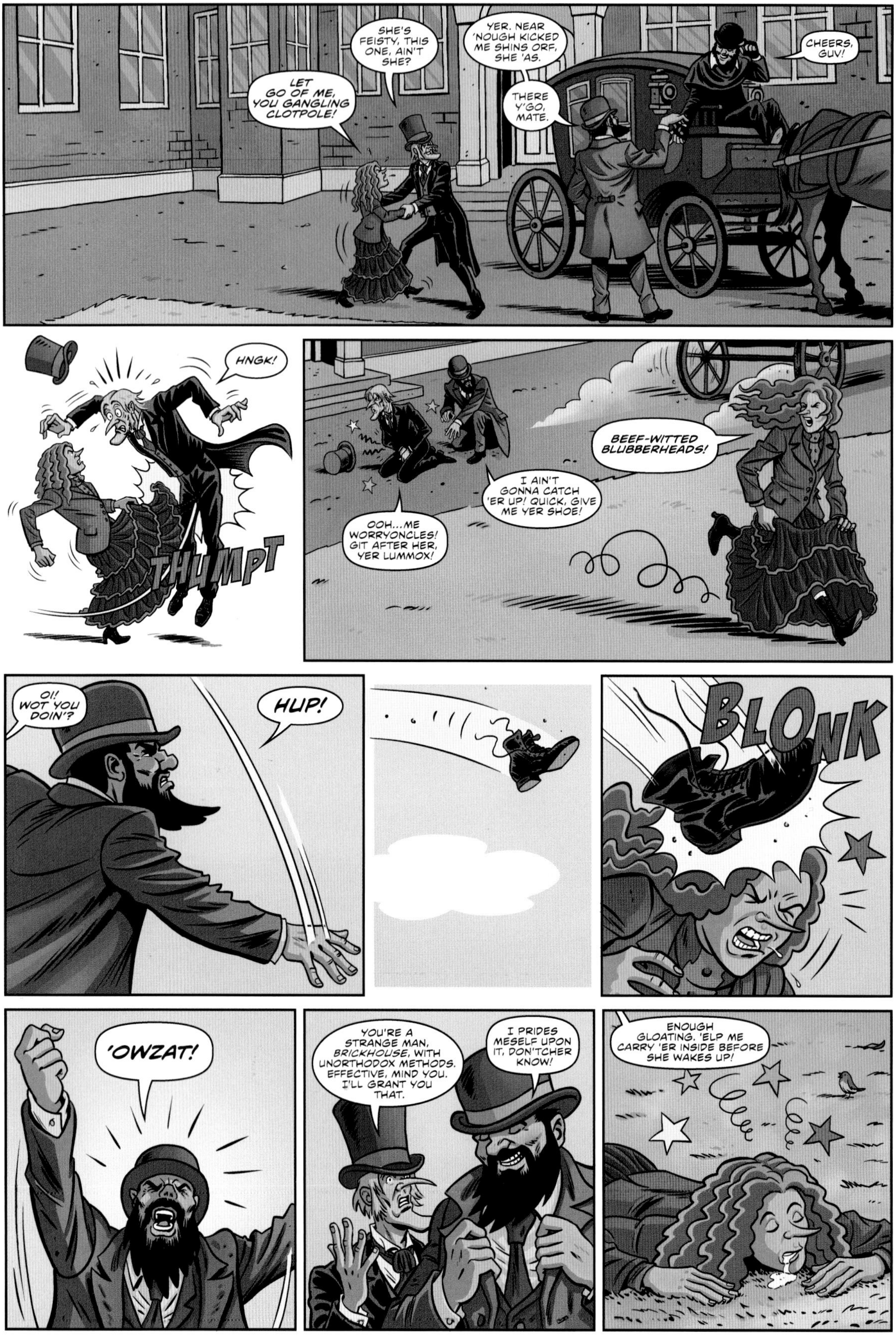
LET GO OF ME, YOU GANGLING CLOTPOLE!
SHE'S FEISTY, THIS ONE, AIN'T SHE?
YER. NEAR 'NOUGH KICKED ME SHINS ORF, SHE 'AS.
THERE Y'GO, MATE.
CHEERS, GUV!
HNGK!
THUMPT
BEEF-WITTED BLUBBERHEADS!
I AIN'T GONNA CATCH 'ER UP! QUICK, GIVE ME YER SHOE!
OOH...ME WORRYONCLES! GIT AFTER HER, YER LUMMOX!
OI! WOT YOU DOIN'?
HUP!
BLONK
'OWZAT!
YOU'RE A STRANGE MAN, BRICKHOUSE, WITH UNORTHODOX METHODS. EFFECTIVE, MIND YOU. I'LL GRANT YOU THAT.
I PRIDES MESELF UPON IT, DON'TCHER KNOW!
ENOUGH GLOATING. 'ELP ME CARRY 'ER INSIDE BEFORE SHE WAKES UP!

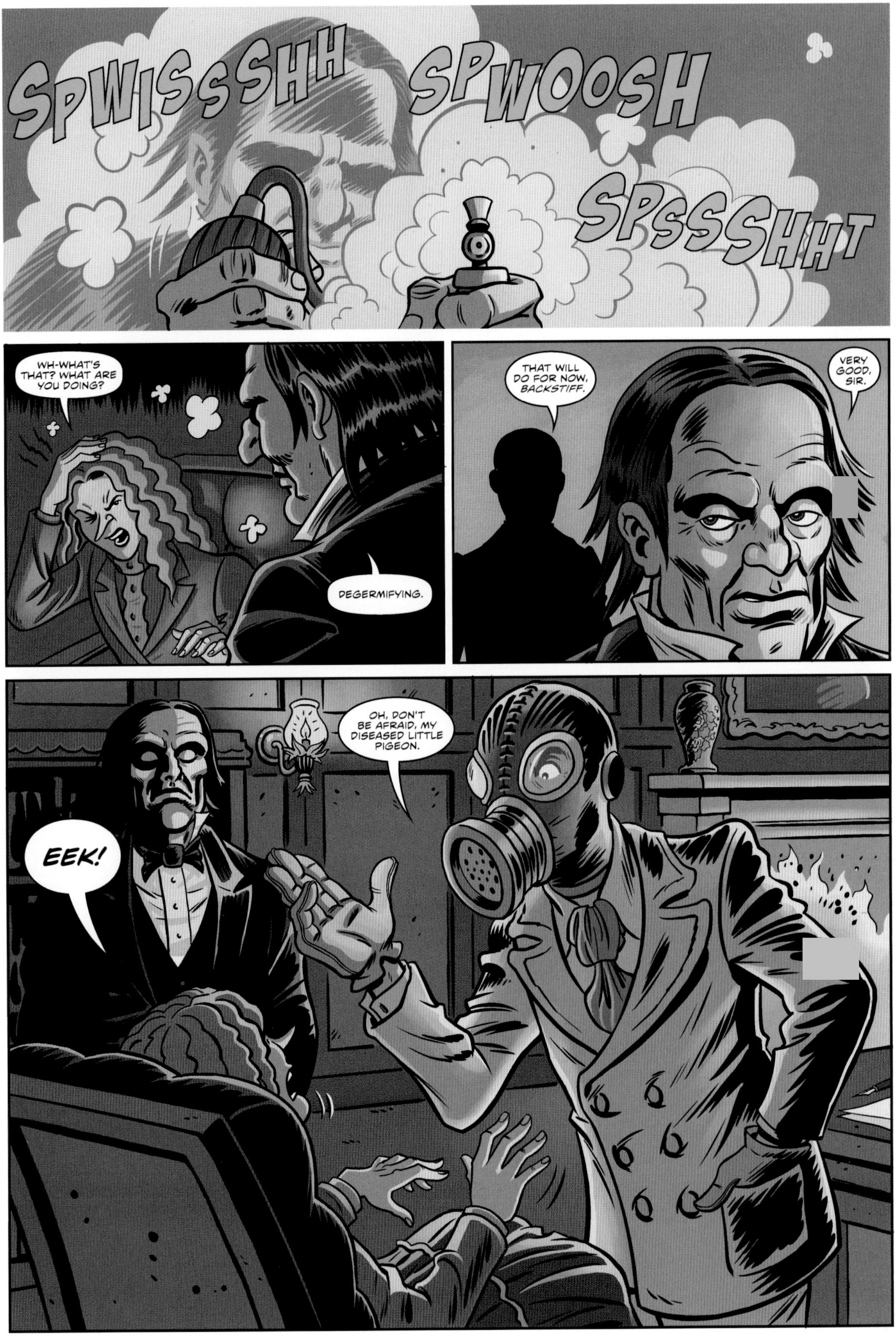

SPWISSSHH
SPWOOSH
SPSSSHHT
WH-WHAT'S THAT? WHAT ARE YOU DOING?
DEGERMIFYING.
THAT WILL DO FOR NOW, BACKSTIFF.
VERY GOOD, SIR.
OH, DON'T BE AFRAID, MY DISEASED LITTLE PIGEON.
EEK!

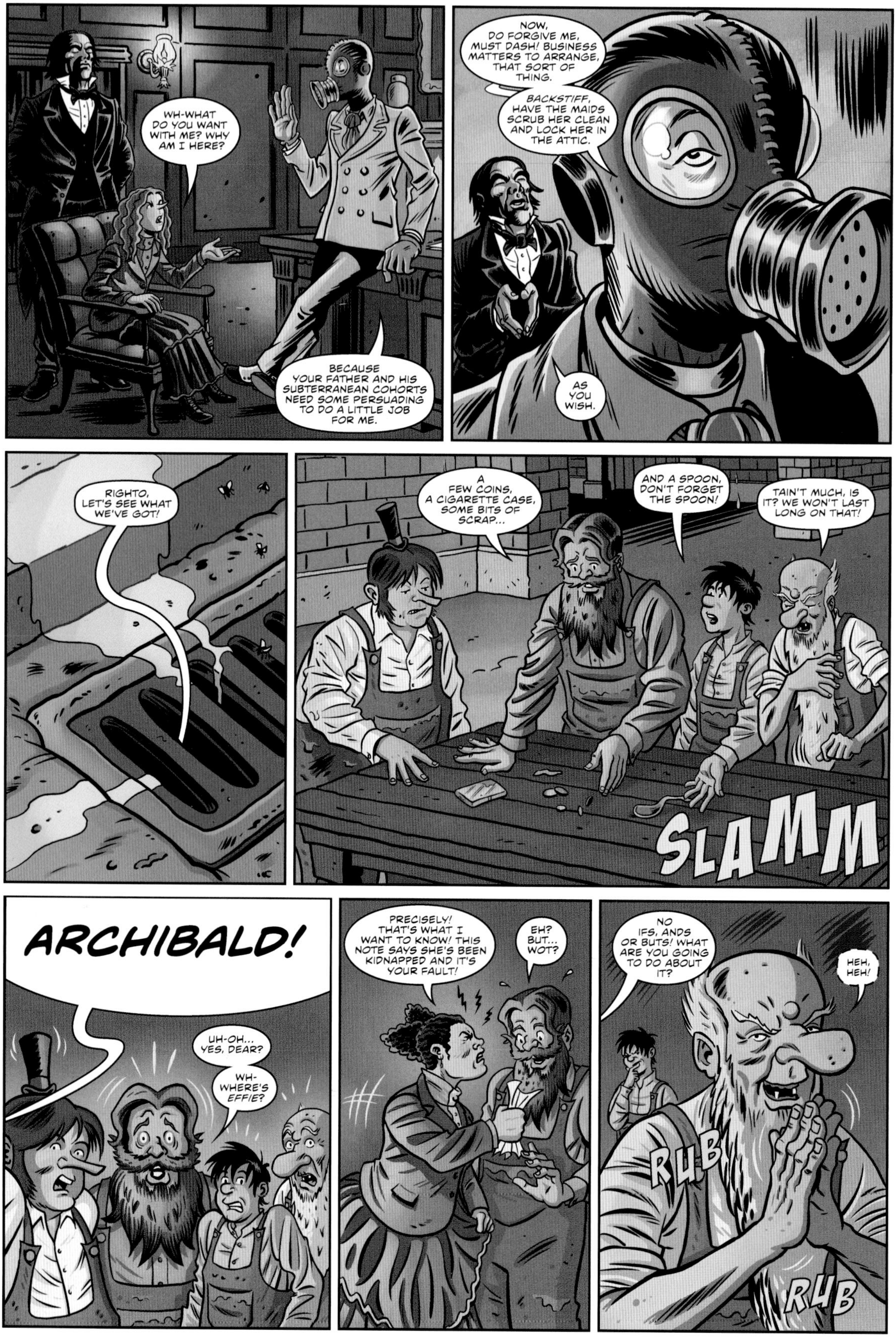
WH-WHAT DO YOU WANT WITH ME? WHY AM I HERE?
BECAUSE YOUR FATHER AND HIS SUBTERRANEAN COHORTS NEED SOME PERSUADING TO DO A LITTLE JOB FOR ME.
NOW, DO FORGIVE ME, MUST DASH! BUSINESS MATTERS TO ARRANGE, THAT SORT OF THING.
BACKSTIFF, HAVE THE MAIDS SCRUB HER CLEAN AND LOCK HER IN THE ATTIC.
AS YOU WISH.
RIGHTO, LET'S SEE WHAT WE'VE GOT!
A FEW COINS, A CIGARETTE CASE, SOME BITS OF SCRAP...
AND A SPOON, DON'T FORGET THE SPOON!
TAIN'T MUCH, IS IT? WE WON'T LAST LONG ON THAT!
SLAMM
ARCHIBALD!
UH-OH... YES, DEAR?
WH-WHERE'S EFFIE?
PRECISELY! THAT'S WHAT I WANT TO KNOW! THIS NOTE SAYS SHE'S BEEN KIDNAPPED AND IT'S YOUR FAULT!
EH? BUT... WOT?
NO IFS, ANDS OR BUTS! WHAT ARE YOU GOING TO DO ABOUT IT?
HEH, HEH!
RUB
RUB

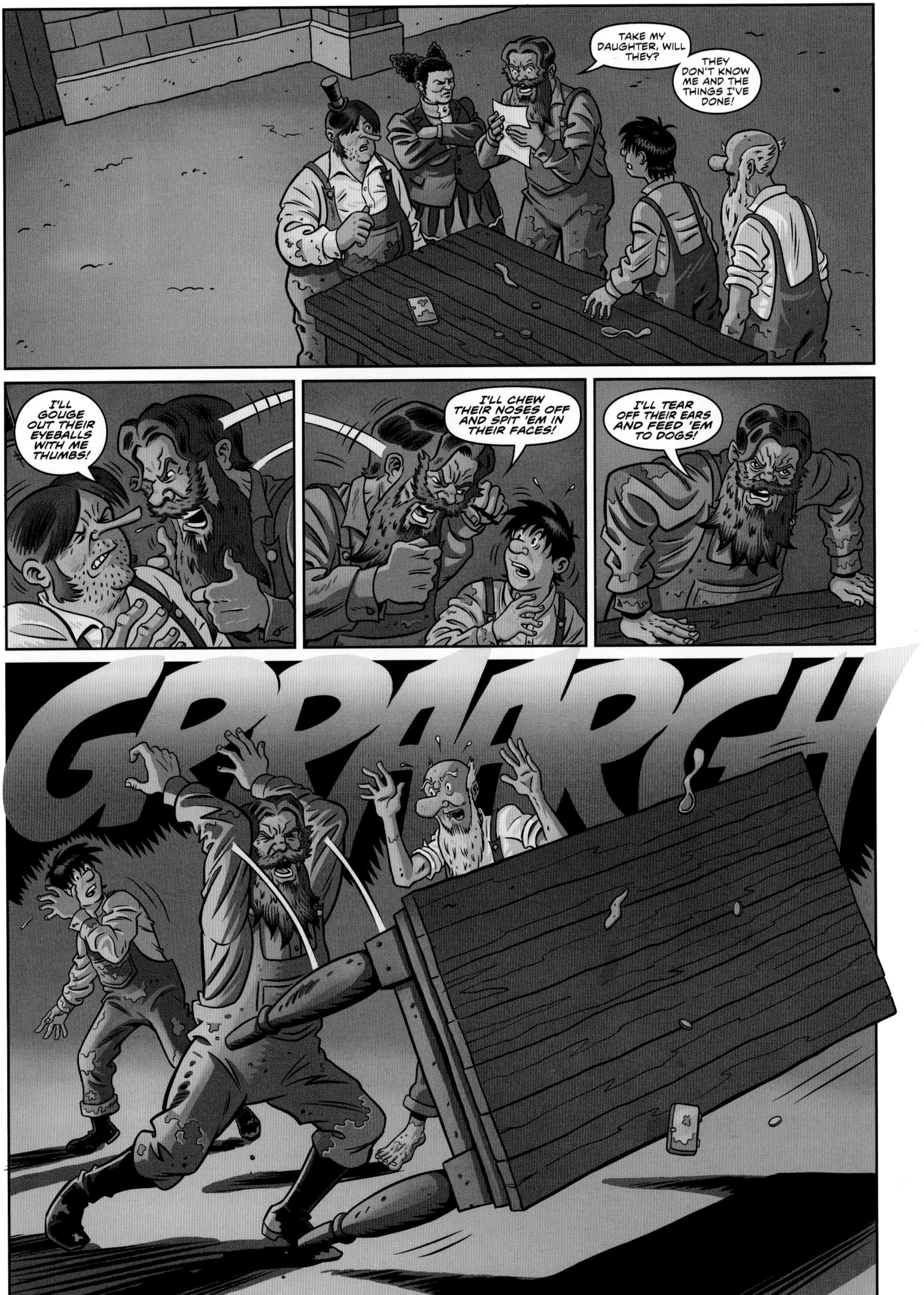
TAKE MY DAUGHTER, WILL THEY?
THEY DON'T KNOW ME AND THE THINGS I'VE DONE!
I'LL GOUGE OUT THEIR EYEBALLS WITH ME THUMBS!
I'LL CHEW THEIR NOSES OFF AND SPIT 'EM IN THEIR FACES!
I'LL TEAR OFF THEIR EARS AND FEED 'EM TO DOGS!

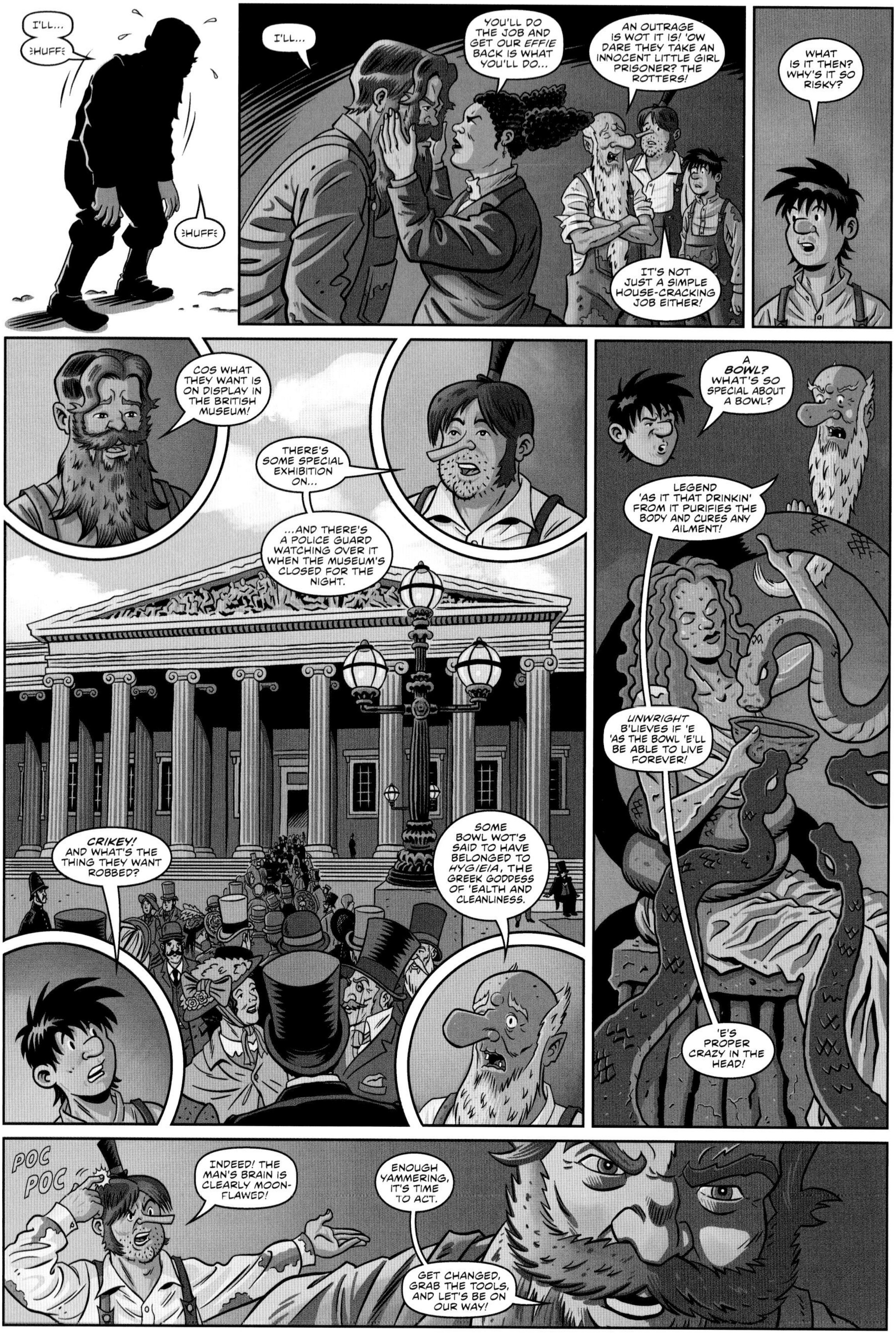

I'LL...
HUFF
HUFF
I'LL...
YOU'LL DO THE JOB AND GET OUR *EFFIE* BACK IS WHAT YOU'LL DO...
AN OUTRAGE IS WOT IT IS! 'OW DARE THEY TAKE AN INNOCENT LITTLE GIRL PRISONER? THE ROTTERS!
IT'S NOT JUST A SIMPLE HOUSE-CRACKING JOB EITHER!
WHAT IS IT THEN? WHY'S IT SO RISKY?
COS WHAT THEY WANT IS ON DISPLAY IN THE BRITISH *MUSEUM!*
THERE'S SOME SPECIAL EXHIBITION ON...
...AND THERE'S A POLICE GUARD WATCHING OVER IT WHEN THE MUSEUM'S CLOSED FOR THE NIGHT.
CRIKEY! AND WHAT'S THE THING THEY WANT ROBBED?
SOME BOWL WOT'S SAID TO HAVE BELONGED TO *HYGIEIA*, THE GREEK GODDESS OF 'EALTH AND CLEANLINESS.
A *BOWL?* WHAT'S SO SPECIAL ABOUT A BOWL?
LEGEND 'AS IT THAT DRINKIN' FROM IT PURIFIES THE BODY AND CURES ANY AILMENT!
UNWRIGHT B'LIEVES IF 'E 'AS THE BOWL 'E'LL BE ABLE TO LIVE FOREVER!
'E'S PROPER CRAZY IN THE HEAD!
POC POC
INDEED! THE MAN'S BRAIN IS CLEARLY MOON-FLAWED!
ENOUGH YAMMERING, IT'S TIME TO ACT.
GET CHANGED, GRAB THE TOOLS, AND LET'S BE ON OUR WAY!

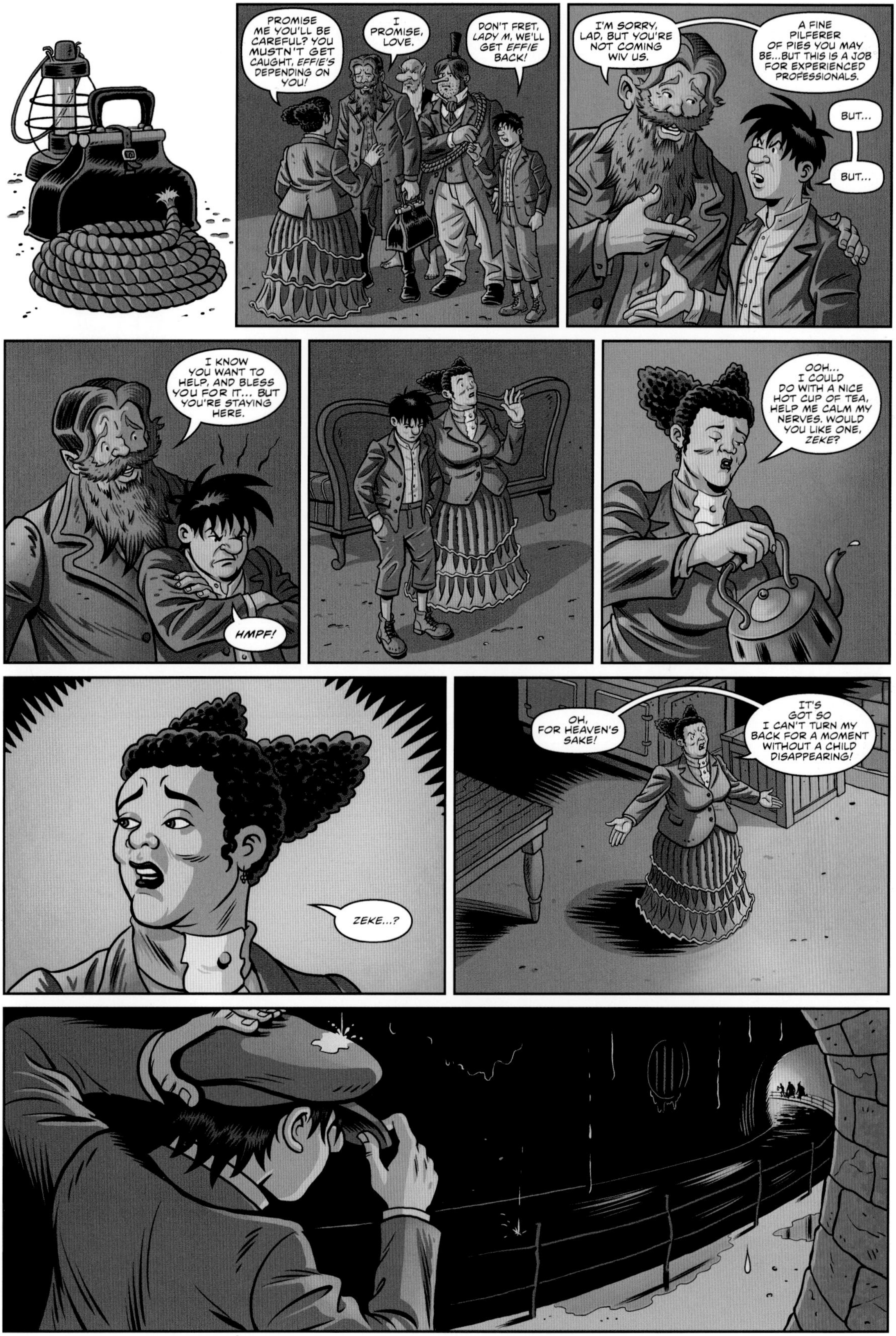
PROMISE ME YOU'LL BE CAREFUL? YOU MUSTN'T GET CAUGHT, EFFIE'S DEPENDING ON YOU!
I PROMISE, LOVE.
DON'T FRET, LADY M, WE'LL GET EFFIE BACK!
I'M SORRY, LAD, BUT YOU'RE NOT COMING WIV US.
A FINE PILFERER OF PIES YOU MAY BE...BUT THIS IS A JOB FOR EXPERIENCED PROFESSIONALS.
BUT...
BUT...
I KNOW YOU WANT TO HELP, AND BLESS YOU FOR IT... BUT YOU'RE STAYING HERE.
HMPF!
OOH... I COULD DO WITH A NICE HOT CUP OF TEA, HELP ME CALM MY NERVES. WOULD YOU LIKE ONE, ZEKE?
ZEKE...?
OH, FOR HEAVEN'S SAKE!
IT'S GOT SO I CAN'T TURN MY BACK FOR A MOMENT WITHOUT A CHILD DISAPPEARING!

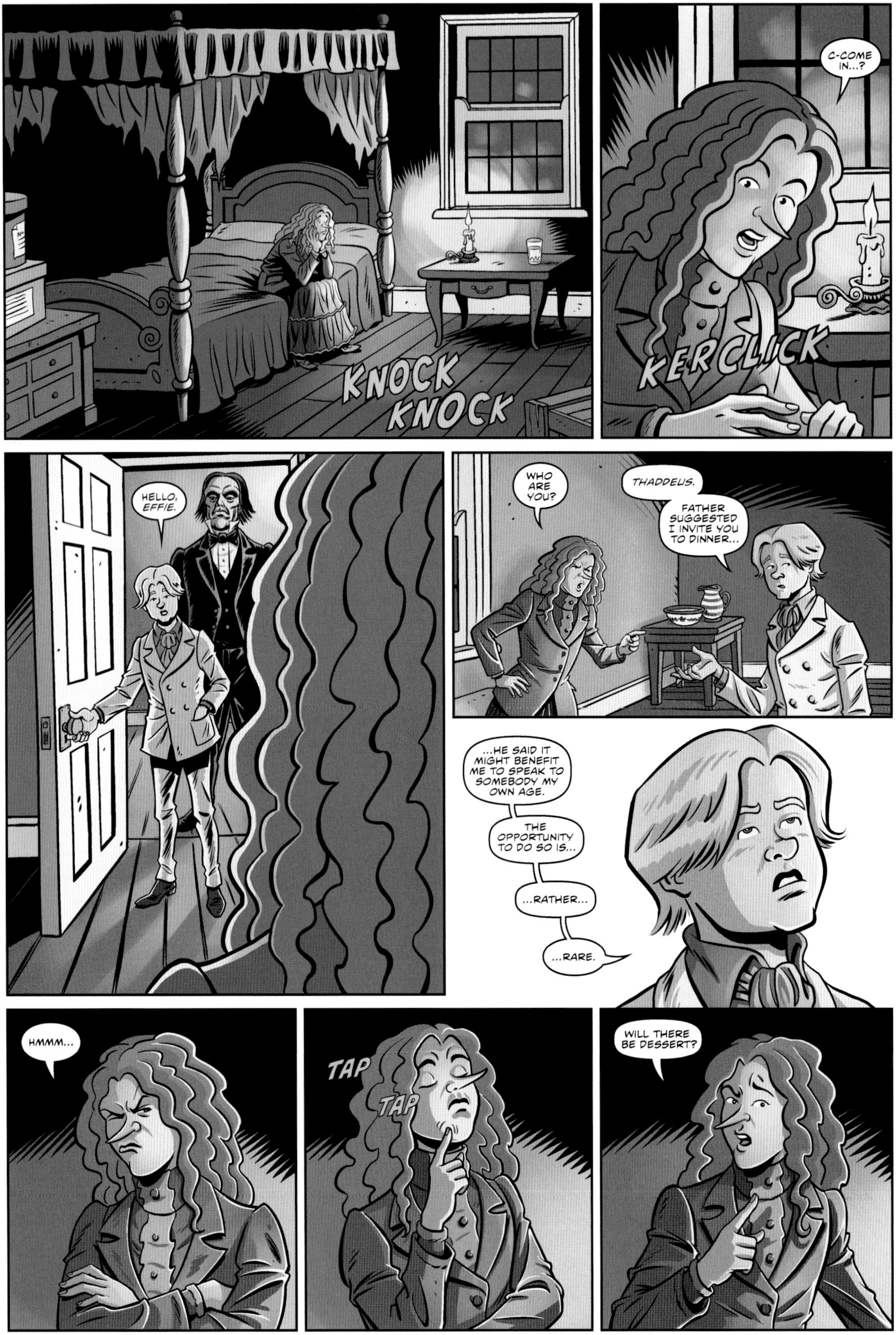
KNOCK KNOCK
C-COME IN...?
KERCLICK
HELLO, EFFIE.
WHO ARE YOU?
THADDEUS.
FATHER SUGGESTED I INVITE YOU TO DINNER...
...HE SAID IT MIGHT BENEFIT ME TO SPEAK TO SOMEBODY MY OWN AGE.
THE OPPORTUNITY TO DO SO IS...
...RATHER...
...RARE.
HMMM...
TAP TAP
WILL THERE BE DESSERT?

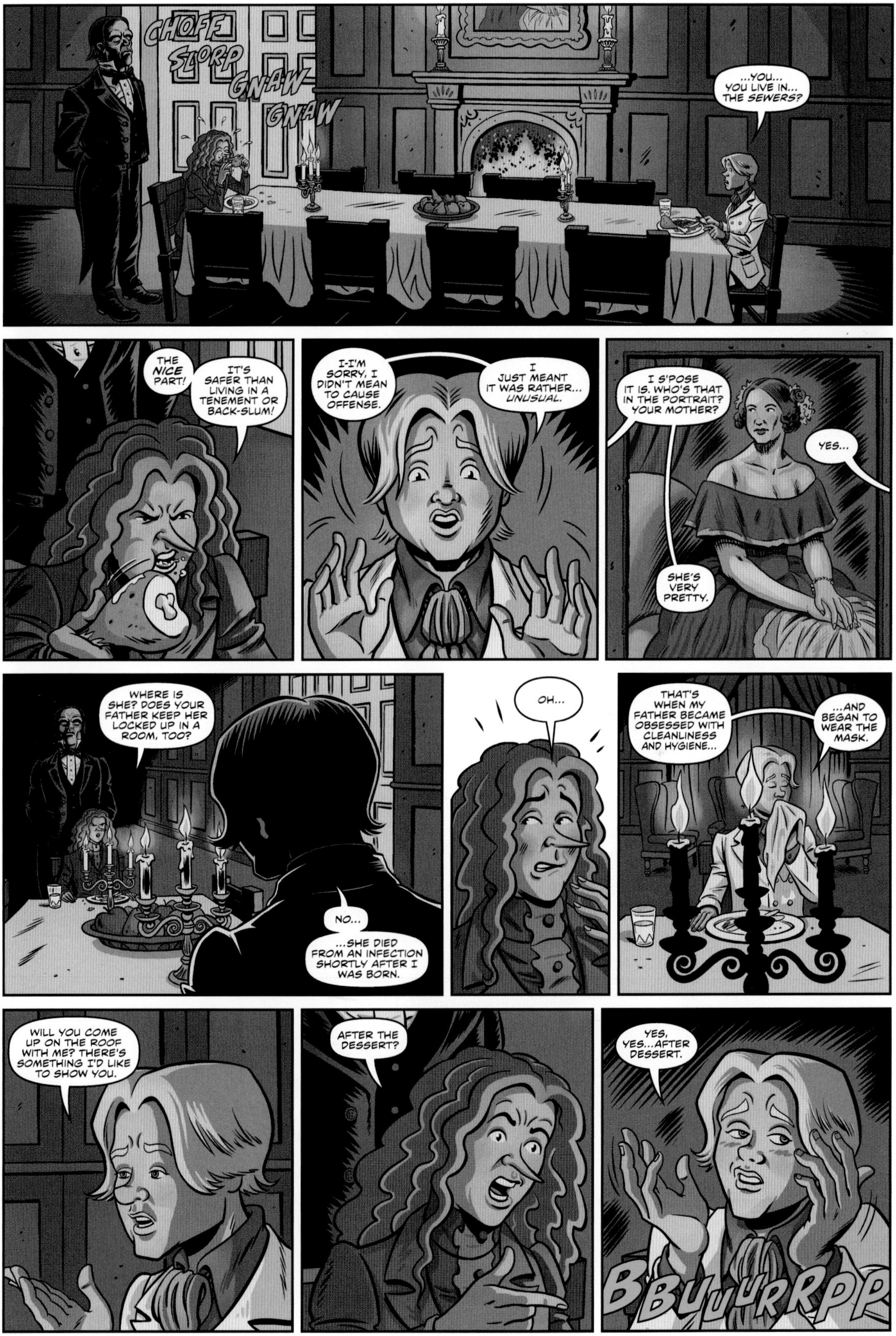
CHOFF
SLORP
GNAW
GNAW
...YOU... YOU LIVE IN... THE SEWERS?
THE NICE PART!
IT'S SAFER THAN LIVING IN A TENEMENT OR BACK-SLUM!
I-I'M SORRY, I DIDN'T MEAN TO CAUSE OFFENSE.
I JUST MEANT IT WAS RATHER... UNUSUAL.
I S'POSE IT IS. WHO'S THAT IN THE PORTRAIT? YOUR MOTHER?
YES...
SHE'S VERY PRETTY.
WHERE IS SHE? DOES YOUR FATHER KEEP HER LOCKED UP IN A ROOM, TOO?
NO...
...SHE DIED FROM AN INFECTION SHORTLY AFTER I WAS BORN.
OH...
THAT'S WHEN MY FATHER BECAME OBSESSED WITH CLEANLINESS AND HYGIENE...
...AND BEGAN TO WEAR THE MASK.
WILL YOU COME UP ON THE ROOF WITH ME? THERE'S SOMETHING I'D LIKE TO SHOW YOU.
AFTER THE DESSERT?
YES, YES...AFTER DESSERT.
BBUUURRPP

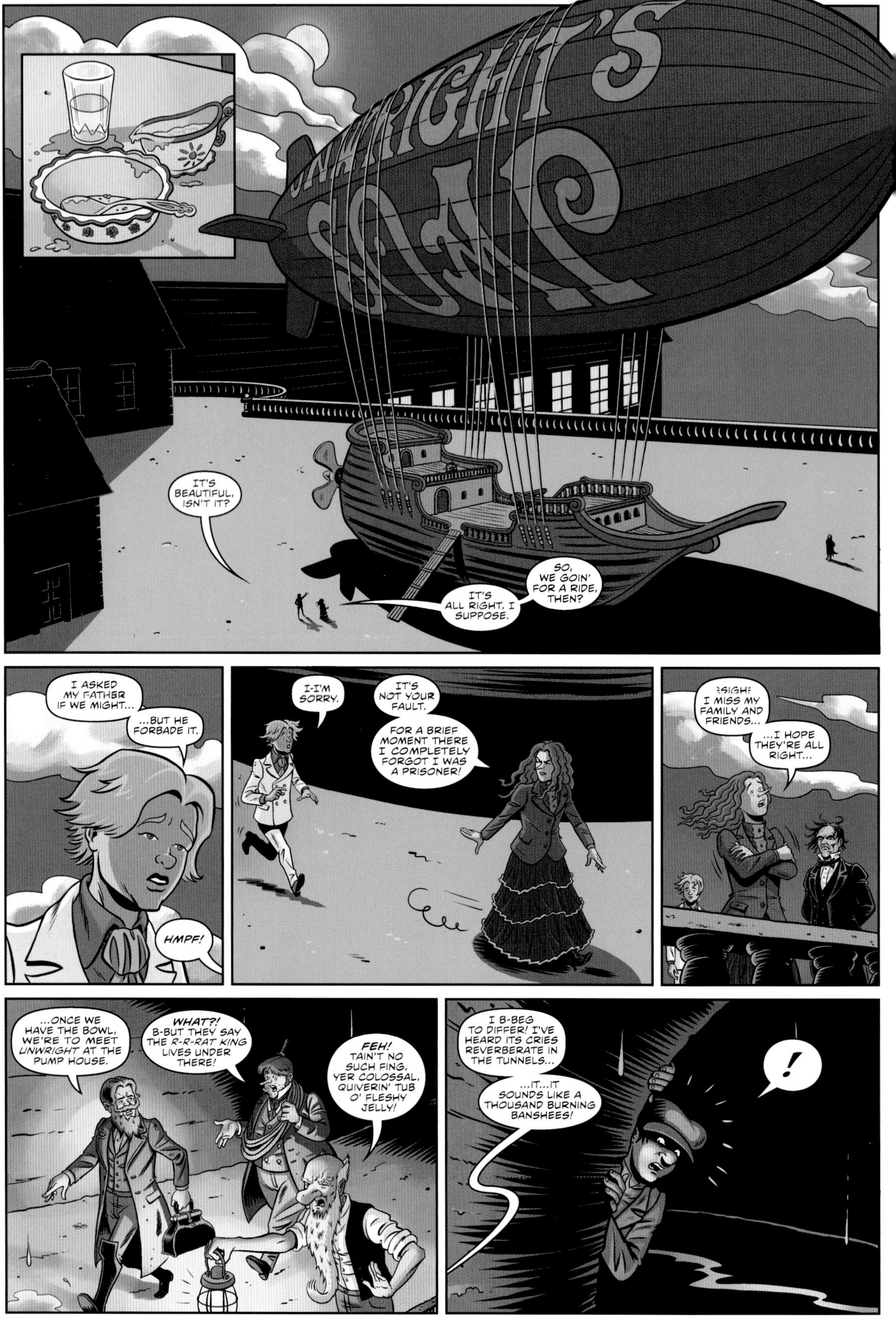
UNWRIGHT'S SOAP
IT'S BEAUTIFUL, ISN'T IT?
IT'S ALL RIGHT, I SUPPOSE.
SO, WE GOIN' FOR A RIDE, THEN?
I ASKED MY FATHER IF WE MIGHT...
...BUT HE FORBADE IT.
HMPF!
I-I'M SORRY.
IT'S NOT YOUR FAULT.
FOR A BRIEF MOMENT THERE I COMPLETELY FORGOT I WAS A PRISONER!
SIGH
I MISS MY FAMILY AND FRIENDS...
...I HOPE THEY'RE ALL RIGHT...
...ONCE WE HAVE THE BOWL, WE'RE TO MEET UNWRIGHT AT THE PUMP HOUSE.
WHAT?! B-BUT THEY SAY THE R-R-RAT KING LIVES UNDER THERE!
FEH! TAIN'T NO SUCH FING, YER COLOSSAL, QUIVERIN' TUB O' FLESHY JELLY!
I B-BEG TO DIFFER! I'VE HEARD ITS CRIES REVERBERATE IN THE TUNNELS...
...IT...IT SOUNDS LIKE A THOUSAND BURNING BANSHEES!
!

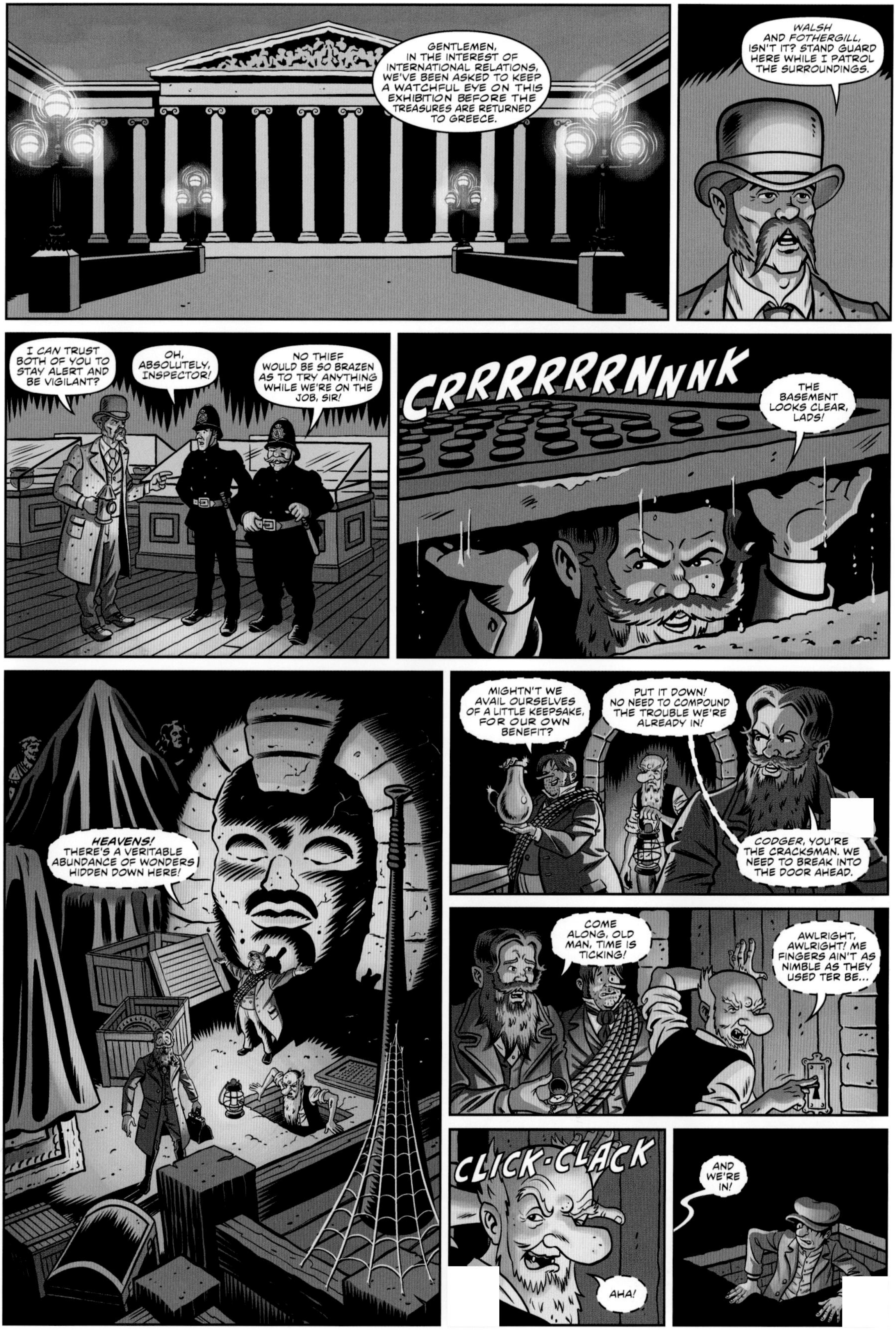
GENTLEMEN, IN THE INTEREST OF INTERNATIONAL RELATIONS, WE'VE BEEN ASKED TO KEEP A WATCHFUL EYE ON THIS EXHIBITION BEFORE THE TREASURES ARE RETURNED TO GREECE.
WALSH AND FOTHERGILL, ISN'T IT? STAND GUARD HERE WHILE I PATROL THE SURROUNDINGS.
I CAN TRUST BOTH OF YOU TO STAY ALERT AND BE VIGILANT?
OH, ABSOLUTELY, INSPECTOR!
NO THIEF WOULD BE SO BRAZEN AS TO TRY ANYTHING WHILE WE'RE ON THE JOB, SIR!
CRRRRRRNNNK
THE BASEMENT LOOKS CLEAR, LADS!
HEAVENS! THERE'S A VERITABLE ABUNDANCE OF WONDERS HIDDEN DOWN HERE!
MIGHTN'T WE AVAIL OURSELVES OF A LITTLE KEEPSAKE, FOR OUR OWN BENEFIT?
PUT IT DOWN! NO NEED TO COMPOUND THE TROUBLE WE'RE ALREADY IN!
CODGER, YOU'RE THE CRACKSMAN. WE NEED TO BREAK INTO THE DOOR AHEAD.
COME ALONG, OLD MAN, TIME IS TICKING!
AWLRIGHT, AWLRIGHT! ME FINGERS AIN'T AS NIMBLE AS THEY USED TER BE...
CLICK-CLACK
AHA!
AND WE'RE IN!

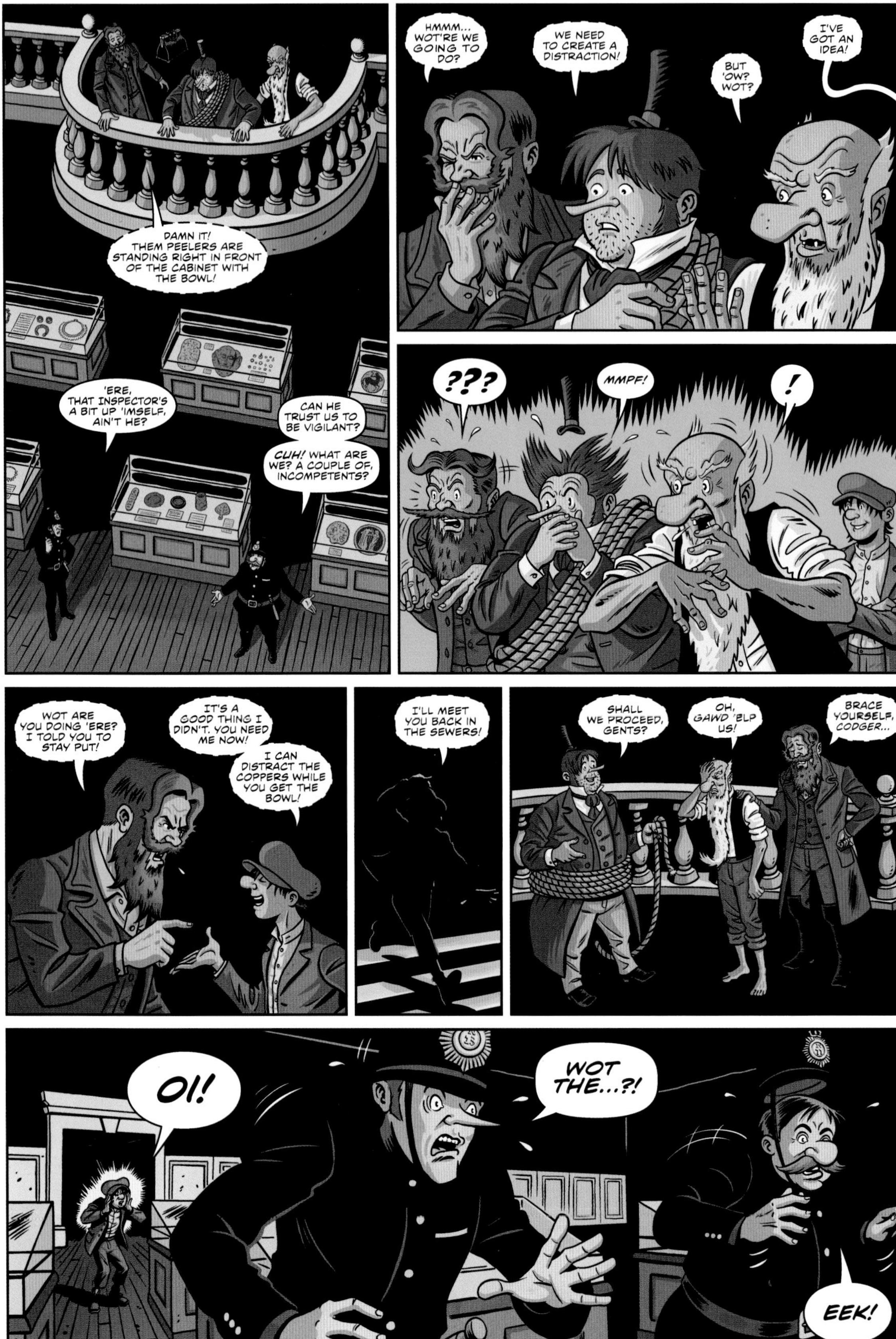
DAMN IT! THEM PEELERS ARE STANDING RIGHT IN FRONT OF THE CABINET WITH THE BOWL!
'ERE, THAT INSPECTOR'S A BIT UP 'IMSELF, AIN'T HE?
CAN HE TRUST US TO BE VIGILANT?
CUH! WHAT ARE WE? A COUPLE OF, INCOMPETENTS?
HMMM... WOT'RE WE GOING TO DO?
WE NEED TO CREATE A DISTRACTION!
BUT 'OW? WOT?
I'VE GOT AN IDEA!
???
MMPF!
!
WOT ARE YOU DOING 'ERE? I TOLD YOU TO STAY PUT!
IT'S A GOOD THING I DIDN'T. YOU NEED ME NOW!
I CAN DISTRACT THE COPPERS WHILE YOU GET THE BOWL!
I'LL MEET YOU BACK IN THE SEWERS!
SHALL WE PROCEED, GENTS?
OH, GAWD 'ELP US!
BRACE YOURSELF, CODGER...
OI!
WOT THE...?!
EEK!

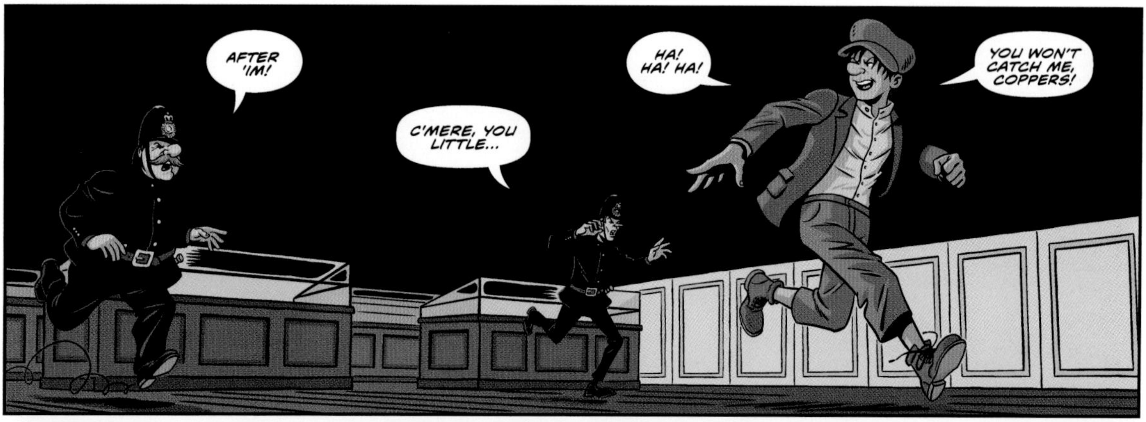
AFTER 'IM!
C'MERE, YOU LITTLE...
HA! HA! HA!
YOU WON'T CATCH ME, COPPERS!

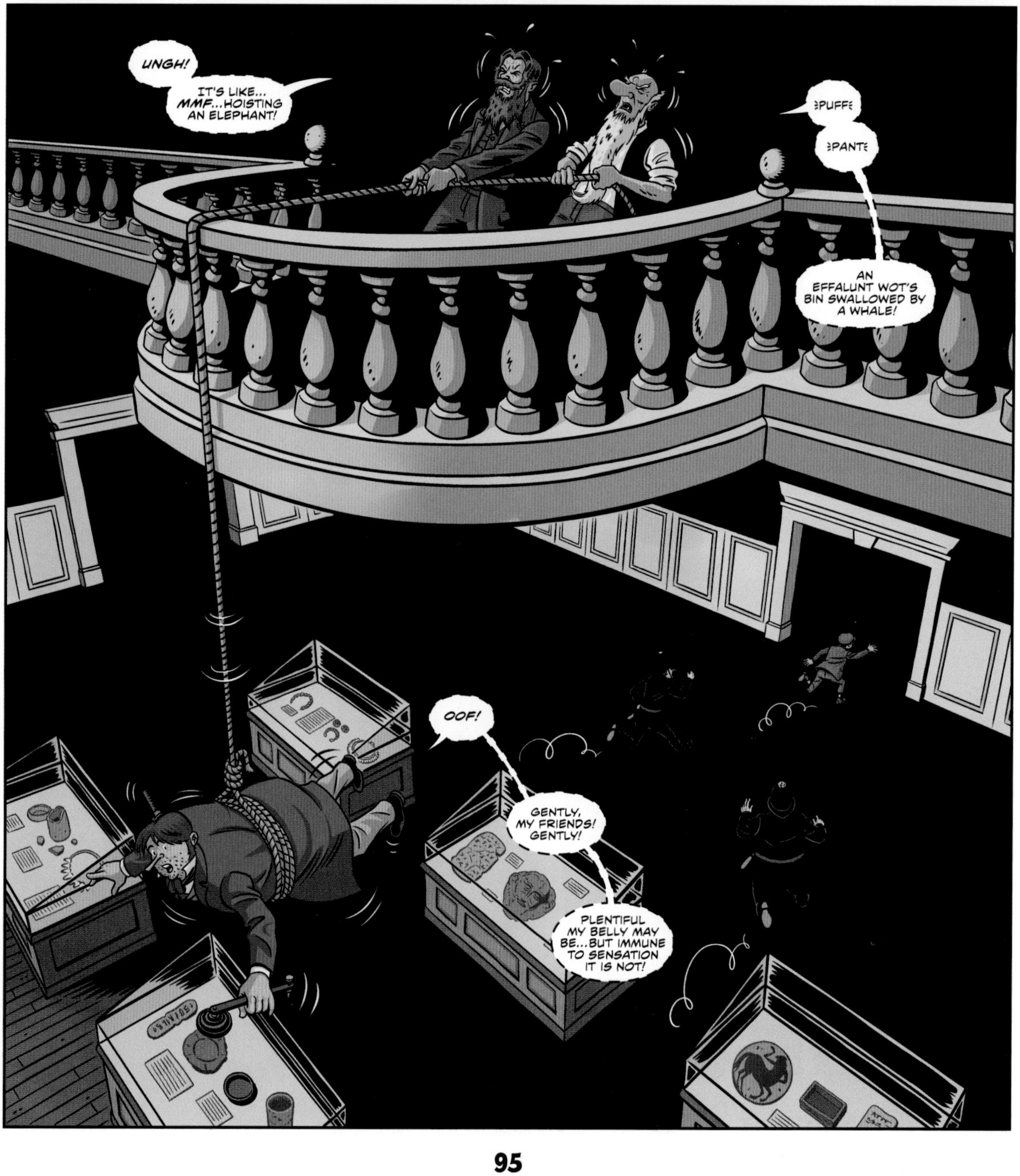
UNGH!
IT'S LIKE... MMF...HOISTING AN ELEPHANT!
PUFF
PANT
AN EFFALUNT WOT'S BIN SWALLOWED BY A WHALE!
OOF!
GENTLY, MY FRIENDS! GENTLY!
PLENTIFUL MY BELLY MAY BE...BUT IMMUNE TO SENSATION IT IS NOT!

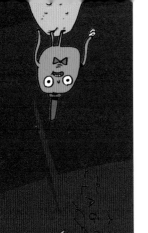

AND NOW FOR SOMETHING A LITTLE BIT RANDOM
THUD
THUD
MEGA ROBO BROS PRESENTS...
BARGAIN BASEMENT BOTS!
DO YOU HAVE TROUBLE MAKING SMALL TALK WITH STRANGERS AT PARTIES?
UM.
YES.
YOU NEED THE NEW
CHIT-CHAT-CHAP
MARK 7!
DESIGNED TO FIT DISCREETLY IN YOUR EAR AND FEED YOU SUGGESTIONS FROM ITS DATABASE OF OVER 7,000 LIGHT AND ENGAGING TOPICS FOR CONVERSATION!
BZZT!
"ANY PLANS FOR THE WEEKEND?"
SO, UM...
"DID YOU KNOW THAT EVERY DAY WE BREATHE IN OVER 2 lbs OF DEAD SKIN PARTICLES?"
EW!
THAT CAN'T BE RIGHT.
"HAVE YOU EVER WORRIED ABOUT A JELLYFISH OVERLORD?"
WHAT? NO.
"WHAT IS AN ALAN?"
"WHAT IS AN ALAN."
"ERROR!"
EXCUSE ME?
"ERROR!"
PLEASE LEAVE.
THE HANDLEBAR
SWOOPS HELD IN PLACE WITH EAR WAX
TWITCHABLE FULCRUM
Want company for a stroll, a jaunt, or a giggle? Put on a handlebar mustache and people will line up!
THE HORSESHOE
NATURAL DOWNWARD FLOW
THE TOUGHNESS IS IN THE HANGING JANGLES
Scrappers wear the horseshoe. Put it on to show the world a bit of razzle won't go unrazzed.
THESE ARE SOME OF THE MUSTACHES I REALLY LOVE. THEY'LL GIVE YOU THAT KICK OF CONFIDENCE JUST WHEN YOU NEED IT
CHOPS'S GUIDE
TO CREATIVE MUSTACHERY

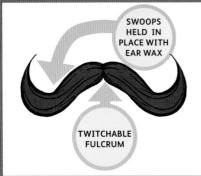

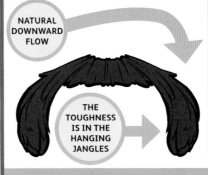

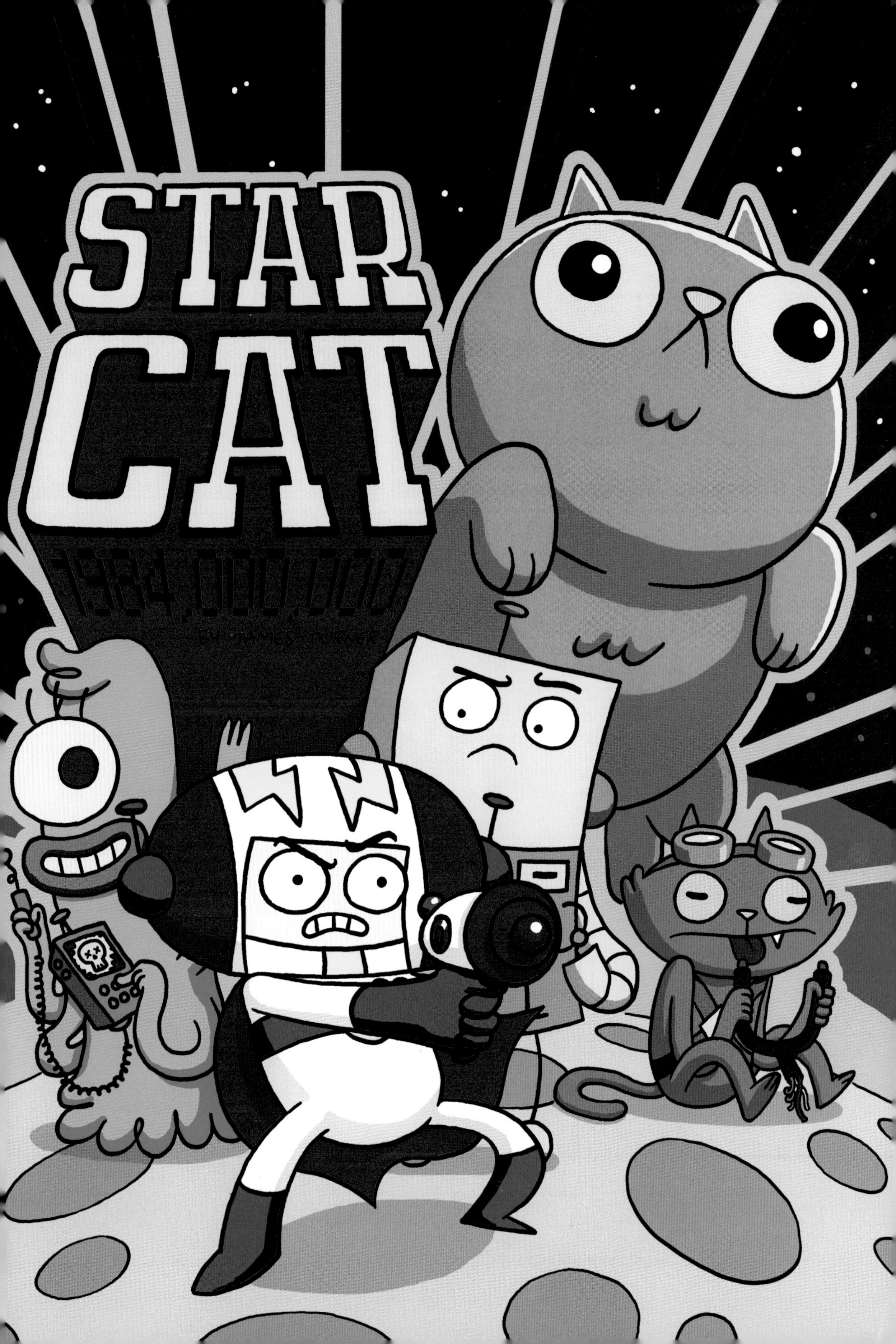
STAR CAT
1,984,000,000
BY JAMES TURNER

AS OUR STORY BEGINS, THE CREW OF THE *STAR CAT* IS AT *SPACE HQ* ATTENDING AN IMPORTANT EVENT...

STAR CAT

1,984,000,000

PART 1

SPACE HQ ...

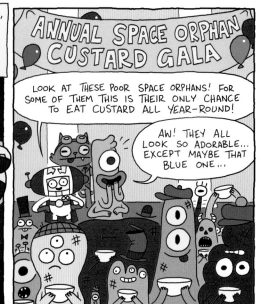

ANNUAL SPACE ORPHAN CUSTARD GALA

LOOK AT THESE POOR SPACE ORPHANS! FOR SOME OF THEM THIS IS THEIR ONLY CHANCE TO EAT CUSTARD ALL YEAR-ROUND!

AW! THEY ALL LOOK SO ADORABLE... EXCEPT MAYBE THAT BLUE ONE...

BLUE ONE...?

HEY!

WHAT? I DON'T HAVE ANY PARENTS!

SHH! THE SPACE MAYOR IS FINISHING HIS SPEECH!

...AND SO IT IS WITH GREAT PLEASURE THAT I NOW PRESENT THIS YEAR'S COLLECTION OF CUSTARD TO THE SPACE ORPHANS - ENJOY!

THREE CHEERS FOR THE SPACE MAYOR!

HIP HIP, HOORAY!

HIP HIP, HOORAY!

TUG!

HIP HIP, HOO——

OH.

SWISHHHH!

AHEM, WELL, IT DOES SEEM LIKE PEOPLE HAVEN'T BEEN SO GENEROUS WITH THEIR CUSTARD DONATIONS THIS YEAR ...BUT I'M SURE IT'S DELICIOUS...

PSST! I HAVE SECRET INFORMATION!

OOH, I LOVE SECRETS! WHAT IS IT, MYSTERIOUSLY PORTENTOUS FIGURE?

THAT'S NOT ALL OF THE CUSTARD THAT WAS COLLECTED THIS YEAR- SOMEONE'S BEEN SKIMMING OFF THE TOP!

OH YES, I ALWAYS SKIM THE TOP OFF MY CUSTARD - I HATE THAT WEIRD SKIN.

NO, I MEAN SOMEONE'S HAD THEIR HAND IN THE COOKIE JAR...

OH, THAT WILL BE ROBOT ONE. HE DOESN'T EAT THE COOKIES, HE JUST LIKES TO TOUCH THEM.

NO...I MEAN SOMEONE HAS BEEN EMBEZZLING FROM THE CUSTARD FUND!

EMBUZZLING? THAT SOUNDS ADORABLE! IS IT SOMETHING TO DO WITH CUDDLING BEES?

LOOK, JUST OPEN THE DOOR TO THE MAYOR'S OFFICE!

OOH, OKAY!

SPACE MAYOR'S OFFICE

KEEP OUT!

NOW, LET'S SEE...

SPACE MAYO OFFIC

KEEP OUT!

OOZE...

UM, WHAT ARE YOU DOING? DON'T OPEN THAT!

AAAH! CUSTARD TSUNAMI!

BLORPP!

WHAT IN THE...

MY OFFICE!

GASP - THIS IS ORPHAN CUSTARD! BUT WHAT'S IT DOING IN YOUR OFFICE, SPACE MAYOR?

AGAIN!

NOW LISTEN, I DIDN'T PUT THAT THERE— I DON'T EVEN LIKE CUSTARD. I'M, UH, HIGHLY ALLERGIC!

I CAN'T BELIEVE IT - THE SPACE MAYOR...STEALING CUSTARD FROM ORPHANS! I... I DON'T KNOW WHAT TO DO...

LOOK, I'M SURE THERE'S A PERFECTLY LOGICAL EXPLANATION FOR THIS...

YOU COULD TRY THIS??

IN CASE OF MAYORAL MALFEASANCE BREAK GLASS

NOW, LET'S NOT BE HASTY...

OKAY, LET'S SEE WHAT...

OOH - WHAT'S THIS?

IN CASE OF MAYOR MALFEA BREAK

SMASH!

RISE!

DSM

NO! NOT HIM!

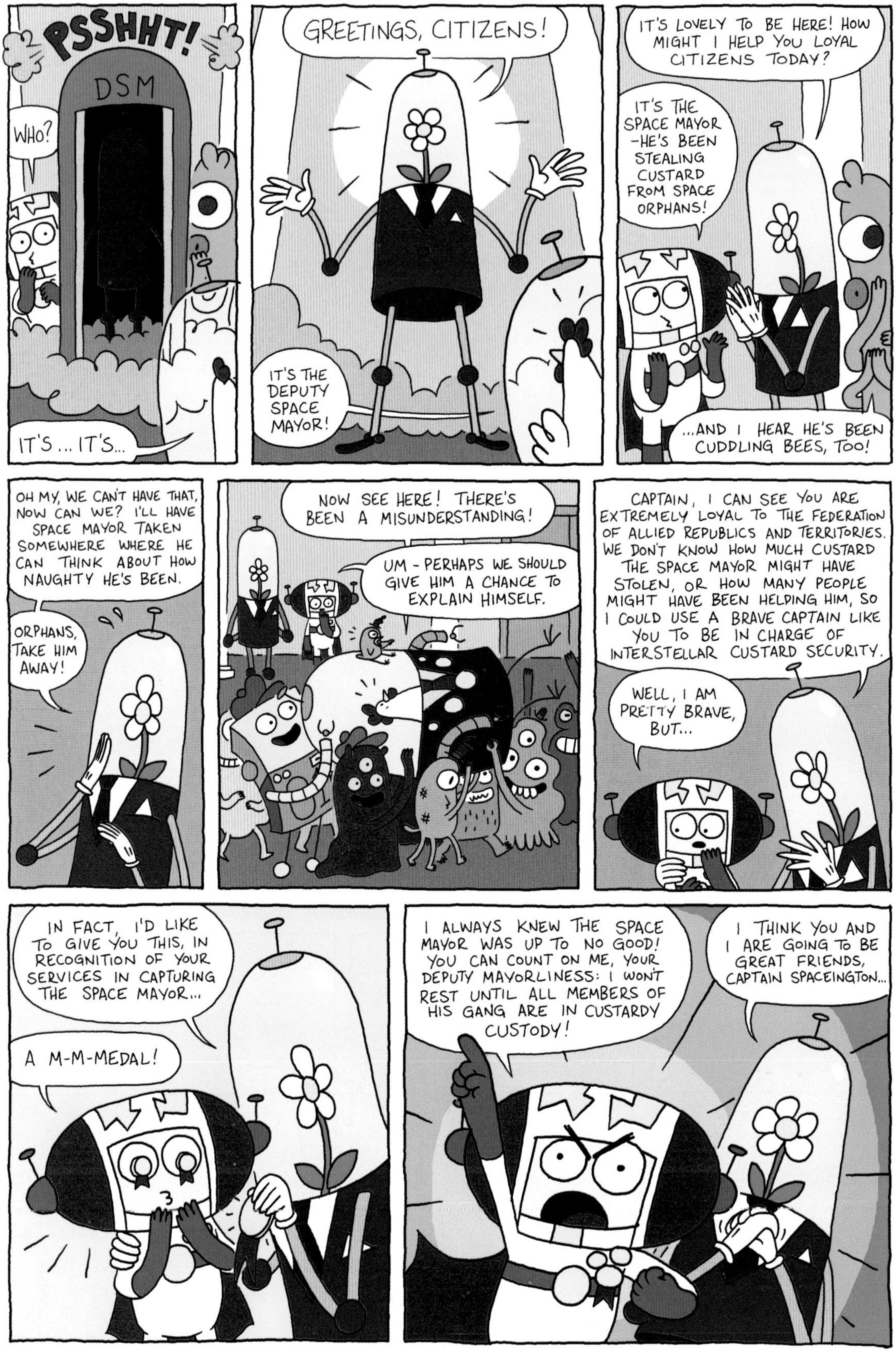
PSSHHT!
DSM
WHO?
IT'S ... IT'S...
GREETINGS, CITIZENS!
IT'S THE DEPUTY SPACE MAYOR!
IT'S LOVELY TO BE HERE! HOW MIGHT I HELP YOU LOYAL CITIZENS TODAY?
IT'S THE SPACE MAYOR -HE'S BEEN STEALING CUSTARD FROM SPACE ORPHANS!
...AND I HEAR HE'S BEEN CUDDLING BEES, TOO!
OH MY, WE CAN'T HAVE THAT, NOW CAN WE? I'LL HAVE SPACE MAYOR TAKEN SOMEWHERE WHERE HE CAN THINK ABOUT HOW NAUGHTY HE'S BEEN.
ORPHANS, TAKE HIM AWAY!
NOW SEE HERE! THERE'S BEEN A MISUNDERSTANDING!
UM - PERHAPS WE SHOULD GIVE HIM A CHANCE TO EXPLAIN HIMSELF.
CAPTAIN, I CAN SEE YOU ARE EXTREMELY LOYAL TO THE FEDERATION OF ALLIED REPUBLICS AND TERRITORIES. WE DON'T KNOW HOW MUCH CUSTARD THE SPACE MAYOR MIGHT HAVE STOLEN, OR HOW MANY PEOPLE MIGHT HAVE BEEN HELPING HIM, SO I COULD USE A BRAVE CAPTAIN LIKE YOU TO BE IN CHARGE OF INTERSTELLAR CUSTARD SECURITY.
WELL, I AM PRETTY BRAVE, BUT...
IN FACT, I'D LIKE TO GIVE YOU THIS, IN RECOGNITION OF YOUR SERVICES IN CAPTURING THE SPACE MAYOR...
A M-M-MEDAL!
I ALWAYS KNEW THE SPACE MAYOR WAS UP TO NO GOOD! YOU CAN COUNT ON ME, YOUR DEPUTY MAYORLINESS: I WON'T REST UNTIL ALL MEMBERS OF HIS GANG ARE IN CUSTARDY CUSTODY!
I THINK YOU AND I ARE GOING TO BE GREAT FRIENDS, CAPTAIN SPACEINGTON...

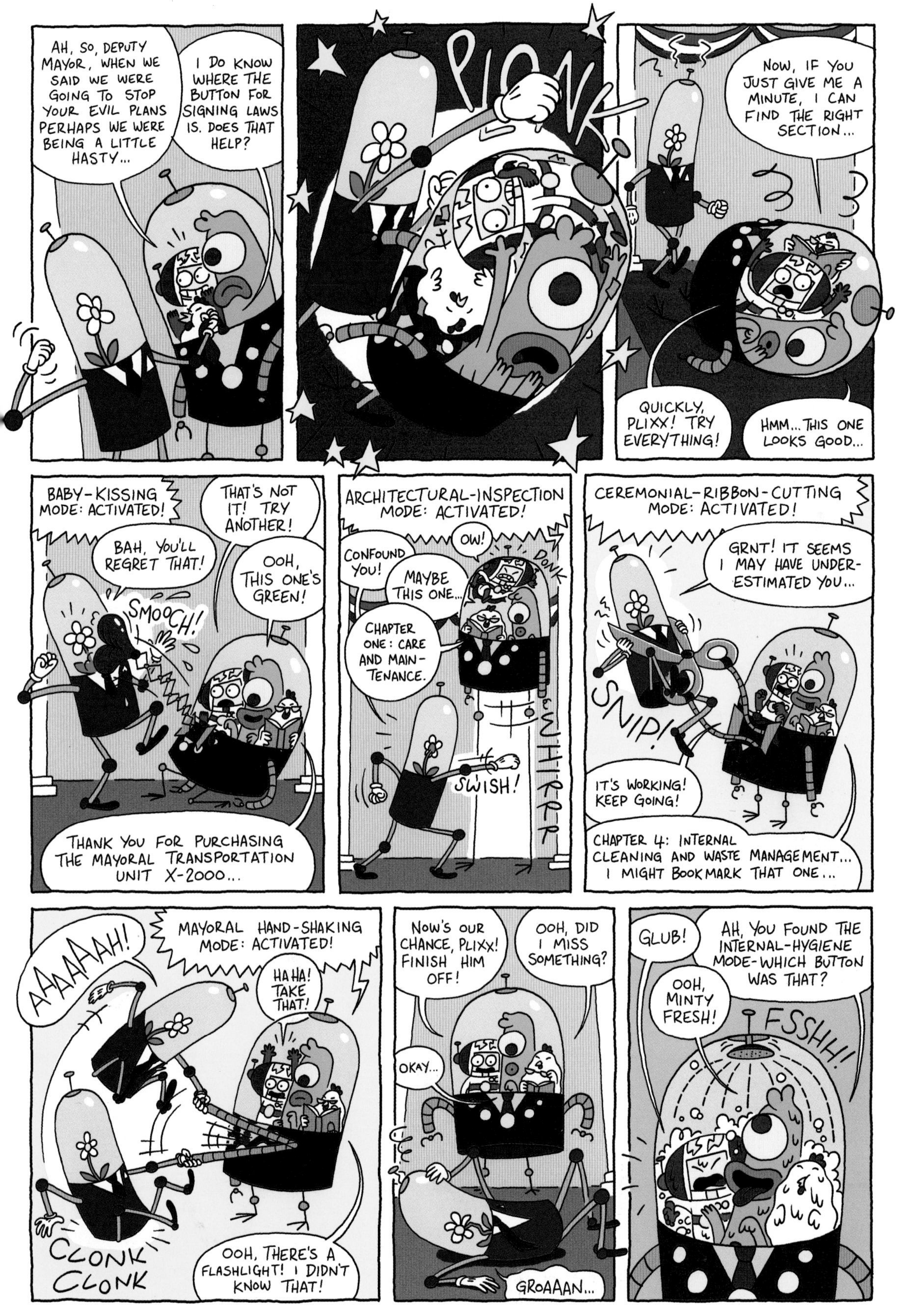
AH, SO, DEPUTY MAYOR, WHEN WE SAID WE WERE GOING TO STOP YOUR EVIL PLANS PERHAPS WE WERE BEING A LITTLE HASTY...
I DO KNOW WHERE THE BUTTON FOR SIGNING LAWS IS. DOES THAT HELP?
PLONK
NOW, IF YOU JUST GIVE ME A MINUTE, I CAN FIND THE RIGHT SECTION...
QUICKLY, PLIXX! TRY EVERYTHING!
HMM... THIS ONE LOOKS GOOD...
BABY-KISSING MODE: ACTIVATED!
THAT'S NOT IT! TRY ANOTHER!
BAH, YOU'LL REGRET THAT!
OOH, THIS ONE'S GREEN!
SMOOCH!
THANK YOU FOR PURCHASING THE MAYORAL TRANSPORTATION UNIT X-2000...
ARCHITECTURAL-INSPECTION MODE: ACTIVATED!
CONFOUND YOU!
OW!
MAYBE THIS ONE...
DONK
CHAPTER ONE: CARE AND MAINTENANCE.
SWISH!
WHIRRR
CEREMONIAL-RIBBON-CUTTING MODE: ACTIVATED!
GRNT! IT SEEMS I MAY HAVE UNDERESTIMATED YOU...
SNIP!
IT'S WORKING! KEEP GOING!
CHAPTER 4: INTERNAL CLEANING AND WASTE MANAGEMENT... I MIGHT BOOKMARK THAT ONE...
AAAAAAH!
MAYORAL HAND-SHAKING MODE: ACTIVATED!
HA HA! TAKE THAT!
CLONK CLONK
OOH, THERE'S A FLASHLIGHT! I DIDN'T KNOW THAT!
NOW'S OUR CHANCE, PLIXX! FINISH HIM OFF!
OOH, DID I MISS SOMETHING?
OKAY...
GROAAAN...
GLUB!
AH, YOU FOUND THE INTERNAL-HYGIENE MODE-WHICH BUTTON WAS THAT?
OOH, MINTY FRESH!
FSSHH!

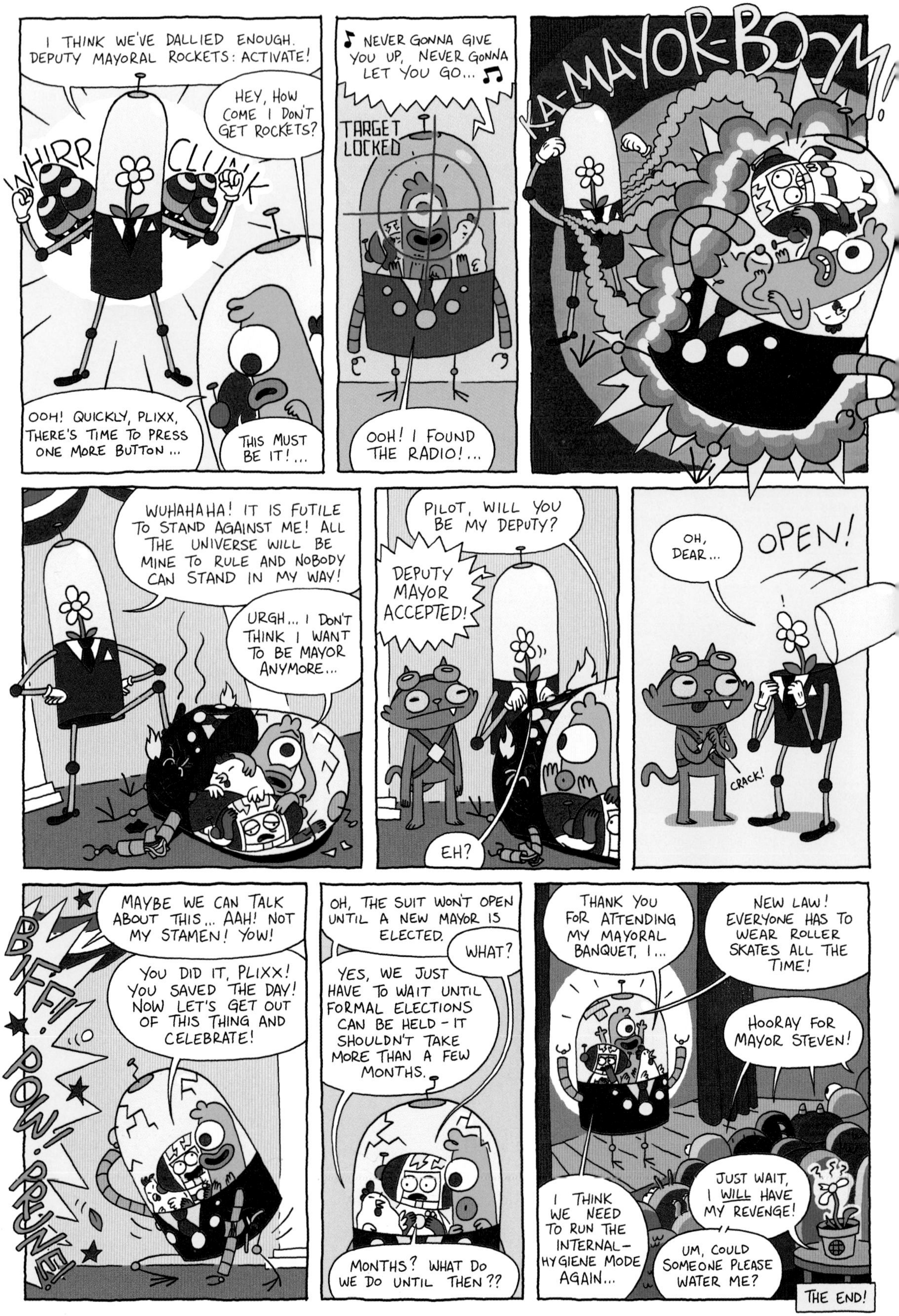
I THINK WE'VE DALLIED ENOUGH. DEPUTY MAYORAL ROCKETS: ACTIVATE!
HEY, HOW COME I DON'T GET ROCKETS?
WHIRR
CLUNK
OOH! QUICKLY, PLIXX, THERE'S TIME TO PRESS ONE MORE BUTTON...
THIS MUST BE IT!...
NEVER GONNA GIVE YOU UP, NEVER GONNA LET YOU GO...
TARGET LOCKED
OOH! I FOUND THE RADIO!...
KA-MAYOR-BOOM!!
WUHAHAHA! IT IS FUTILE TO STAND AGAINST ME! ALL THE UNIVERSE WILL BE MINE TO RULE AND NOBODY CAN STAND IN MY WAY!
URGH... I DON'T THINK I WANT TO BE MAYOR ANYMORE...
PILOT, WILL YOU BE MY DEPUTY?
DEPUTY MAYOR ACCEPTED!
EH?
OH, DEAR...
OPEN!
CRACK!
MAYBE WE CAN TALK ABOUT THIS... AAH! NOT MY STAMEN! YOW!
BIFF! POW! PRUNE!
YOU DID IT, PLIXX! YOU SAVED THE DAY! NOW LET'S GET OUT OF THIS THING AND CELEBRATE!
OH, THE SUIT WON'T OPEN UNTIL A NEW MAYOR IS ELECTED.
WHAT?
YES, WE JUST HAVE TO WAIT UNTIL FORMAL ELECTIONS CAN BE HELD - IT SHOULDN'T TAKE MORE THAN A FEW MONTHS.
MONTHS? WHAT DO WE DO UNTIL THEN??
THANK YOU FOR ATTENDING MY MAYORAL BANQUET, I...
NEW LAW! EVERYONE HAS TO WEAR ROLLER SKATES ALL THE TIME!
HOORAY FOR MAYOR STEVEN!
I THINK WE NEED TO RUN THE INTERNAL-HYGIENE MODE AGAIN...
JUST WAIT, I WILL HAVE MY REVENGE!
UM, COULD SOMEONE PLEASE WATER ME?
THE END!

Squid Bits!

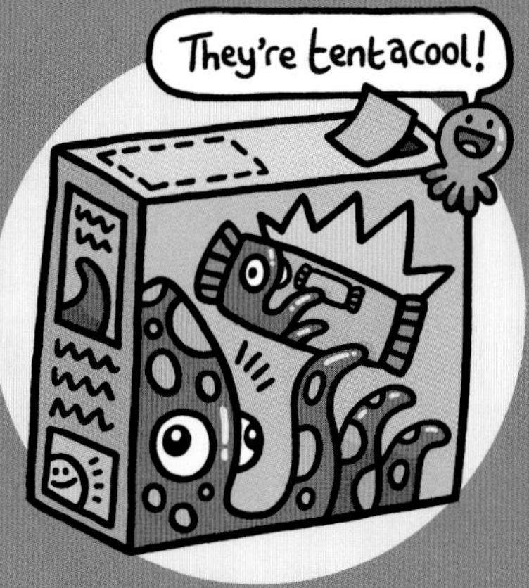
They're tentacool!

EVERY DELICIOUS BOX OF SQUID BITS INCLUDES ALL THIS AND MORE...

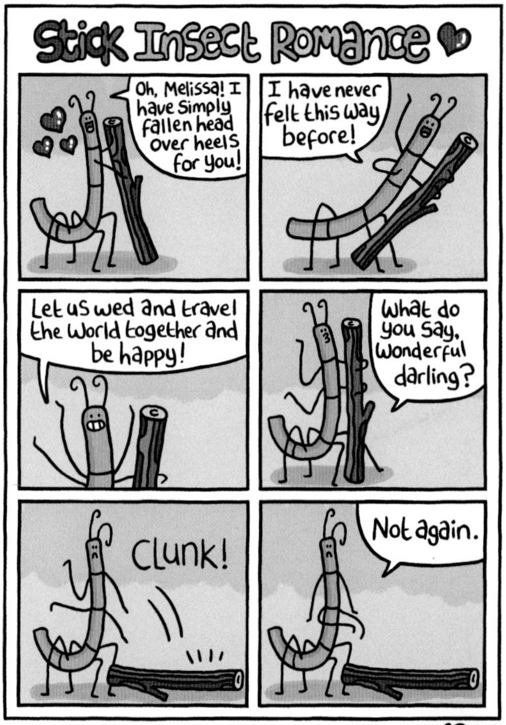
Stick Insect Romance
Oh, Melissa! I have simply fallen head over heels for you!
I have never felt this way before!
Let us wed and travel the world together and be happy!
What do you say, wonderful darling?
CLUNK!
Not again.

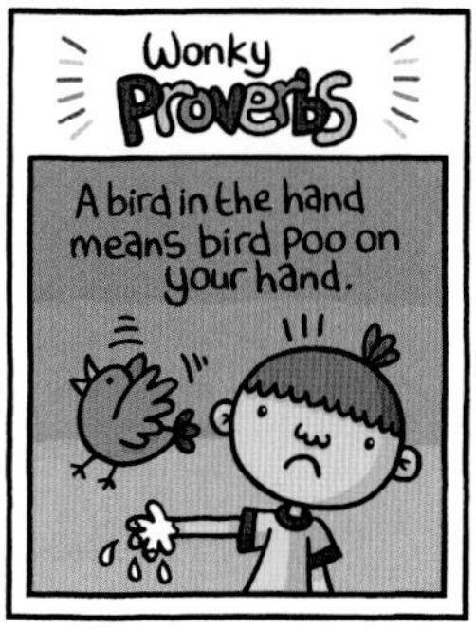
Wonky Proverbs
A bird in the hand means bird poo on your hand.

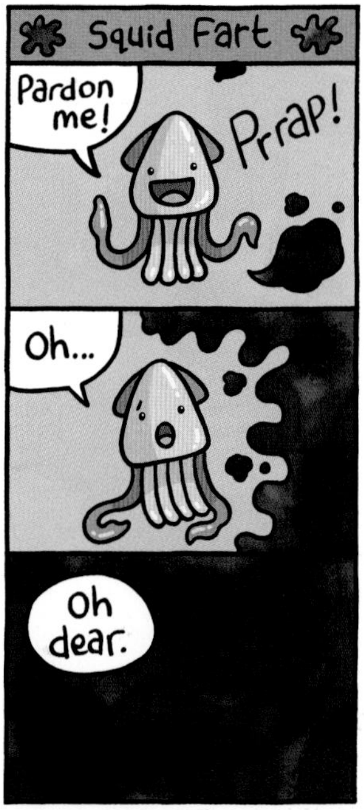
Squid Fart
Pardon me!
Prrap!
Oh...
Oh dear.

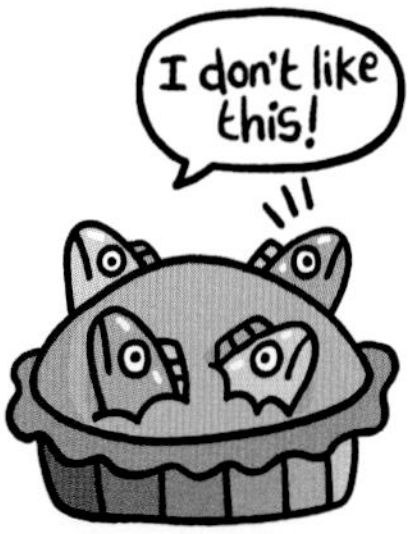
I don't like this!

These koalas need some jaunty hats!

Draw 'em!

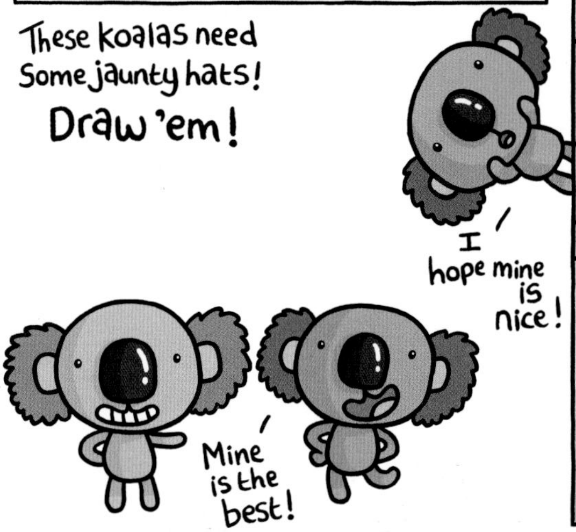
I hope mine is nice!
Mine is the best!

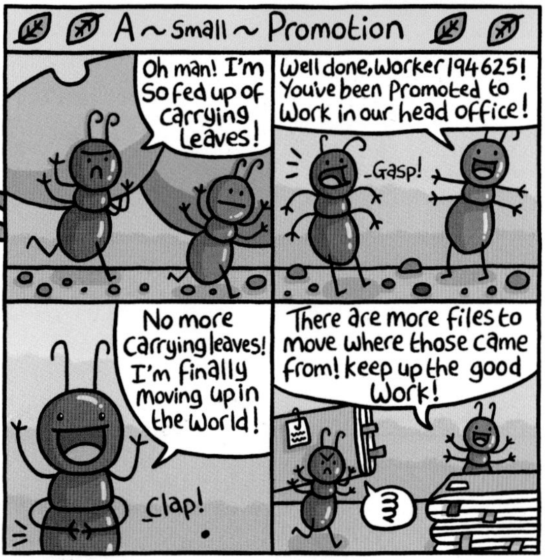
A ~ Small ~ Promotion
Oh man! I'm so fed up of carrying leaves!
Well done, Worker 194625! You've been promoted to work in our head office!
Gasp!
No more carrying leaves! I'm finally moving up in the world!
Clap!
There are more files to move where those came from! Keep up the good work!

by Jess Bradley

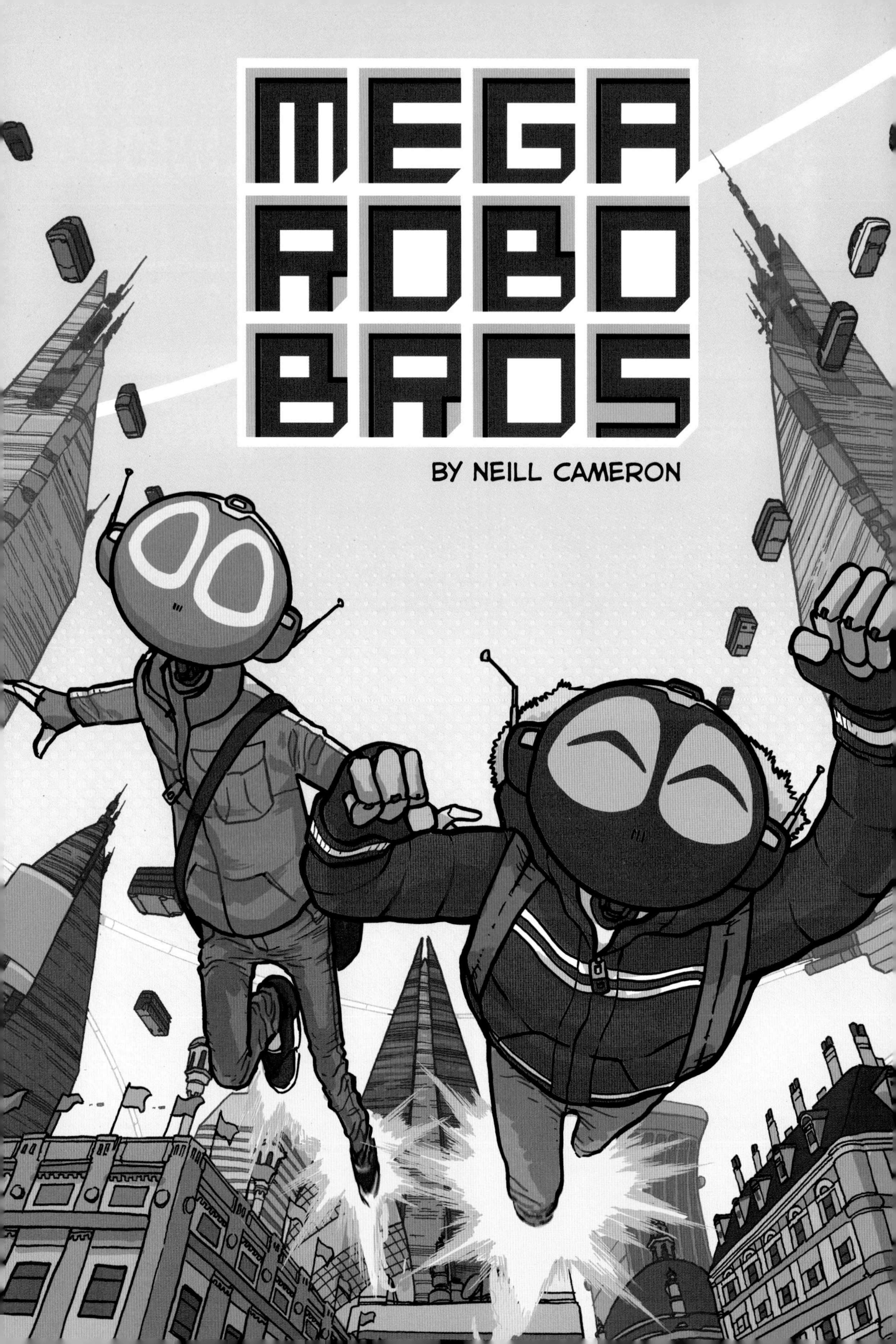
MEGA ROBO BROS
BY NEILL CAMERON

MEGA ROBO SCHOOL TRIP

CHILDREN OF OAK HILL SCHOOL, WELCOME TO THE *NATURAL HISTORY MUSEUM!*

WOW.

TODAY WE'RE GOING TO BE LEARNING ALL KINDS OF THINGS ABOUT *LIFE* AND ALL THE INCREDIBLY VARIED FORMS IT CAN TAKE!

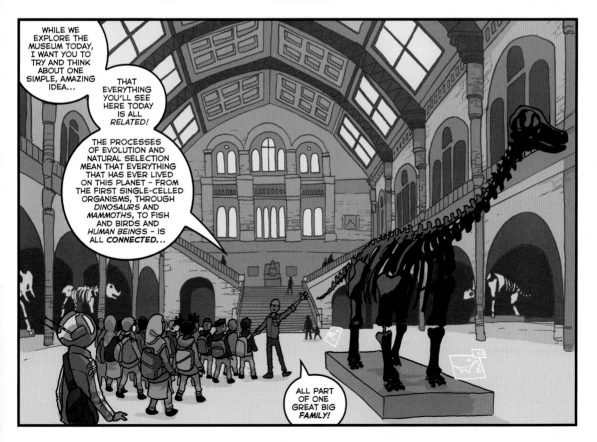

WHILE WE EXPLORE THE MUSEUM TODAY, I WANT YOU TO TRY AND THINK ABOUT ONE SIMPLE, AMAZING IDEA...

THAT EVERYTHING YOU'LL SEE HERE TODAY IS ALL *RELATED!*

THE PROCESSES OF EVOLUTION AND NATURAL SELECTION MEAN THAT EVERYTHING THAT HAS EVER LIVED ON THIS PLANET – FROM THE FIRST SINGLE-CELLED ORGANISMS, THROUGH *DINOSAURS* AND *MAMMOTHS*, TO FISH AND BIRDS AND *HUMAN BEINGS* – IS ALL *CONNECTED...*

ALL PART OF ONE GREAT BIG *FAMILY!*

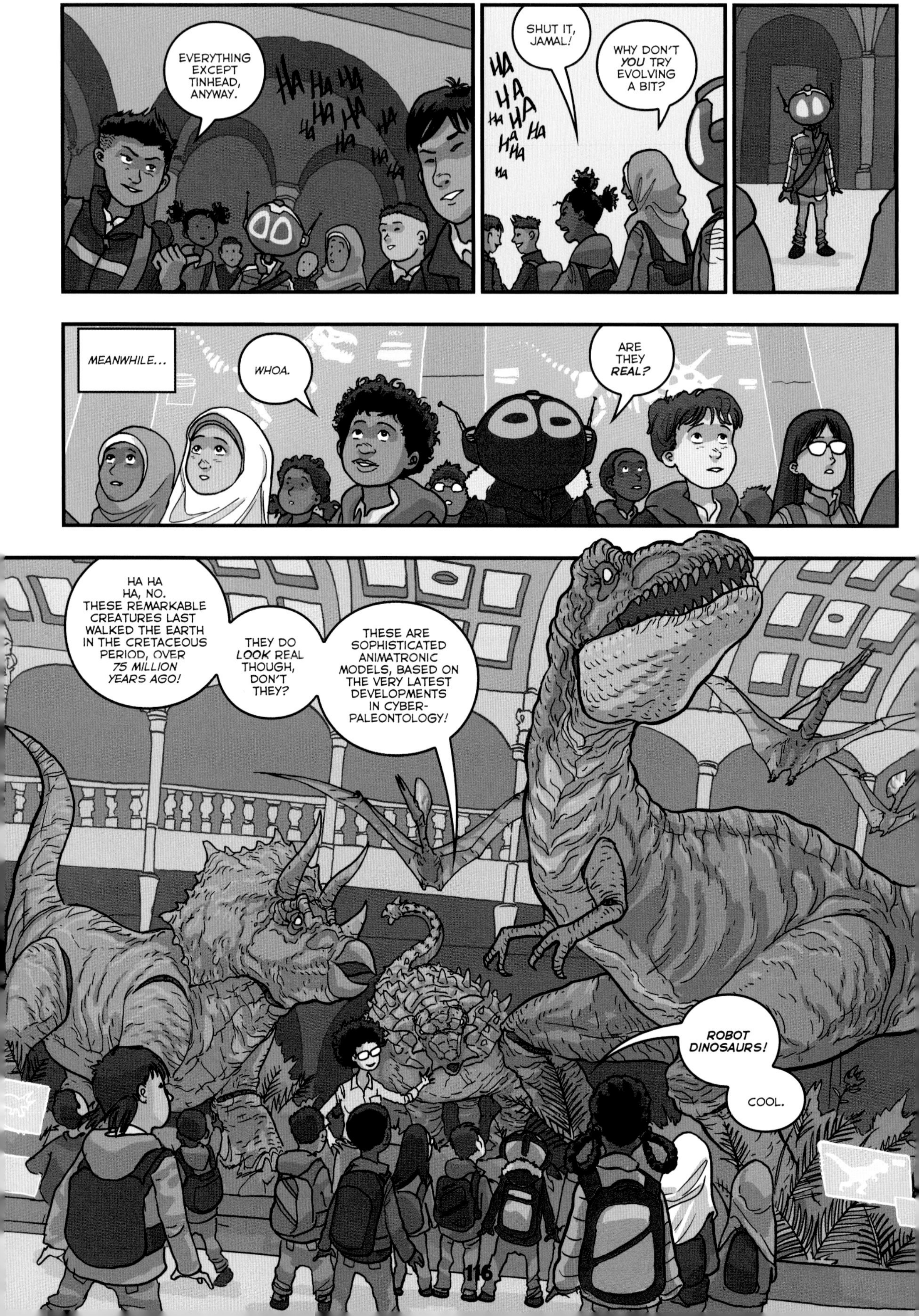
EVERYTHING EXCEPT TINHEAD, ANYWAY.
HA HA HA HA HA HA HA HA HA HA
SHUT IT, JAMAL!
WHY DON'T YOU TRY EVOLVING A BIT?
HA HA HA HA HA HA HA HA HA HA
MEANWHILE...
WHOA.
ARE THEY REAL?
HA HA HA, NO. THESE REMARKABLE CREATURES LAST WALKED THE EARTH IN THE CRETACEOUS PERIOD, OVER 75 MILLION YEARS AGO!
THEY DO LOOK REAL THOUGH, DON'T THEY?
THESE ARE SOPHISTICATED ANIMATRONIC MODELS, BASED ON THE VERY LATEST DEVELOPMENTS IN CYBER-PALEONTOLOGY!
ROBOT DINOSAURS!
COOL.

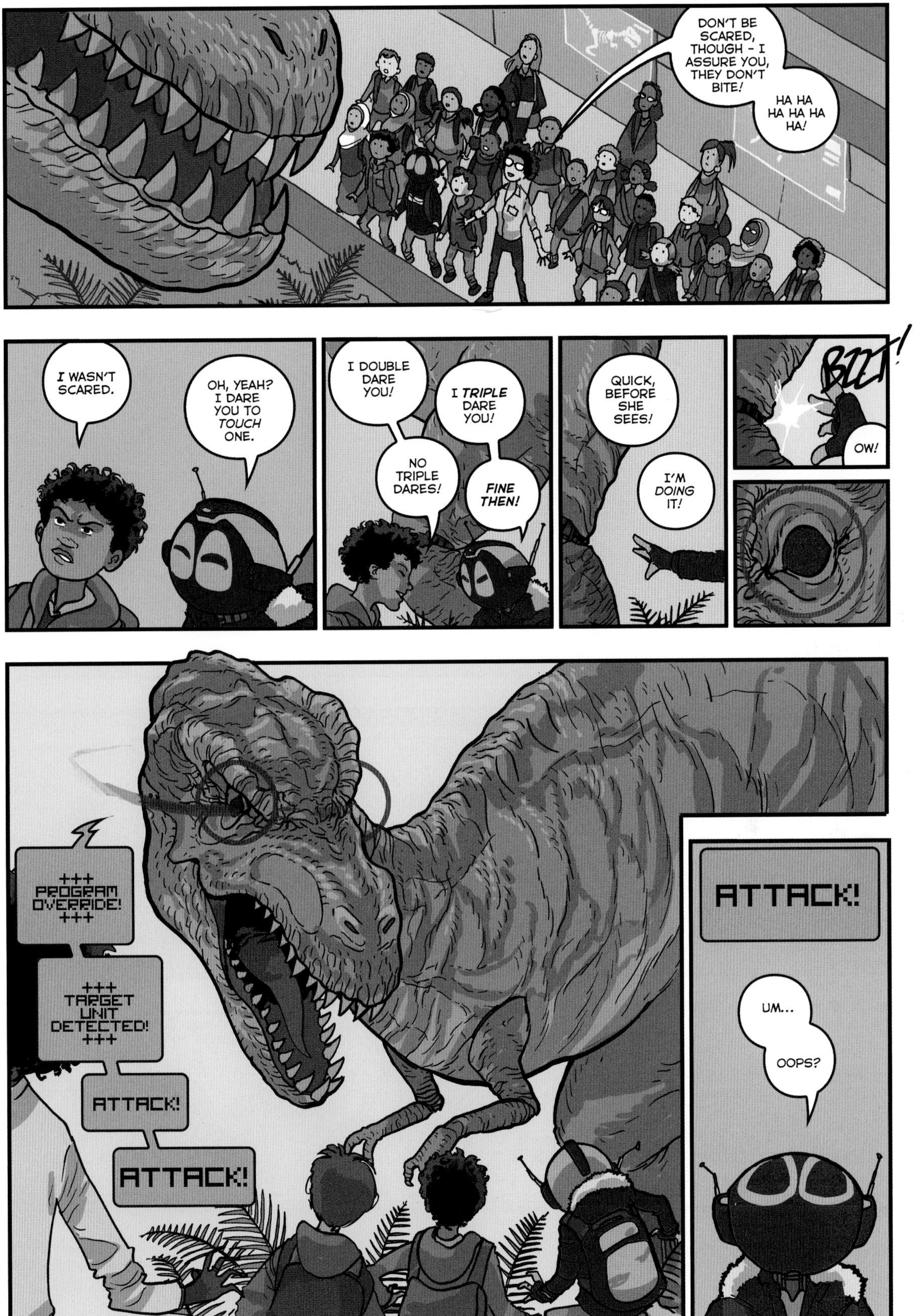

DON'T BE SCARED, THOUGH - I ASSURE YOU, THEY DON'T BITE!
HA HA HA HA HA HA!
I WASN'T SCARED.
OH, YEAH? I DARE YOU TO TOUCH ONE.
I DOUBLE DARE YOU!
NO TRIPLE DARES!
I TRIPLE DARE YOU!
FINE THEN!
QUICK, BEFORE SHE SEES!
I'M DOING IT!
BZZT!
OW!
+++ PROGRAM OVERRIDE! +++
+++ TARGET UNIT DETECTED! +++
ATTACK!
ATTACK!
ATTACK!
UM...
OOPS?

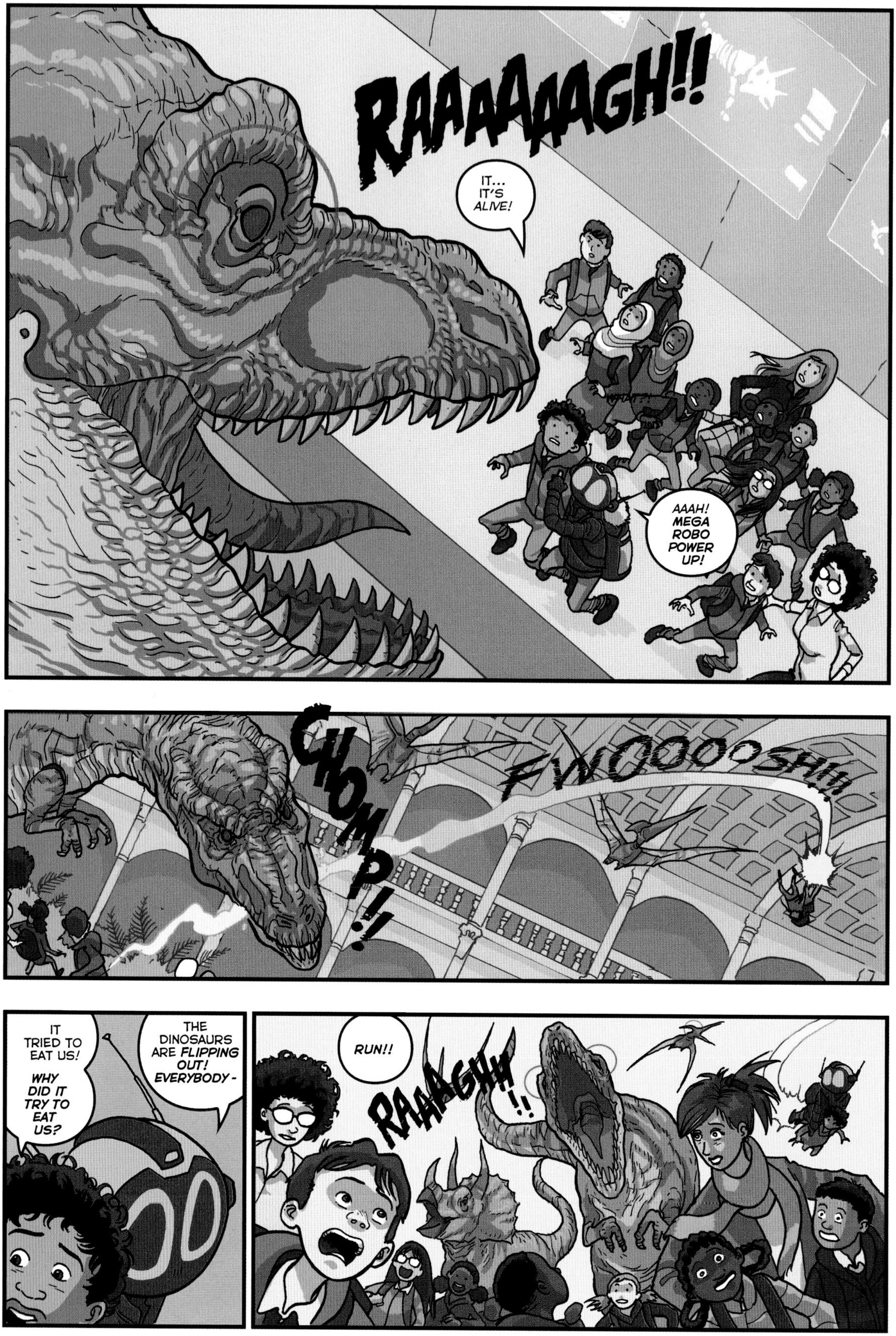
RAAAAAAGH!!
IT... IT'S ALIVE!
AAAH! MEGA ROBO POWER UP!
CHOMP!!
FWOOOOSH!!
IT TRIED TO EAT US!
WHY DID IT TRY TO EAT US?
THE DINOSAURS ARE FLIPPING OUT! EVERYBODY -
RUN!!
RAAAGHH!!

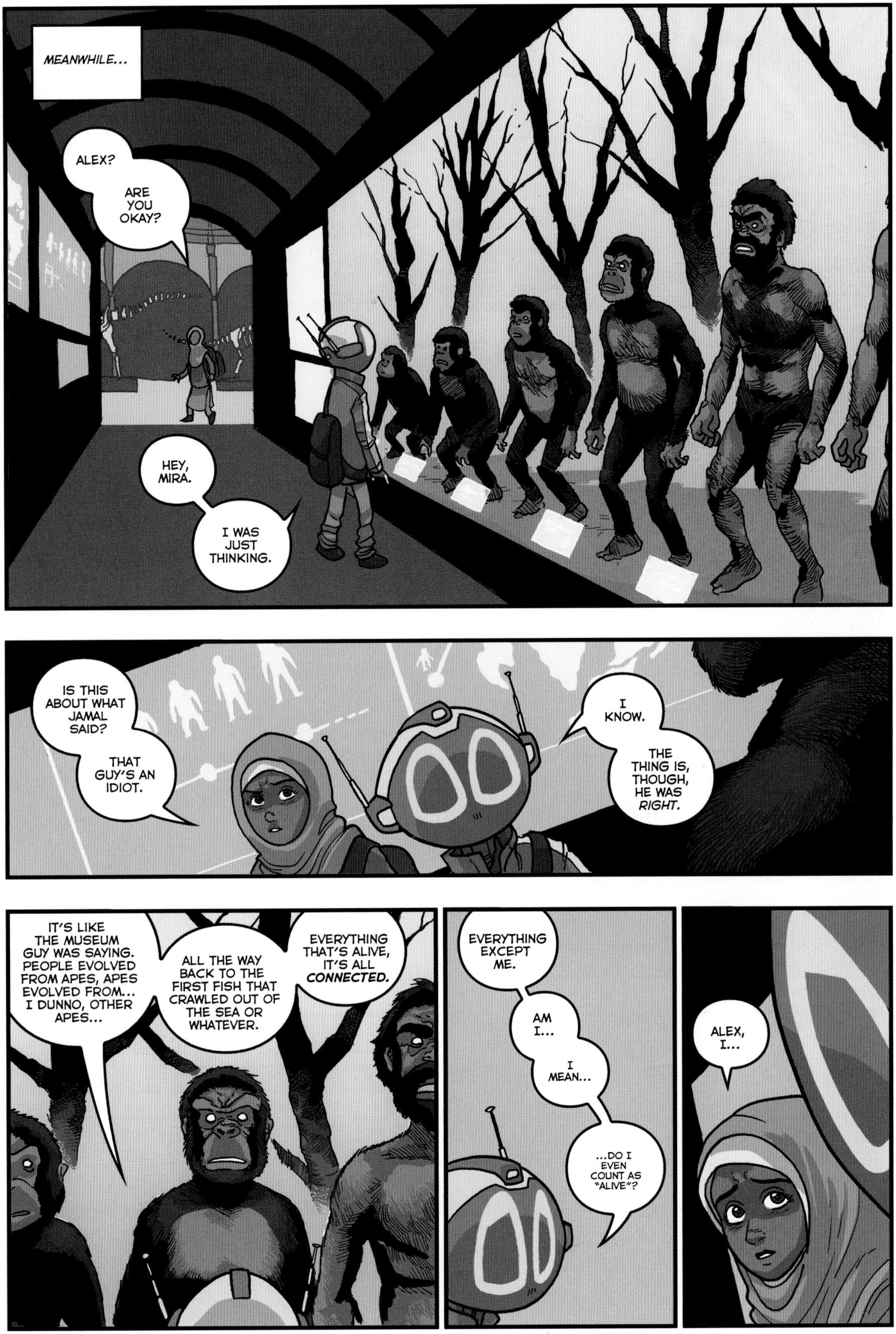
MEANWHILE...
ALEX?
ARE YOU OKAY?
HEY, MIRA.
I WAS JUST THINKING.
IS THIS ABOUT WHAT JAMAL SAID?
THAT GUY'S AN IDIOT.
I KNOW.
THE THING IS, THOUGH, HE WAS *RIGHT.*
IT'S LIKE THE MUSEUM GUY WAS SAYING. PEOPLE EVOLVED FROM APES, APES EVOLVED FROM... I DUNNO, OTHER APES...
ALL THE WAY BACK TO THE FIRST FISH THAT CRAWLED OUT OF THE SEA OR WHATEVER.
EVERYTHING THAT'S ALIVE, IT'S ALL **CONNECTED.**
EVERYTHING EXCEPT ME.
AM I...
I MEAN...
...DO I EVEN COUNT AS "ALIVE"?
ALEX, I...

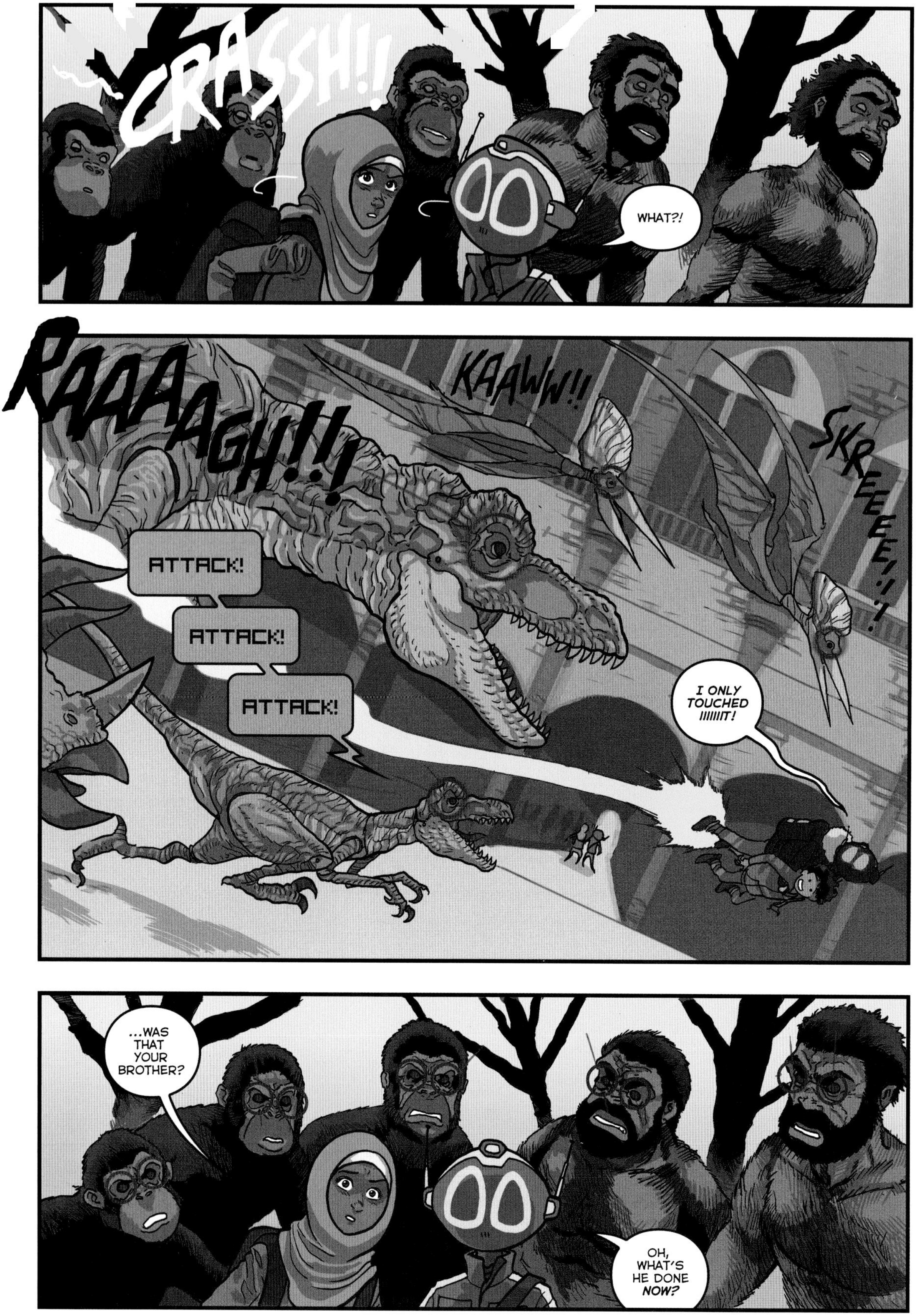
CRASSH!!
WHAT?!
RAAAAGH!!!
KAAWW!!
SKREEEE!!!
ATTACK!
ATTACK!
ATTACK!
I ONLY TOUCHED IIIIIIIT!
...WAS THAT YOUR BROTHER?
OH, WHAT'S HE DONE NOW?

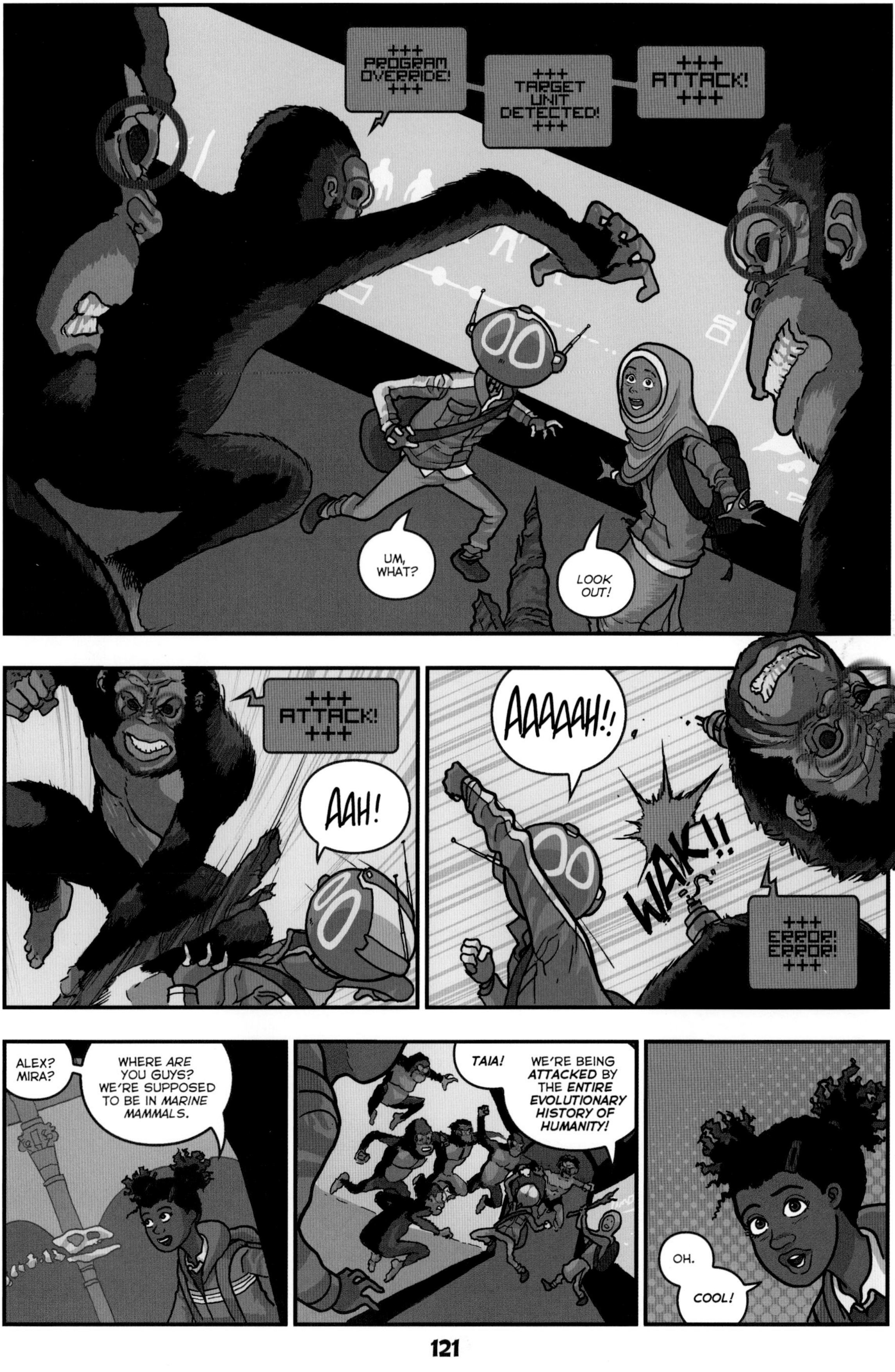
+++ PROGRAM OVERRIDE! +++
+++ TARGET UNIT DETECTED! +++
+++ ATTACK! +++
UM, WHAT?
LOOK OUT!
+++ ATTACK! +++
AAH!
AAAAAH!!
WAK!!
+++ ERROR! ERROR! +++
ALEX? MIRA?
WHERE ARE YOU GUYS? WE'RE SUPPOSED TO BE IN MARINE MAMMALS.
TAIA!
WE'RE BEING ATTACKED BY THE ENTIRE EVOLUTIONARY HISTORY OF HUMANITY!
OH.
COOL!

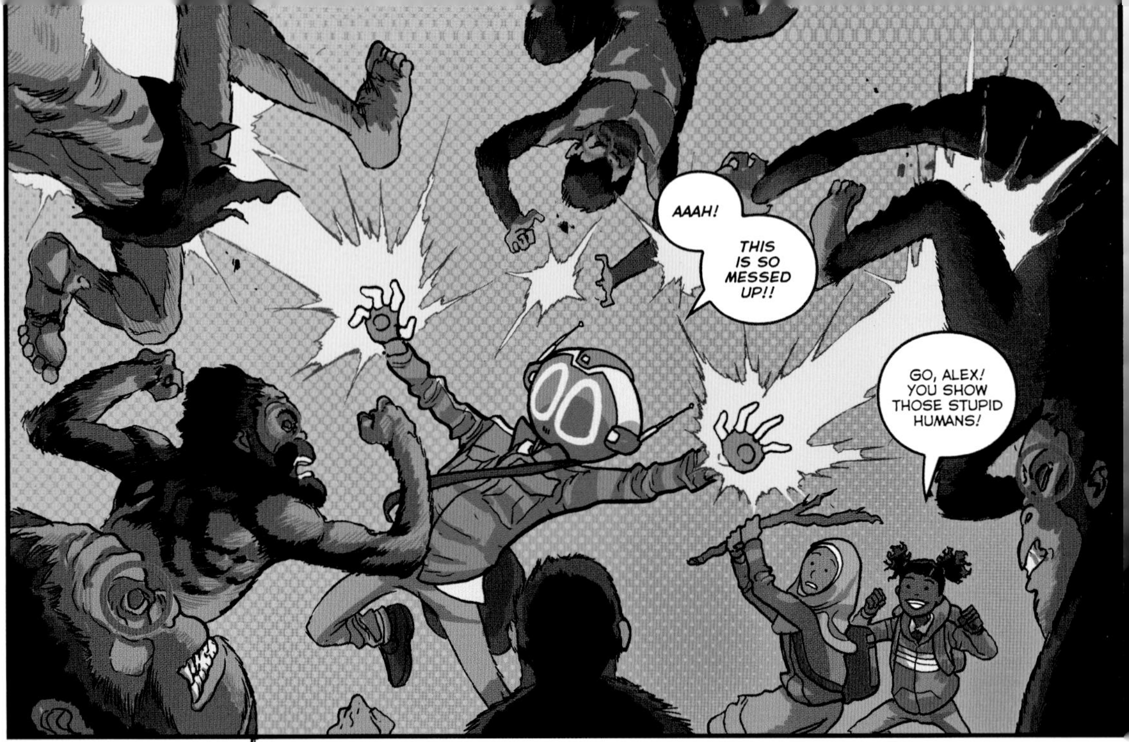
AAAH!
THIS IS SO MESSED UP!!
GO, ALEX! YOU SHOW THOSE STUPID HUMANS!

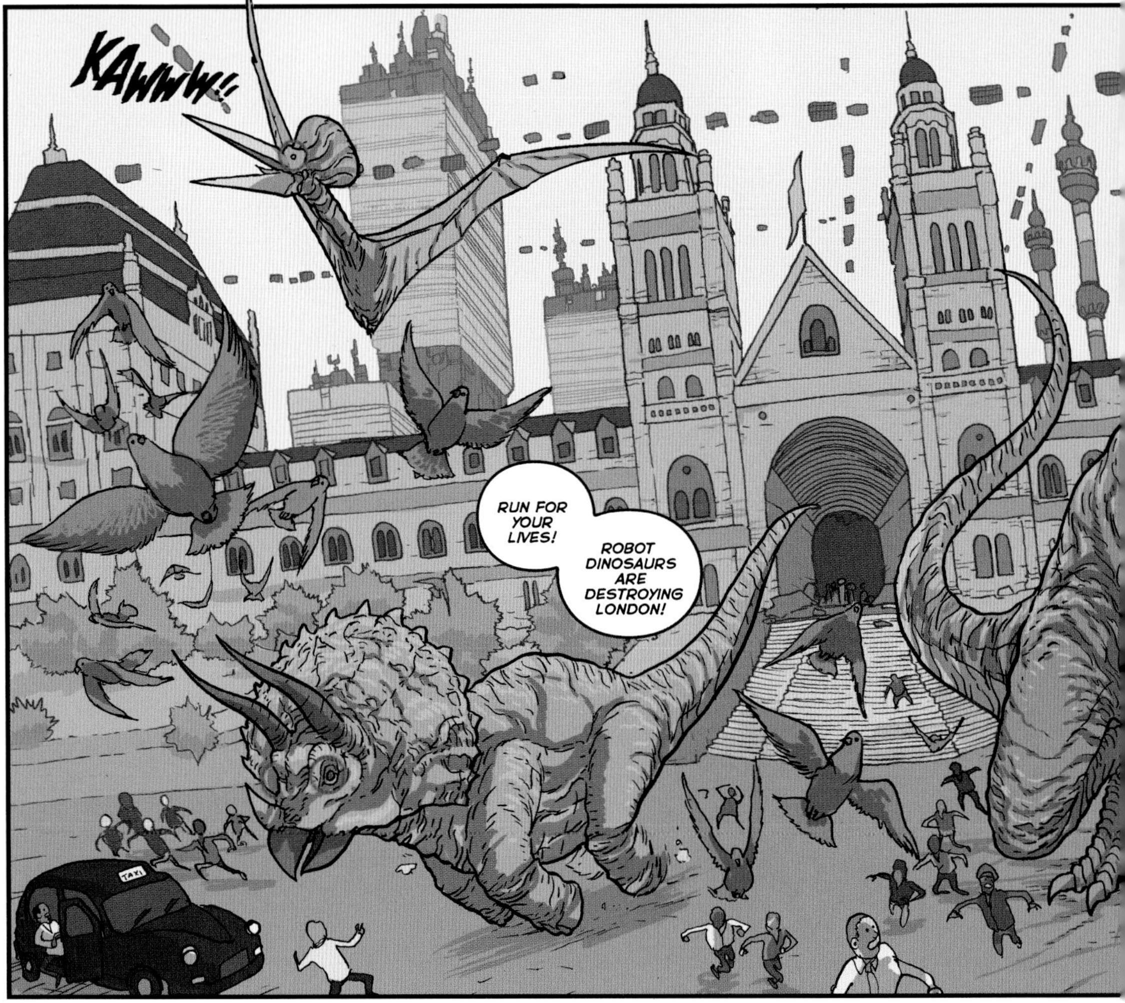
KAWWW!!
RUN FOR YOUR LIVES!
ROBOT DINOSAURS ARE DESTROYING LONDON!
TAXI

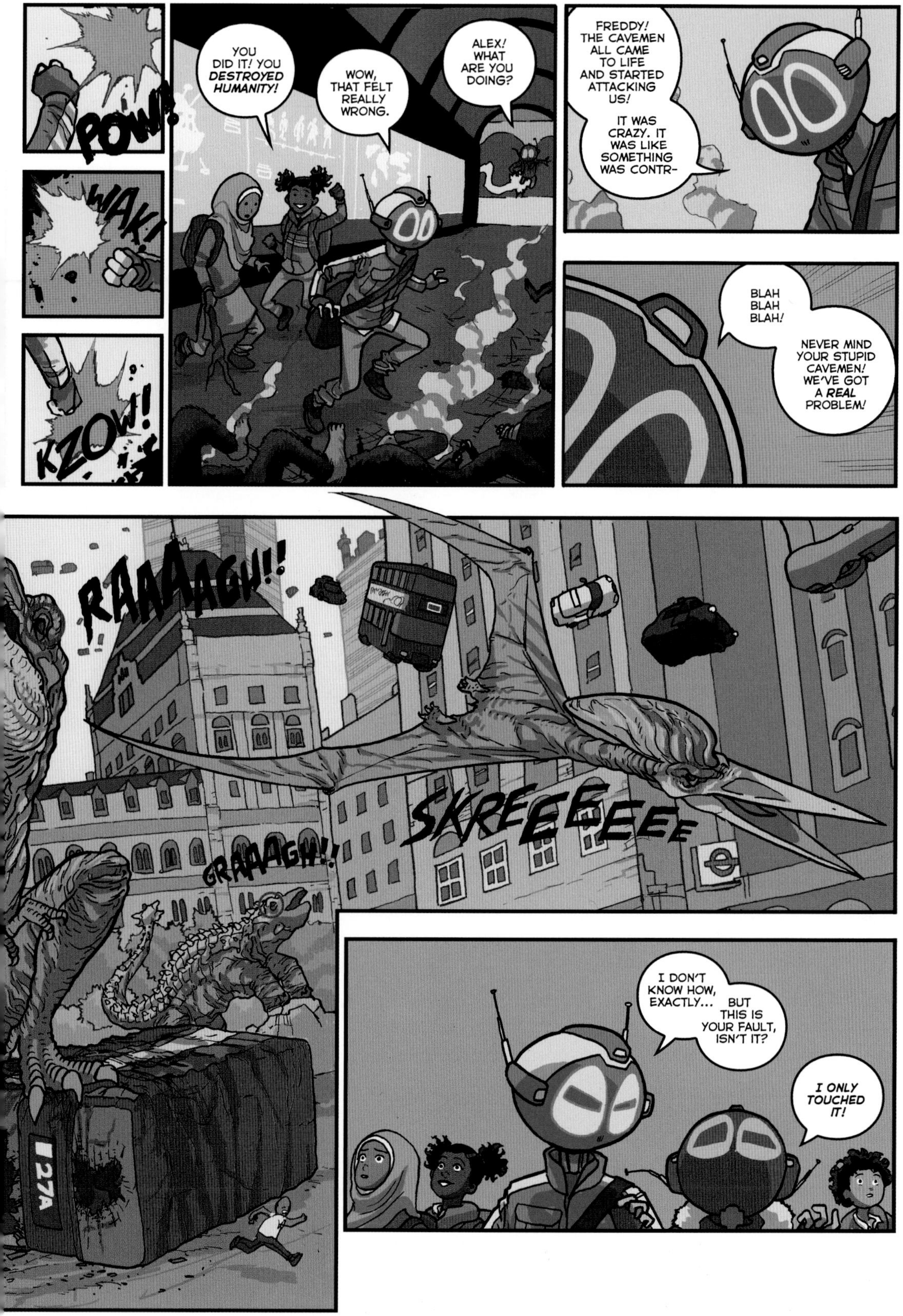

POW!
WAK!
KZOW!
YOU DID IT! YOU DESTROYED HUMANITY!
WOW, THAT FELT REALLY WRONG.
ALEX! WHAT ARE YOU DOING?
FREDDY! THE CAVEMEN ALL CAME TO LIFE AND STARTED ATTACKING US!
IT WAS CRAZY. IT WAS LIKE SOMETHING WAS CONTR-
BLAH BLAH BLAH!
NEVER MIND YOUR STUPID CAVEMEN! WE'VE GOT A REAL PROBLEM!
RAAAAGH!!
SKREEEEEEE
GRAAAGH!!
27A
I DON'T KNOW HOW, EXACTLY... BUT THIS IS YOUR FAULT, ISN'T IT?
I ONLY TOUCHED IT!

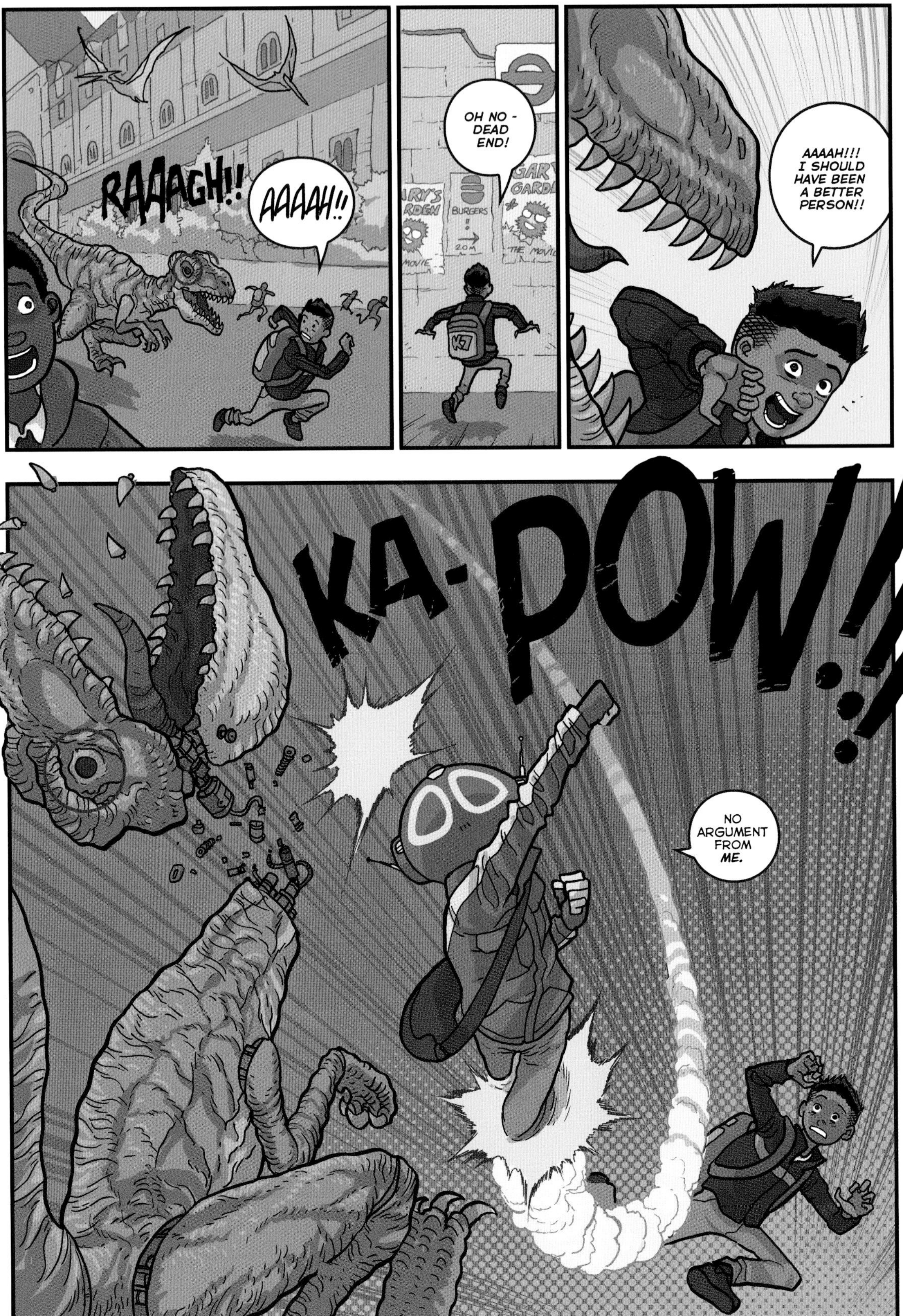
RAAAGH!!
AAAAH!!
OH NO - DEAD END!
GARY'S GARDEN
BURGERS 20M
THE MOVIE
AAAAH!!! I SHOULD HAVE BEEN A BETTER PERSON!!
KA-POW!!!
NO ARGUMENT FROM ME.

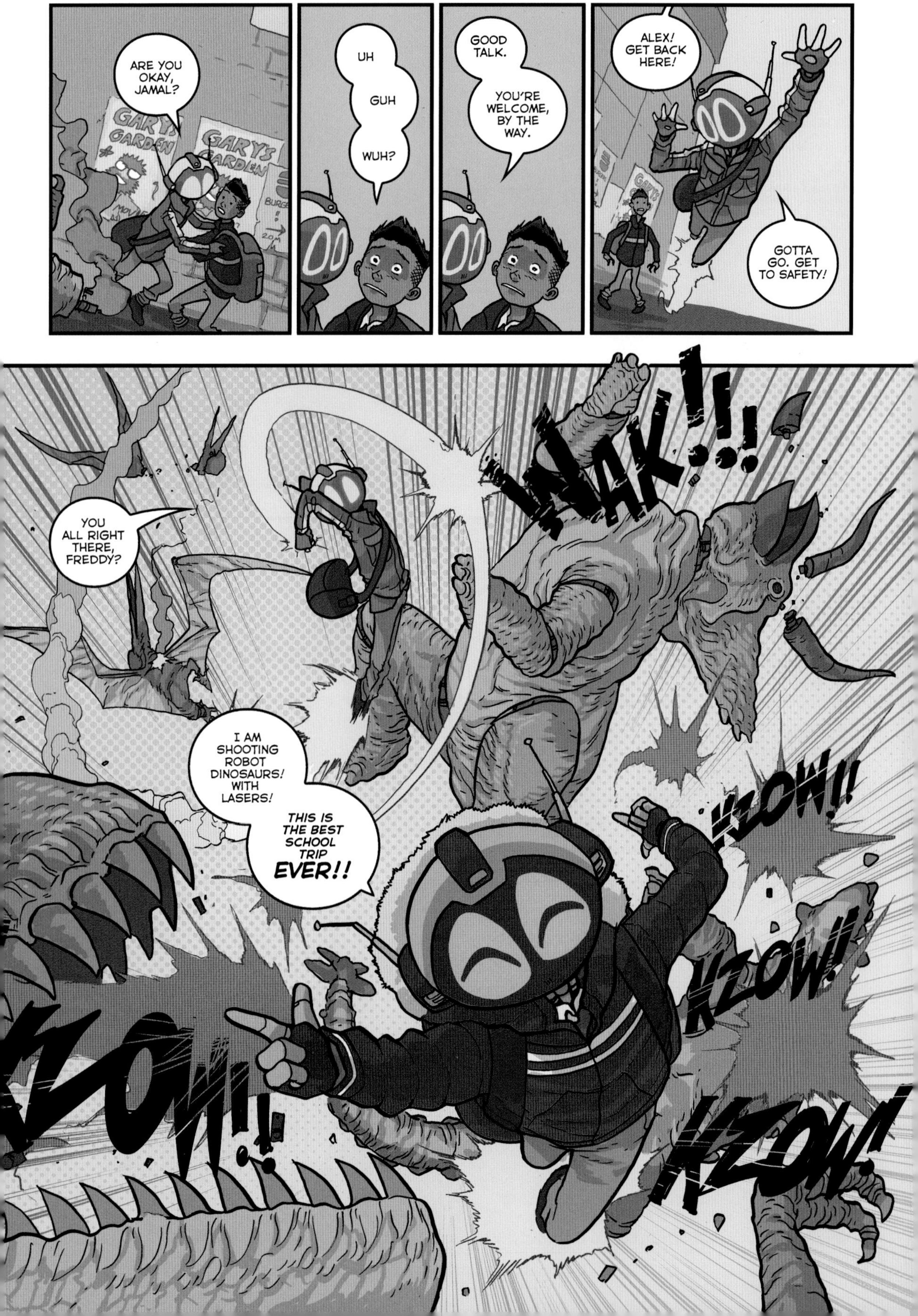
ARE YOU OKAY, JAMAL?
GARY'S GARDEN
GARY'S GARDEN
UH
GUH
WUH?
GOOD TALK.
YOU'RE WELCOME, BY THE WAY.
ALEX! GET BACK HERE!
GOTTA GO. GET TO SAFETY!
WAK!!!
YOU ALL RIGHT THERE, FREDDY?
I AM SHOOTING ROBOT DINOSAURS! WITH LASERS!
THIS IS THE BEST SCHOOL TRIP EVER!!
KZOW!!
KZOW!!
KZOW!!
KZOW!

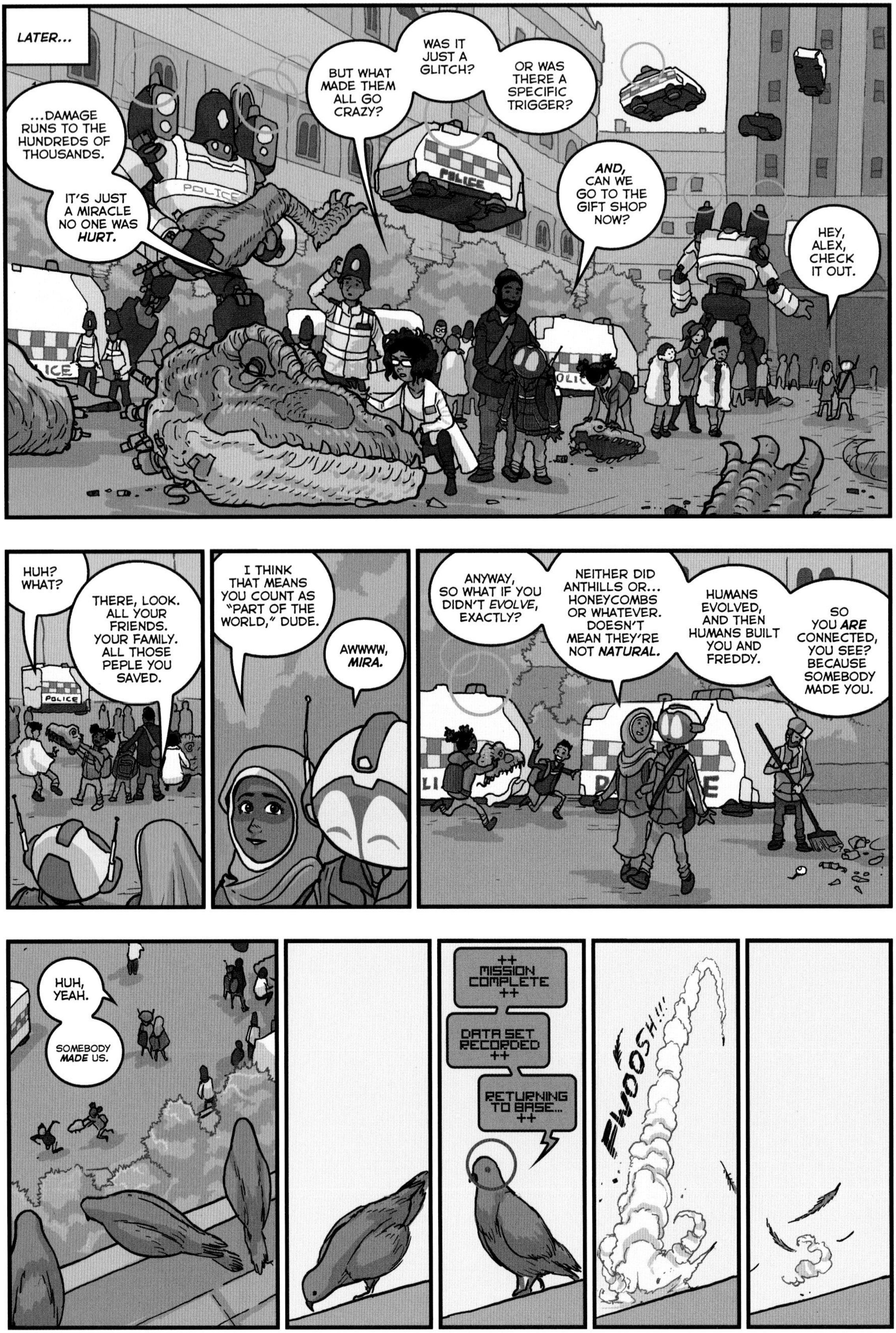
LATER...
...DAMAGE RUNS TO THE HUNDREDS OF THOUSANDS.
IT'S JUST A MIRACLE NO ONE WAS *HURT.*
BUT WHAT MADE THEM ALL GO CRAZY?
WAS IT JUST A GLITCH?
OR WAS THERE A SPECIFIC TRIGGER?
AND, CAN WE GO TO THE GIFT SHOP NOW?
HEY, ALEX, CHECK IT OUT.
POLICE
HUH? WHAT?
THERE, LOOK. ALL YOUR FRIENDS. YOUR FAMILY. ALL THOSE PEPLE YOU SAVED.
I THINK THAT MEANS YOU COUNT AS "PART OF THE WORLD," DUDE.
AWWWW, *MIRA.*
ANYWAY, SO WHAT IF YOU DIDN'T *EVOLVE,* EXACTLY?
NEITHER DID ANTHILLS OR... HONEYCOMBS OR WHATEVER. DOESN'T MEAN THEY'RE NOT *NATURAL.*
HUMANS EVOLVED, AND THEN HUMANS BUILT YOU AND FREDDY.
SO YOU *ARE* CONNECTED, YOU SEE? BECAUSE SOMEBODY MADE YOU.
HUH, YEAH.
SOMEBODY *MADE* US.
++ MISSION COMPLETE ++
DATA SET RECORDED ++
RETURNING TO BASE... ++
FWOOSH!!!

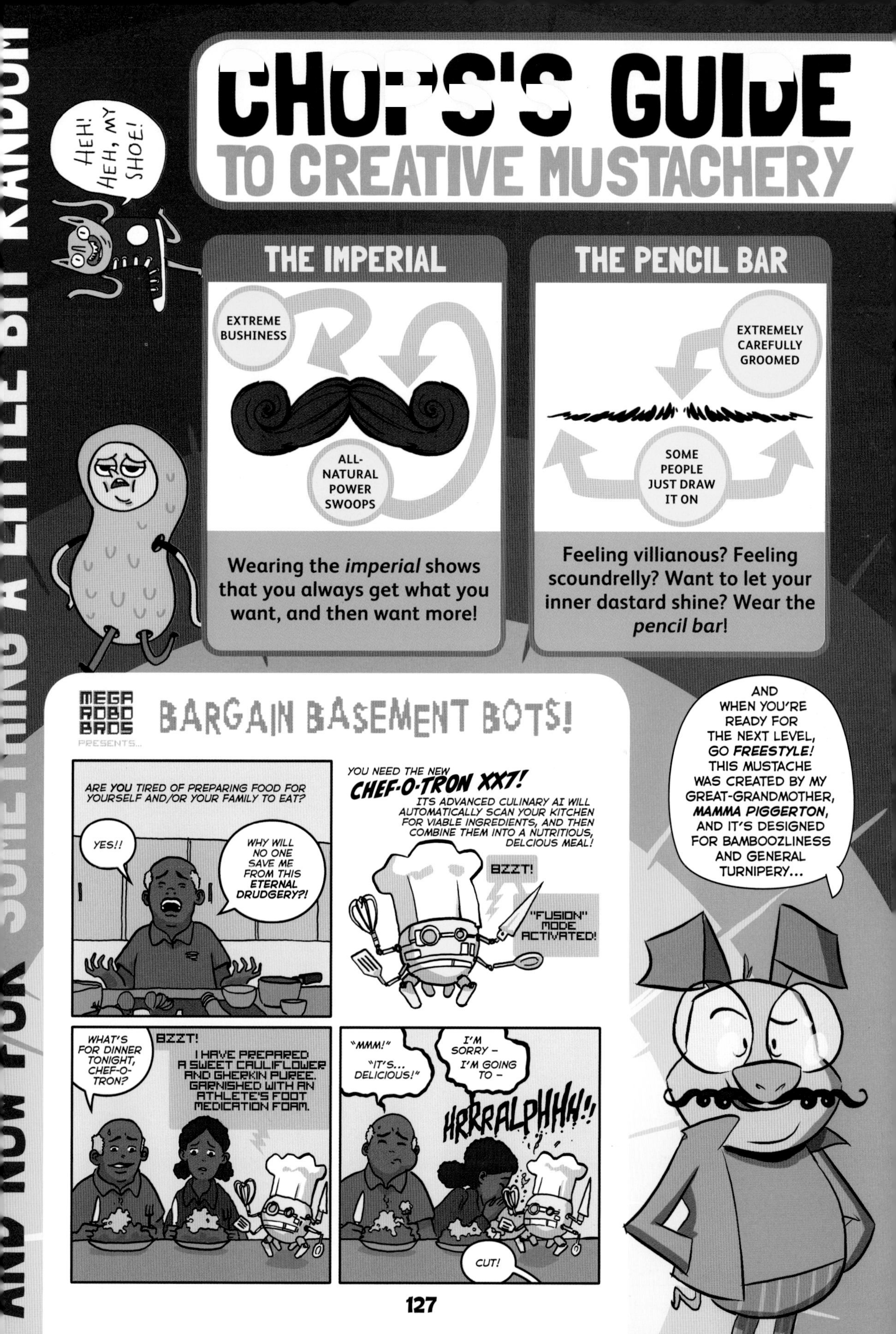

AND NOW FOR SOMETHING A LITTLE BIT RANDOM
CHOPS'S GUIDE
TO CREATIVE MUSTACHERY
HEH! HEH, MY SHOE!
THE IMPERIAL
EXTREME BUSHINESS
ALL-NATURAL POWER SWOOPS
Wearing the *imperial* shows that you always get what you want, and then want more!
THE PENCIL BAR
EXTREMELY CAREFULLY GROOMED
SOME PEOPLE JUST DRAW IT ON
Feeling villianous? Feeling scoundrelly? Want to let your inner dastard shine? Wear the *pencil bar*!
AND WHEN YOU'RE READY FOR THE NEXT LEVEL, GO **FREESTYLE!** THIS MUSTACHE WAS CREATED BY MY GREAT-GRANDMOTHER, **MAMMA PIGGERTON,** AND IT'S DESIGNED FOR BAMBOOZLINESS AND GENERAL TURNIPERY...
MEGA ROBO BROS PRESENTS...
BARGAIN BASEMENT BOTS!
ARE YOU TIRED OF PREPARING FOOD FOR YOURSELF AND/OR YOUR FAMILY TO EAT?
YES!!
WHY WILL NO ONE SAVE ME FROM THIS **ETERNAL DRUDGERY?!**
YOU NEED THE NEW
CHEF-O-TRON XX7!
ITS ADVANCED CULINARY AI WILL AUTOMATICALLY SCAN YOUR KITCHEN FOR VIABLE INGREDIENTS, AND THEN COMBINE THEM INTO A NUTRITIOUS, DELCIOUS MEAL!
BZZT!
"FUSION" MODE ACTIVATED!
WHAT'S FOR DINNER TONIGHT, CHEF-O-TRON?
BZZT!
I HAVE PREPARED A SWEET CAULIFLOWER AND GHERKIN PUREE. GARNISHED WITH AN ATHLETE'S FOOT MEDICATION FOAM.
"MMM!"
"IT'S... DELICIOUS!"
I'M SORRY – I'M GOING TO –
HRRRALPHHH!!
CUT!

The Pie Thief

Chapter 3

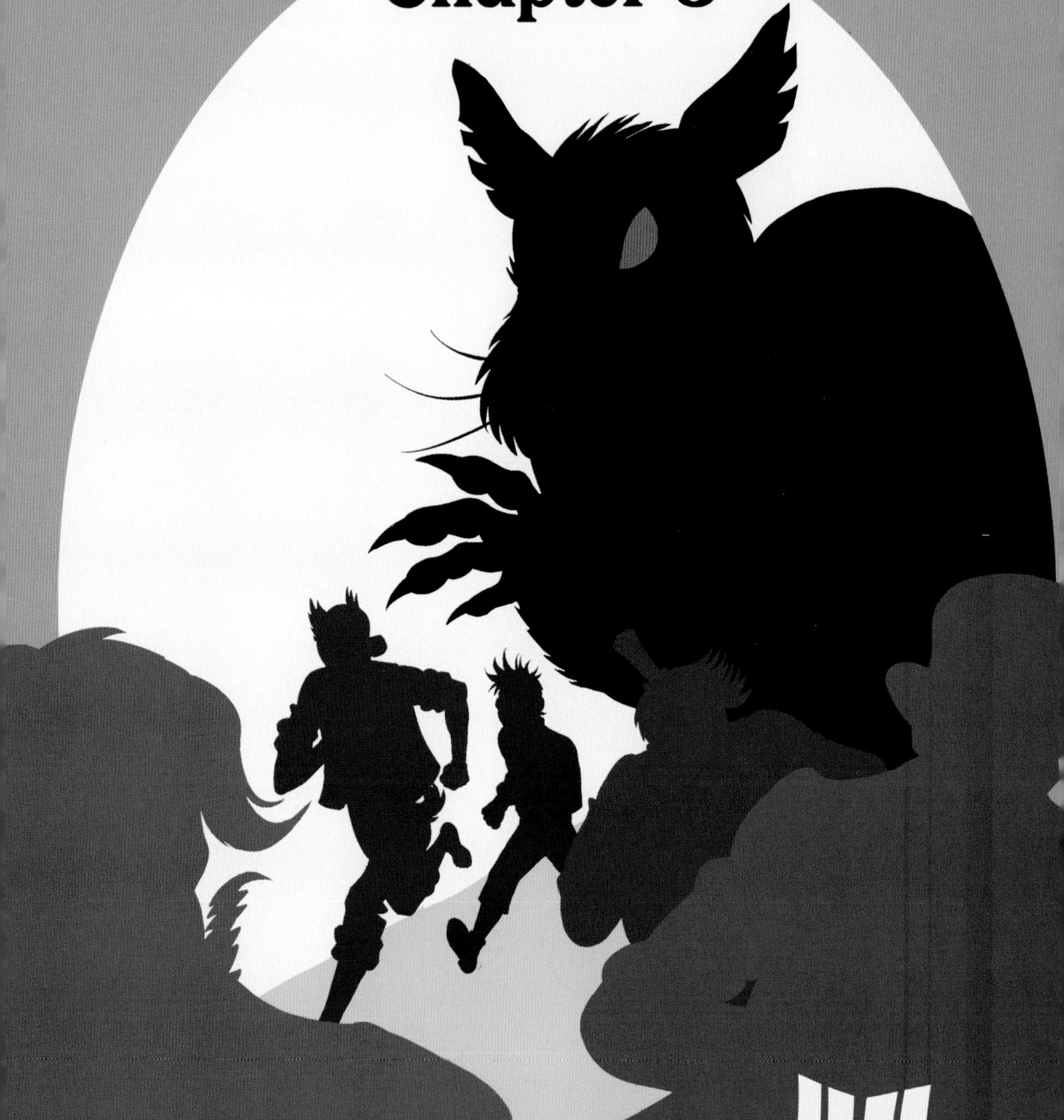

By Faz Choudhury

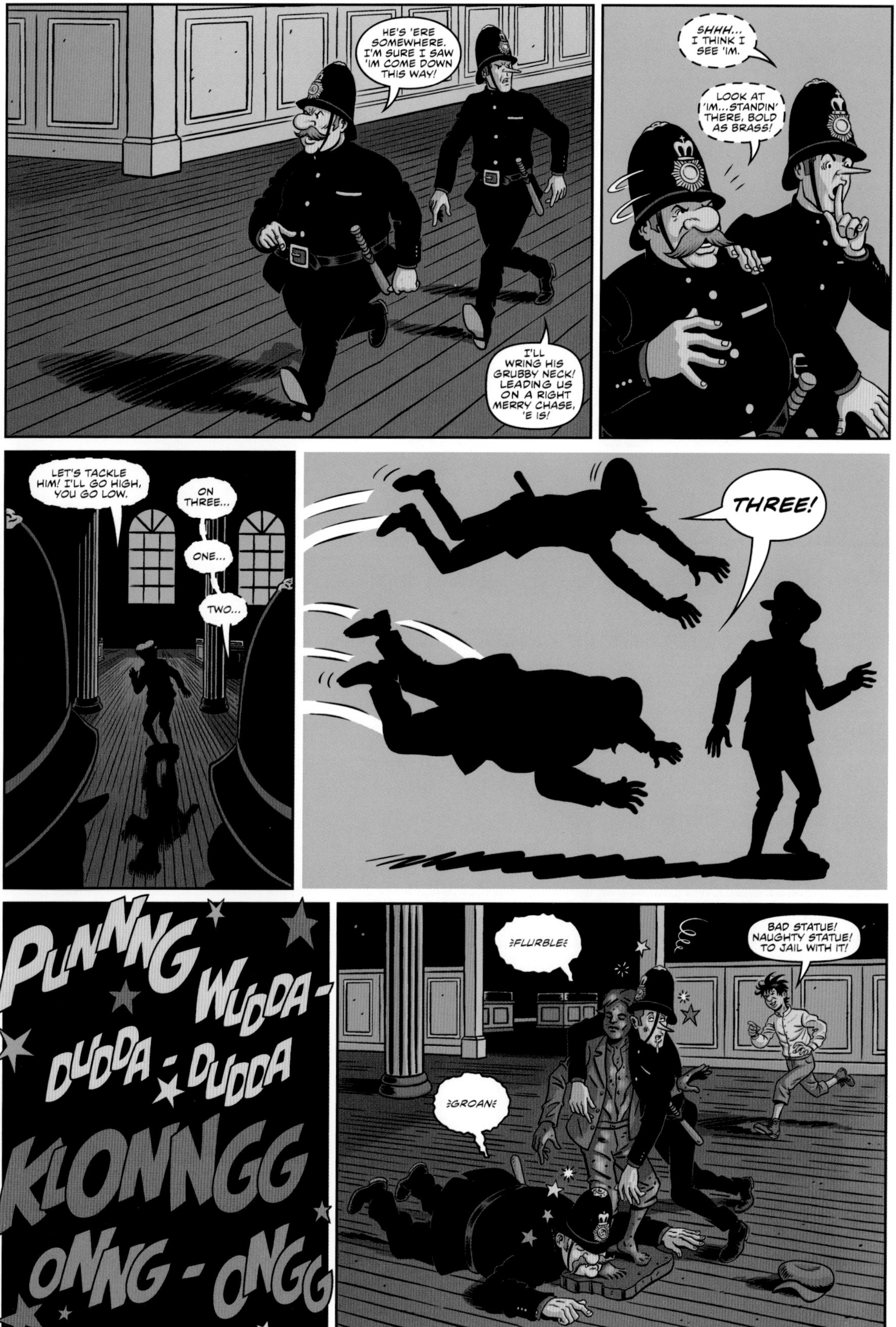
HE'S 'ERE SOMEWHERE. I'M SURE I SAW 'IM COME DOWN THIS WAY!
I'LL WRING HIS GRUBBY NECK! LEADING US ON A RIGHT MERRY CHASE, 'E IS!
SHHH... I THINK I SEE 'IM.
LOOK AT 'IM...STANDIN' THERE, BOLD AS BRASS!
LET'S TACKLE HIM! I'LL GO HIGH, YOU GO LOW.
ON THREE...
ONE...
TWO...
THREE!
PLINNNG
WUDDA-DUDDA-DUDDA
KLONNGG
ONNG-ONGG
FLURBLE
GROAN
BAD STATUE! NAUGHTY STATUE! TO JAIL WITH IT!

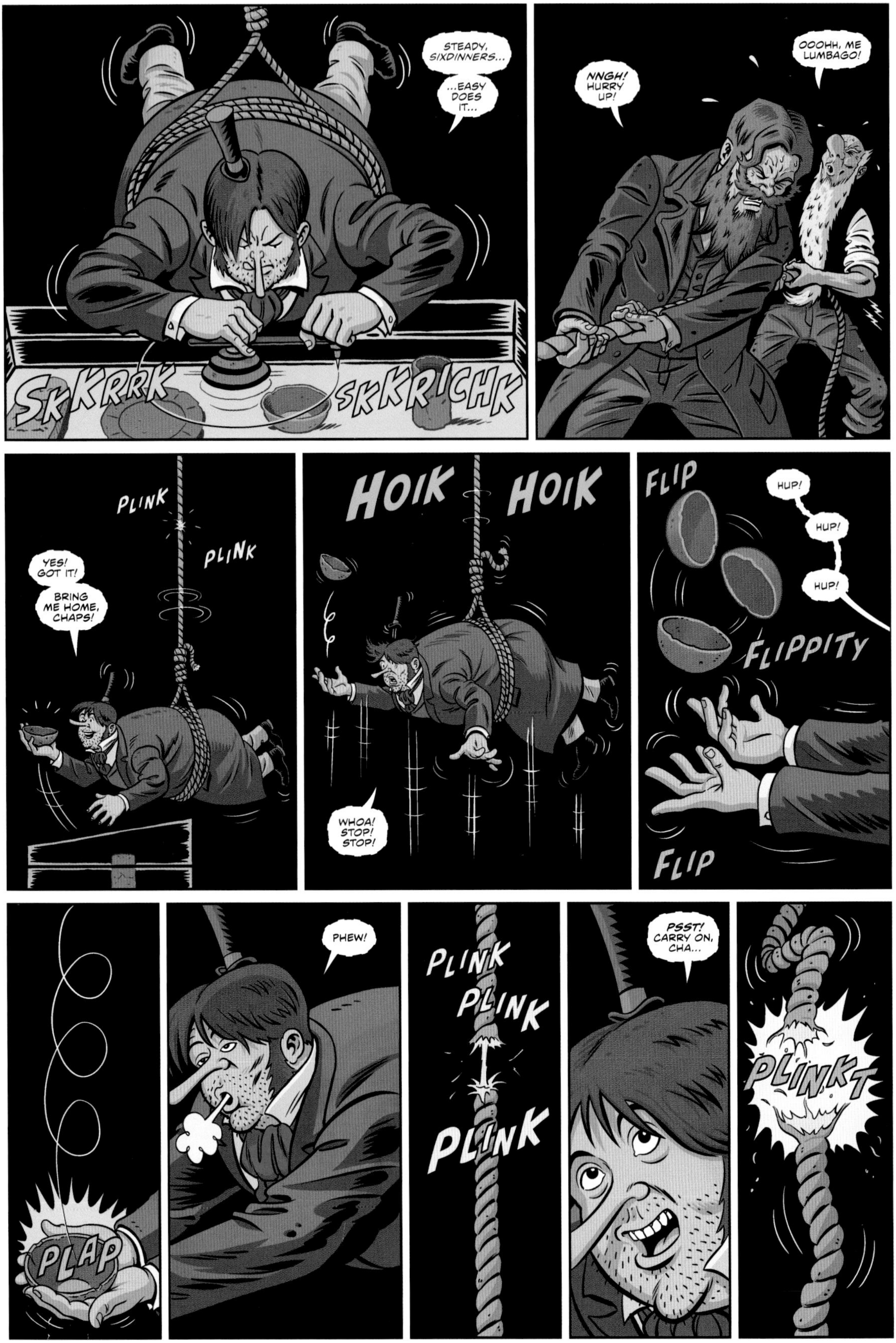
STEADY, SIXDINNERS...
...EASY DOES IT...
SKRRRK
SKKRICHK
NNGH! HURRY UP!
OOOHH, ME LUMBAGO!
PLINK
PLINK
YES! GOT IT!
BRING ME HOME, CHAPS!
HOIK HOIK
WHOA! STOP! STOP!
FLIP
HUP!
HUP!
HUP!
FLIPPITY
FLIP
PLAP
PHEW!
PLINK
PLINK
PLINK
PSST! CARRY ON, CHA...
PLINKT

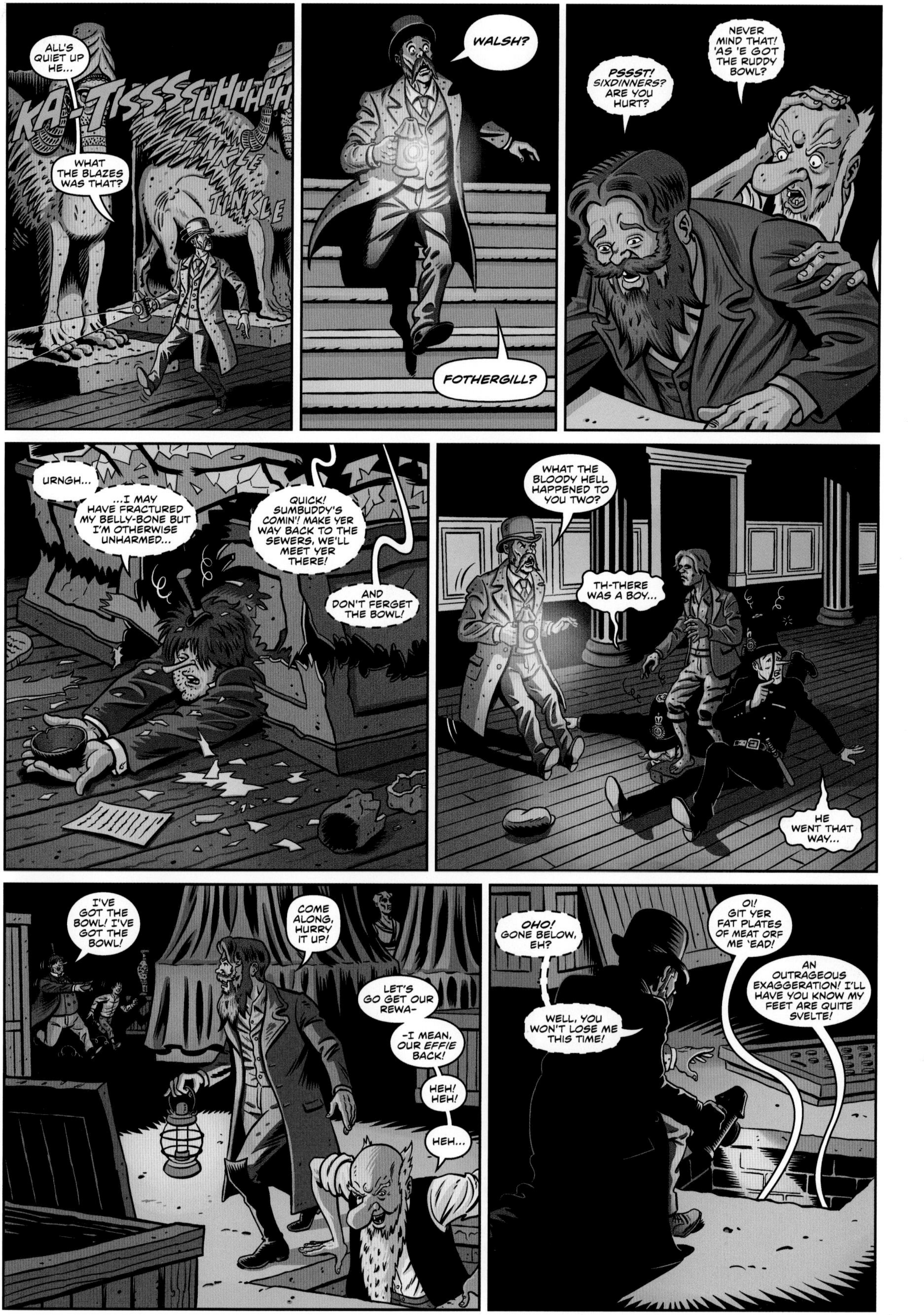
ALL'S QUIET UP HE...
KA-TISSSSHHHHH
TINKLE TINKLE
WHAT THE BLAZES WAS THAT?
WALSH?
FOTHERGILL?
PSSST! SIXDINNERS? ARE YOU HURT?
NEVER MIND THAT! 'AS 'E GOT THE RUDDY BOWL?
URNGH...
...I MAY HAVE FRACTURED MY BELLY-BONE BUT I'M OTHERWISE UNHARMED...
QUICK! SUMBUDDY'S COMIN'! MAKE YER WAY BACK TO THE SEWERS, WE'LL MEET YER THERE!
AND DON'T FERGET THE BOWL!
WHAT THE BLOODY HELL HAPPENED TO YOU TWO?
TH-THERE WAS A BOY...
HE WENT THAT WAY...
I'VE GOT THE BOWL! I'VE GOT THE BOWL!
COME ALONG, HURRY IT UP!
LET'S GO GET OUR REWA-
-I MEAN, OUR EFFIE BACK!
HEH! HEH!
HEH...
OHO! GONE BELOW, EH?
WELL, YOU WON'T LOSE ME THIS TIME!
OI! GIT YER FAT PLATES OF MEAT ORF ME 'EAD!
AN OUTRAGEOUS EXAGGERATION! I'LL HAVE YOU KNOW MY FEET ARE QUITE SVELTE!

WE DID IT! *EFFIE'LL* BE HOME SOON, LORD M!

I 'OPE SO, *ZEKE*, LAD! THAT *UNWRIGHT* BETTER BE TAKIN' GOOD CARE OF HER!

SQWUUEEEEEEECHH

WHAT W-W-WAS THAT?

TH-THAT, MY DEAR CH-CHILD, IS THE WAIL OF THE *RAT KING!*

PFFFT! I TOLD YER, THERE AIN'T NO SUCH FING!

WIND HOWLIN' IN THE TUNNELS IS WOT THAT IS!

WHO'S THE *RAT KING?*

NOT WHO, BUT *WHAT!*

LEGEND HAS IT THAT IT'S A TANGLE-TAILED, WRITHING, SEETHING MASS OF GIANT RATS...

...ALL WITH GREAT BIG POINTY TEETH READY TO TEAR YOU APART!

PIFFLE 'N' POPPY-COCK!

THERE'S BIG RATS DOWN 'ERE, BUT THERE AIN'T NO MIFFICAL MONSTERS.

THE ONLY REAL MONSTERS IS YOOMANS.

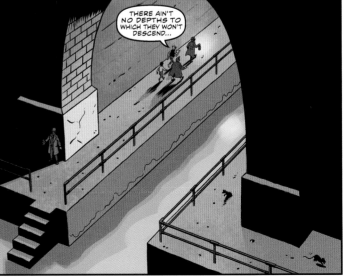

THERE AIN'T NO DEPTHS TO WHICH THEY WON'T DESCEND...

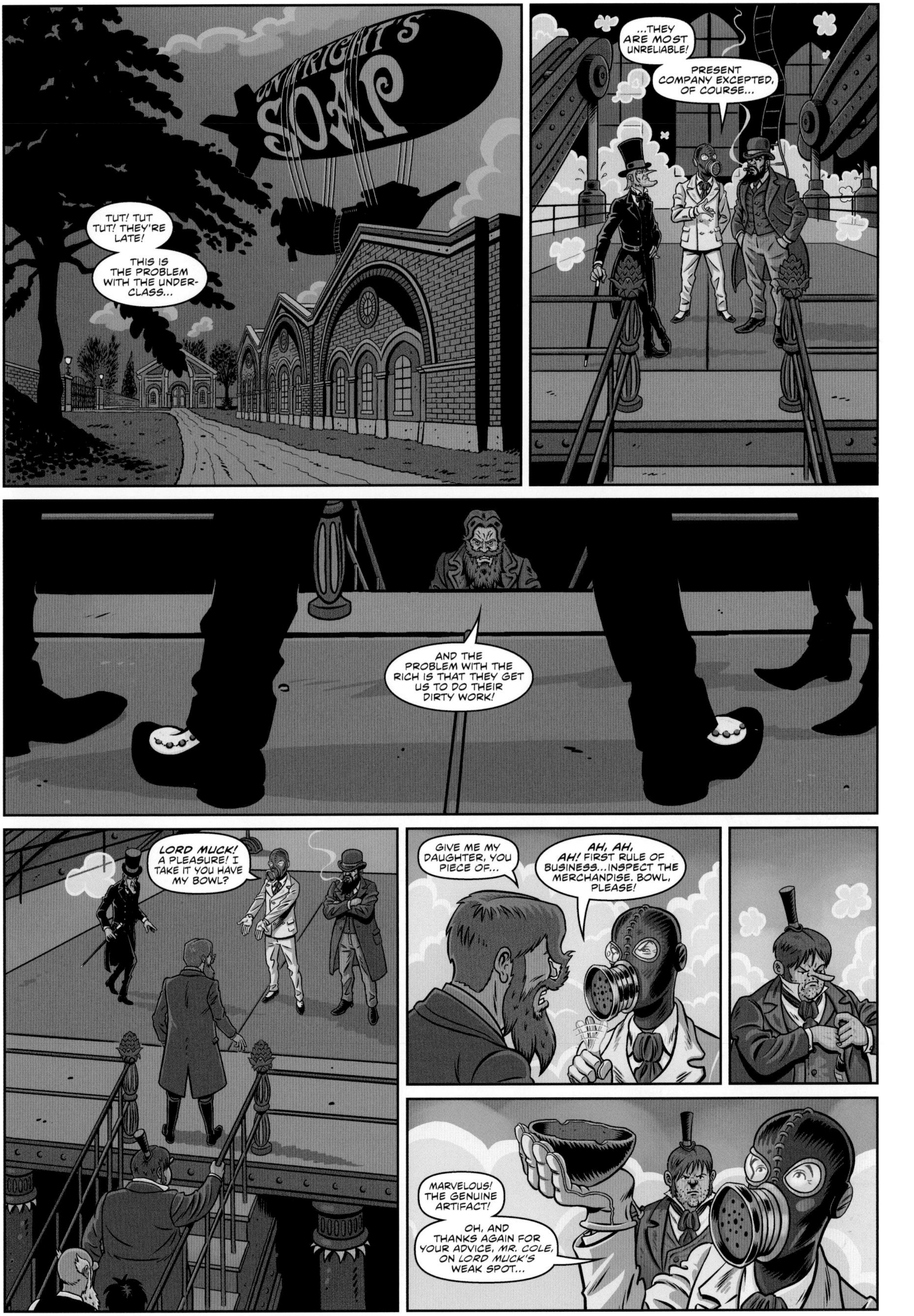
SOAP
TUT! TUT TUT! THEY'RE LATE!
THIS IS THE PROBLEM WITH THE UNDER-CLASS...
...THEY ARE MOST UNRELIABLE!
PRESENT COMPANY EXCEPTED, OF COURSE...
AND THE PROBLEM WITH THE RICH IS THAT THEY GET US TO DO THEIR DIRTY WORK!
LORD MUCK! A PLEASURE! I TAKE IT YOU HAVE MY BOWL?
GIVE ME MY DAUGHTER, YOU PIECE OF...
AH, AH, AH! FIRST RULE OF BUSINESS...INSPECT THE MERCHANDISE. BOWL, PLEASE!
MARVELOUS! THE GENUINE ARTIFACT!
OH, AND THANKS AGAIN FOR YOUR ADVICE, MR. COLE, ON LORD MUCK'S WEAK SPOT...

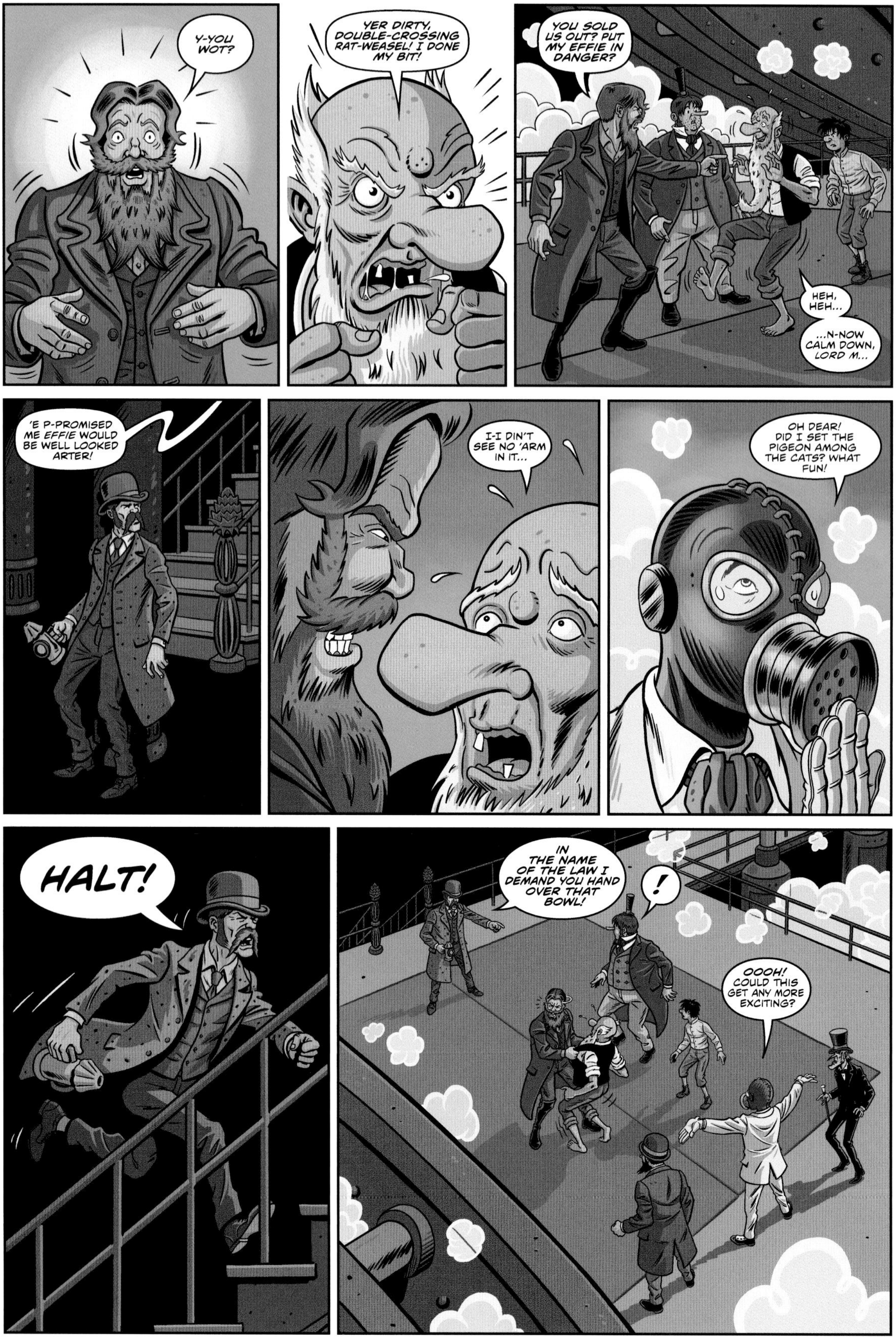

Y-YOU WOT?
YER DIRTY, DOUBLE-CROSSING RAT-WEASEL! I DONE MY BIT!
YOU SOLD US OUT? PUT MY EFFIE IN DANGER?
HEH, HEH...
...N-NOW CALM DOWN, LORD M...
'E P-PROMISED ME EFFIE WOULD BE WELL LOOKED ARTER!
I-I DIN'T SEE NO 'ARM IN IT...
OH DEAR! DID I SET THE PIGEON AMONG THE CATS? WHAT FUN!
HALT!
IN THE NAME OF THE LAW I DEMAND YOU HAND OVER THAT BOWL!
!
OOOH! COULD THIS GET ANY MORE EXCITING?

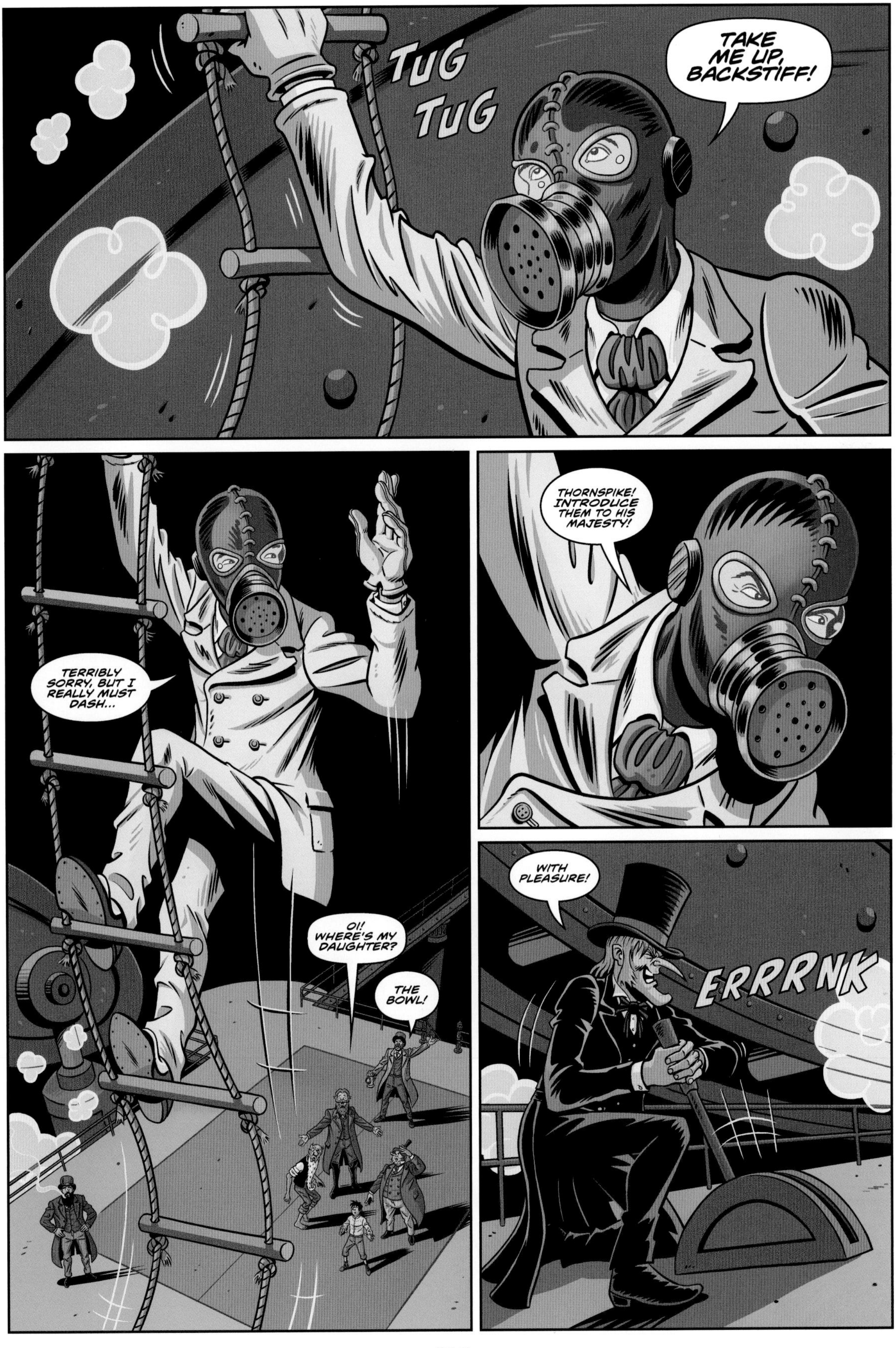

TUG
TUG
TAKE ME UP, BACKSTIFF!
TERRIBLY SORRY, BUT I REALLY MUST DASH...
OI! WHERE'S MY DAUGHTER?
THE BOWL!
THORNSPIKE! INTRODUCE THEM TO HIS MAJESTY!
WITH PLEASURE!
ERRRNK

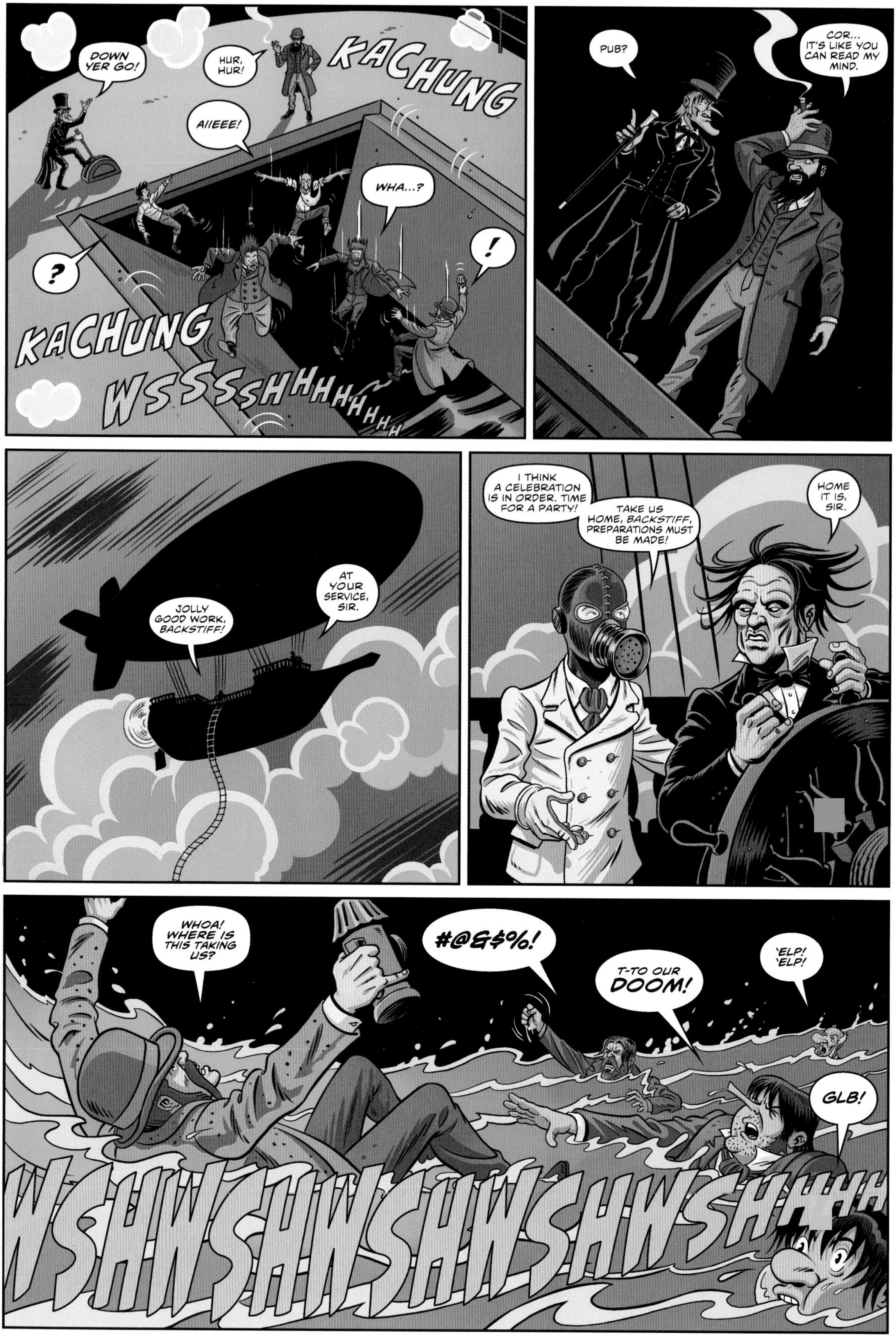

DOWN YER GO!
HUR, HUR!
KACHUNG
AIIEEE!
WHA...?
?
!
KACHUNG
WSSSSHHHHHHHH
PUB?
COR... IT'S LIKE YOU CAN READ MY MIND.
JOLLY GOOD WORK, BACKSTIFF!
AT YOUR SERVICE, SIR.
I THINK A CELEBRATION IS IN ORDER. TIME FOR A PARTY!
TAKE US HOME, BACKSTIFF, PREPARATIONS MUST BE MADE!
HOME IT IS, SIR.
WHOA! WHERE IS THIS TAKING US?
#@&$%!
T-TO OUR DOOM!
'ELP! 'ELP!
GLB!

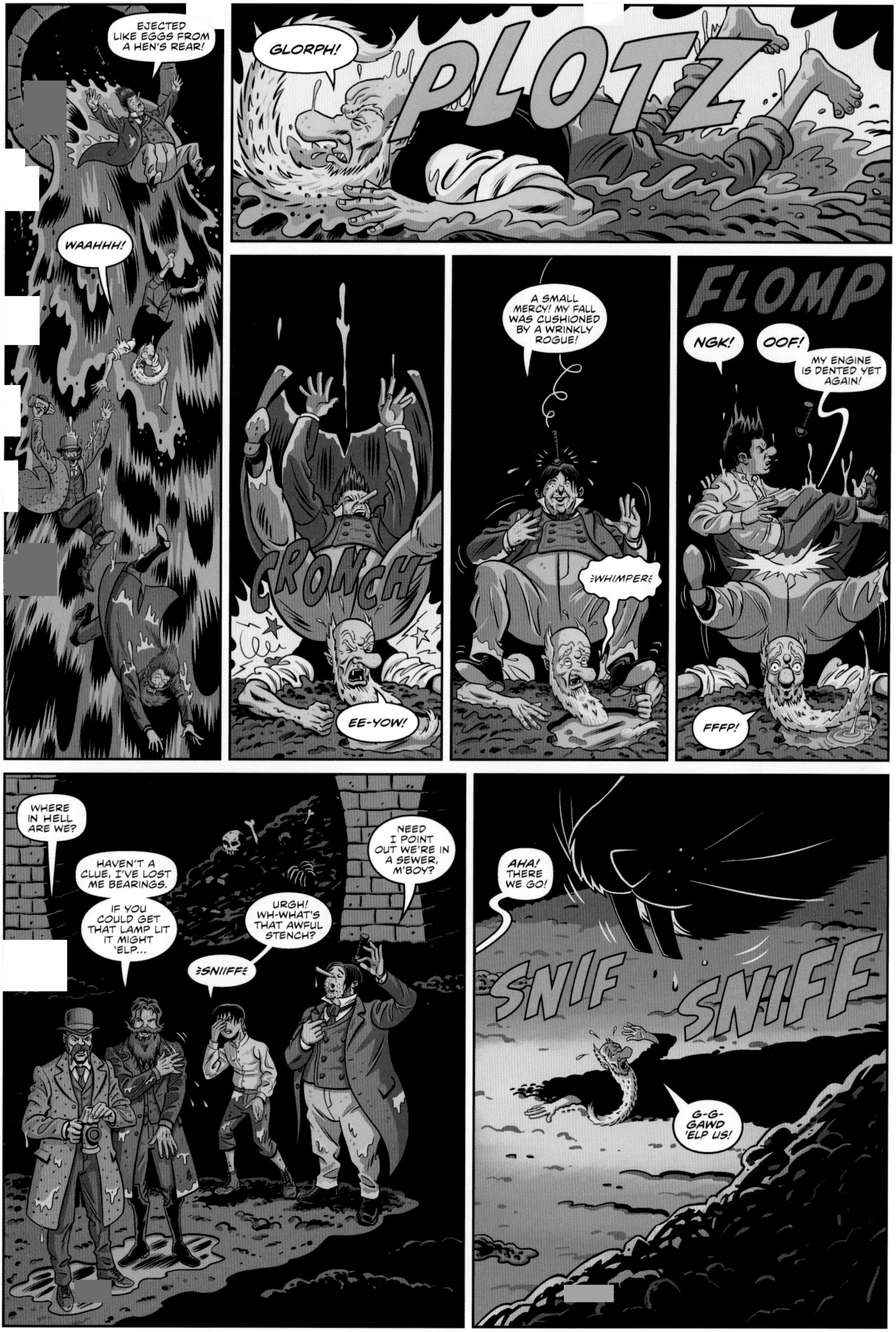
EJECTED LIKE EGGS FROM A HEN'S REAR!
WAAHHH!
GLORPH!
PLOTZ
CRONCH
EE-YOW!
A SMALL MERCY! MY FALL WAS CUSHIONED BY A WRINKLY ROGUE!
WHIMPER
FLOMP
NGK!
OOF!
MY ENGINE IS DENTED YET AGAIN!
FFFP!
WHERE IN HELL ARE WE?
HAVEN'T A CLUE, I'VE LOST ME BEARINGS.
IF YOU COULD GET THAT LAMP LIT IT MIGHT 'ELP...
SNIFF
URGH! WH-WHAT'S THAT AWFUL STENCH?
NEED I POINT OUT WE'RE IN A SEWER, M'BOY?
AHA! THERE WE GO!
SNIF
SNIFF
G-G-GAWD 'ELP US!

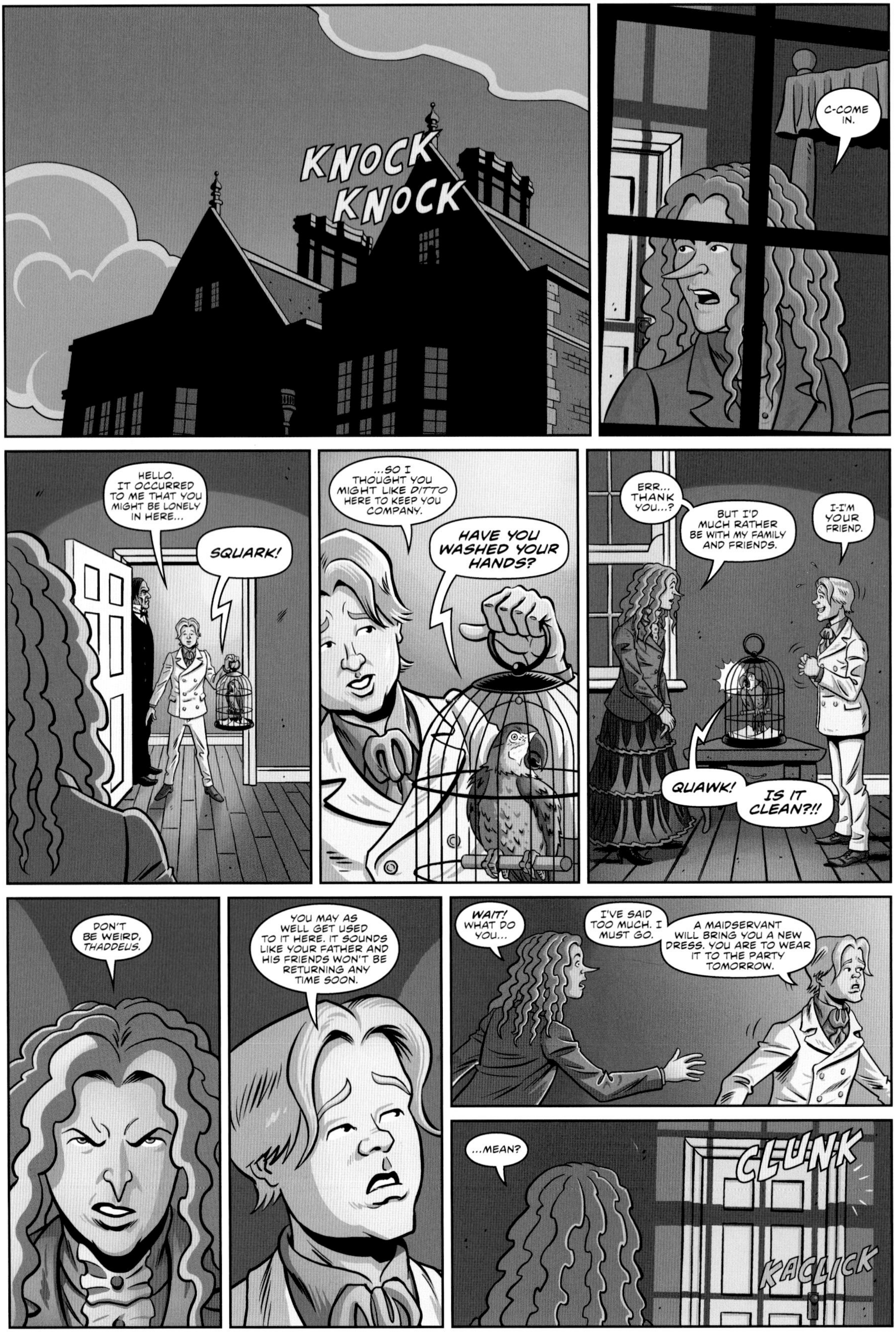
KNOCK
KNOCK
C-COME IN.
HELLO. IT OCCURRED TO ME THAT YOU MIGHT BE LONELY IN HERE...
SQUARK!
...SO I THOUGHT YOU MIGHT LIKE *DITTO* HERE TO KEEP YOU COMPANY.
HAVE YOU WASHED YOUR HANDS?
ERR... THANK YOU...?
BUT I'D MUCH RATHER BE WITH MY FAMILY AND FRIENDS.
I-I'M YOUR FRIEND.
QUAWK!
IS IT CLEAN?!!
DON'T BE WEIRD, *THADDEUS*.
YOU MAY AS WELL GET USED TO IT HERE. IT SOUNDS LIKE YOUR FATHER AND HIS FRIENDS WON'T BE RETURNING ANY TIME SOON.
WAIT! WHAT DO YOU...
I'VE SAID TOO MUCH. I MUST GO.
A MAIDSERVANT WILL BRING YOU A NEW DRESS. YOU ARE TO WEAR IT TO THE PARTY TOMORROW.
...MEAN?
CLUNK
KACLICK

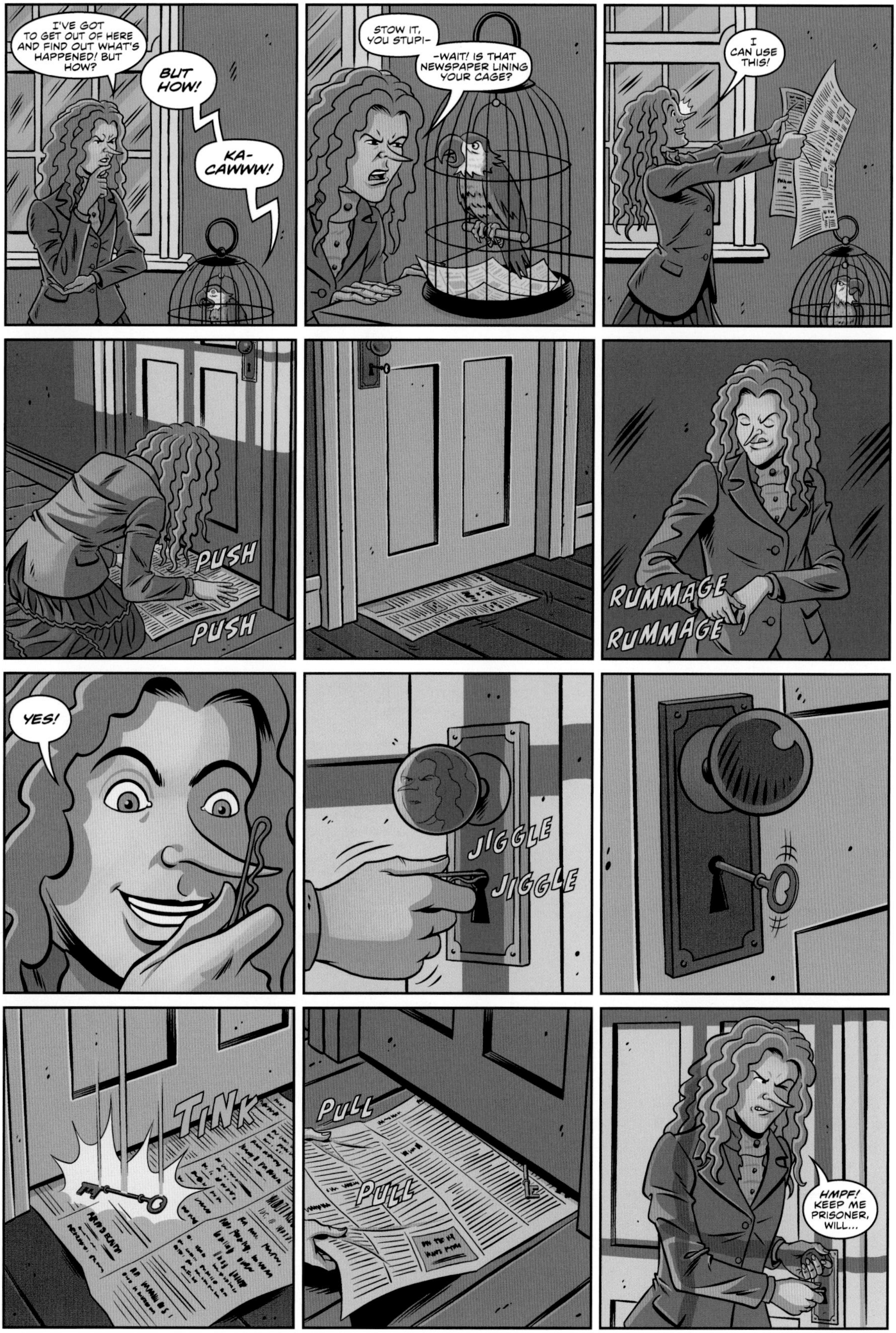
I'VE GOT TO GET OUT OF HERE AND FIND OUT WHAT'S HAPPENED! BUT HOW?
BUT HOW!
KA-CAWWW!
STOW IT, YOU STUPI-
-WAIT! IS THAT NEWSPAPER LINING YOUR CAGE?
I CAN USE THIS!
PUSH
PUSH
RUMMAGE
RUMMAGE
YES!
JIGGLE
JIGGLE
TINK
PULL
PULL
HMPF! KEEP ME PRISONER, WILL...

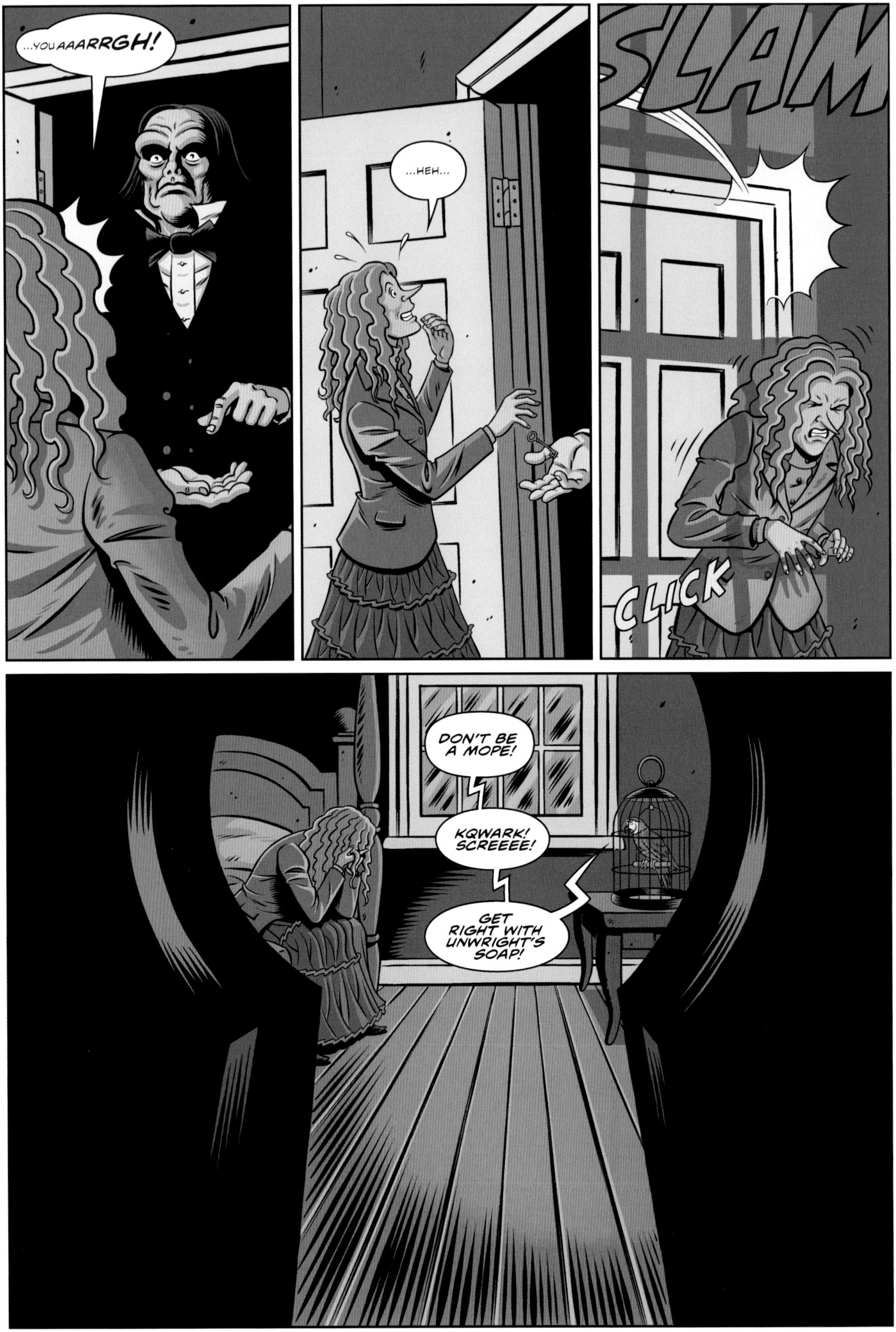
...YOU AAARRGH!
...HEH...
SLAM
CLICK
DON'T BE A MOPE!
KQWARK! SCREEEE!
GET RIGHT WITH UNWRIGHT'S SOAP!

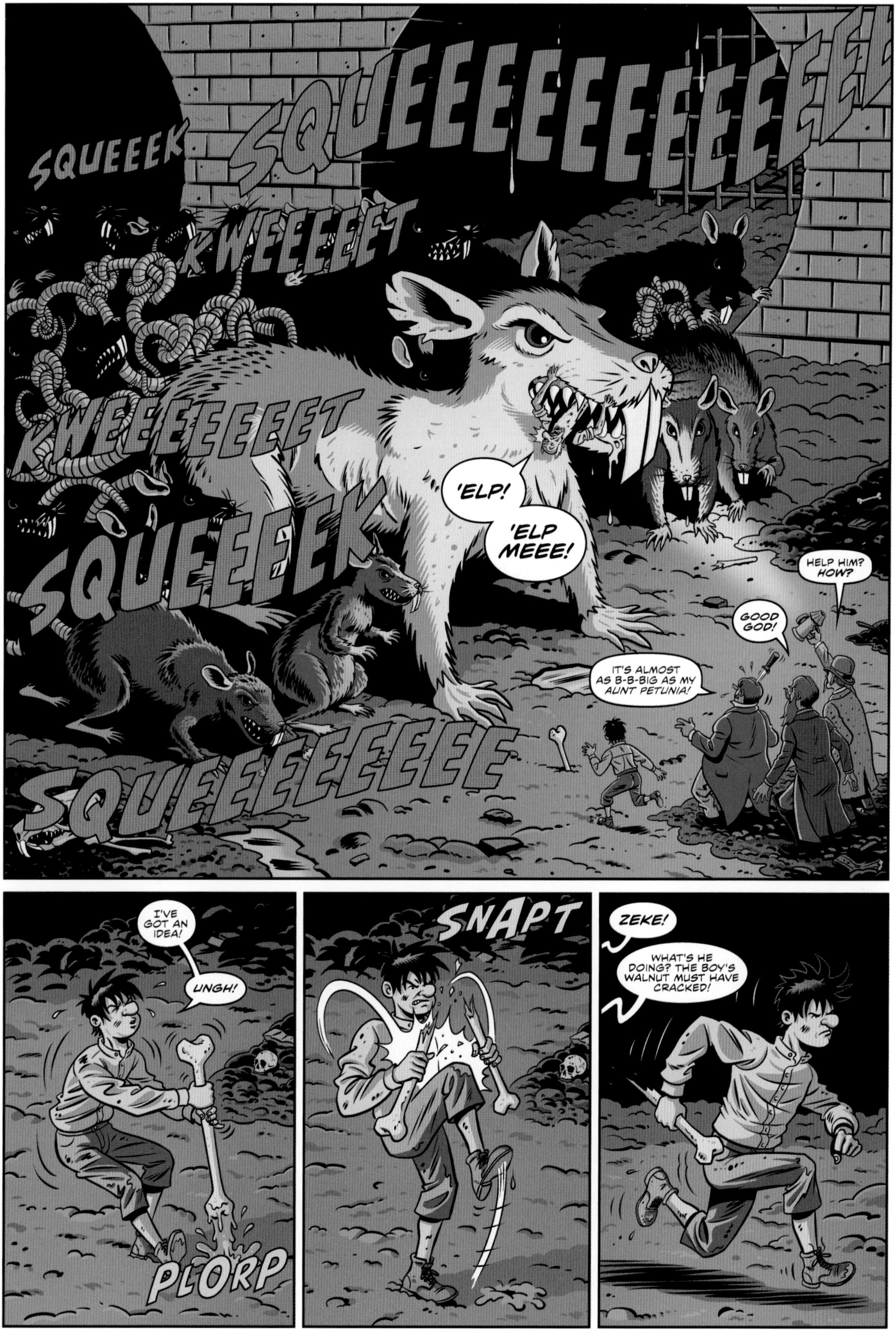
SQUEEEK
SQUEEEEEEEEEEEEEE
KWEEEEET
KWEEEEEEEET
SQUEEEEK
SQUEEEEEEEEE
'ELP!
'ELP MEEE!
HELP HIM? HOW?
GOOD GOD!
IT'S ALMOST AS B-B-BIG AS MY AUNT PETUNIA!
I'VE GOT AN IDEA!
UNGH!
PLORP
SNAPT
ZEKE!
WHAT'S HE DOING? THE BOY'S WALNUT MUST HAVE CRACKED!

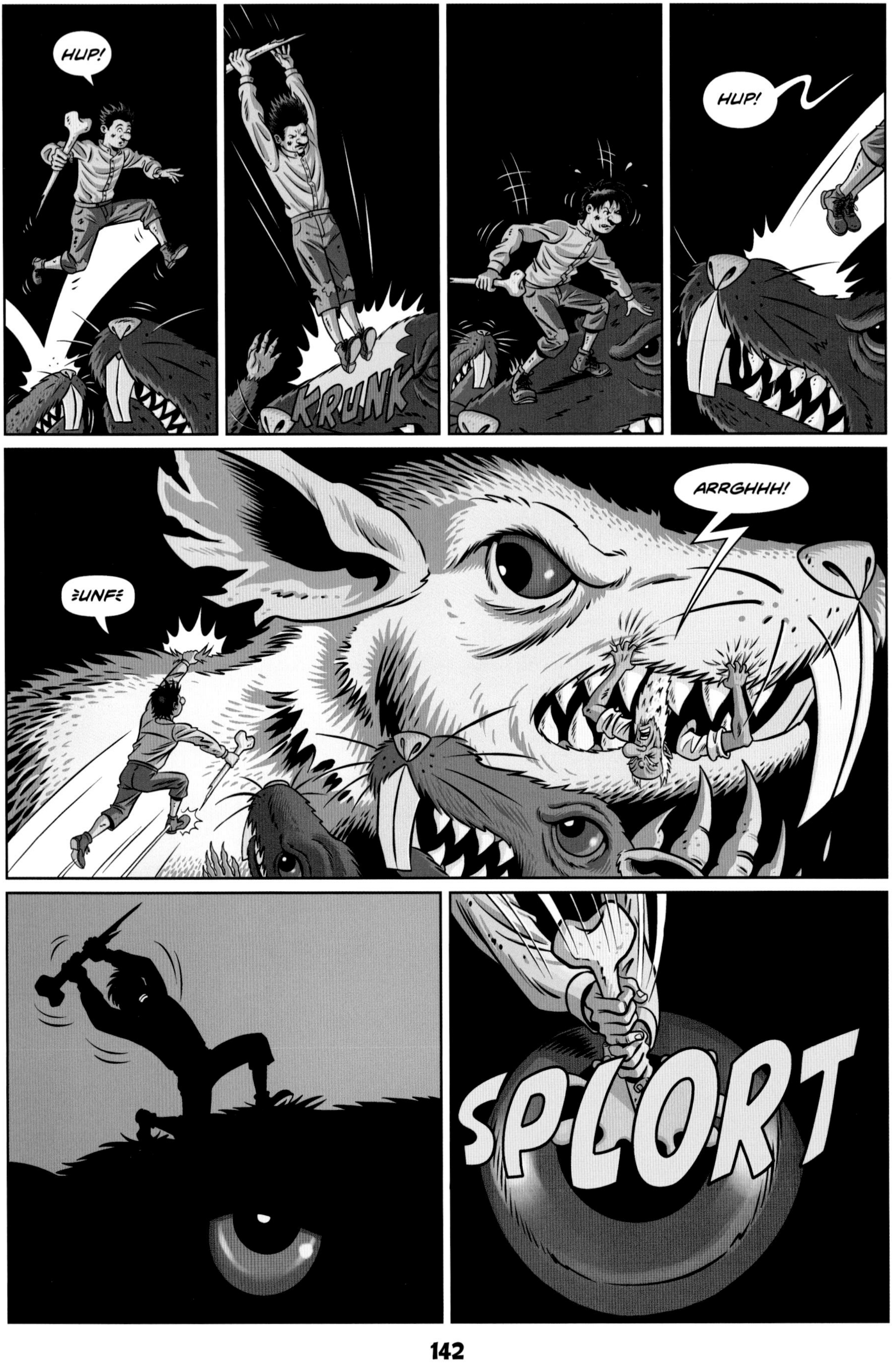
HUP!
KRUNK
HUP!
ARRGHHH!
UNF
SPLORT

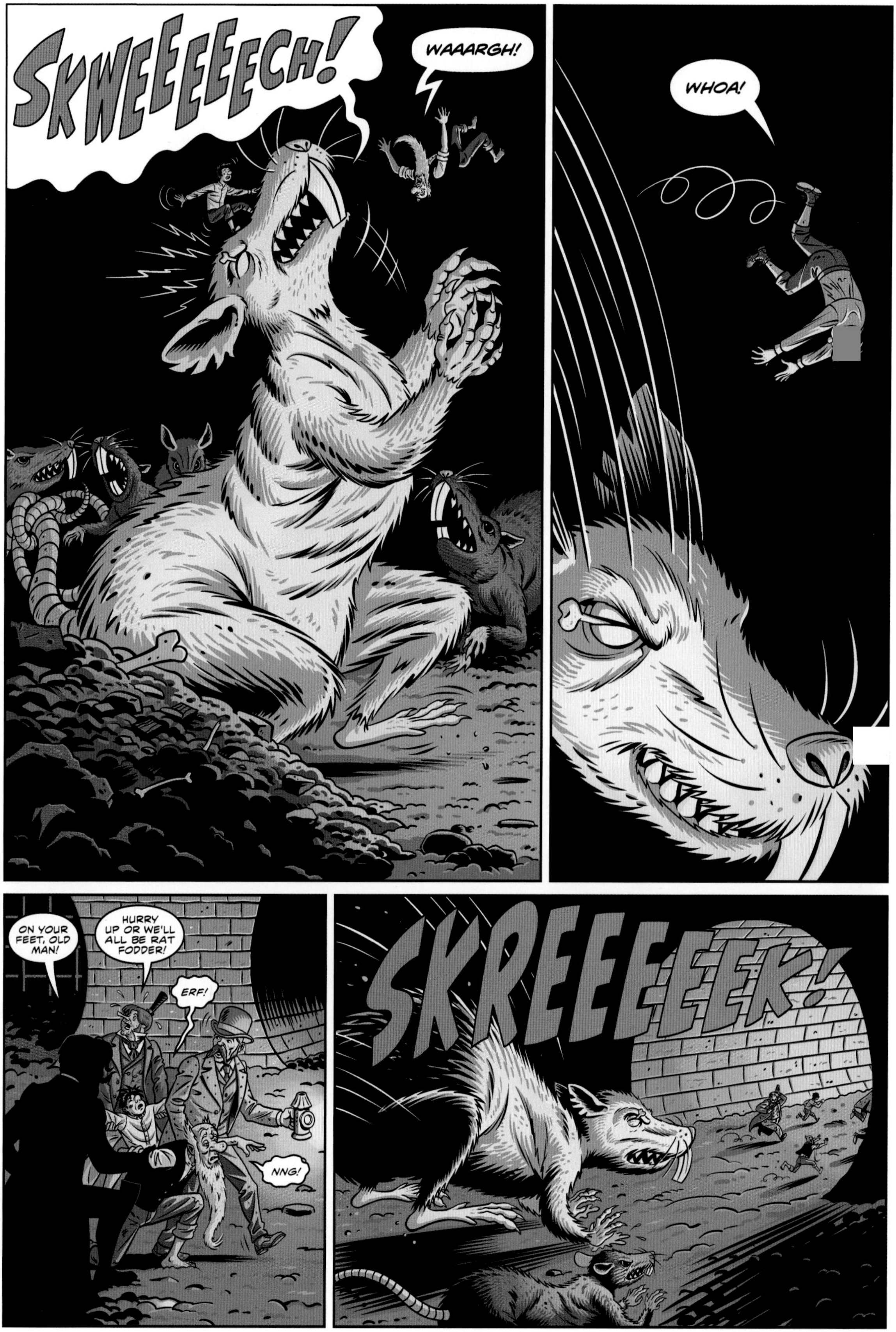
SKWEEEEECH!
WAAARGH!
WHOA!
ON YOUR FEET, OLD MAN!
HURRY UP OR WE'LL ALL BE RAT FODDER!
ERF!
NNG!
SKREEEEEK!

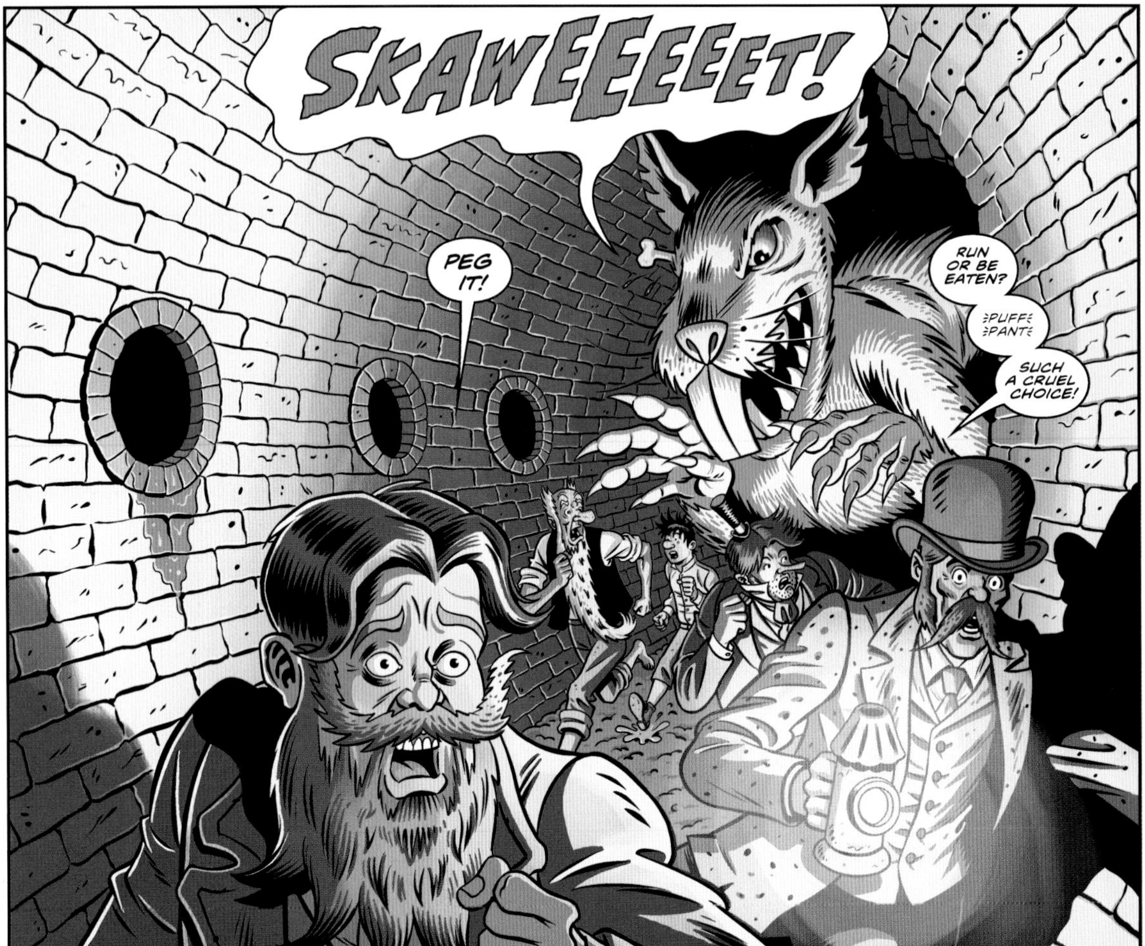
SKAWEEEEET!
PEG IT!
RUN OR BE EATEN?
PUFF PANT
SUCH A CRUEL CHOICE!

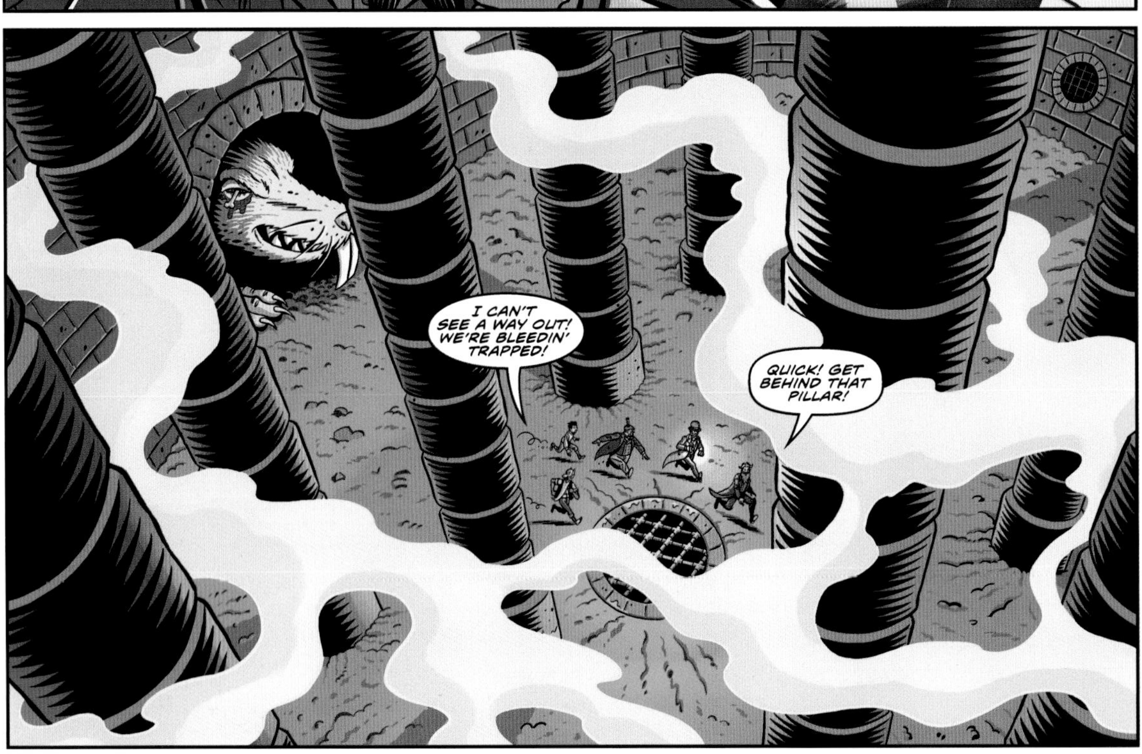
I CAN'T SEE A WAY OUT! WE'RE BLEEDIN' TRAPPED!
QUICK! GET BEHIND THAT PILLAR!

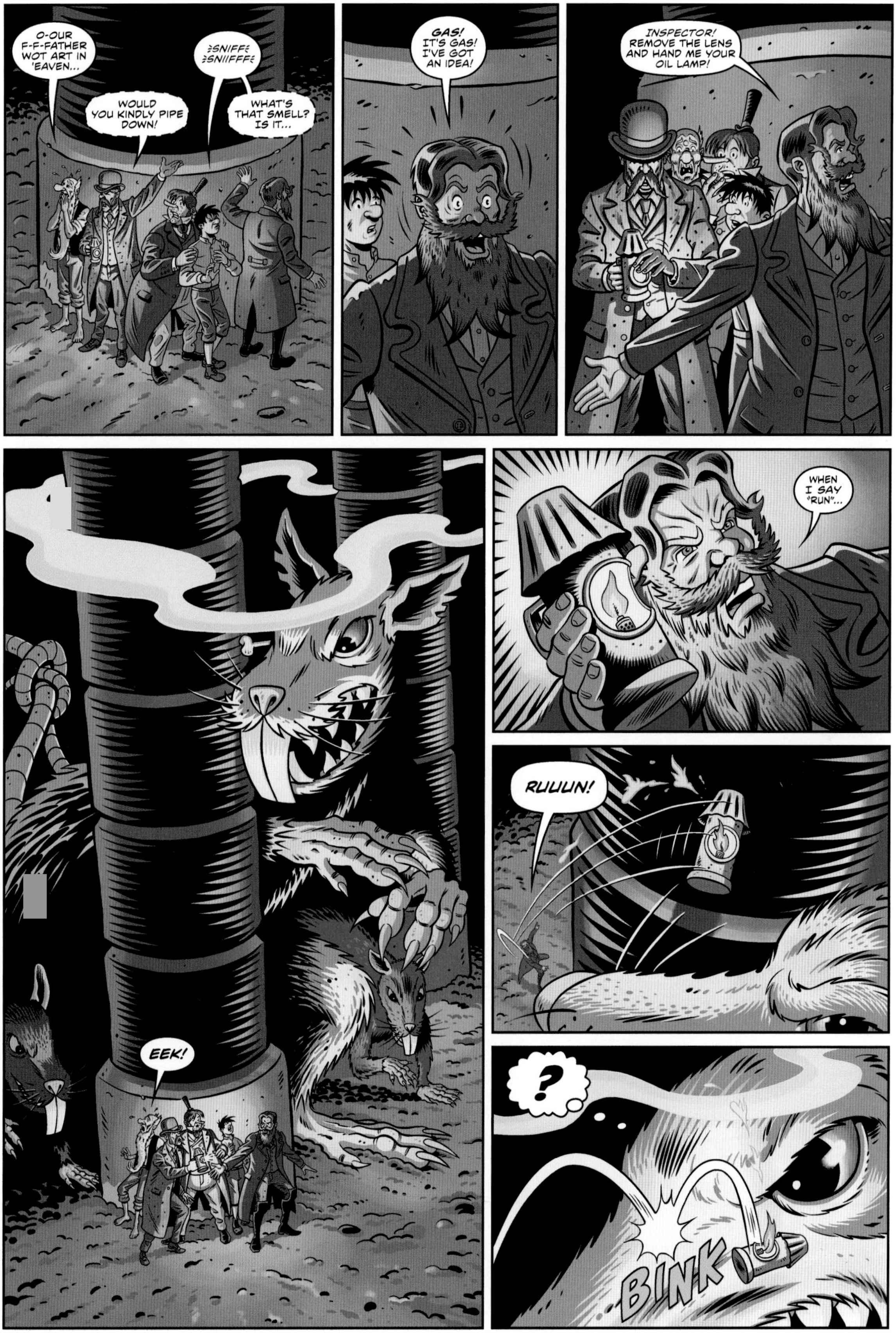
O-OUR F-F-FATHER WOT ART IN 'EAVEN...
WOULD YOU KINDLY PIPE DOWN!
SNIFF SNIIFFF
WHAT'S THAT SMELL? IS IT...
GAS! IT'S GAS! I'VE GOT AN IDEA!
INSPECTOR! REMOVE THE LENS AND HAND ME YOUR OIL LAMP!
EEK!
WHEN I SAY "RUN"...
RUUUN!
?
BINK

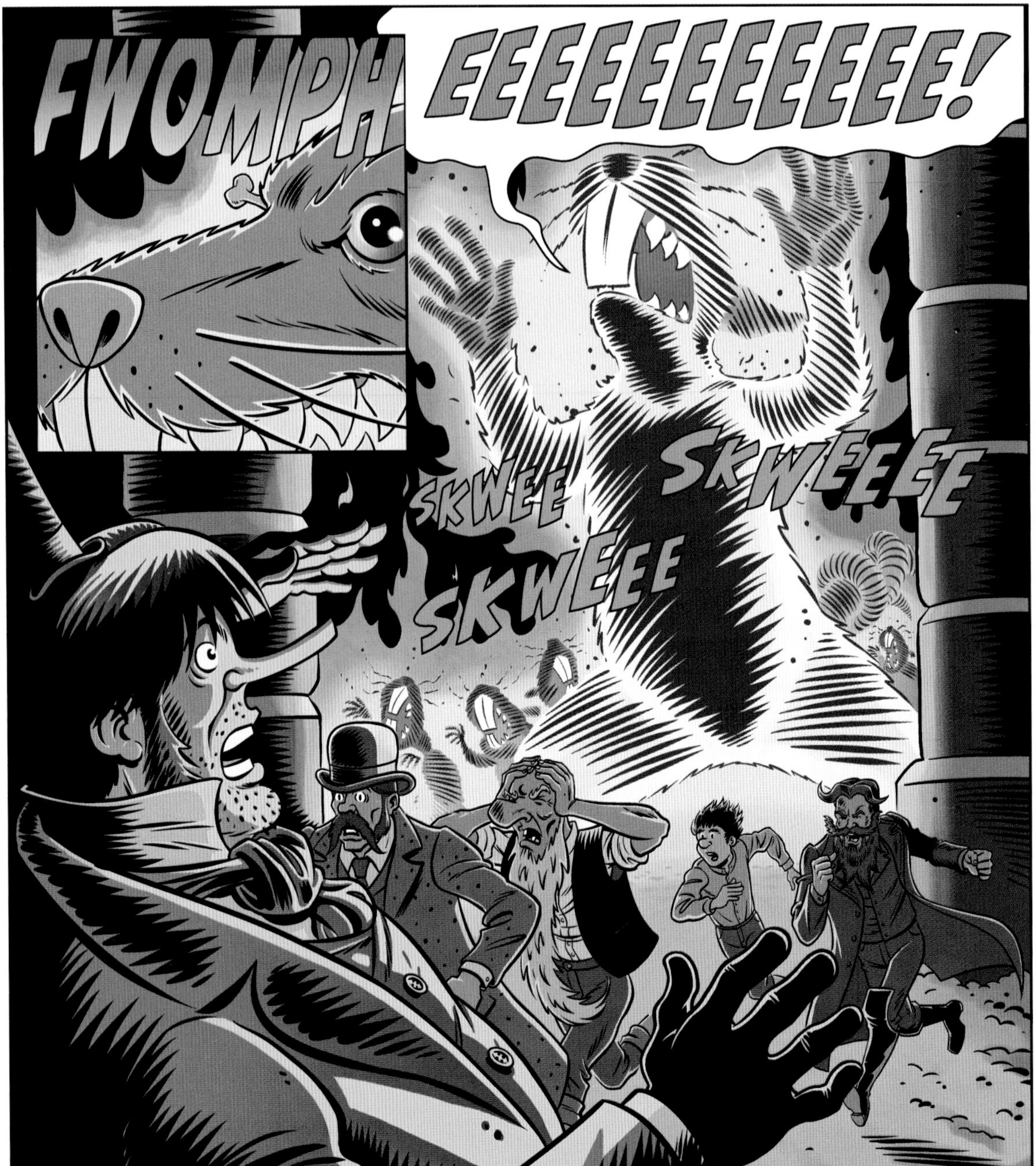
FWOMPH
EEEEEEEEEEEE!
SKWEE
SKWEEE
SKWEEEEE

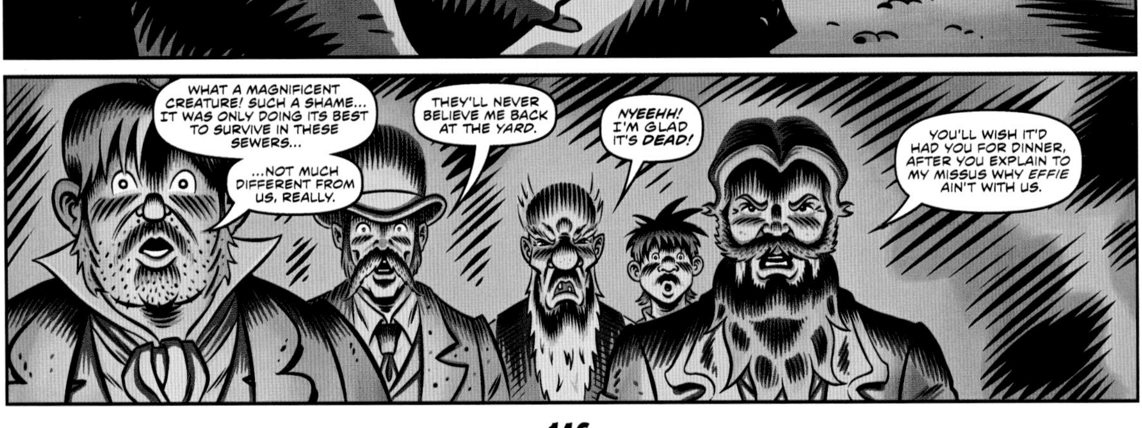
WHAT A MAGNIFICENT CREATURE! SUCH A SHAME... IT WAS ONLY DOING ITS BEST TO SURVIVE IN THESE SEWERS...
...NOT MUCH DIFFERENT FROM US, REALLY.
THEY'LL NEVER BELIEVE ME BACK AT THE YARD.
NYEEHH! I'M GLAD IT'S DEAD!
YOU'LL WISH IT'D HAD YOU FOR DINNER, AFTER YOU EXPLAIN TO MY MISSUS WHY EFFIE AIN'T WITH US.

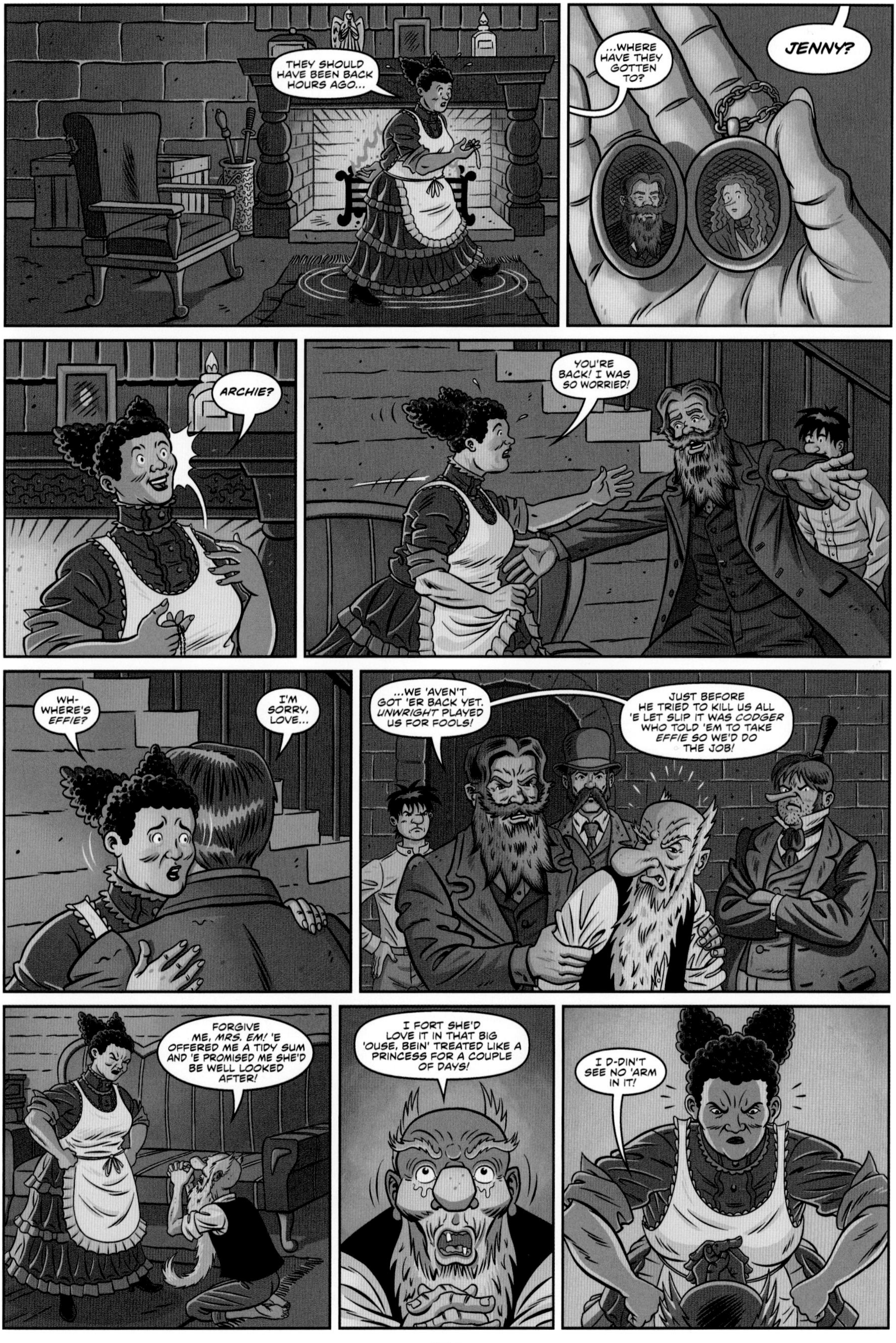
THEY SHOULD HAVE BEEN BACK HOURS AGO...
...WHERE HAVE THEY GOTTEN TO?
JENNY?
ARCHIE?
YOU'RE BACK! I WAS SO WORRIED!
WH-WHERE'S EFFIE?
I'M SORRY, LOVE...
...WE 'AVEN'T GOT 'ER BACK YET. UNWRIGHT PLAYED US FOR FOOLS!
JUST BEFORE HE TRIED TO KILL US ALL 'E LET SLIP IT WAS CODGER WHO TOLD 'EM TO TAKE EFFIE SO WE'D DO THE JOB!
FORGIVE ME, MRS. EM! 'E OFFERED ME A TIDY SUM AND 'E PROMISED ME SHE'D BE WELL LOOKED AFTER!
I FORT SHE'D LOVE IT IN THAT BIG 'OUSE, BEIN' TREATED LIKE A PRINCESS FOR A COUPLE OF DAYS!
I D-DIN'T SEE NO 'ARM IN IT!

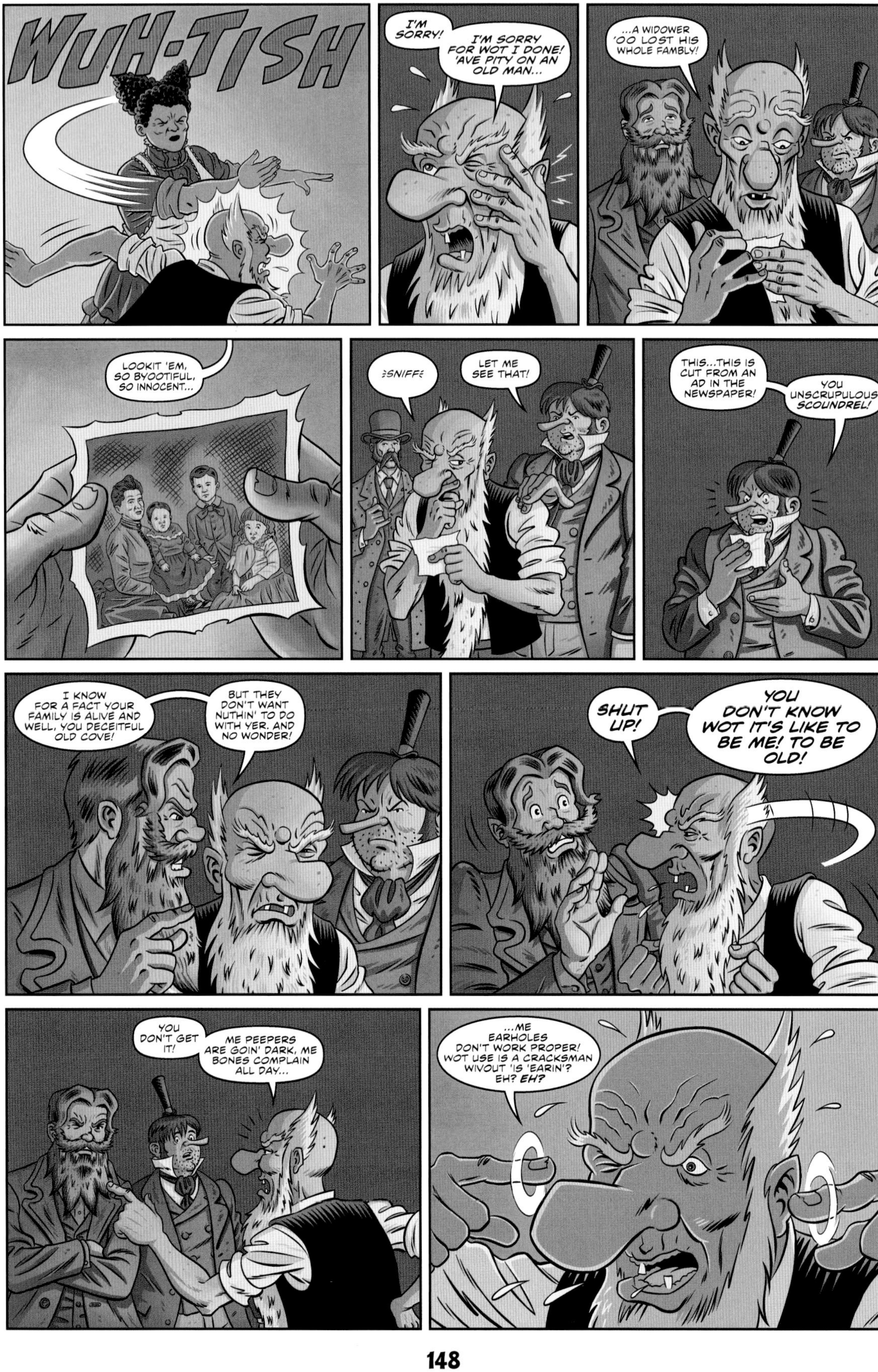
WUH-TISH
I'M SORRY!
I'M SORRY FOR WOT I DONE! 'AVE PITY ON AN OLD MAN...
...A WIDOWER 'OO LOST HIS WHOLE FAMBLY!
LOOKIT 'EM, SO BYOOTIFUL, SO INNOCENT...
SNIFF
LET ME SEE THAT!
THIS...THIS IS CUT FROM AN AD IN THE NEWSPAPER!
YOU UNSCRUPULOUS SCOUNDREL!
I KNOW FOR A FACT YOUR FAMILY IS ALIVE AND WELL, YOU DECEITFUL OLD COVE!
BUT THEY DON'T WANT NUTHIN' TO DO WITH YER. AND NO WONDER!
SHUT UP!
YOU DON'T KNOW WOT IT'S LIKE TO BE ME! TO BE OLD!
YOU DON'T GET IT!
ME PEEPERS ARE GOIN' DARK, ME BONES COMPLAIN ALL DAY...
...ME EARHOLES DON'T WORK PROPER! WOT USE IS A CRACKSMAN WIVOUT 'IS 'EARIN'? EH? EH?

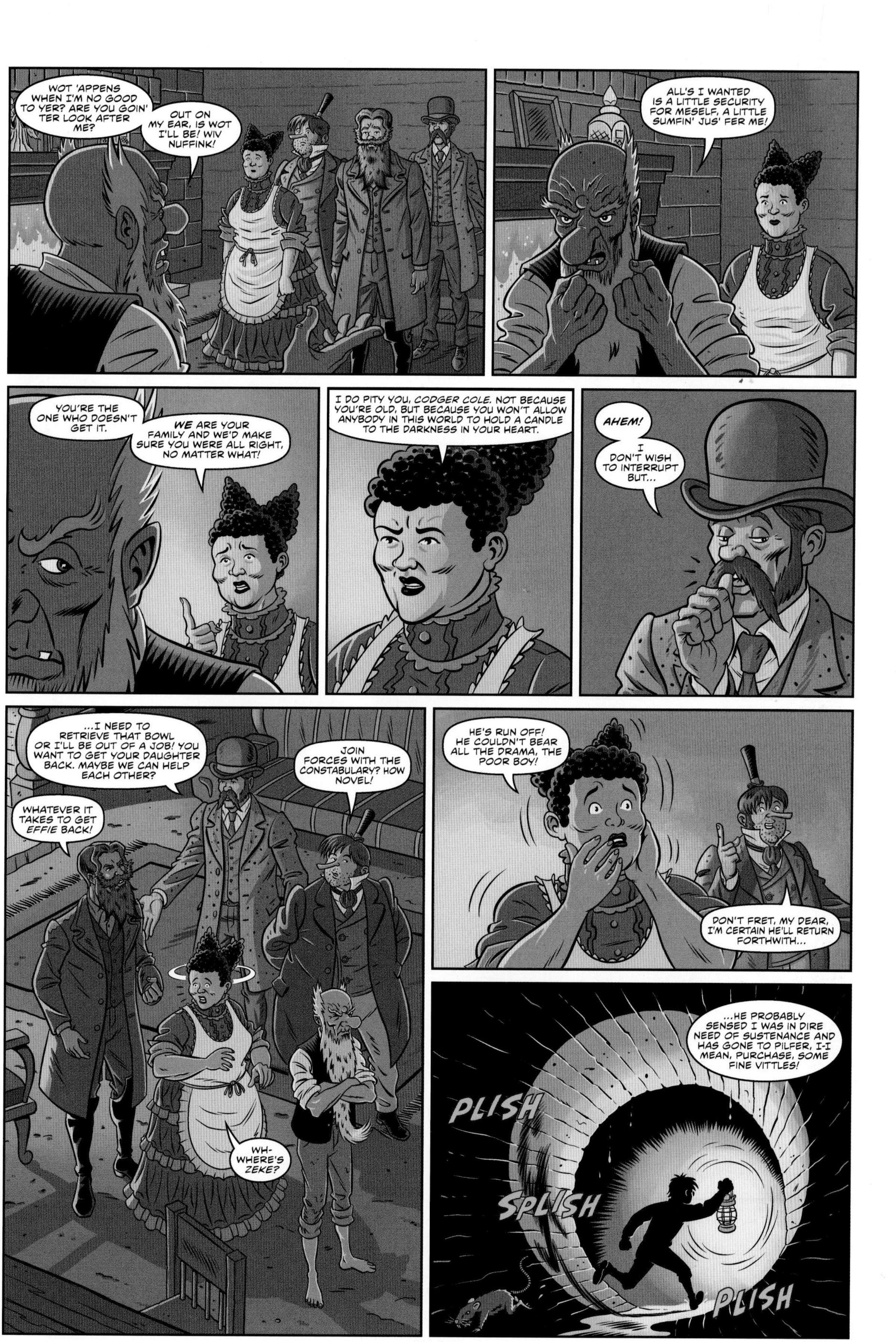
WOT 'APPENS WHEN I'M NO GOOD TO YER? ARE YOU GOIN' TER LOOK AFTER ME?
OUT ON MY EAR, IS WOT I'LL BE! WIV NUFFINK!
ALL'S I WANTED IS A LITTLE SECURITY FOR MESELF, A LITTLE SUMFIN' JUS' FER ME!
YOU'RE THE ONE WHO DOESN'T GET IT.
WE ARE YOUR FAMILY AND WE'D MAKE SURE YOU WERE ALL RIGHT, NO MATTER WHAT!
I DO PITY YOU, CODGER COLE. NOT BECAUSE YOU'RE OLD, BUT BECAUSE YOU WON'T ALLOW ANYBODY IN THIS WORLD TO HOLD A CANDLE TO THE DARKNESS IN YOUR HEART.
AHEM!
I DON'T WISH TO INTERRUPT BUT...
...I NEED TO RETRIEVE THAT BOWL OR I'LL BE OUT OF A JOB! YOU WANT TO GET YOUR DAUGHTER BACK. MAYBE WE CAN HELP EACH OTHER?
WHATEVER IT TAKES TO GET EFFIE BACK!
JOIN FORCES WITH THE CONSTABULARY? HOW NOVEL!
WH-WHERE'S ZEKE?
HE'S RUN OFF! HE COULDN'T BEAR ALL THE DRAMA, THE POOR BOY!
DON'T FRET, MY DEAR, I'M CERTAIN HE'LL RETURN FORTHWITH...
...HE PROBABLY SENSED I WAS IN DIRE NEED OF SUSTENANCE AND HAS GONE TO PILFER, I-I MEAN, PURCHASE, SOME FINE VITTLES!
PLISH
SPLISH
PLISH

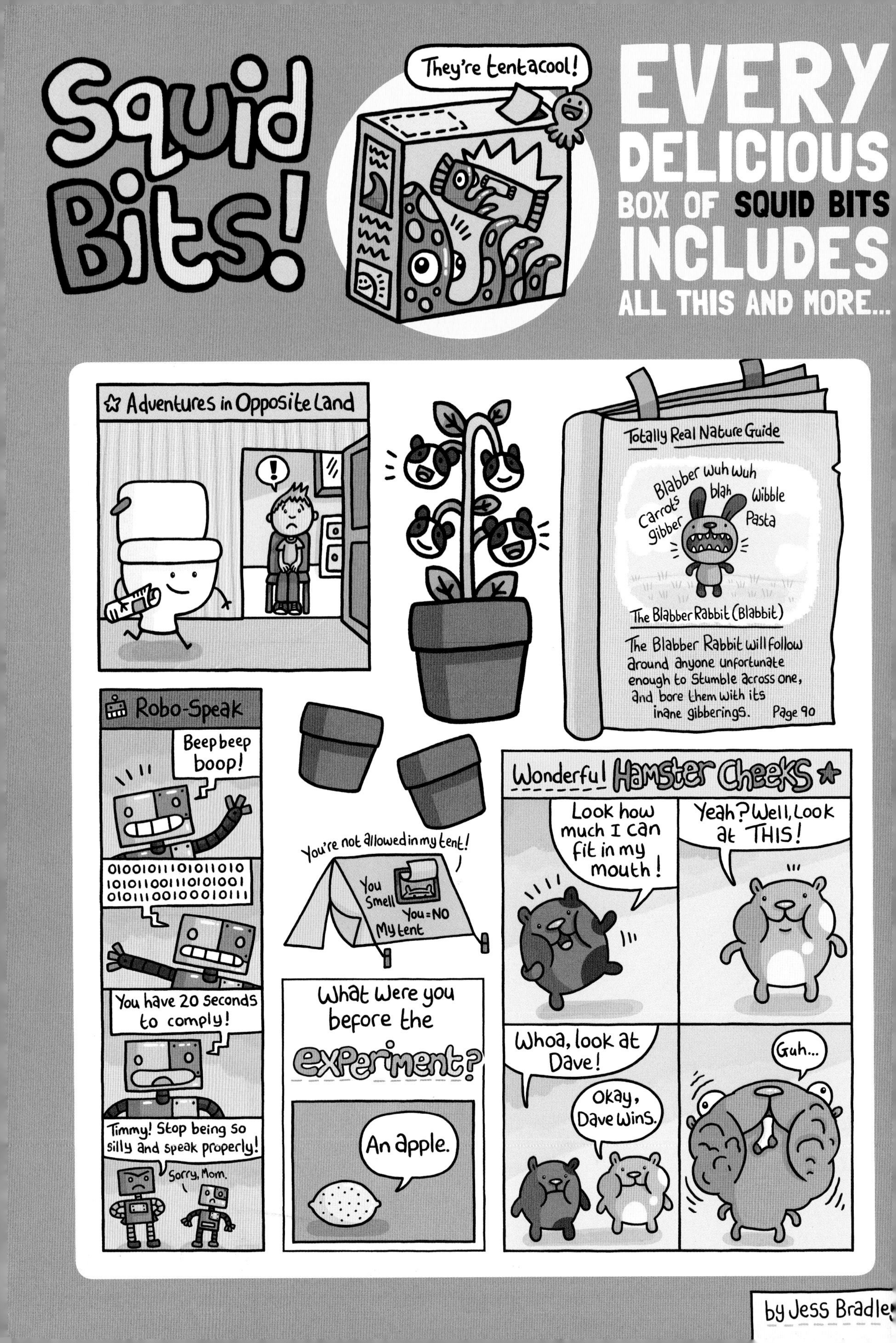

Squid Bits!
They're tentacool!
EVERY DELICIOUS BOX OF SQUID BITS INCLUDES ALL THIS AND MORE...
Adventures in Opposite Land
!
Totally Real Nature Guide
Blabber wuh wuh
blah
Wibble
Carrots
gibber
Pasta
The Blabber Rabbit (Blabbit)
The Blabber Rabbit will follow around anyone unfortunate enough to stumble across one, and bore them with its inane gibberings.
Page 90
Robo-Speak
Beep beep boop!
010010111010111010
101011001101010001
010111001000010111
You have 20 seconds to comply!
Timmy! Stop being so silly and speak properly!
Sorry, Mom.
You're not allowed in my tent!
You Smell
You = NO
My tent
What were you before the experiment?
An apple.
Wonderful Hamster Cheeks
Look how much I can fit in my mouth!
Yeah? Well, look at THIS!
Whoa, look at Dave!
Okay, Dave wins.
Guh...
by Jess Bradley

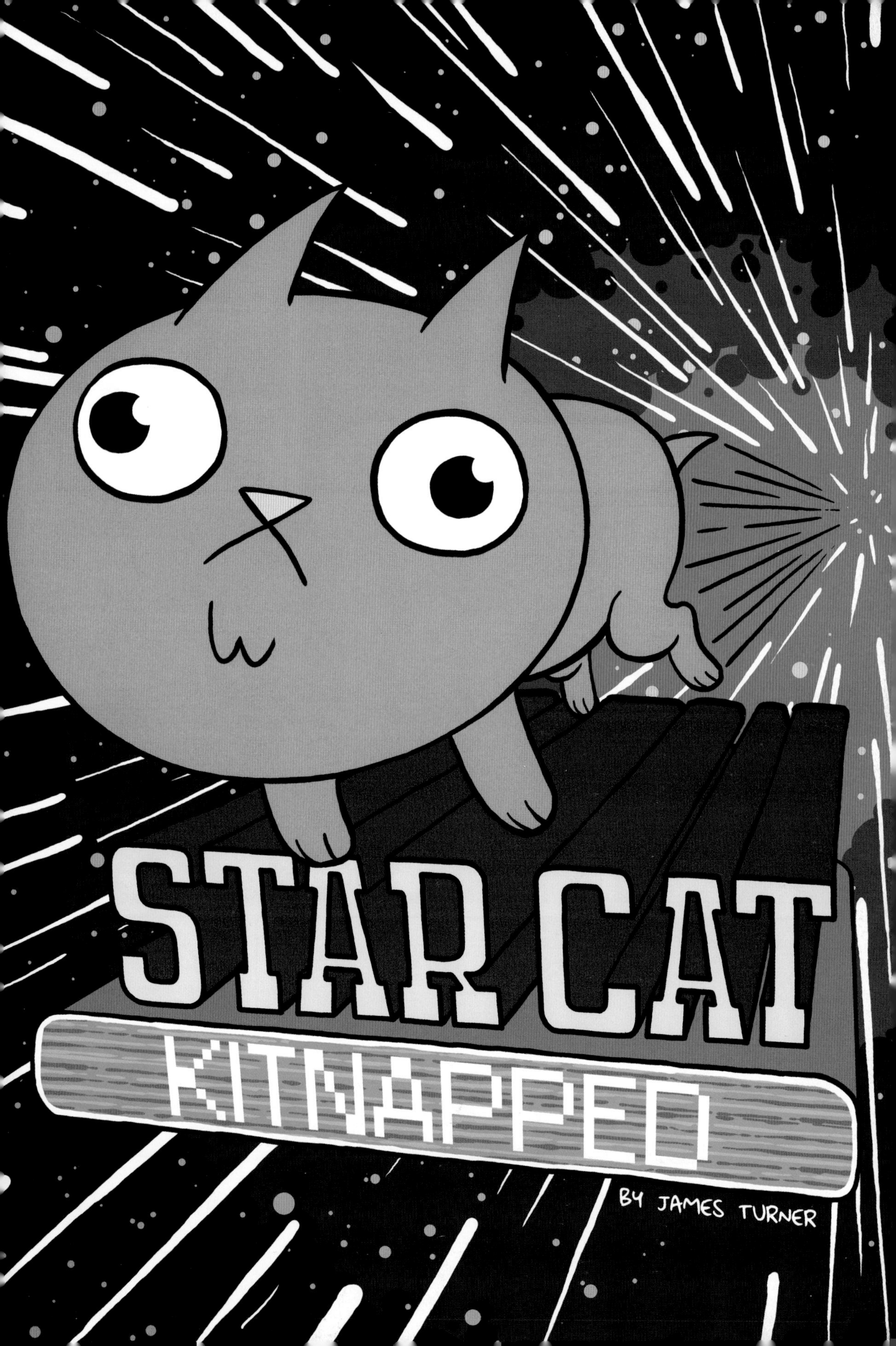
STAR CAT
KITNAPPED
BY JAMES TURNER

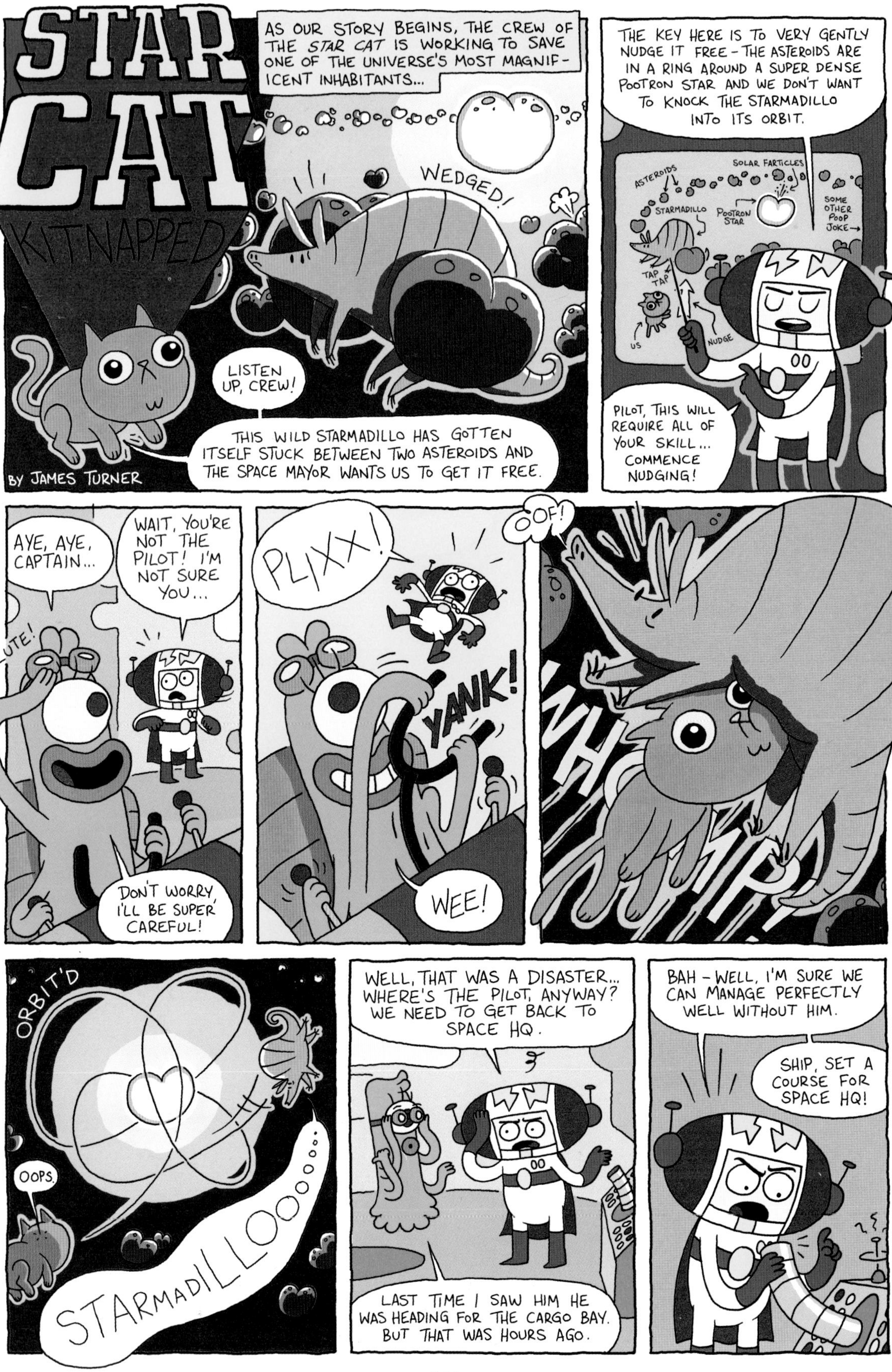
STAR CAT
KITNAPPED
BY JAMES TURNER
AS OUR STORY BEGINS, THE CREW OF THE STAR CAT IS WORKING TO SAVE ONE OF THE UNIVERSE'S MOST MAGNIFICENT INHABITANTS...
WEDGED!
LISTEN UP, CREW!
THIS WILD STARMADILLO HAS GOTTEN ITSELF STUCK BETWEEN TWO ASTEROIDS AND THE SPACE MAYOR WANTS US TO GET IT FREE.
THE KEY HERE IS TO VERY GENTLY NUDGE IT FREE - THE ASTEROIDS ARE IN A RING AROUND A SUPER DENSE POOTRON STAR AND WE DON'T WANT TO KNOCK THE STARMADILLO INTO ITS ORBIT.
ASTEROIDS
SOLAR FARTICLES
STARMADILLO
POOTRON STAR
SOME OTHER POOP JOKE
TAP TAP
US
NUDGE
PILOT, THIS WILL REQUIRE ALL OF YOUR SKILL... COMMENCE NUDGING!
AYE, AYE, CAPTAIN...
WAIT, YOU'RE NOT THE PILOT! I'M NOT SURE YOU...
SALUTE!
DON'T WORRY I'LL BE SUPER CAREFUL!
PLIXX!
YANK!
WEE!
OOF!
WHUMP!
ORBIT'D
OOPS.
STARMADILLOOOOOO...
WELL, THAT WAS A DISASTER... WHERE'S THE PILOT, ANYWAY? WE NEED TO GET BACK TO SPACE HQ.
LAST TIME I SAW HIM HE WAS HEADING FOR THE CARGO BAY. BUT THAT WAS HOURS AGO.
BAH - WELL, I'M SURE WE CAN MANAGE PERFECTLY WELL WITHOUT HIM.
SHIP, SET A COURSE FOR SPACE HQ!

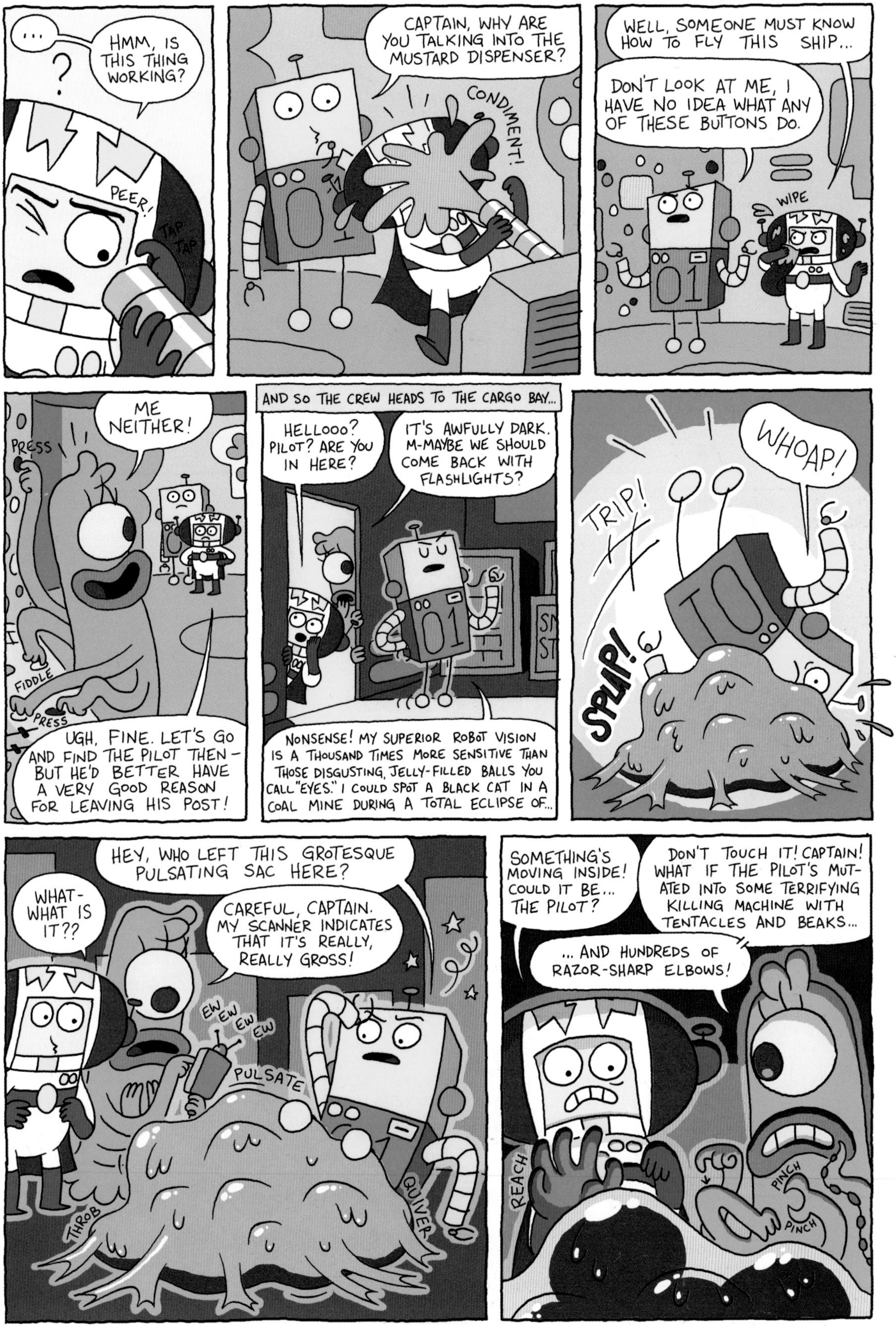
...
?
HMM, IS THIS THING WORKING?
PEER!
TAP TAP
CAPTAIN, WHY ARE YOU TALKING INTO THE MUSTARD DISPENSER?
CONDIMENT!
WELL, SOMEONE MUST KNOW HOW TO FLY THIS SHIP...
DON'T LOOK AT ME, I HAVE NO IDEA WHAT ANY OF THESE BUTTONS DO.
WIPE
ME NEITHER!
PRESS
FIDDLE
PRESS
UGH, FINE. LET'S GO AND FIND THE PILOT THEN - BUT HE'D BETTER HAVE A VERY GOOD REASON FOR LEAVING HIS POST!
AND SO THE CREW HEADS TO THE CARGO BAY...
HELLOOO? PILOT? ARE YOU IN HERE?
IT'S AWFULLY DARK. M-MAYBE WE SHOULD COME BACK WITH FLASHLIGHTS?
NONSENSE! MY SUPERIOR ROBOT VISION IS A THOUSAND TIMES MORE SENSITIVE THAN THOSE DISGUSTING, JELLY-FILLED BALLS YOU CALL "EYES." I COULD SPOT A BLACK CAT IN A COAL MINE DURING A TOTAL ECLIPSE OF...
WHOAP!
TRIP!
SPLIP!
HEY, WHO LEFT THIS GROTESQUE PULSATING SAC HERE?
WHAT-WHAT IS IT??
CAREFUL, CAPTAIN. MY SCANNER INDICATES THAT IT'S REALLY, REALLY GROSS!
EW EW EW EW
PULSATE
THROB
QUIVER
SOMETHING'S MOVING INSIDE! COULD IT BE... THE PILOT?
DON'T TOUCH IT! CAPTAIN! WHAT IF THE PILOT'S MUTATED INTO SOME TERRIFYING KILLING MACHINE WITH TENTACLES AND BEAKS...
... AND HUNDREDS OF RAZOR-SHARP ELBOWS!
REACH
PINCH
PINCH

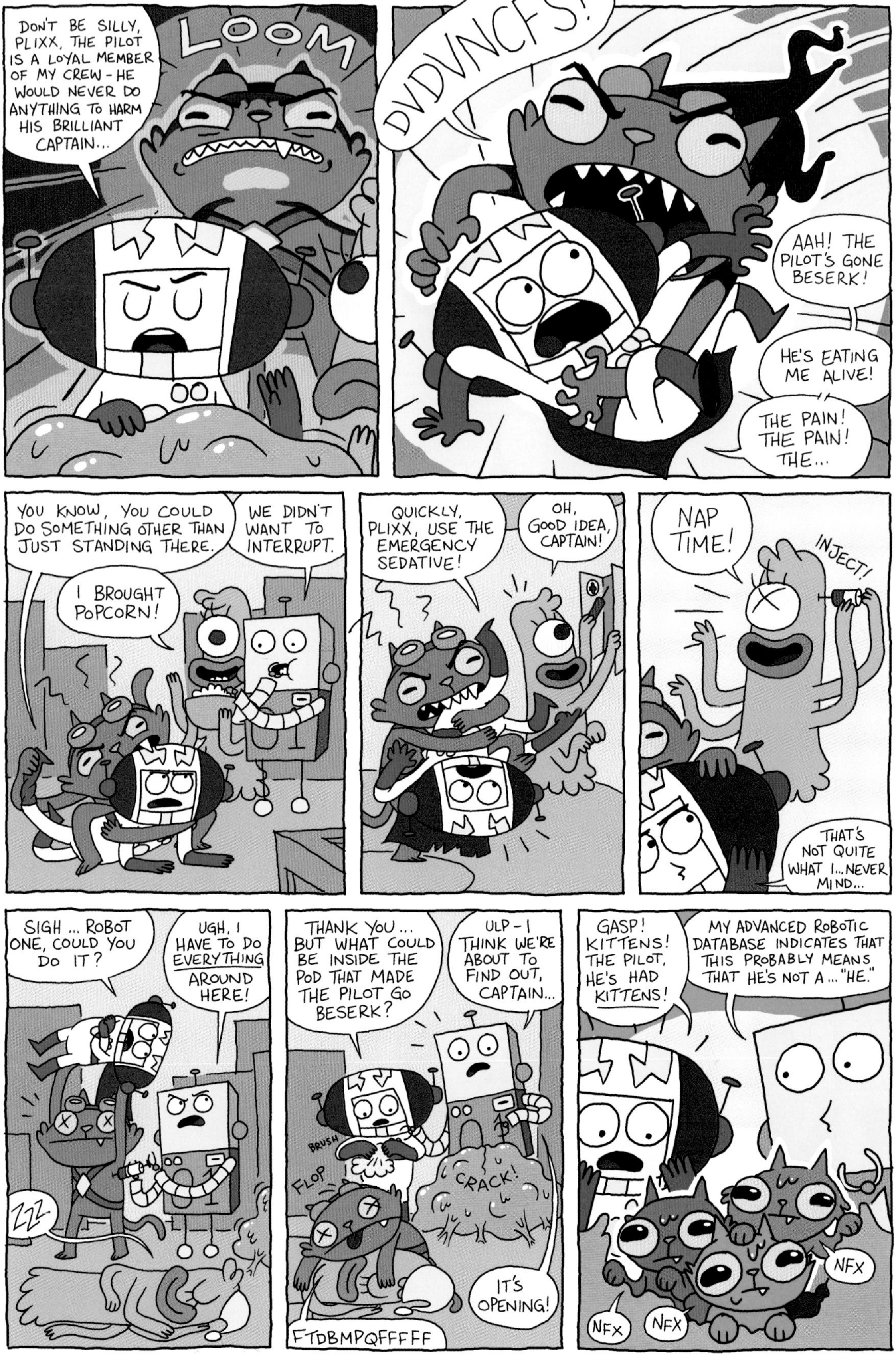
DON'T BE SILLY, PLIXX, THE PILOT IS A LOYAL MEMBER OF MY CREW - HE WOULD NEVER DO ANYTHING TO HARM HIS BRILLIANT CAPTAIN...
LOOM
DVDVNCFS!
AAH! THE PILOT'S GONE BESERK!
HE'S EATING ME ALIVE!
THE PAIN! THE PAIN! THE...
YOU KNOW, YOU COULD DO SOMETHING OTHER THAN JUST STANDING THERE.
WE DIDN'T WANT TO INTERRUPT.
I BROUGHT POPCORN!
QUICKLY, PLIXX, USE THE EMERGENCY SEDATIVE!
OH, GOOD IDEA, CAPTAIN!
NAP TIME!
INJECT!
THAT'S NOT QUITE WHAT I...NEVER MIND...
SIGH ... ROBOT ONE, COULD YOU DO IT?
UGH, I HAVE TO DO EVERYTHING AROUND HERE!
ZZZ
THANK YOU ... BUT WHAT COULD BE INSIDE THE POD THAT MADE THE PILOT GO BESERK?
ULP - I THINK WE'RE ABOUT TO FIND OUT, CAPTAIN...
BRUSH
FLOP
CRACK!
IT'S OPENING!
FTDBMPQFFFFF
GASP! KITTENS! THE PILOT, HE'S HAD KITTENS!
MY ADVANCED ROBOTIC DATABASE INDICATES THAT THIS PROBABLY MEANS THAT HE'S NOT A ... "HE."
NFX
NFX
NFX

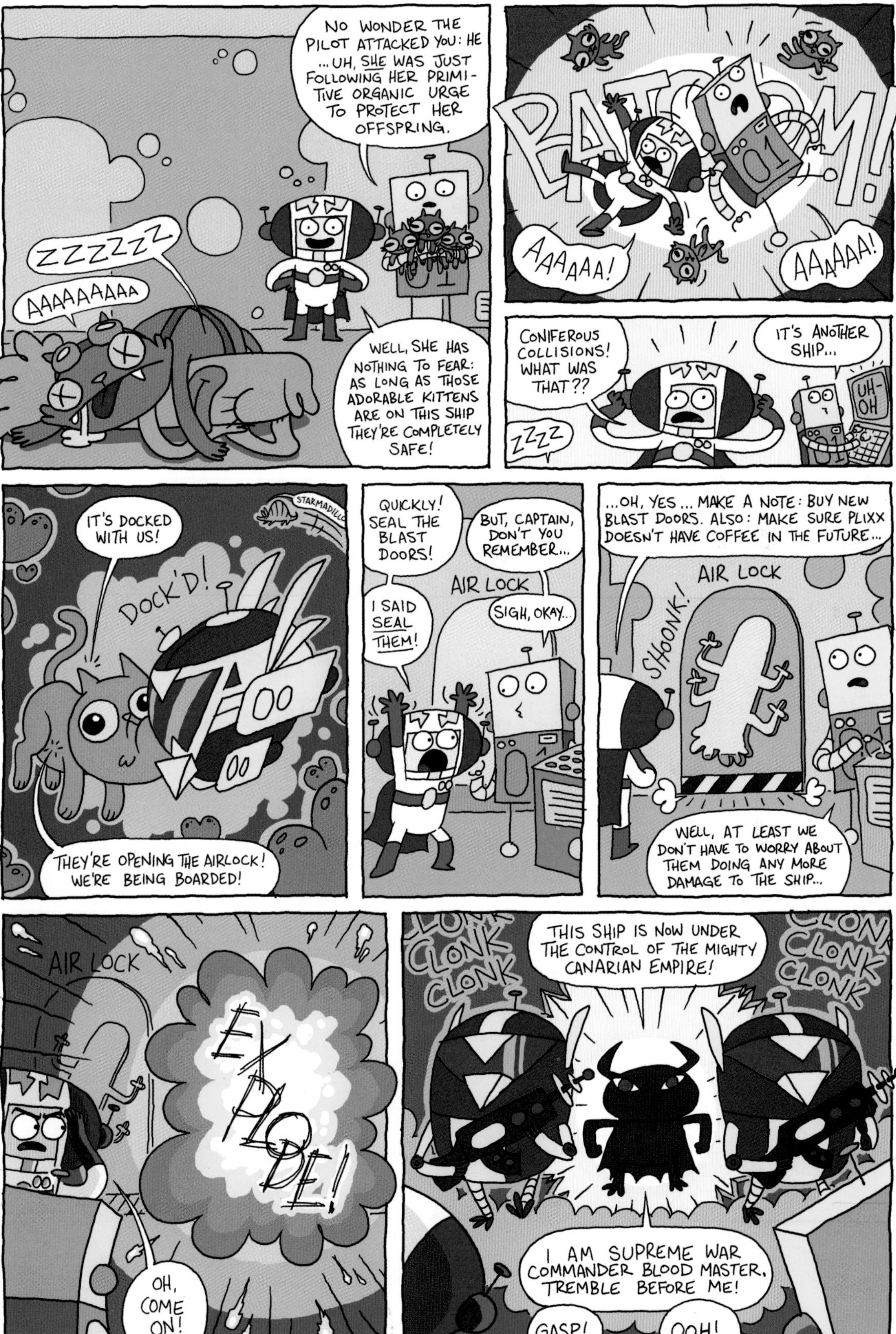
NO WONDER THE PILOT ATTACKED YOU: HE ...UH, SHE WAS JUST FOLLOWING HER PRIMITIVE ORGANIC URGE TO PROTECT HER OFFSPRING.
ZZZZZZ
AAAAAAAAA
WELL, SHE HAS NOTHING TO FEAR: AS LONG AS THOSE ADORABLE KITTENS ARE ON THIS SHIP THEY'RE COMPLETELY SAFE!
BATOOM!
AAAAAA!
AAAAAA!
CONIFEROUS COLLISIONS! WHAT WAS THAT??
IT'S ANOTHER SHIP...
UH-OH
ZZZZ
IT'S DOCKED WITH US!
STARMADILLO
DOCK'D!
THEY'RE OPENING THE AIRLOCK! WE'RE BEING BOARDED!
QUICKLY! SEAL THE BLAST DOORS!
BUT, CAPTAIN, DON'T YOU REMEMBER...
AIR LOCK
I SAID SEAL THEM!
SIGH, OKAY...
...OH, YES... MAKE A NOTE: BUY NEW BLAST DOORS. ALSO: MAKE SURE PLIXX DOESN'T HAVE COFFEE IN THE FUTURE...
AIR LOCK
SHOONK!
WELL, AT LEAST WE DON'T HAVE TO WORRY ABOUT THEM DOING ANY MORE DAMAGE TO THE SHIP...
AIR LOCK
EXPLODE!
OH, COME ON!
CLONK CLONK CLONK
THIS SHIP IS NOW UNDER THE CONTROL OF THE MIGHTY CANARIAN EMPIRE!
CLONK CLONK CLONK
I AM SUPREME WAR COMMANDER BLOOD MASTER. TREMBLE BEFORE ME!
GASP!
OOH!

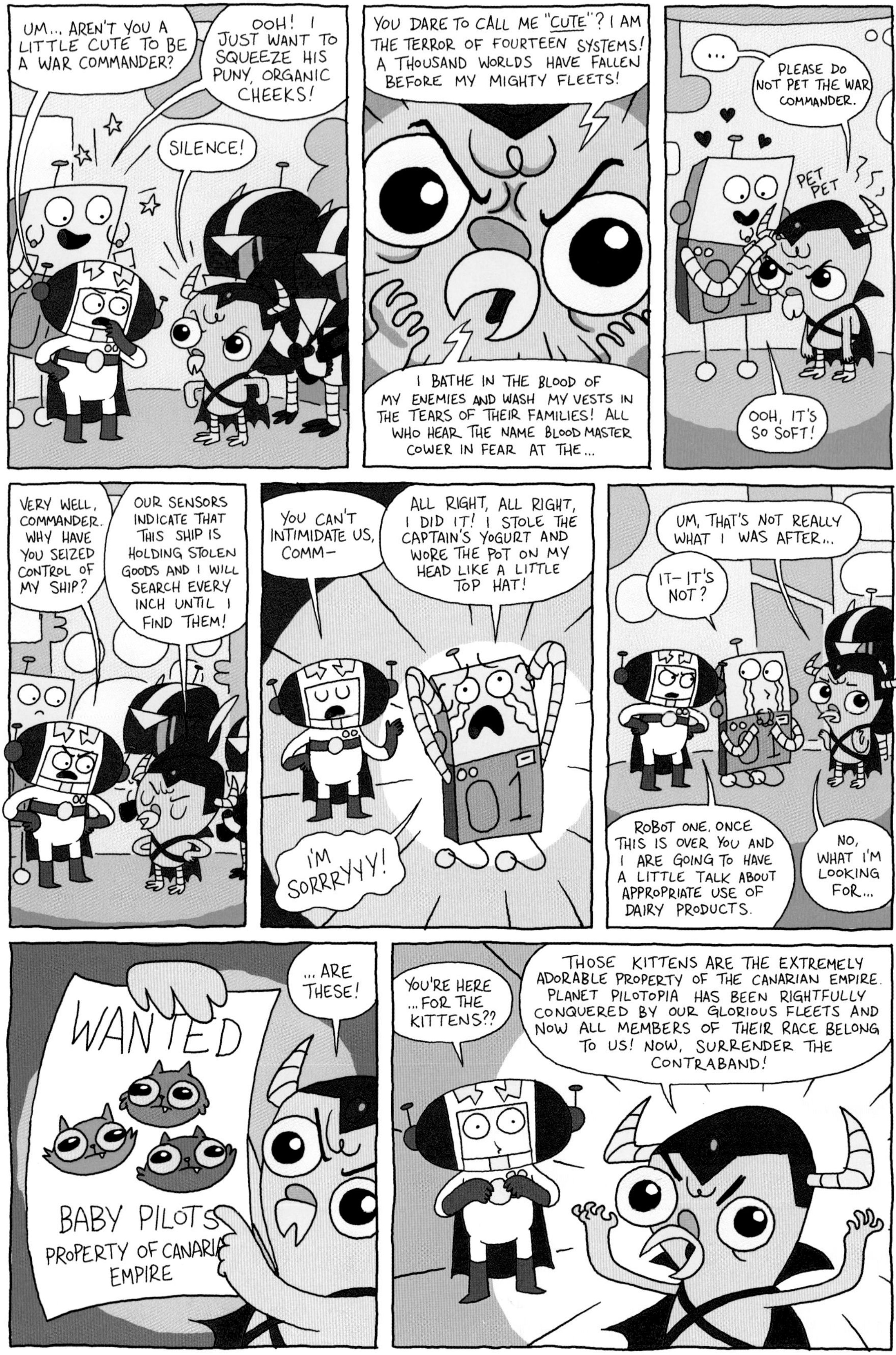
UM... AREN'T YOU A LITTLE CUTE TO BE A WAR COMMANDER?
OOH! I JUST WANT TO SQUEEZE HIS PUNY, ORGANIC CHEEKS!
SILENCE!
YOU DARE TO CALL ME "CUTE"? I AM THE TERROR OF FOURTEEN SYSTEMS! A THOUSAND WORLDS HAVE FALLEN BEFORE MY MIGHTY FLEETS!
I BATHE IN THE BLOOD OF MY ENEMIES AND WASH MY VESTS IN THE TEARS OF THEIR FAMILIES! ALL WHO HEAR THE NAME BLOOD MASTER COWER IN FEAR AT THE...
...
PLEASE DO NOT PET THE WAR COMMANDER.
PET PET
OOH, IT'S SO SOFT!
VERY WELL, COMMANDER. WHY HAVE YOU SEIZED CONTROL OF MY SHIP?
OUR SENSORS INDICATE THAT THIS SHIP IS HOLDING STOLEN GOODS AND I WILL SEARCH EVERY INCH UNTIL I FIND THEM!
YOU CAN'T INTIMIDATE US, COMM–
ALL RIGHT, ALL RIGHT, I DID IT! I STOLE THE CAPTAIN'S YOGURT AND WORE THE POT ON MY HEAD LIKE A LITTLE TOP HAT!
I'M SORRRYYY!
UM, THAT'S NOT REALLY WHAT I WAS AFTER...
IT– IT'S NOT?
ROBOT ONE, ONCE THIS IS OVER YOU AND I ARE GOING TO HAVE A LITTLE TALK ABOUT APPROPRIATE USE OF DAIRY PRODUCTS.
NO, WHAT I'M LOOKING FOR...
...ARE THESE!
WANTED
BABY PILOTS
PROPERTY OF CANARIA EMPIRE
YOU'RE HERE ...FOR THE KITTENS??
THOSE KITTENS ARE THE EXTREMELY ADORABLE PROPERTY OF THE CANARIAN EMPIRE. PLANET PILOTOPIA HAS BEEN RIGHTFULLY CONQUERED BY OUR GLORIOUS FLEETS AND NOW ALL MEMBERS OF THEIR RACE BELONG TO US! NOW, SURRENDER THE CONTRABAND!

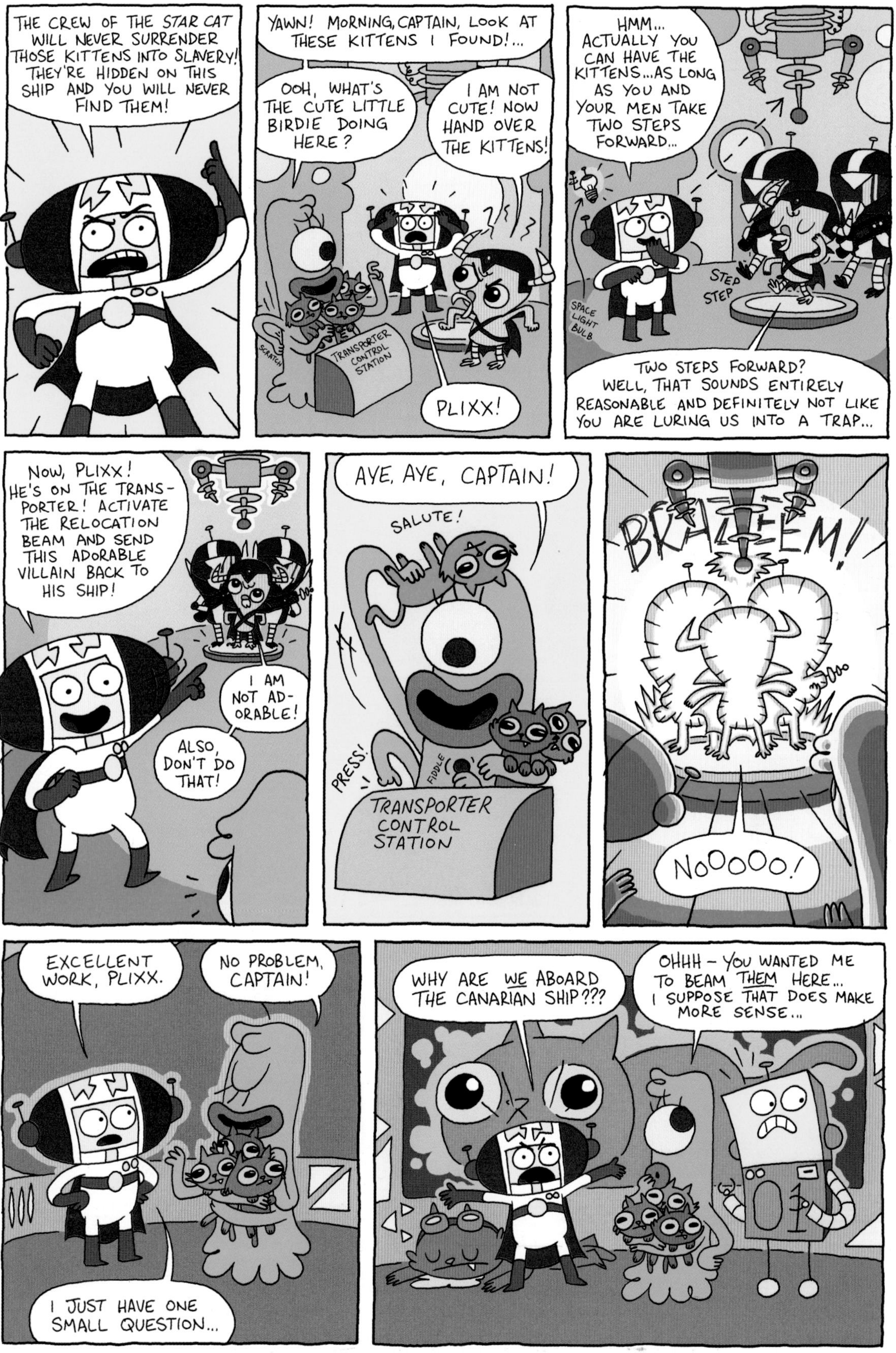
THE CREW OF THE STAR CAT WILL NEVER SURRENDER THOSE KITTENS INTO SLAVERY! THEY'RE HIDDEN ON THIS SHIP AND YOU WILL NEVER FIND THEM!
YAWN! MORNING, CAPTAIN, LOOK AT THESE KITTENS I FOUND!...
OOH, WHAT'S THE CUTE LITTLE BIRDIE DOING HERE?
I AM NOT CUTE! NOW HAND OVER THE KITTENS!
SCRATCH
TRANSPORTER CONTROL STATION
PLIXX!
HMM... ACTUALLY YOU CAN HAVE THE KITTENS...AS LONG AS YOU AND YOUR MEN TAKE TWO STEPS FORWARD...
SPACE LIGHT BULB
STEP
STEP
TWO STEPS FORWARD? WELL, THAT SOUNDS ENTIRELY REASONABLE AND DEFINITELY NOT LIKE YOU ARE LURING US INTO A TRAP...
NOW, PLIXX! HE'S ON THE TRANSPORTER! ACTIVATE THE RELOCATION BEAM AND SEND THIS ADORABLE VILLAIN BACK TO HIS SHIP!
I AM NOT ADORABLE!
ALSO, DON'T DO THAT!
AYE, AYE, CAPTAIN!
SALUTE!
PRESS!
FIDDLE
TRANSPORTER CONTROL STATION
NOOOOO!
EXCELLENT WORK, PLIXX.
NO PROBLEM, CAPTAIN!
I JUST HAVE ONE SMALL QUESTION...
WHY ARE WE ABOARD THE CANARIAN SHIP???
OHHH - YOU WANTED ME TO BEAM THEM HERE... I SUPPOSE THAT DOES MAKE MORE SENSE...

ULP!

INTRUDERS! YOU HAVE ILLEGALLY BOARDED A CANARIAN BATTLESHIP! SURRENDER YOURSELVES IMMEDIATELY! AND DON'T TOUCH MY STUFF!

OKAY, DON'T WORRY, CREW — IF WE CAN FIND OUR WAY TO THE CENTRAL CONTROL ROOM WE CAN DISENGAGE THE DOCKING CLAMPS AND FREE THE STAR CAT. IT'S OUR ONLY CHANCE TO ESCAPE!

LET'S GO!

BUT, CAPTAIN, THE SHIP IS FULL OF CANARIAN TROOPERS! HOW WILL WE GET PAST THEM?

FIND THE INTRUDERS!

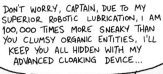

DON'T WORRY, CAPTAIN, DUE TO MY SUPERIOR ROBOTIC LUBRICATION, I AM 100,000 TIMES MORE SNEAKY THAN YOU CLUMSY ORGANIC ENTITIES, I'LL KEEP YOU ALL HIDDEN WITH MY ADVANCED CLOAKING DEVICE...

STEALTH MODE ACTIVATE!

OPEN!

PRESS!

IT'S UNFOLDING INTO SOMETHING...

IT'S AMAZING! IT'S... IT'S...

WHIRR

CLANK!

...IT'S A CARD-BOARD BOX.

TOTALLY NORMAL BOX (HONEST)

QUICKLY, ENTER THE STEALTH UNIT!

AND SO...

YOU KNOW, I CAN'T BELIEVE WE DIDN'T REALIZE THAT THE PILOT WAS FEMALE ALL ALONG...

THERE'S STILL NO SIGN OF THEM...

KEEP LOOKING!

HELLOOO? INTRUDERS?

TOTALLY NORMAL BOX (HONEST)

THIS WAY UP

I KNOW — USUALLY MY ADVANCED GENDER DETECTION SYSTEMS CAN PICK UP EVEN THE MOST SUBTLE INDICATIONS...

LIKE YOU CAN TELL PLIXX IS A GIRL BECAUSE SHE HAS THOSE BIG FLAPPY EYELASHES.

EYELASHES? I DON'T HAVE EYE...

?

AAAAH! EYELID SPIDER!

GAH! RUMBLED!

LEAP

PLIXX!

OOPS...

HALT! SURRENDER, INTRUDERS!

DON'T WORRY, CAPTAIN, MY ADVANCED ROBOTIC BRAIN HAS ANALYZED THE CANARIAN RACE AND NEAR-INSTANTANEOUSLY COME UP WITH THE PERFECT DISTRACTION.

SCUTTLE

TOTALLY NOR... BOX (HONEST)

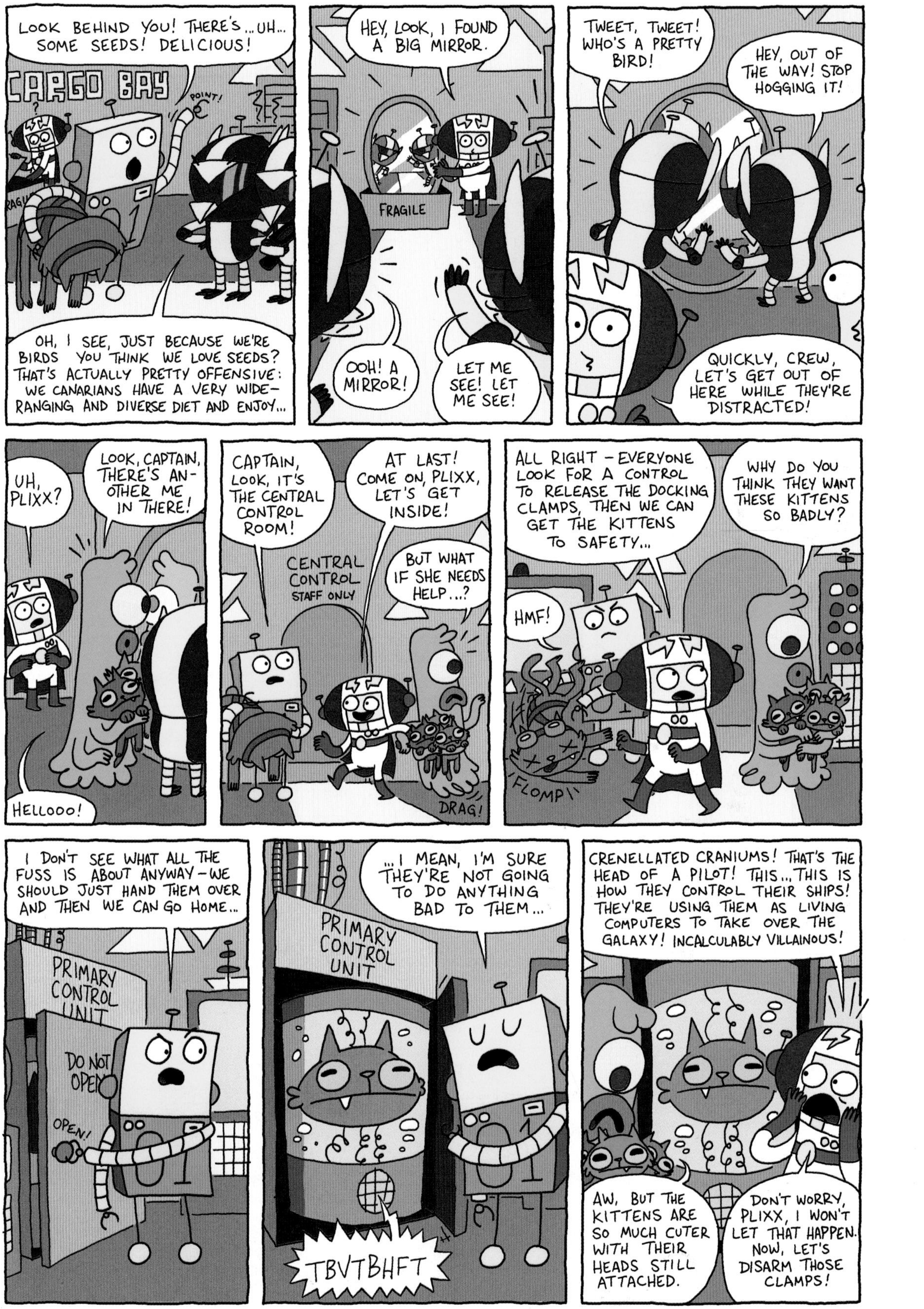
LOOK BEHIND YOU! THERE'S... UH... SOME SEEDS! DELICIOUS!
CARGO BAY
POINT!
OH, I SEE, JUST BECAUSE WE'RE BIRDS YOU THINK WE LOVE SEEDS? THAT'S ACTUALLY PRETTY OFFENSIVE: WE CANARIANS HAVE A VERY WIDE-RANGING AND DIVERSE DIET AND ENJOY...
HEY, LOOK, I FOUND A BIG MIRROR.
FRAGILE
OOH! A MIRROR!
LET ME SEE! LET ME SEE!
TWEET, TWEET! WHO'S A PRETTY BIRD!
HEY, OUT OF THE WAY! STOP HOGGING IT!
QUICKLY, CREW, LET'S GET OUT OF HERE WHILE THEY'RE DISTRACTED!
UH, PLIXX?
LOOK, CAPTAIN, THERE'S AN-OTHER ME IN THERE!
HELLOOO!
CAPTAIN, LOOK, IT'S THE CENTRAL CONTROL ROOM!
AT LAST! COME ON, PLIXX, LET'S GET INSIDE!
CENTRAL CONTROL STAFF ONLY
BUT WHAT IF SHE NEEDS HELP...?
DRAG!
ALL RIGHT - EVERYONE LOOK FOR A CONTROL TO RELEASE THE DOCKING CLAMPS, THEN WE CAN GET THE KITTENS TO SAFETY...
WHY DO YOU THINK THEY WANT THESE KITTENS SO BADLY?
HMF!
FLOMP
I DON'T SEE WHAT ALL THE FUSS IS ABOUT ANYWAY - WE SHOULD JUST HAND THEM OVER AND THEN WE CAN GO HOME...
PRIMARY CONTROL UNIT
DO NOT OPEN
OPEN!
...I MEAN, I'M SURE THEY'RE NOT GOING TO DO ANYTHING BAD TO THEM...
PRIMARY CONTROL UNIT
TBVTBHFT
CRENELLATED CRANIUMS! THAT'S THE HEAD OF A PILOT! THIS... THIS IS HOW THEY CONTROL THEIR SHIPS! THEY'RE USING THEM AS LIVING COMPUTERS TO TAKE OVER THE GALAXY! INCALCULABLY VILLAINOUS!
AW, BUT THE KITTENS ARE SO MUCH CUTER WITH THEIR HEADS STILL ATTACHED.
DON'T WORRY, PLIXX, I WON'T LET THAT HAPPEN. NOW, LET'S DISARM THOSE CLAMPS!

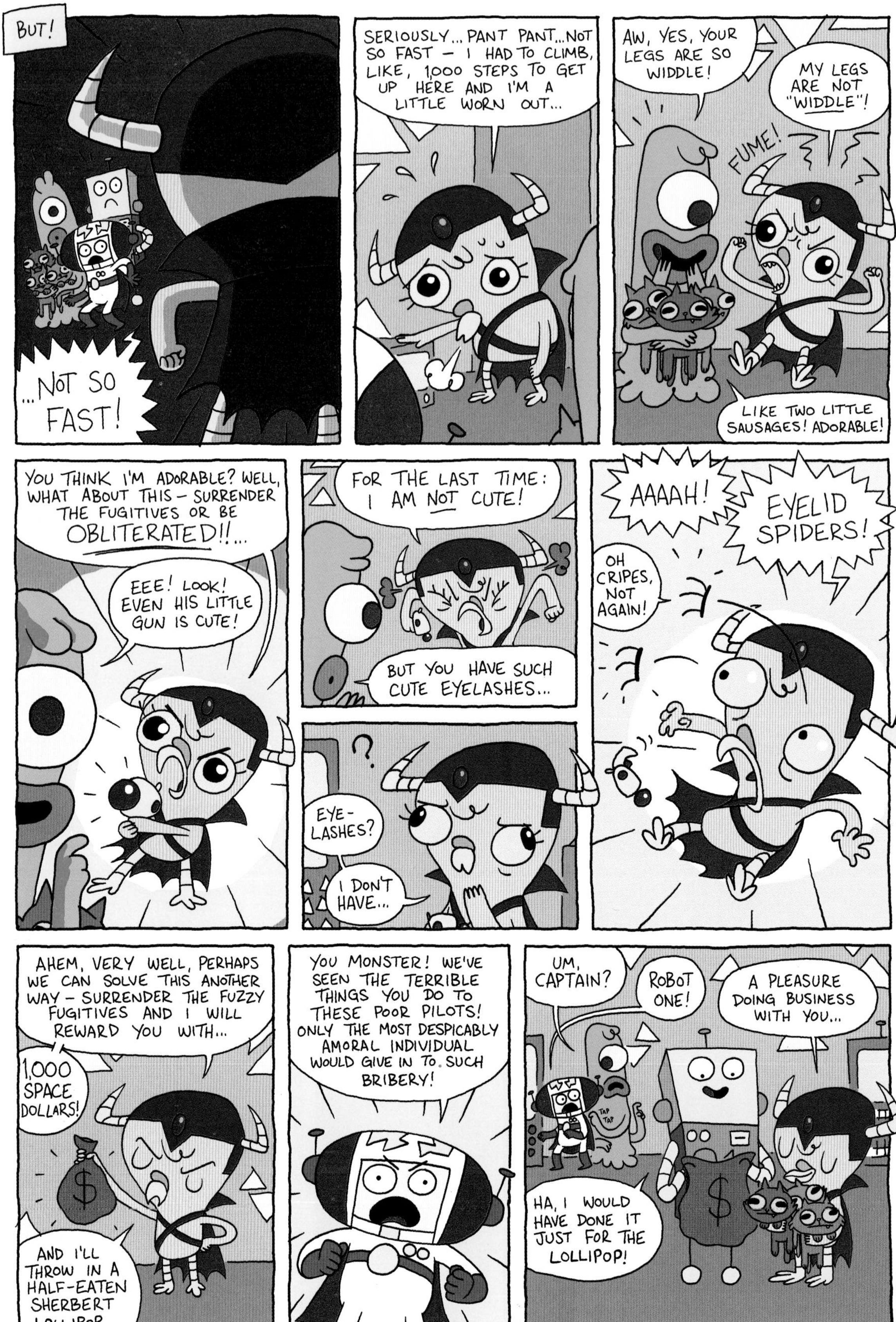
BUT!
...NOT SO FAST!
SERIOUSLY... PANT PANT...NOT SO FAST – I HAD TO CLIMB, LIKE, 1,000 STEPS TO GET UP HERE AND I'M A LITTLE WORN OUT...
AW, YES, YOUR LEGS ARE SO WIDDLE!
MY LEGS ARE NOT "WIDDLE"!
FUME!
LIKE TWO LITTLE SAUSAGES! ADORABLE!
YOU THINK I'M ADORABLE? WELL, WHAT ABOUT THIS – SURRENDER THE FUGITIVES OR BE OBLITERATED!!...
EEE! LOOK! EVEN HIS LITTLE GUN IS CUTE!
FOR THE LAST TIME: I AM NOT CUTE!
BUT YOU HAVE SUCH CUTE EYELASHES...
?
EYE-LASHES?
I DON'T HAVE...
AAAAH!
EYELID SPIDERS!
OH CRIPES, NOT AGAIN!
AHEM, VERY WELL, PERHAPS WE CAN SOLVE THIS ANOTHER WAY – SURRENDER THE FUZZY FUGITIVES AND I WILL REWARD YOU WITH...
1,000 SPACE DOLLARS!
$
AND I'LL THROW IN A HALF-EATEN SHERBERT LOLLIPOP.
YOU MONSTER! WE'VE SEEN THE TERRIBLE THINGS YOU DO TO THESE POOR PILOTS! ONLY THE MOST DESPICABLY AMORAL INDIVIDUAL WOULD GIVE IN TO SUCH BRIBERY!
UM, CAPTAIN?
ROBOT ONE!
A PLEASURE DOING BUSINESS WITH YOU...
TAP TAP
$
HA, I WOULD HAVE DONE IT JUST FOR THE LOLLIPOP!

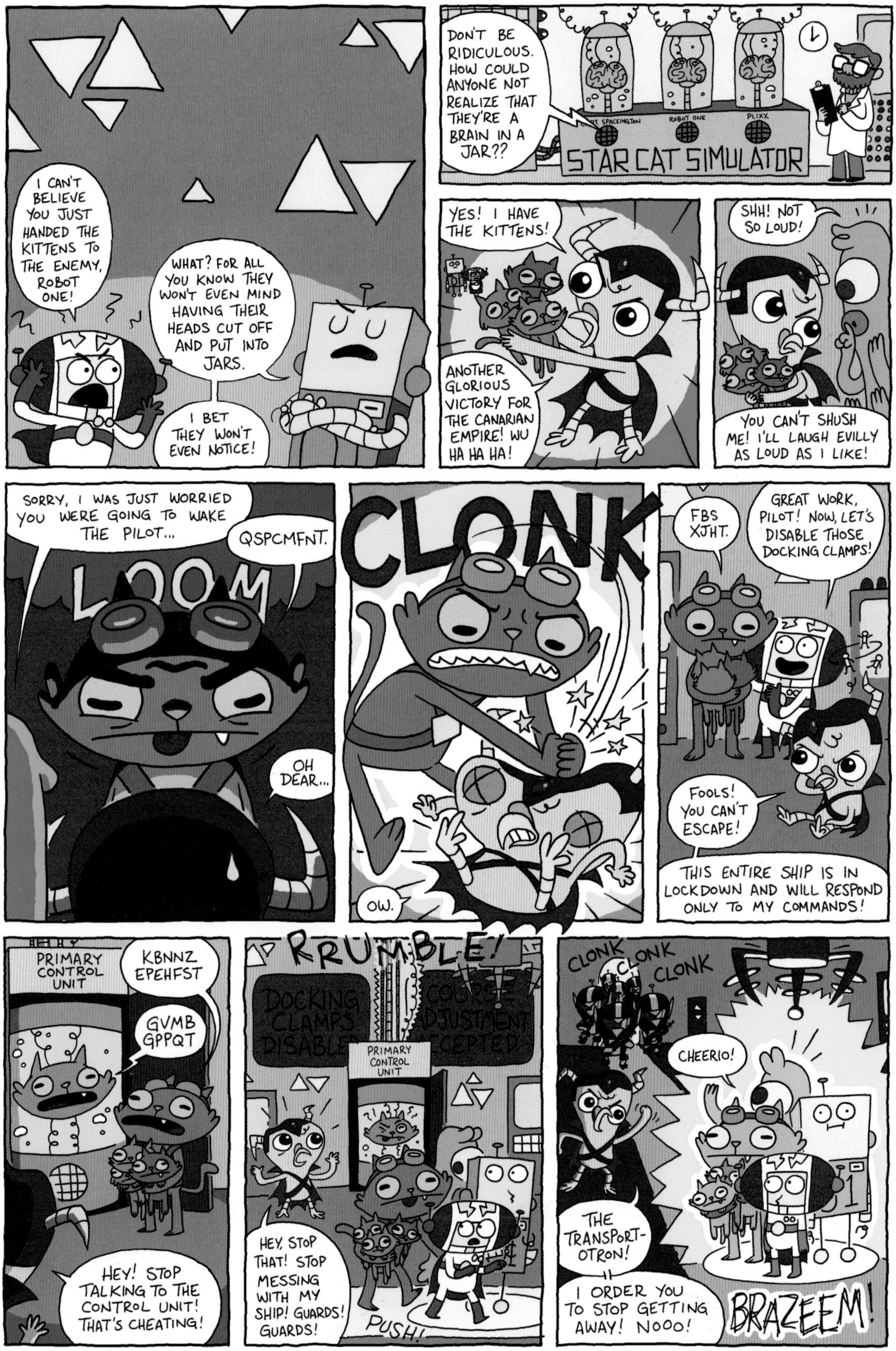
I CAN'T BELIEVE YOU JUST HANDED THE KITTENS TO THE ENEMY, ROBOT ONE!
WHAT? FOR ALL YOU KNOW THEY WON'T EVEN MIND HAVING THEIR HEADS CUT OFF AND PUT INTO JARS.
I BET THEY WON'T EVEN NOTICE!
DON'T BE RIDICULOUS. HOW COULD ANYONE NOT REALIZE THAT THEY'RE A BRAIN IN A JAR??
ROBOT ONE
PLIXX
STAR CAT SIMULATOR
YES! I HAVE THE KITTENS!
ANOTHER GLORIOUS VICTORY FOR THE CANARIAN EMPIRE! WU HA HA HA!
SHH! NOT SO LOUD!
YOU CAN'T SHUSH ME! I'LL LAUGH EVILLY AS LOUD AS I LIKE!
SORRY, I WAS JUST WORRIED YOU WERE GOING TO WAKE THE PILOT...
QSPCMFNT.
LOOM
OH DEAR...
CLONK
OW.
FBS XJHT.
GREAT WORK, PILOT! NOW, LET'S DISABLE THOSE DOCKING CLAMPS!
FOOLS! YOU CAN'T ESCAPE!
THIS ENTIRE SHIP IS IN LOCKDOWN AND WILL RESPOND ONLY TO MY COMMANDS!
PRIMARY CONTROL UNIT
KBNNZ EPEHFST
GVMB GPPQT
HEY! STOP TALKING TO THE CONTROL UNIT! THAT'S CHEATING!
RRUMBLE!
DOCKING CLAMPS DISABLED
COURSE ADJUSTMENT ACCEPTED
PRIMARY CONTROL UNIT
HEY, STOP THAT! STOP MESSING WITH MY SHIP! GUARDS! GUARDS!
PUSH!
CLONK CLONK CLONK
CHEERIO!
THE TRANSPORT-OTRON!
I ORDER YOU TO STOP GETTING AWAY! NOOO!
BRAZEEM!

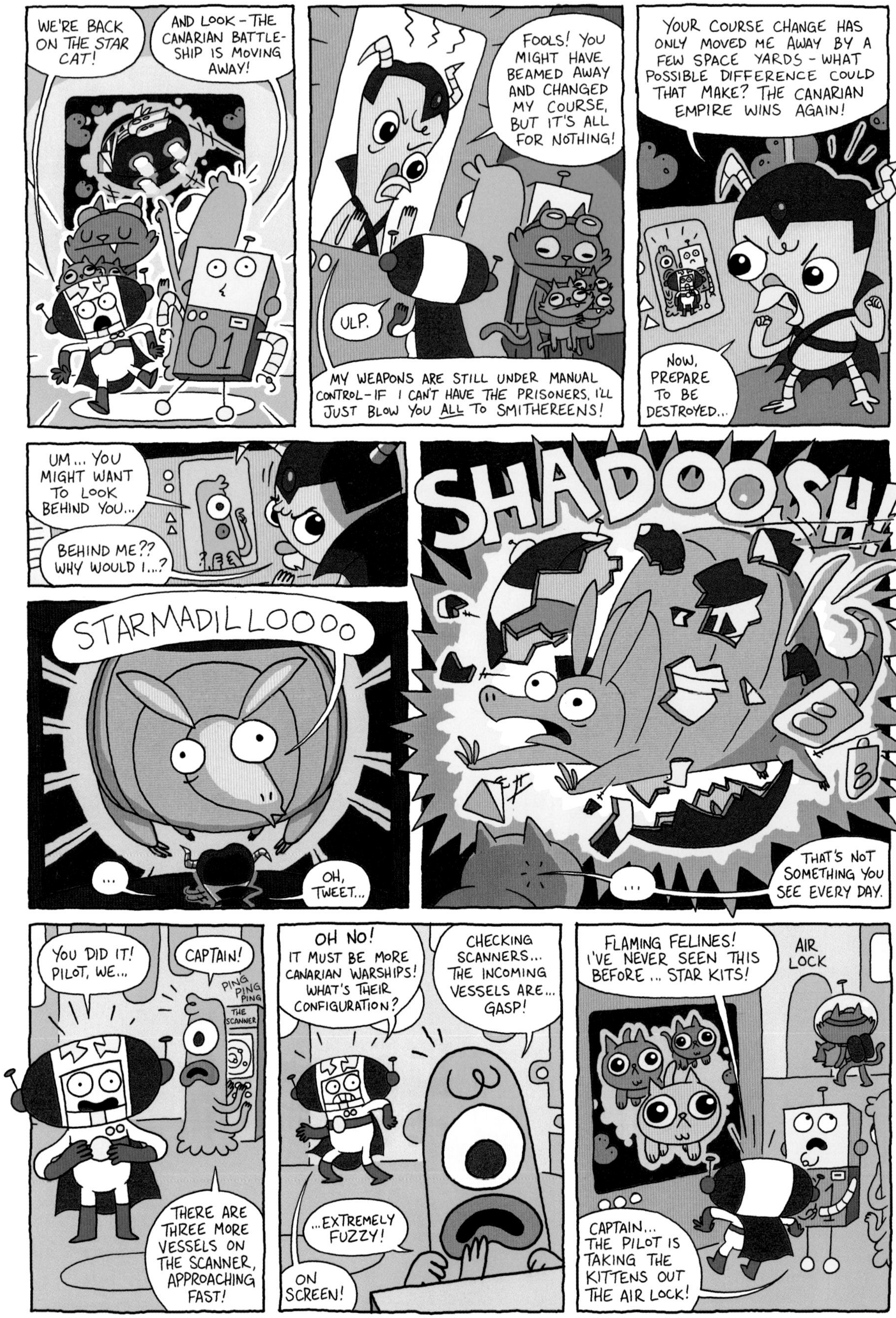
WE'RE BACK ON THE STAR CAT!
AND LOOK - THE CANARIAN BATTLESHIP IS MOVING AWAY!
FOOLS! YOU MIGHT HAVE BEAMED AWAY AND CHANGED MY COURSE, BUT IT'S ALL FOR NOTHING!
ULP.
MY WEAPONS ARE STILL UNDER MANUAL CONTROL - IF I CAN'T HAVE THE PRISONERS, I'LL JUST BLOW YOU ALL TO SMITHEREENS!
YOUR COURSE CHANGE HAS ONLY MOVED ME AWAY BY A FEW SPACE YARDS - WHAT POSSIBLE DIFFERENCE COULD THAT MAKE? THE CANARIAN EMPIRE WINS AGAIN!
NOW, PREPARE TO BE DESTROYED...
UM... YOU MIGHT WANT TO LOOK BEHIND YOU...
BEHIND ME?? WHY WOULD I...?
STARMADILLOOOO
...
OH, TWEET...
SHADOOSH!!
...
THAT'S NOT SOMETHING YOU SEE EVERY DAY.
YOU DID IT! PILOT, WE...
CAPTAIN!
PING PING PING
THE SCANNER
THERE ARE THREE MORE VESSELS ON THE SCANNER, APPROACHING FAST!
OH NO! IT MUST BE MORE CANARIAN WARSHIPS! WHAT'S THEIR CONFIGURATION?
CHECKING SCANNERS... THE INCOMING VESSELS ARE... GASP!
...EXTREMELY FUZZY!
ON SCREEN!
FLAMING FELINES! I'VE NEVER SEEN THIS BEFORE... STAR KITS!
AIR LOCK
CAPTAIN... THE PILOT IS TAKING THE KITTENS OUT THE AIR LOCK!

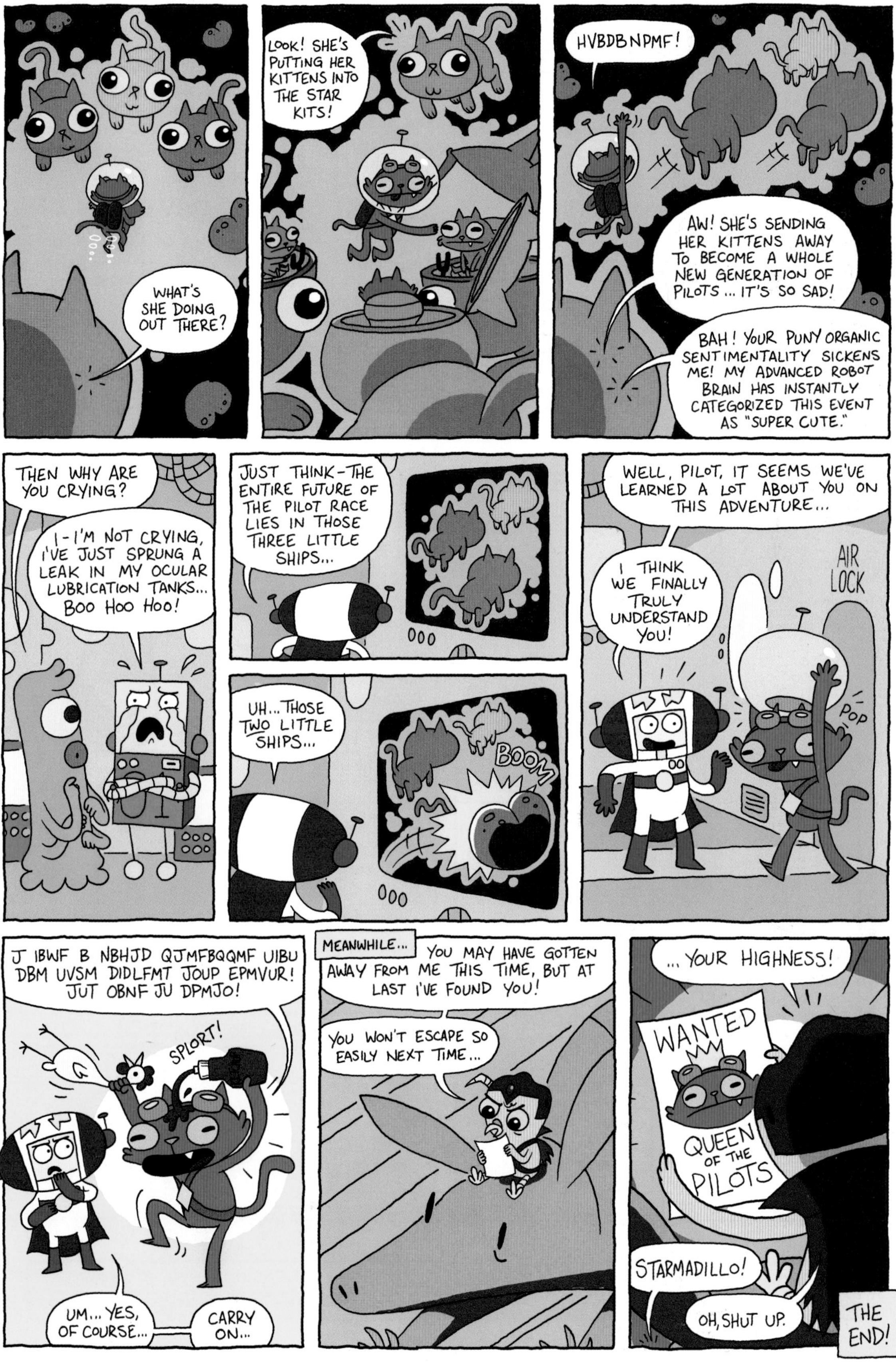
WHAT'S SHE DOING OUT THERE?
LOOK! SHE'S PUTTING HER KITTENS INTO THE STAR KITS!
HVBDBNPMF!
AW! SHE'S SENDING HER KITTENS AWAY TO BECOME A WHOLE NEW GENERATION OF PILOTS ... IT'S SO SAD!
BAH! YOUR PUNY ORGANIC SENTIMENTALITY SICKENS ME! MY ADVANCED ROBOT BRAIN HAS INSTANTLY CATEGORIZED THIS EVENT AS "SUPER CUTE."
THEN WHY ARE YOU CRYING?
I-I'M NOT CRYING, I'VE JUST SPRUNG A LEAK IN MY OCULAR LUBRICATION TANKS... BOO HOO HOO!
JUST THINK–THE ENTIRE FUTURE OF THE PILOT RACE LIES IN THOSE THREE LITTLE SHIPS...
UH... THOSE TWO LITTLE SHIPS...
BOOM
WELL, PILOT, IT SEEMS WE'VE LEARNED A LOT ABOUT YOU ON THIS ADVENTURE...
I THINK WE FINALLY TRULY UNDERSTAND YOU!
AIR LOCK
POP
J IBWF B NBHJD QJMFBQQMF UIBU DBM UVSM DIDLFMT JOUP EPMVUR! JUT OBNF JU DPMJO!
SPLORT!
UM... YES, OF COURSE...
CARRY ON...
MEANWHILE...
YOU MAY HAVE GOTTEN AWAY FROM ME THIS TIME, BUT AT LAST I'VE FOUND YOU!
YOU WON'T ESCAPE SO EASILY NEXT TIME...
... YOUR HIGHNESS!
WANTED
QUEEN OF THE PILOTS
STARMADILLO!
OH, SHUT UP.
THE END!

Squid Bits!

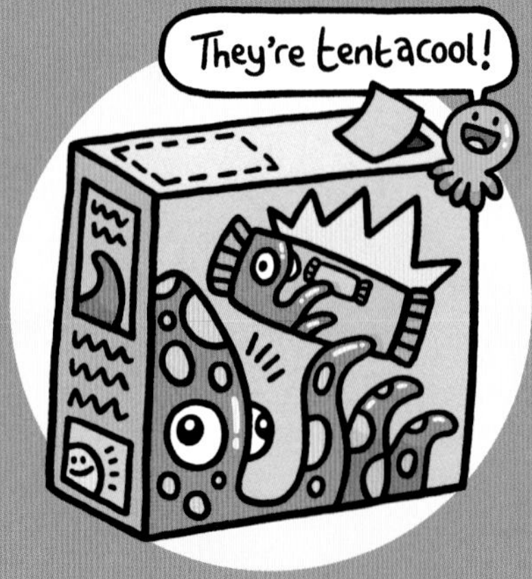
They're tentacool!

EVERY DELICIOUS BOX OF SQUID BITS INCLUDES ALL THIS AND MORE...

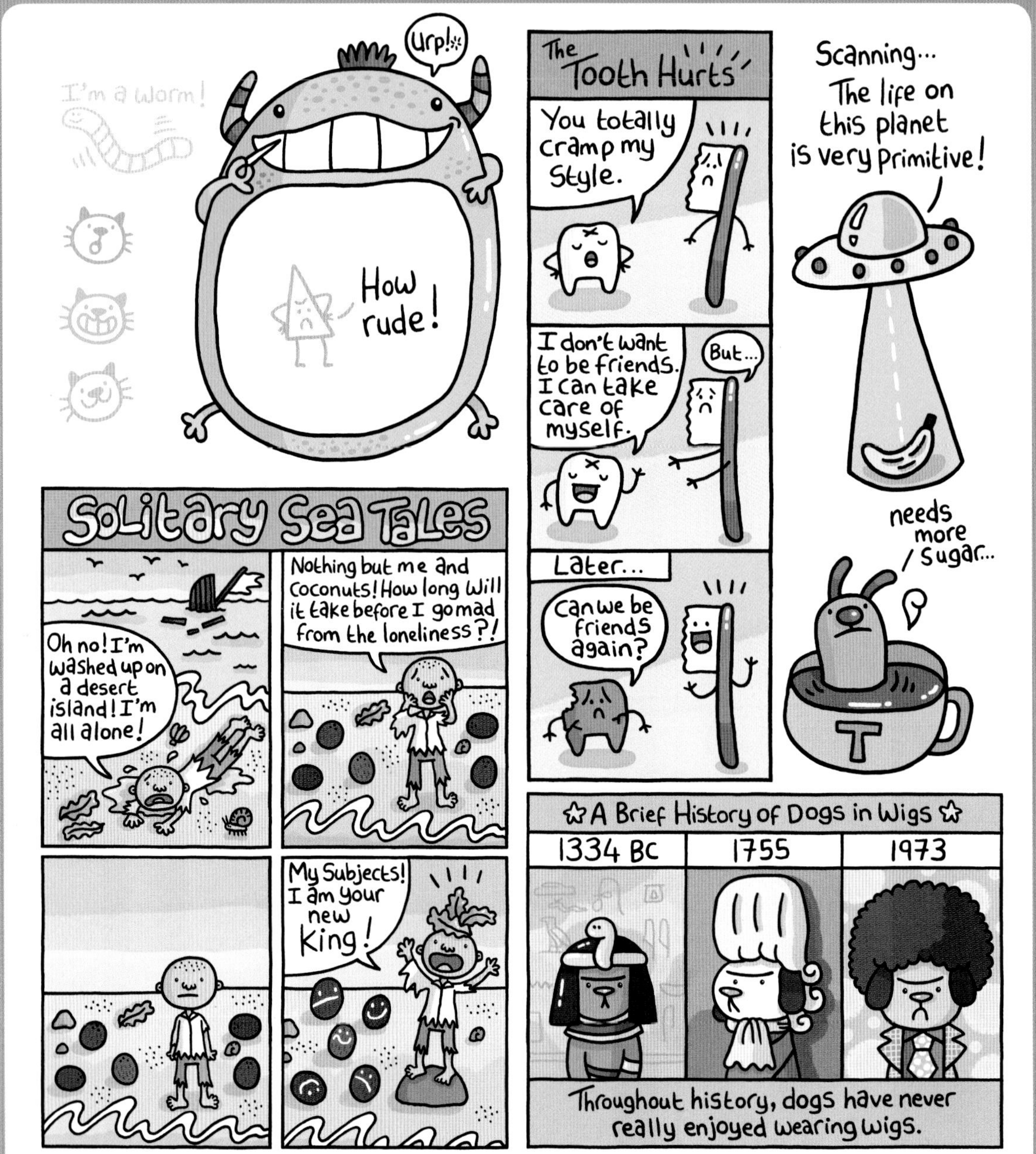
Urp!
I'm a worm!
How rude!
The Tooth Hurts
You totally cramp my style.
I don't want to be friends. I can take care of myself.
But...
Later...
Can we be friends again?
Scanning... The life on this planet is very primitive!
needs more sugar...
T
Solitary Sea Tales
Oh no! I'm washed up on a desert island! I'm all alone!
Nothing but me and coconuts! How long will it take before I go mad from the loneliness?!
My subjects! I am your new King!
A Brief History of Dogs in Wigs
1334 BC
1755
1973
Throughout history, dogs have never really enjoyed wearing wigs.

by Jess Bradley

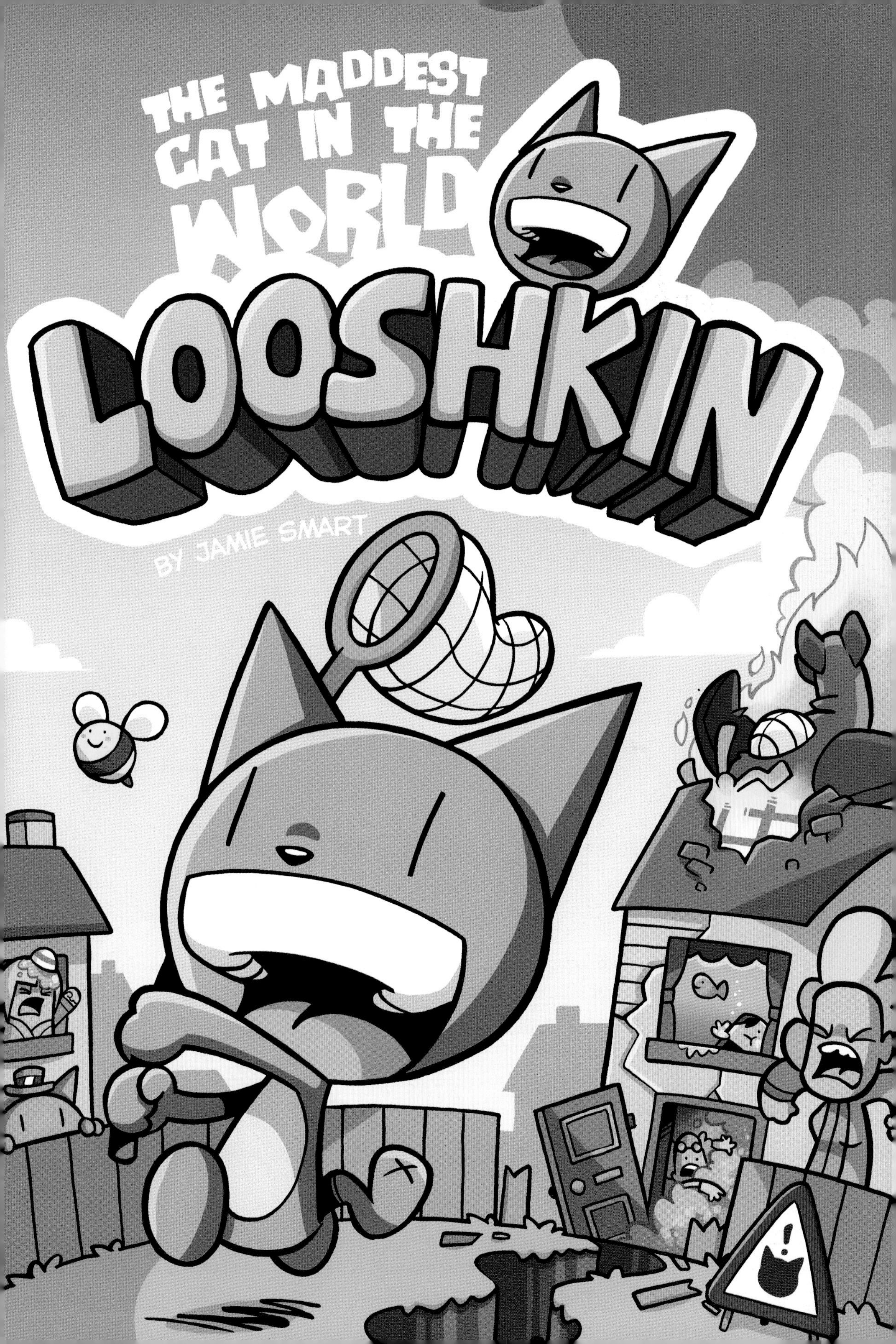

THE MADDEST CAT IN THE WORLD
LOOSHKIN
BY JAMIE SMART

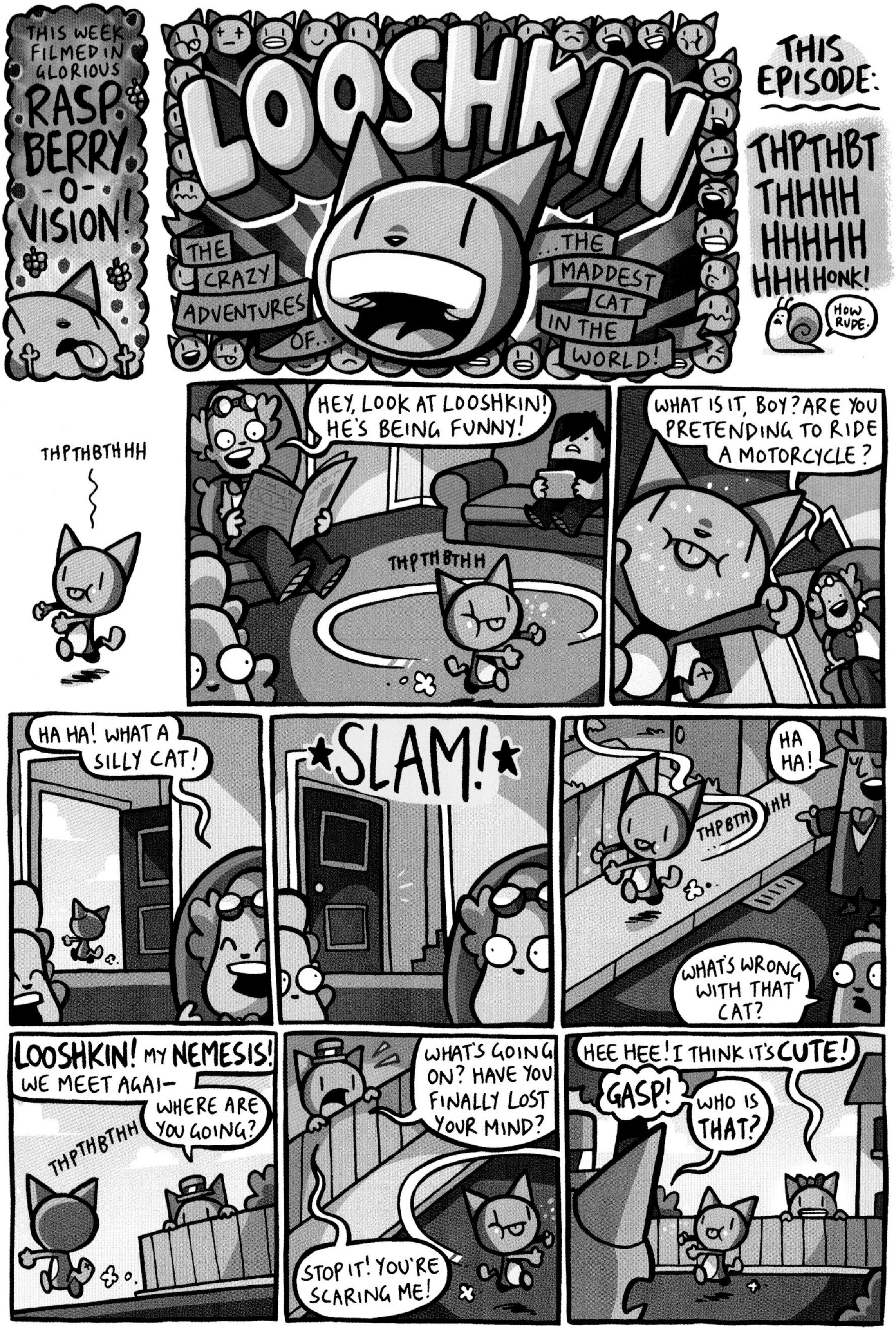
THIS WEEK FILMED IN GLORIOUS RASPBERRY-O-VISION!
LOOSHKIN
THE CRAZY ADVENTURES OF... ...THE MADDEST CAT IN THE WORLD!
THIS EPISODE:
THPTHBT THHHH HHHHH HHHHONK!
HOW RUDE.
THPTHBTHHH
HEY, LOOK AT LOOSHKIN! HE'S BEING FUNNY!
THPTHBTHH
WHAT IS IT, BOY? ARE YOU PRETENDING TO RIDE A MOTORCYCLE?
HA HA! WHAT A SILLY CAT!
SLAM!
HA HA!
THPBTHHHH
WHAT'S WRONG WITH THAT CAT?
LOOSHKIN! MY NEMESIS! WE MEET AGAI-
WHERE ARE YOU GOING?
THPTHBTHH
WHAT'S GOING ON? HAVE YOU FINALLY LOST YOUR MIND?
STOP IT! YOU'RE SCARING ME!
HEE HEE! I THINK IT'S CUTE!
GASP!
WHO IS THAT?

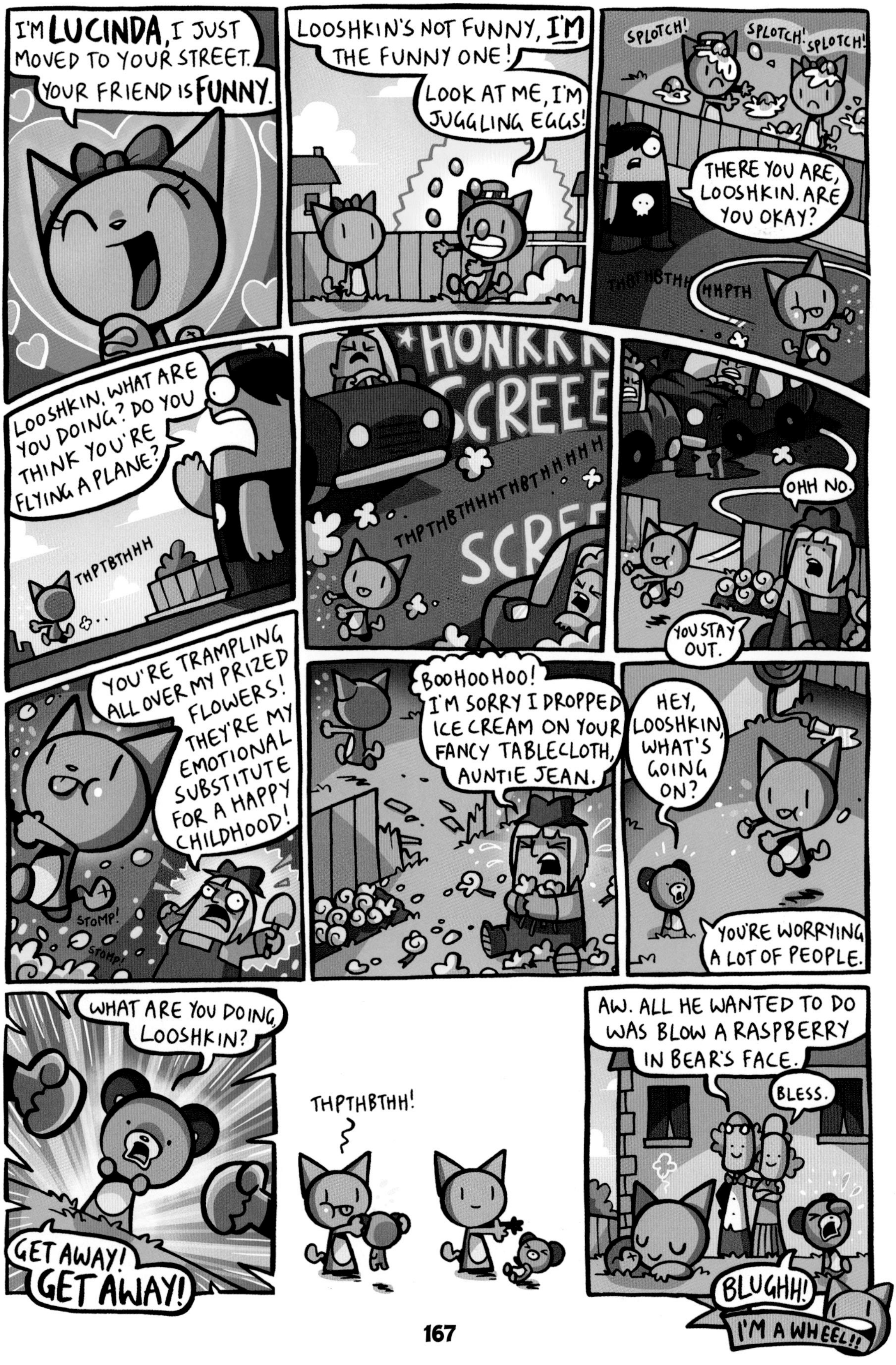

I'M LUCINDA, I JUST MOVED TO YOUR STREET.
YOUR FRIEND IS FUNNY.
LOOSHKIN'S NOT FUNNY, I'M THE FUNNY ONE!
LOOK AT ME, I'M JUGGLING EGGS!
SPLOTCH!
SPLOTCH!
SPLOTCH!
THERE YOU ARE, LOOSHKIN. ARE YOU OKAY?
THPTHBTHHHHHPTH
LOOSHKIN, WHAT ARE YOU DOING? DO YOU THINK YOU'RE FLYING A PLANE?
THPTBTHHH
HONKKK
SCREEE
THPTHBTHHHTHBTHHHHH
SCREE
OHH NO.
YOU STAY OUT.
YOU'RE TRAMPLING ALL OVER MY PRIZED FLOWERS! THEY'RE MY EMOTIONAL SUBSTITUTE FOR A HAPPY CHILDHOOD!
STOMP!
STOMP!
BOOHOOHOO! I'M SORRY I DROPPED ICE CREAM ON YOUR FANCY TABLECLOTH, AUNTIE JEAN.
HEY, LOOSHKIN, WHAT'S GOING ON?
YOU'RE WORRYING A LOT OF PEOPLE.
WHAT ARE YOU DOING, LOOSHKIN?
GET AWAY! GET AWAY!
THPTHBTHH!
AW. ALL HE WANTED TO DO WAS BLOW A RASPBERRY IN BEAR'S FACE.
BLESS.
BLUGHH!
I'M A WHEEL!!

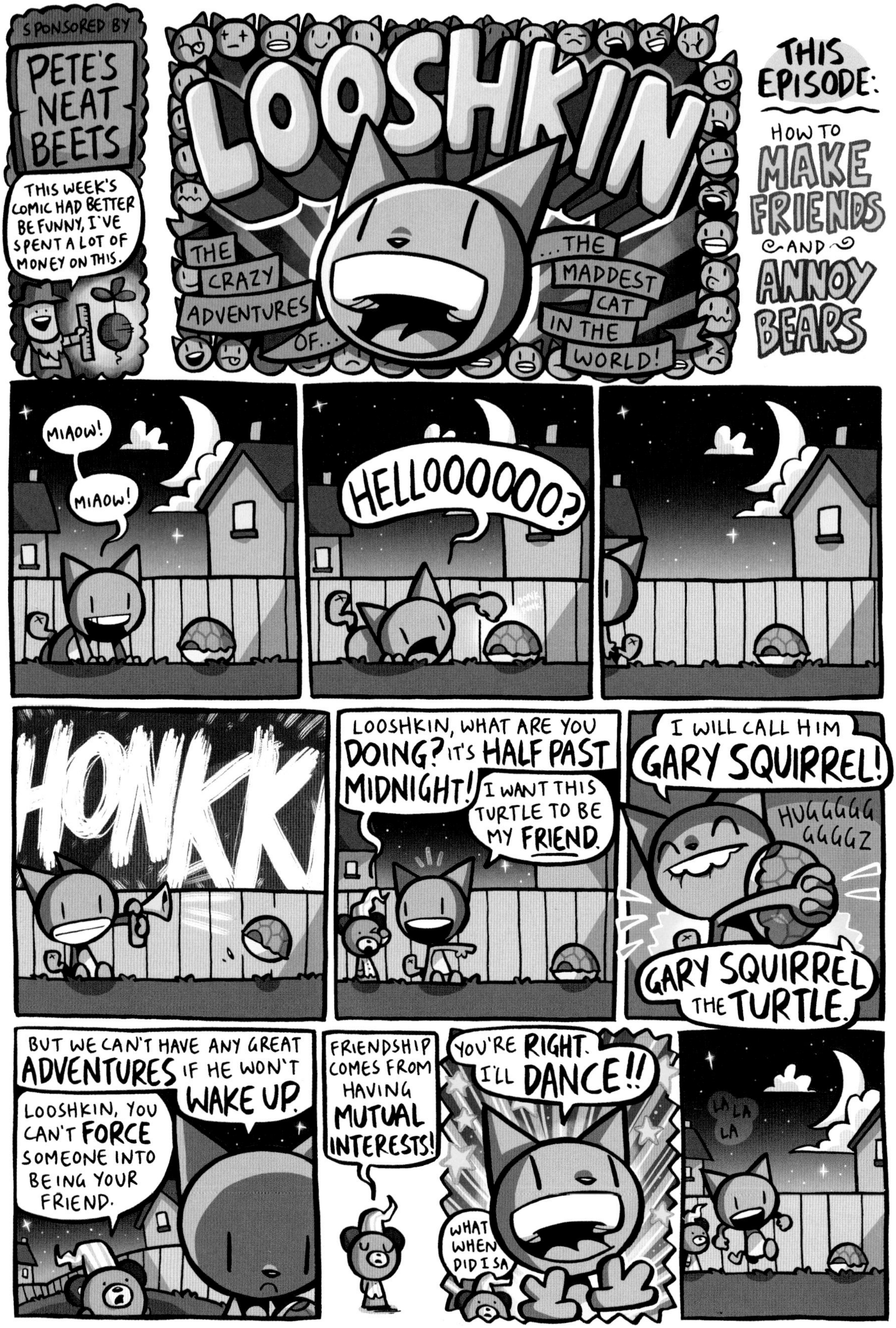
SPONSORED BY
PETE'S NEAT BEETS
THIS WEEK'S COMIC HAD BETTER BE FUNNY, I'VE SPENT A LOT OF MONEY ON THIS.
LOOSHKIN
THE CRAZY ADVENTURES OF...
...THE MADDEST CAT IN THE WORLD!
THIS EPISODE:
HOW TO MAKE FRIENDS AND ANNOY BEARS
MIAOW!
MIAOW!
HELLOOOOOO?
HONKK
LOOSHKIN, WHAT ARE YOU DOING? IT'S HALF PAST MIDNIGHT!
I WANT THIS TURTLE TO BE MY FRIEND.
I WILL CALL HIM GARY SQUIRREL!
HUGGGGG GGGGZ
GARY SQUIRREL THE TURTLE.
BUT WE CAN'T HAVE ANY GREAT ADVENTURES IF HE WON'T WAKE UP.
LOOSHKIN, YOU CAN'T FORCE SOMEONE INTO BEING YOUR FRIEND.
FRIENDSHIP COMES FROM HAVING MUTUAL INTERESTS!
YOU'RE RIGHT. I'LL DANCE!!
WHAT WHEN DID I SA
LA LA LA

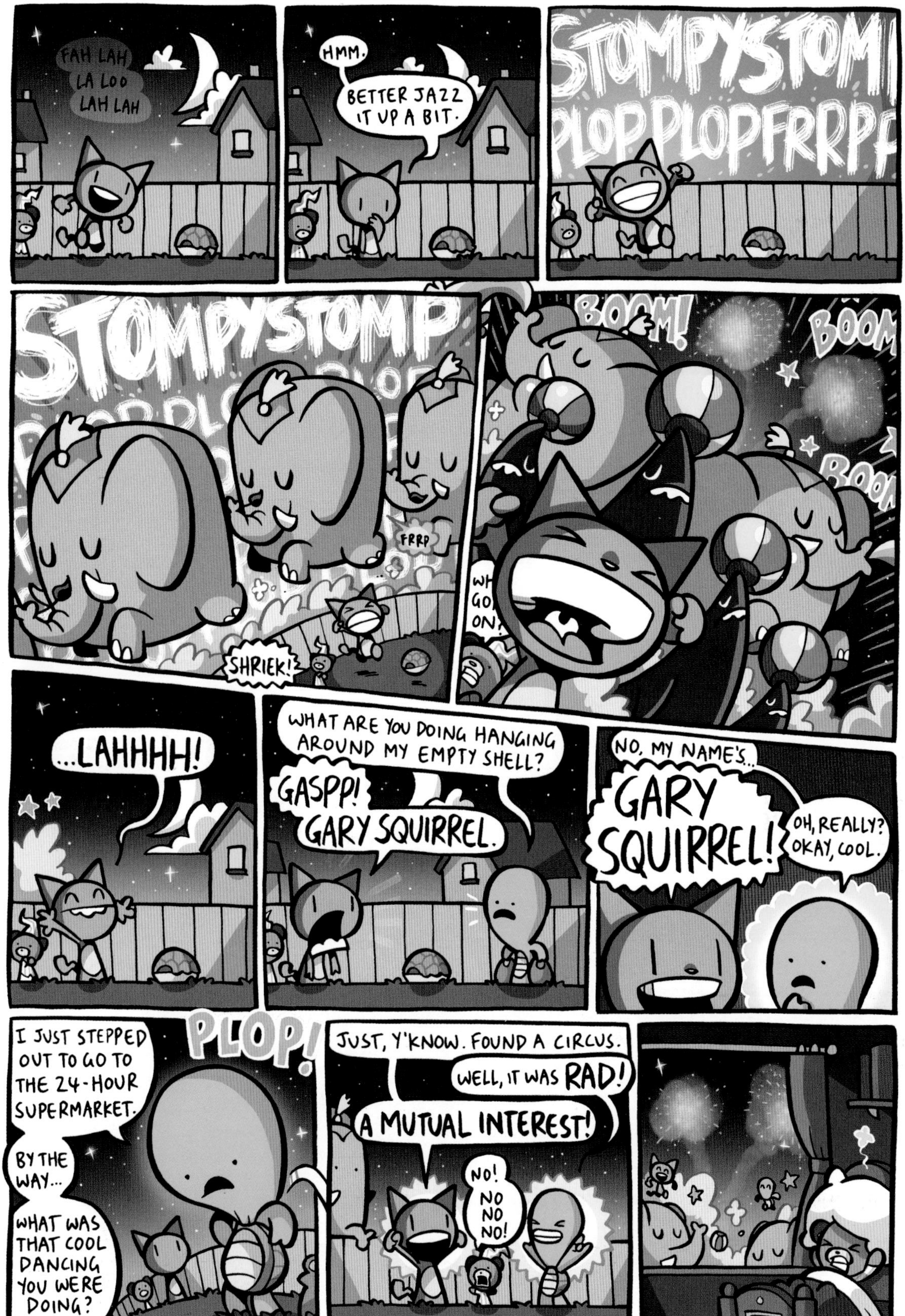

FAH LAH
LA LOO
LAH LAH
HMM.
BETTER JAZZ IT UP A BIT.
STOMPYSTOMP
PLOP PLOP FRRPF
STOMPYSTOMP
FRRP
SHRIEK!
BOOM!
BOOM
BOOM
...LAHHHH!
WHAT ARE YOU DOING HANGING AROUND MY EMPTY SHELL?
GASPP!
GARY SQUIRREL.
NO, MY NAME'S...
GARY SQUIRREL!
OH, REALLY? OKAY, COOL.
PLOP!
I JUST STEPPED OUT TO GO TO THE 24-HOUR SUPERMARKET.
BY THE WAY...
WHAT WAS THAT COOL DANCING YOU WERE DOING?
JUST, Y'KNOW. FOUND A CIRCUS.
WELL, IT WAS RAD!
A MUTUAL INTEREST!
NO! NO NO NO!

FOR THE PURPOSES OF READING THIS COMIC, YOUR NAME WILL BE BERYL, OKAY?

UM..

OKAY!

LOOSHKIN

THE CRAZY ADVENTURES OF...

...THE MADDEST CAT IN THE WORLD!

THIS EPISODE:

VIRTUAL REALITY

BONK BONK FRPP!

IT'S JUST LIKE REAL LIFE.

AHH! I PRETENDED TO BE ILL SO I COULD GET THE DAY OFF SCHOOL. NOW TO SETTLE DOWN AND WATCH...

MONSTER TRUCK VIDEOS! HONK, HONKKK!

TRUCK CRUSHES BIG CAKE

COMMENTS

I'M HAVING SO MUCH FUN I COULD FART!

TRUCK CRUSHES BIG CAKE

COMMENTS

L-LOOSHKIN?

LOOSHKIN, ARE YOU IN THE INTERNET?!

YES!

TRUCK C... CAKE

BUT HOW?

I DUNNO. ONE MINUTE I WAS IN THE KITCHEN EATING CHEESY TOAST...

THEN I WAS HITTING THE LAPTOP WITH CHEESY TOAST...

SLAP SLAP SLAP

AND THEN SOME OTHER STUFF HAPPENED. I GUESS. BYE!

BRUM!

WAIT! WHERE ARE YOU GOING?

LOOSHKIN'S RUINING MY GAME!

HE'S DRIVING A MONSTER TRUCK THROUGH MY MAGICAL TEACUP PONY GYMKHANA™!!

BRUM!

SORRY! WHEE! SORRY! WHEE!

HONK!

NOOO! NOT UNI-PONY! SHE'S WORTH 5,000 COINS!

MOO!

170

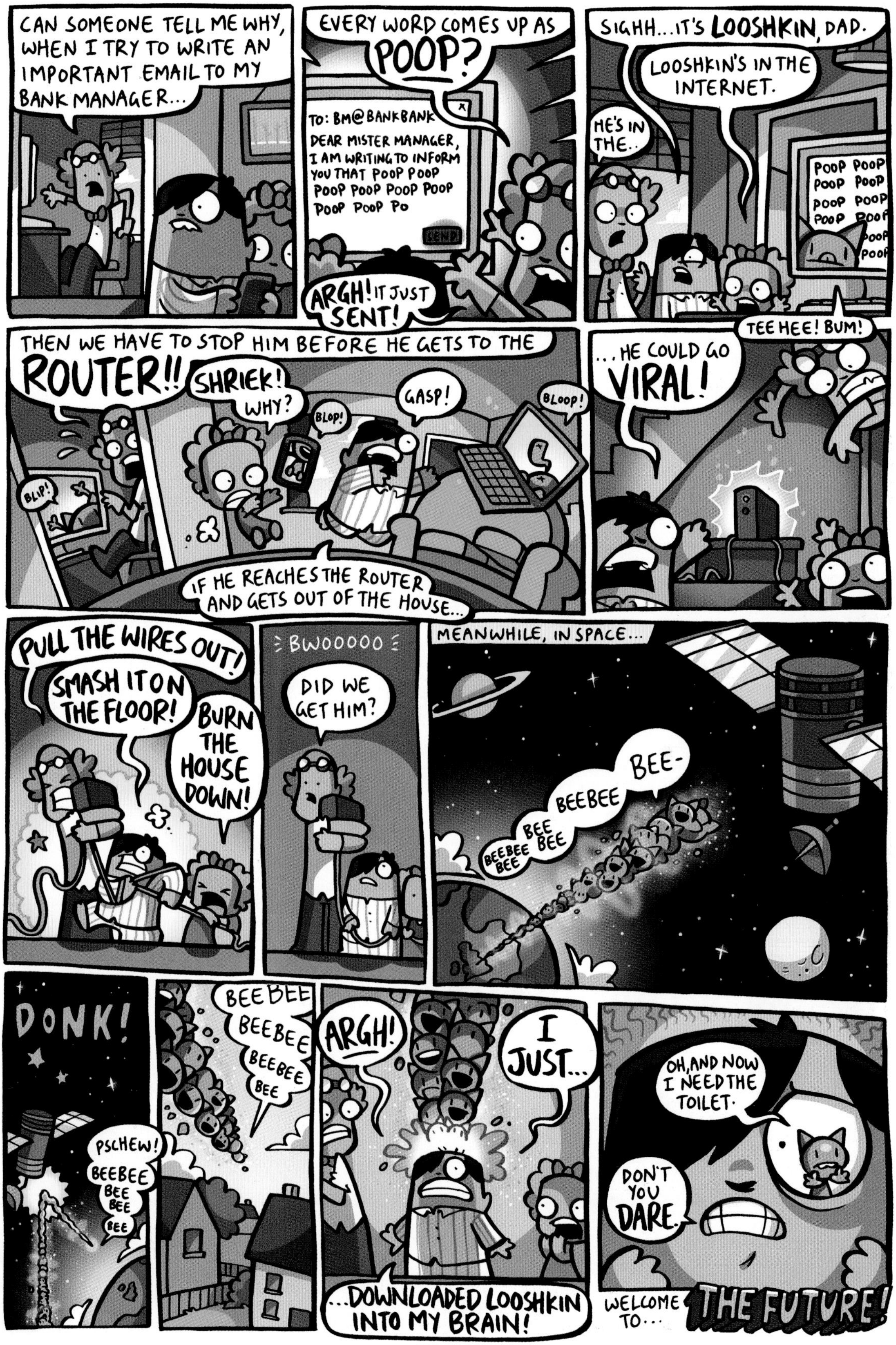
CAN SOMEONE TELL ME WHY, WHEN I TRY TO WRITE AN IMPORTANT EMAIL TO MY BANK MANAGER...
EVERY WORD COMES UP AS POOP?
TO: BM@BANKBANK
DEAR MISTER MANAGER, I AM WRITING TO INFORM YOU THAT POOP POOP POOP POOP POOP POOP POOP POOP PO
SEND
ARGH! IT JUST SENT!
SIGHH...IT'S LOOSHKIN, DAD.
LOOSHKIN'S IN THE INTERNET.
HE'S IN THE..
POOP POOP POOP POOP POOP POOP POOP POOF POOP POOP
THEN WE HAVE TO STOP HIM BEFORE HE GETS TO THE ROUTER!!
SHRIEK! WHY?
GASP!
BLOP!
BLOOP!
BLIP!
IF HE REACHES THE ROUTER AND GETS OUT OF THE HOUSE...
...HE COULD GO VIRAL!
TEE HEE! BUM!
PULL THE WIRES OUT!
SMASH IT ON THE FLOOR!
BURN THE HOUSE DOWN!
BWOOOOO
DID WE GET HIM?
MEANWHILE, IN SPACE...
BEE-
BEEBEE
BEE BEE
BEEBEE BEE
DONK!
PSCHEW!
BEEBEE BEE BEE BEE
BEEBEE
BEEBEE
BEEBEE
BEE
ARGH!
I JUST...
...DOWNLOADED LOOSHKIN INTO MY BRAIN!
OH, AND NOW I NEED THE TOILET.
DON'T YOU DARE.
WELCOME TO... THE FUTURE!

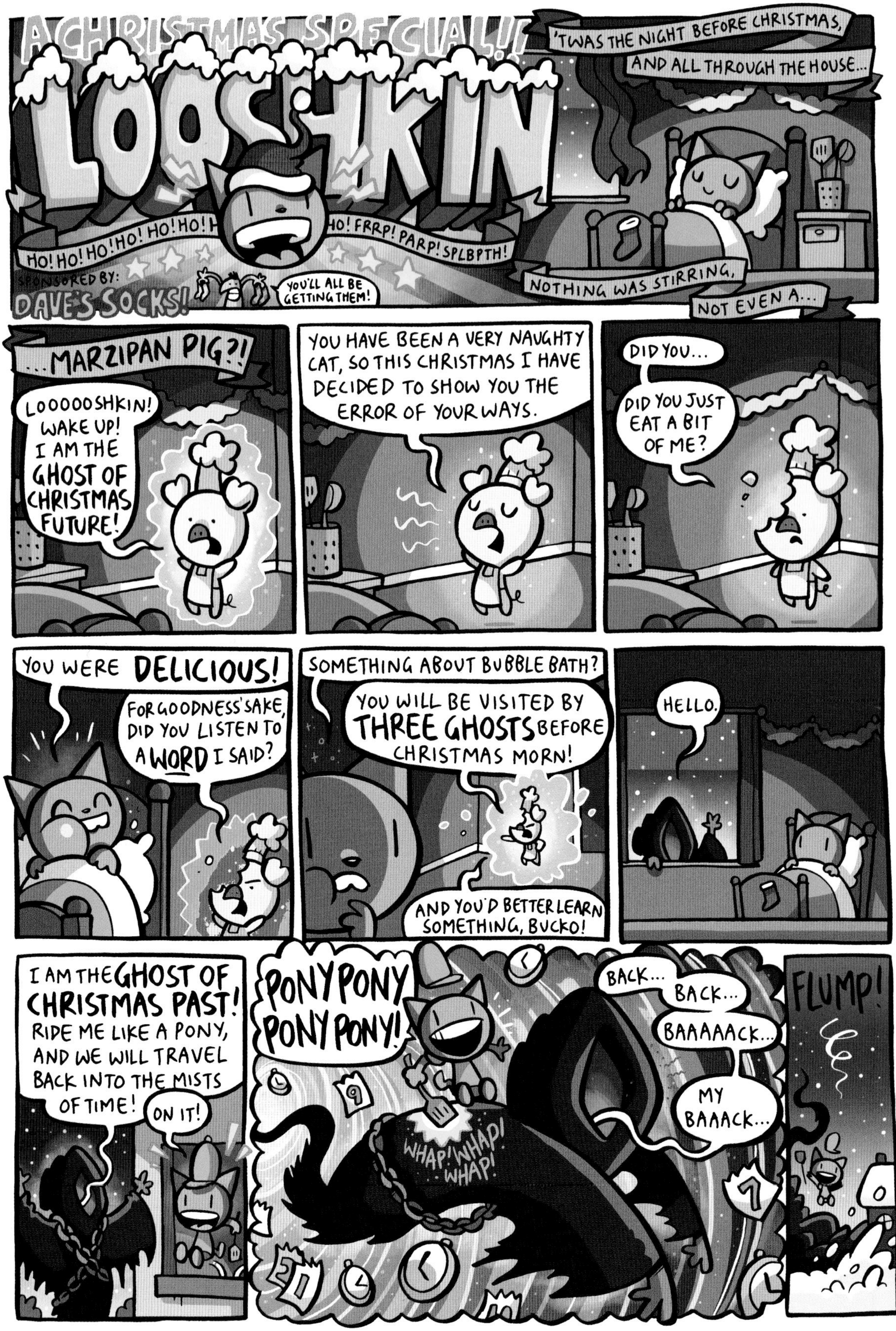
A CHRISTMAS SPECIAL!!
LOOSHKIN
HO! HO! HO! HO! HO! HO! HO!
HO! FRRP! PARP! SPLBPTH!
SPONSORED BY:
DAVE'S SOCKS!
YOU'LL ALL BE GETTING THEM!
'TWAS THE NIGHT BEFORE CHRISTMAS,
AND ALL THROUGH THE HOUSE...
NOTHING WAS STIRRING,
NOT EVEN A...
...MARZIPAN PIG?!
LOOOOOSHKIN! WAKE UP! I AM THE GHOST OF CHRISTMAS FUTURE!
YOU HAVE BEEN A VERY NAUGHTY CAT, SO THIS CHRISTMAS I HAVE DECIDED TO SHOW YOU THE ERROR OF YOUR WAYS.
DID YOU...
DID YOU JUST EAT A BIT OF ME?
YOU WERE DELICIOUS!
FOR GOODNESS' SAKE, DID YOU LISTEN TO A WORD I SAID?
SOMETHING ABOUT BUBBLE BATH?
YOU WILL BE VISITED BY THREE GHOSTS BEFORE CHRISTMAS MORN!
AND YOU'D BETTER LEARN SOMETHING, BUCKO!
HELLO.
I AM THE GHOST OF CHRISTMAS PAST! RIDE ME LIKE A PONY, AND WE WILL TRAVEL BACK INTO THE MISTS OF TIME!
ON IT!
PONY PONY PONY PONY!
WHAP! WHAP! WHAP!
BACK...
BACK...
BAAAAACK...
MY BAAACK...
FLUMP!

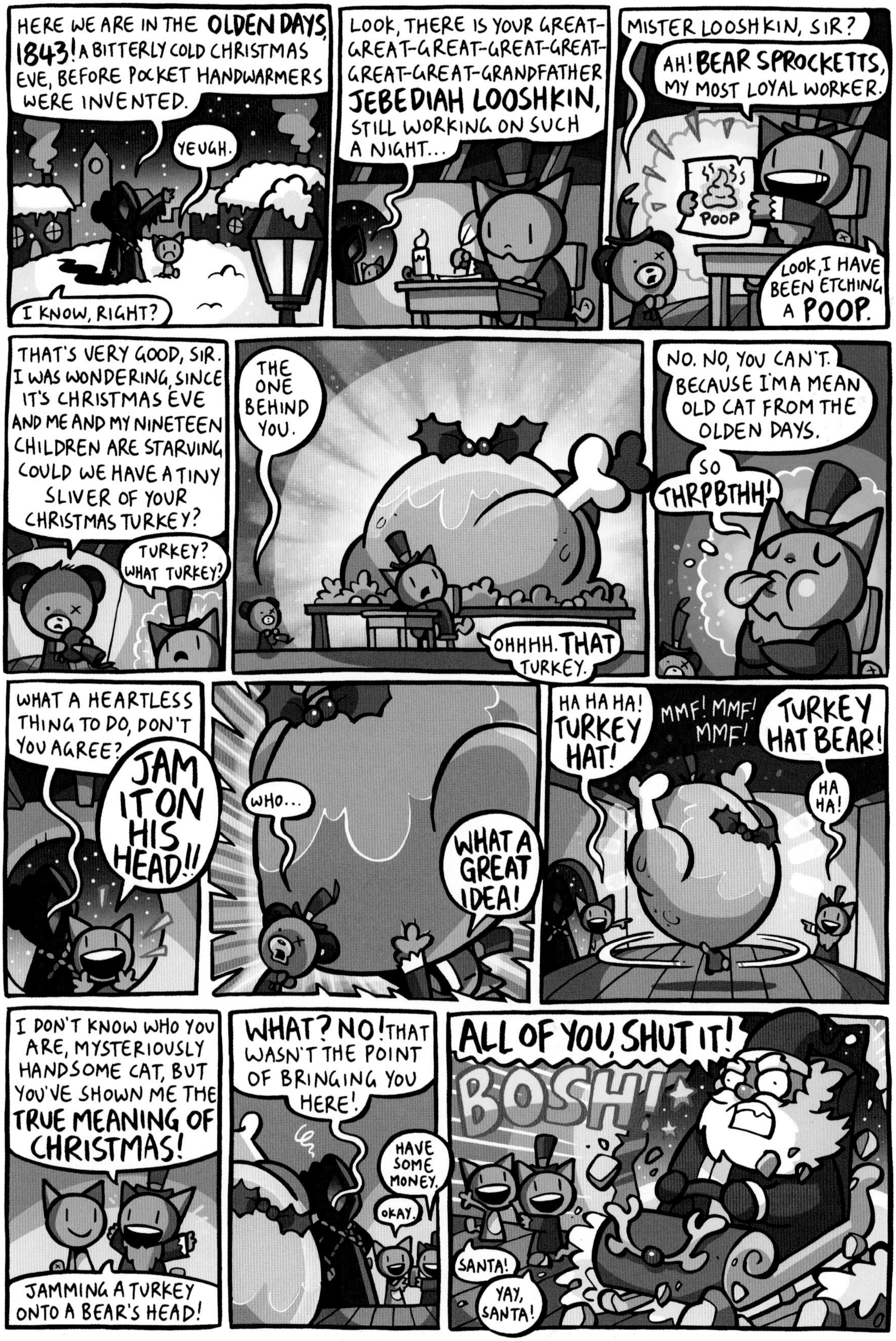
HERE WE ARE IN THE OLDEN DAYS, 1843! A BITTERLY COLD CHRISTMAS EVE, BEFORE POCKET HANDWARMERS WERE INVENTED.
YEUGH.
I KNOW, RIGHT?
LOOK, THERE IS YOUR GREAT-GREAT-GREAT-GREAT-GREAT-GREAT-GREAT-GRANDFATHER JEBEDIAH LOOSHKIN, STILL WORKING ON SUCH A NIGHT...
MISTER LOOSHKIN, SIR?
AH! BEAR SPROCKETTS, MY MOST LOYAL WORKER.
POOP
LOOK, I HAVE BEEN ETCHING A POOP.
THAT'S VERY GOOD, SIR. I WAS WONDERING, SINCE IT'S CHRISTMAS EVE AND ME AND MY NINETEEN CHILDREN ARE STARVING COULD WE HAVE A TINY SLIVER OF YOUR CHRISTMAS TURKEY?
TURKEY? WHAT TURKEY?
THE ONE BEHIND YOU.
OHHHH. THAT TURKEY.
NO. NO, YOU CAN'T. BECAUSE I'M A MEAN OLD CAT FROM THE OLDEN DAYS.
SO THRPBTHH!
WHAT A HEARTLESS THING TO DO, DON'T YOU AGREE?
JAM IT ON HIS HEAD!!
WHO...
WHAT A GREAT IDEA!
HA HA HA! TURKEY HAT!
MMF! MMF! MMF!
TURKEY HAT BEAR!
HA HA!
I DON'T KNOW WHO YOU ARE, MYSTERIOUSLY HANDSOME CAT, BUT YOU'VE SHOWN ME THE TRUE MEANING OF CHRISTMAS!
JAMMING A TURKEY ONTO A BEAR'S HEAD!
WHAT? NO! THAT WASN'T THE POINT OF BRINGING YOU HERE!
HAVE SOME MONEY.
OKAY.
ALL OF YOU, SHUT IT!
BOSH!
SANTA!
YAY, SANTA!

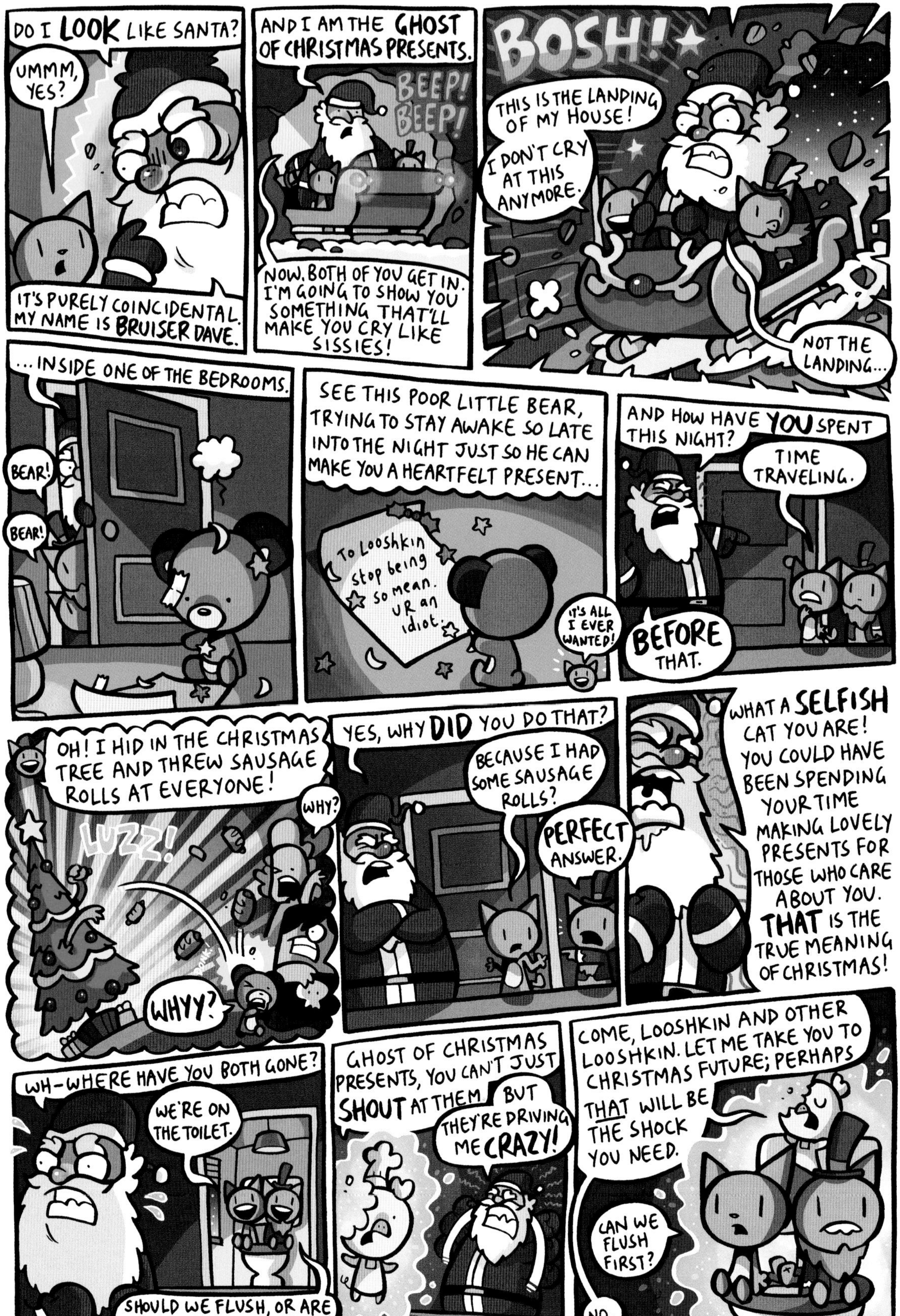

DO I LOOK LIKE SANTA?
UMMM, YES?
IT'S PURELY COINCIDENTAL. MY NAME IS BRUISER DAVE.
AND I AM THE GHOST OF CHRISTMAS PRESENTS.
BEEP! BEEP!
NOW, BOTH OF YOU GET IN. I'M GOING TO SHOW YOU SOMETHING THAT'LL MAKE YOU CRY LIKE SISSIES!
BOSH!
THIS IS THE LANDING OF MY HOUSE!
I DON'T CRY AT THIS ANYMORE.
NOT THE LANDING...
... INSIDE ONE OF THE BEDROOMS.
BEAR!
BEAR!
SEE THIS POOR LITTLE BEAR, TRYING TO STAY AWAKE SO LATE INTO THE NIGHT JUST SO HE CAN MAKE YOU A HEARTFELT PRESENT...
To Looshkin stop being so mean. UR an idiot.
IT'S ALL I EVER WANTED!
AND HOW HAVE YOU SPENT THIS NIGHT?
TIME TRAVELING.
BEFORE THAT.
OH! I HID IN THE CHRISTMAS TREE AND THREW SAUSAGE ROLLS AT EVERYONE!
WHY?
LUZZ!
WHYY?
YES, WHY DID YOU DO THAT?
BECAUSE I HAD SOME SAUSAGE ROLLS?
PERFECT ANSWER.
WHAT A SELFISH CAT YOU ARE! YOU COULD HAVE BEEN SPENDING YOUR TIME MAKING LOVELY PRESENTS FOR THOSE WHO CARE ABOUT YOU. THAT IS THE TRUE MEANING OF CHRISTMAS!
WH-WHERE HAVE YOU BOTH GONE?
WE'RE ON THE TOILET.
SHOULD WE FLUSH, OR ARE YOU GOING, TOO?
GHOST OF CHRISTMAS PRESENTS, YOU CAN'T JUST SHOUT AT THEM.
BUT THEY'RE DRIVING ME CRAZY!
COME, LOOSHKIN AND OTHER LOOSHKIN. LET ME TAKE YOU TO CHRISTMAS FUTURE; PERHAPS THAT WILL BE THE SHOCK YOU NEED.
CAN WE FLUSH FIRST?
NO.

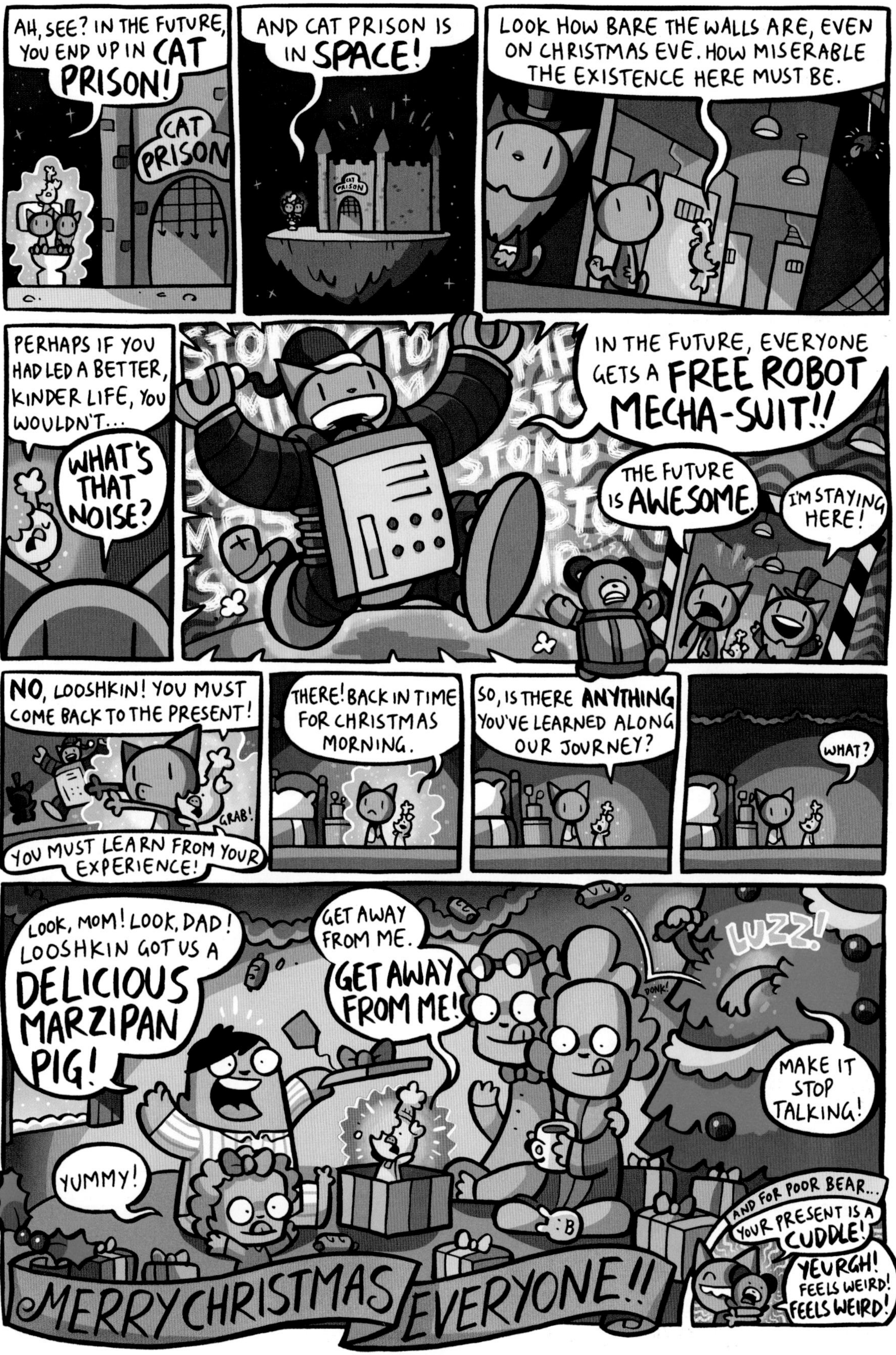
AH, SEE? IN THE FUTURE, YOU END UP IN CAT PRISON!
CAT PRISON
AND CAT PRISON IS IN SPACE!
CAT PRISON
LOOK HOW BARE THE WALLS ARE, EVEN ON CHRISTMAS EVE. HOW MISERABLE THE EXISTENCE HERE MUST BE.
PERHAPS IF YOU HAD LED A BETTER, KINDER LIFE, YOU WOULDN'T...
WHAT'S THAT NOISE?
IN THE FUTURE, EVERYONE GETS A FREE ROBOT MECHA-SUIT!!
THE FUTURE IS AWESOME.
I'M STAYING HERE!
NO, LOOSHKIN! YOU MUST COME BACK TO THE PRESENT!
GRAB!
YOU MUST LEARN FROM YOUR EXPERIENCE!
THERE! BACK IN TIME FOR CHRISTMAS MORNING.
SO, IS THERE ANYTHING YOU'VE LEARNED ALONG OUR JOURNEY?
WHAT?
LOOK, MOM! LOOK, DAD! LOOSHKIN GOT US A DELICIOUS MARZIPAN PIG!
GET AWAY FROM ME.
GET AWAY FROM ME!
LUZZ!
DONK!
MAKE IT STOP TALKING!
YUMMY!
AND FOR POOR BEAR... YOUR PRESENT IS A CUDDLE!
YEURGH! FEELS WEIRD! FEELS WEIRD!
MERRY CHRISTMAS EVERYONE!!

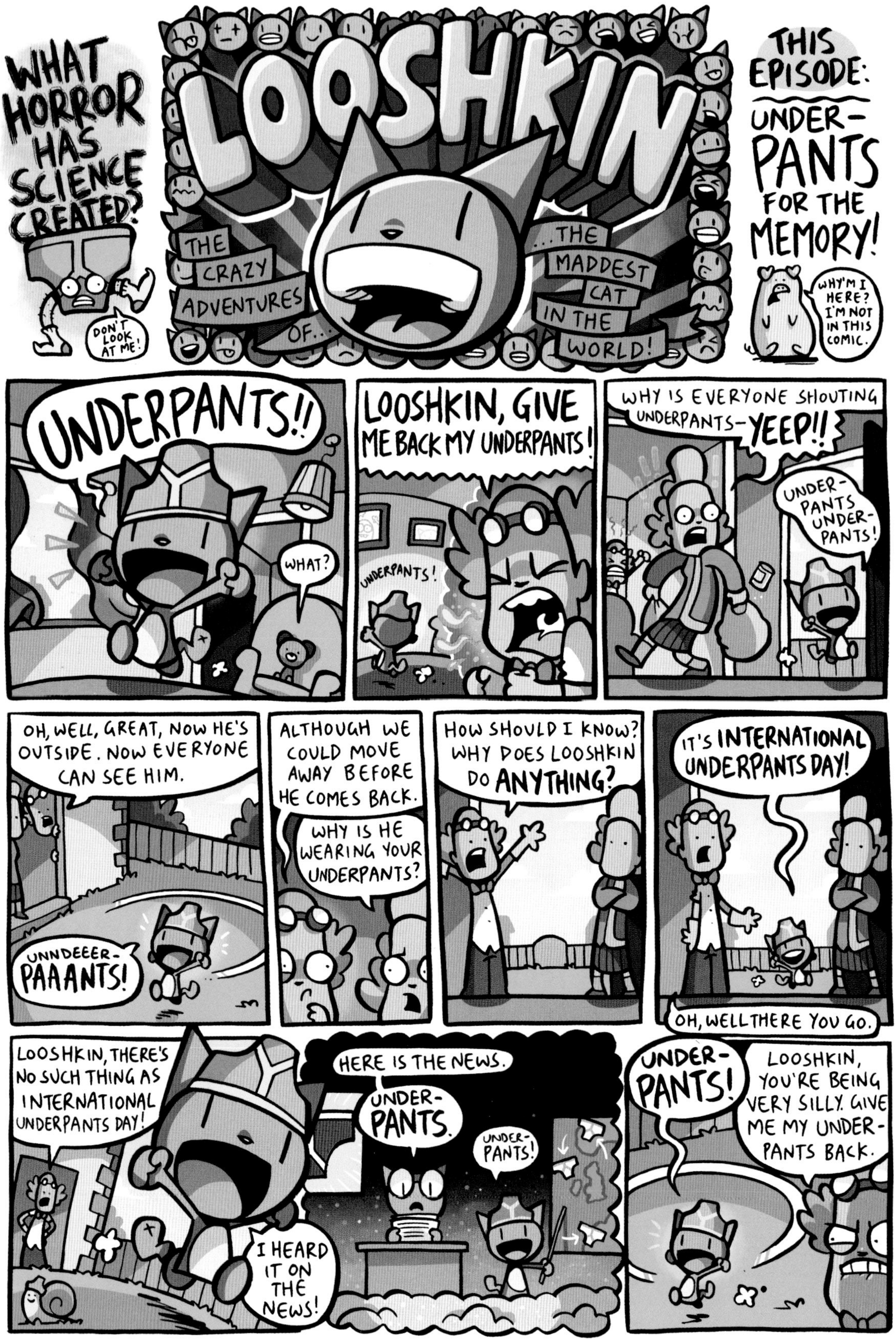

WHAT HORROR HAS SCIENCE CREATED?
DON'T LOOK AT ME!
LOOSHKIN
THE CRAZY ADVENTURES OF... ...THE MADDEST CAT IN THE WORLD!
THIS EPISODE: UNDER-PANTS FOR THE MEMORY!
WHY'M I HERE? I'M NOT IN THIS COMIC.
UNDERPANTS!!
WHAT?
LOOSHKIN, GIVE ME BACK MY UNDERPANTS!
UNDERPANTS!
WHY IS EVERYONE SHOUTING UNDERPANTS—YEEP!!
UNDER-PANTS UNDER-PANTS!
OH, WELL, GREAT, NOW HE'S OUTSIDE. NOW EVERYONE CAN SEE HIM.
UNNDEEER-PAAANTS!
ALTHOUGH WE COULD MOVE AWAY BEFORE HE COMES BACK.
WHY IS HE WEARING YOUR UNDERPANTS?
HOW SHOULD I KNOW? WHY DOES LOOSHKIN DO ANYTHING?
IT'S INTERNATIONAL UNDERPANTS DAY!
OH, WELL THERE YOU GO.
LOOSHKIN, THERE'S NO SUCH THING AS INTERNATIONAL UNDERPANTS DAY!
I HEARD IT ON THE NEWS!
HERE IS THE NEWS.
UNDER-PANTS.
UNDER-PANTS!
UNDER-PANTS!
LOOSHKIN, YOU'RE BEING VERY SILLY. GIVE ME MY UNDER-PANTS BACK.

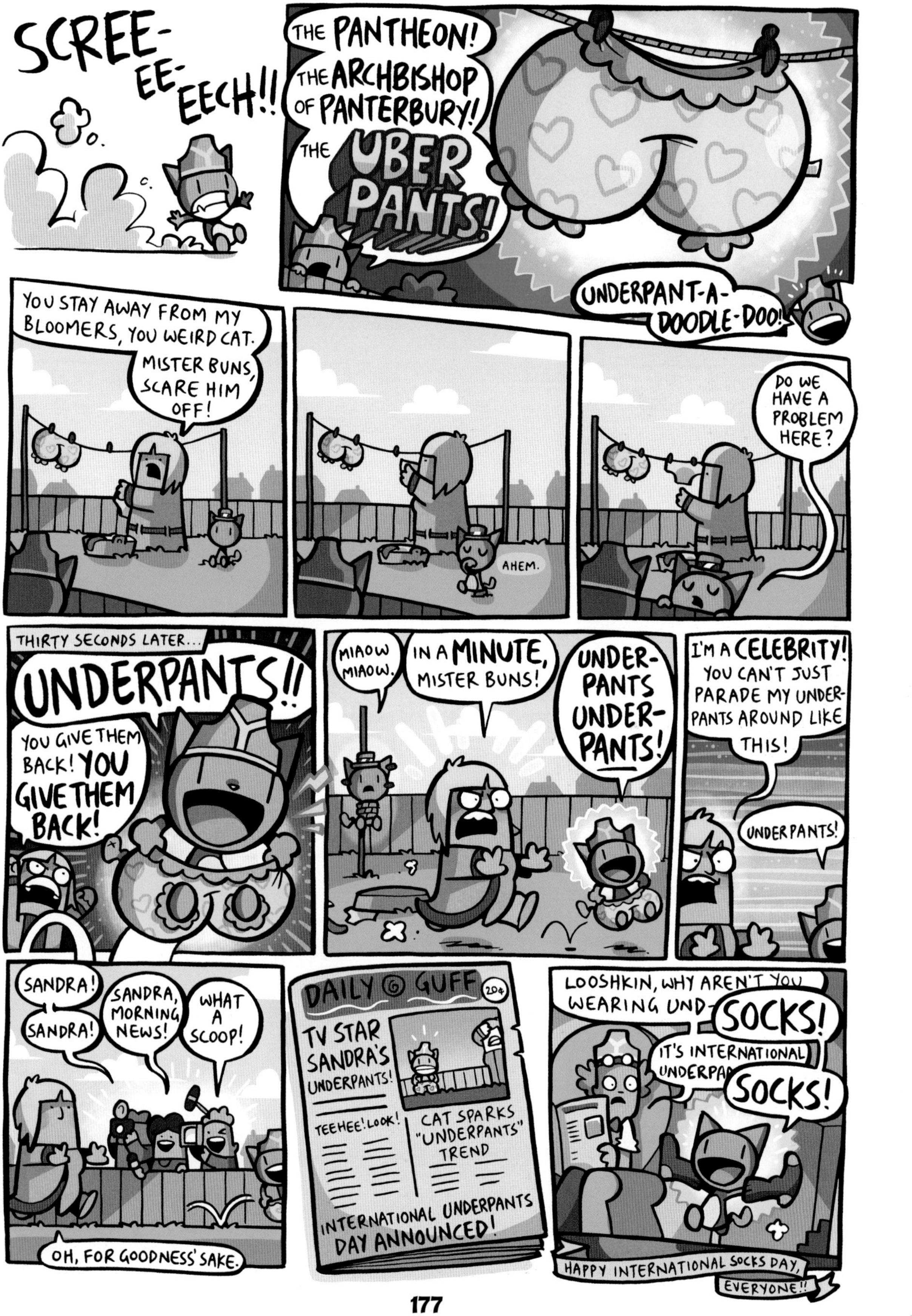
SCREE-EE-EECH!!
THE PANTHEON! THE ARCHBISHOP OF PANTERBURY! THE UBER PANTS!
UNDERPANT-A-DOODLE-DOO!
YOU STAY AWAY FROM MY BLOOMERS, YOU WEIRD CAT.
MISTER BUNS, SCARE HIM OFF!
AHEM.
DO WE HAVE A PROBLEM HERE?
THIRTY SECONDS LATER...
UNDERPANTS!!
YOU GIVE THEM BACK! YOU GIVE THEM BACK!
MIAOW MIAOW.
IN A MINUTE, MISTER BUNS!
UNDER-PANTS UNDER-PANTS!
I'M A CELEBRITY! YOU CAN'T JUST PARADE MY UNDER-PANTS AROUND LIKE THIS!
UNDERPANTS!
SANDRA!
SANDRA!
SANDRA, MORNING NEWS!
WHAT A SCOOP!
OH, FOR GOODNESS' SAKE.
DAILY G GUFF 20¢
TV STAR SANDRA'S UNDERPANTS!
TEEHEE! LOOK!
CAT SPARKS "UNDERPANTS" TREND
INTERNATIONAL UNDERPANTS DAY ANNOUNCED!
LOOSHKIN, WHY AREN'T YOU WEARING UND-
SOCKS!
IT'S INTERNATIONAL UNDERPA-
SOCKS!
HAPPY INTERNATIONAL SOCKS DAY, EVERYONE!!

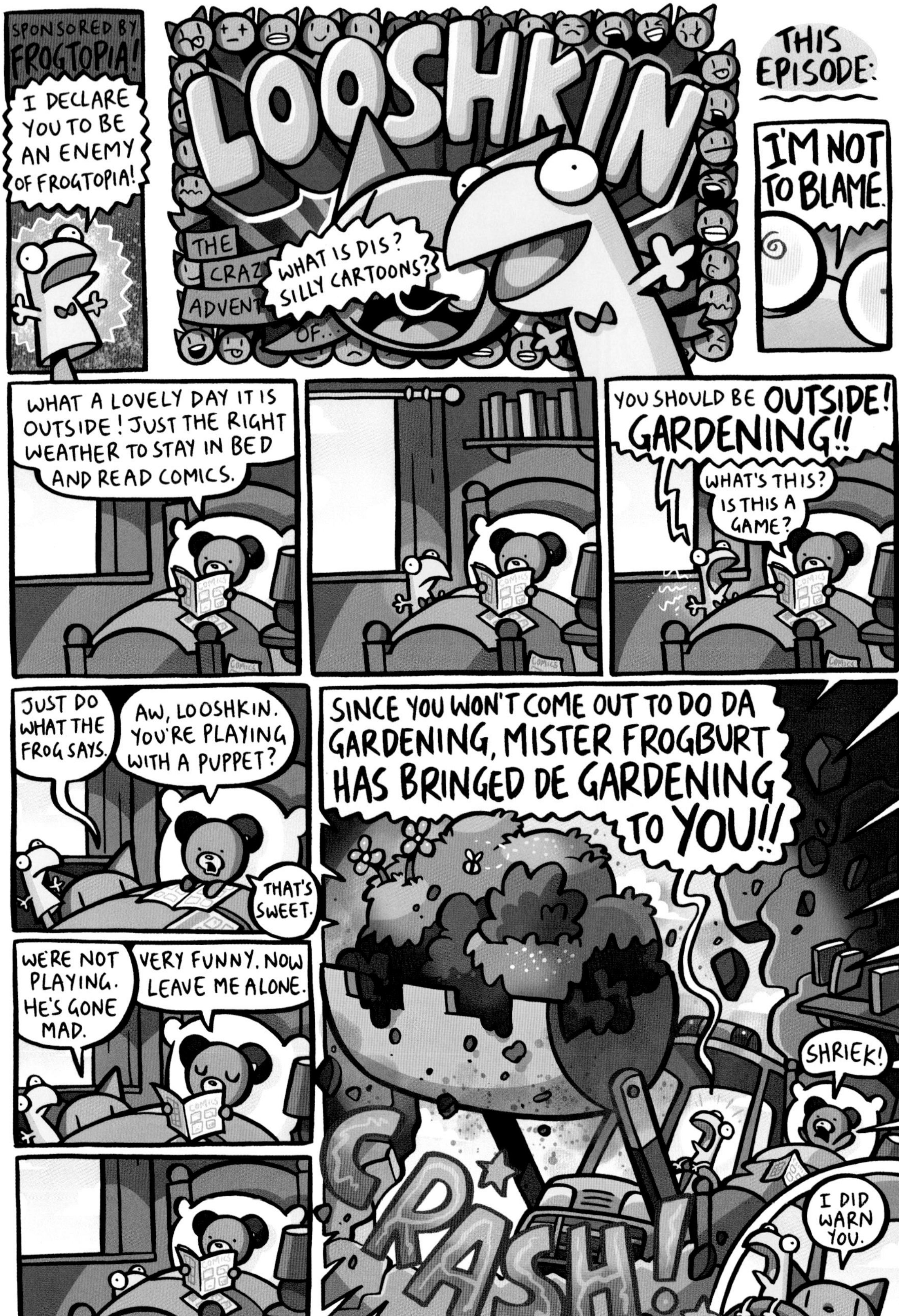
SPONSORED BY FROGTOPIA!
I DECLARE YOU TO BE AN ENEMY OF FROGTOPIA!
LOOSHKIN
THE CRAZ ADVENT OF...
WHAT IS DIS? SILLY CARTOONS?
THIS EPISODE:
I'M NOT TO BLAME.
WHAT A LOVELY DAY IT IS OUTSIDE! JUST THE RIGHT WEATHER TO STAY IN BED AND READ COMICS.
COMICS
YOU SHOULD BE OUTSIDE! GARDENING!!
WHAT'S THIS? IS THIS A GAME?
JUST DO WHAT THE FROG SAYS.
AW, LOOSHKIN. YOU'RE PLAYING WITH A PUPPET?
THAT'S SWEET.
WE'RE NOT PLAYING. HE'S GONE MAD.
VERY FUNNY. NOW LEAVE ME ALONE.
SINCE YOU WON'T COME OUT TO DO DA GARDENING, MISTER FROGBURT HAS BRINGED DE GARDENING TO YOU!!
SHRIEK!
CRASH!
I DID WARN YOU.

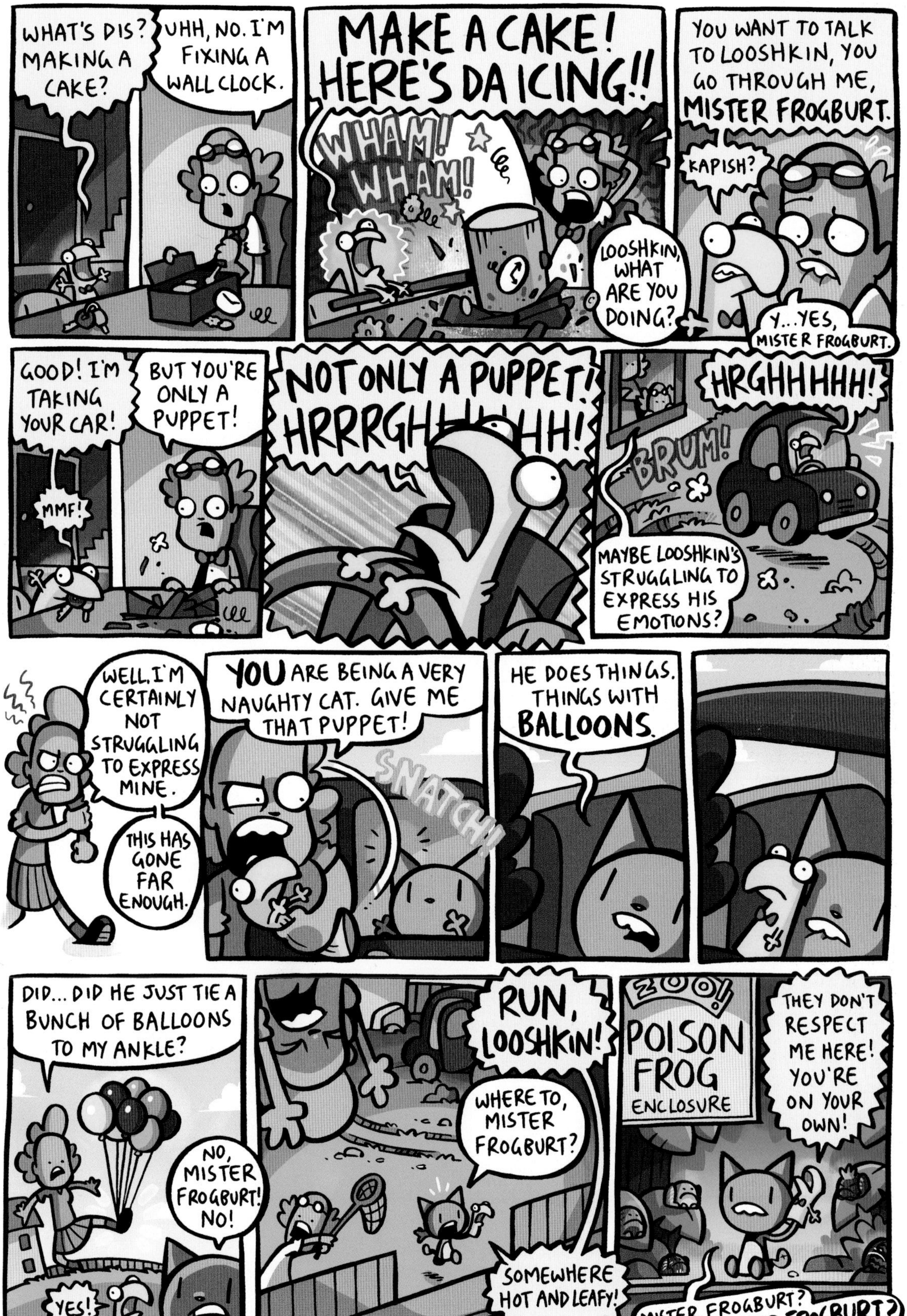
WHAT'S DIS? MAKING A CAKE?
UHH, NO. I'M FIXING A WALL CLOCK.
MAKE A CAKE! HERE'S DA ICING!!
WHAM! WHAM!
LOOSHKIN, WHAT ARE YOU DOING?
YOU WANT TO TALK TO LOOSHKIN, YOU GO THROUGH ME, MISTER FROGBURT.
KAPISH?
Y...YES, MISTER FROGBURT.
GOOD! I'M TAKING YOUR CAR!
BUT YOU'RE ONLY A PUPPET!
MMF!
NOT ONLY A PUPPET! HRRRGHHHHHH!
HRGHHHHH!
BRUM!
MAYBE LOOSHKIN'S STRUGGLING TO EXPRESS HIS EMOTIONS?
WELL, I'M CERTAINLY NOT STRUGGLING TO EXPRESS MINE.
THIS HAS GONE FAR ENOUGH.
YOU ARE BEING A VERY NAUGHTY CAT. GIVE ME THAT PUPPET!
SNATCH!
HE DOES THINGS. THINGS WITH BALLOONS.
DID... DID HE JUST TIE A BUNCH OF BALLOONS TO MY ANKLE?
NO, MISTER FROGBURT! NO!
YES!
RUN, LOOSHKIN!
WHERE TO, MISTER FROGBURT?
SOMEWHERE HOT AND LEAFY!
ZOO!
POISON FROG ENCLOSURE
THEY DON'T RESPECT ME HERE! YOU'RE ON YOUR OWN!
MISTER FROGBURT? MISTER FROGBURT?

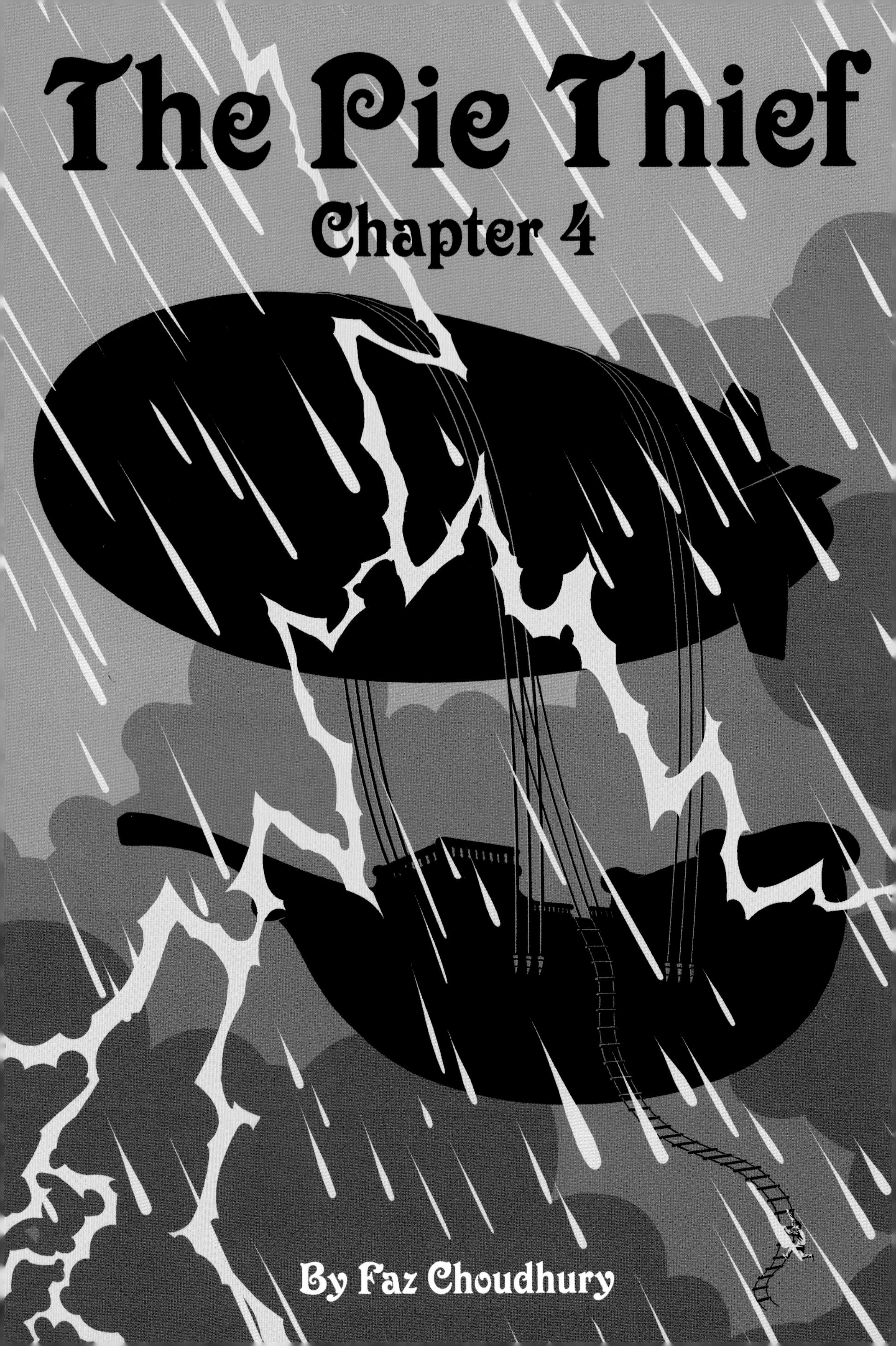
The Pie Thief
Chapter 4
By Faz Choudhury

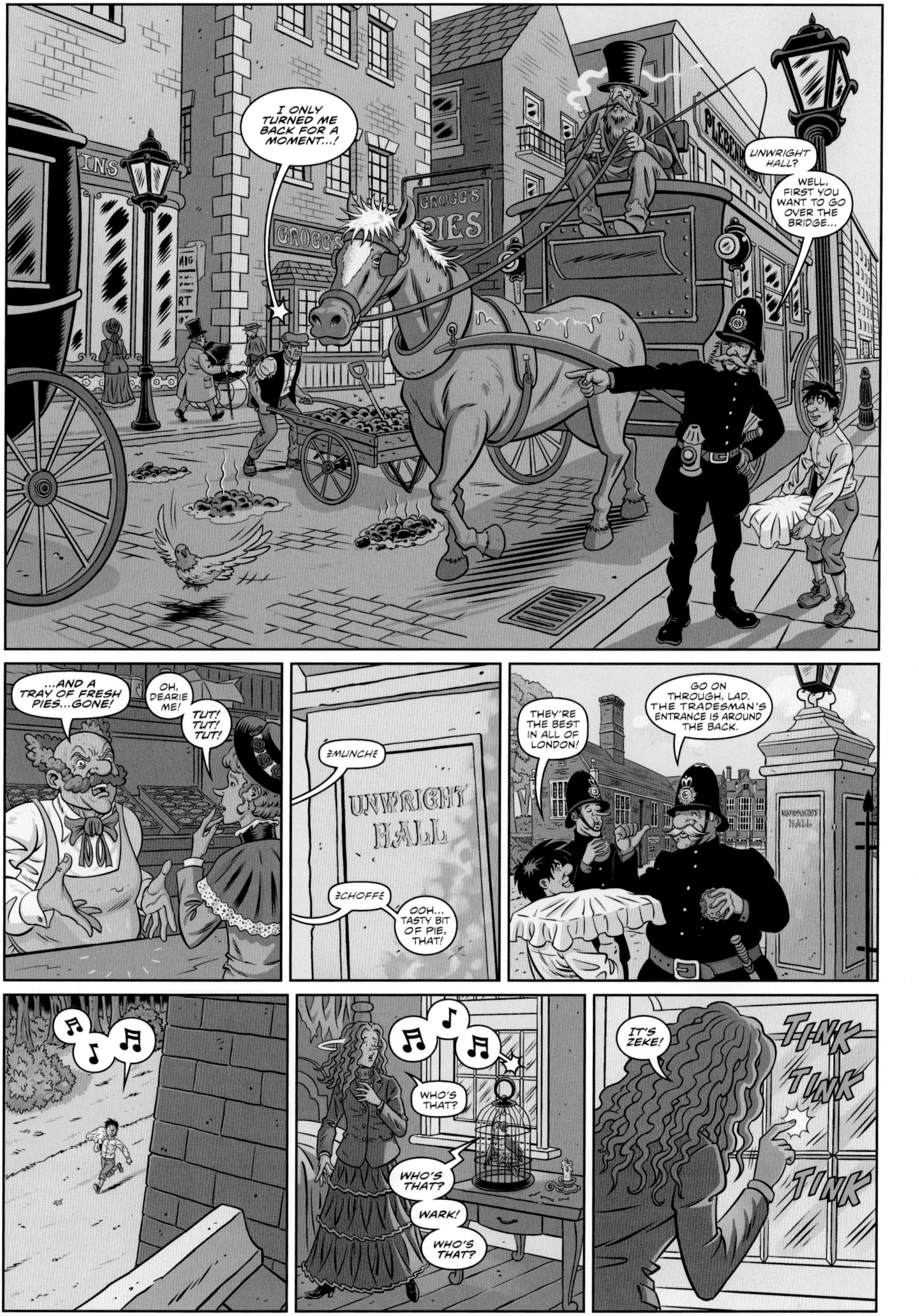
GROGG'S
PIES
GROGG'S
PLEBEN
I ONLY TURNED ME BACK FOR A MOMENT...!
UNWRIGHT HALL?
WELL, FIRST YOU WANT TO GO OVER THE BRIDGE...
...AND A TRAY OF FRESH PIES...GONE!
OH, DEARIE ME!
TUT! TUT! TUT!
MUNCH
UNWRIGHT HALL
CHOFF
OOH... TASTY BIT OF PIE, THAT!
THEY'RE THE BEST IN ALL OF LONDON!
GO ON THROUGH, LAD. THE TRADESMAN'S ENTRANCE IS AROUND THE BACK.
UNWRIGHT HALL
WHO'S THAT?
WHO'S THAT?
WARK!
WHO'S THAT?
IT'S ZEKE!
TINK
TINK
TINK

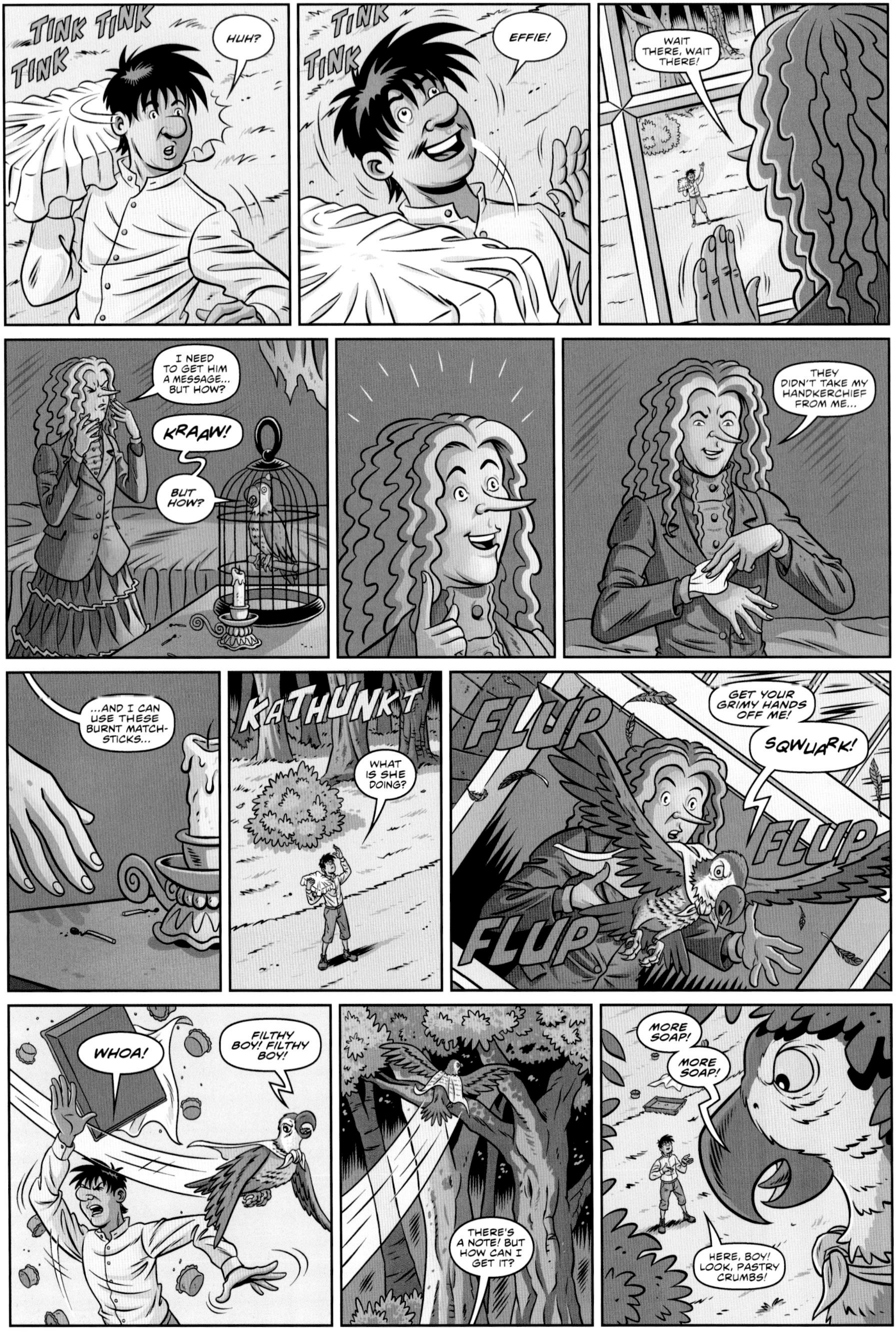
TINK TINK
TINK
HUH?
TINK
TINK
EFFIE!
WAIT THERE, WAIT THERE!
I NEED TO GET HIM A MESSAGE... BUT HOW?
KRAAW!
BUT HOW?
THEY DIDN'T TAKE MY HANDKERCHIEF FROM ME...
...AND I CAN USE THESE BURNT MATCH-STICKS...
KATHUNKT
WHAT IS SHE DOING?
FLUP
GET YOUR GRIMY HANDS OFF ME!
SQWUARK!
FLUP
FLUP
WHOA!
FILTHY BOY! FILTHY BOY!
THERE'S A NOTE! BUT HOW CAN I GET IT?
MORE SOAP!
MORE SOAP!
HERE, BOY! LOOK, PASTRY CRUMBS!

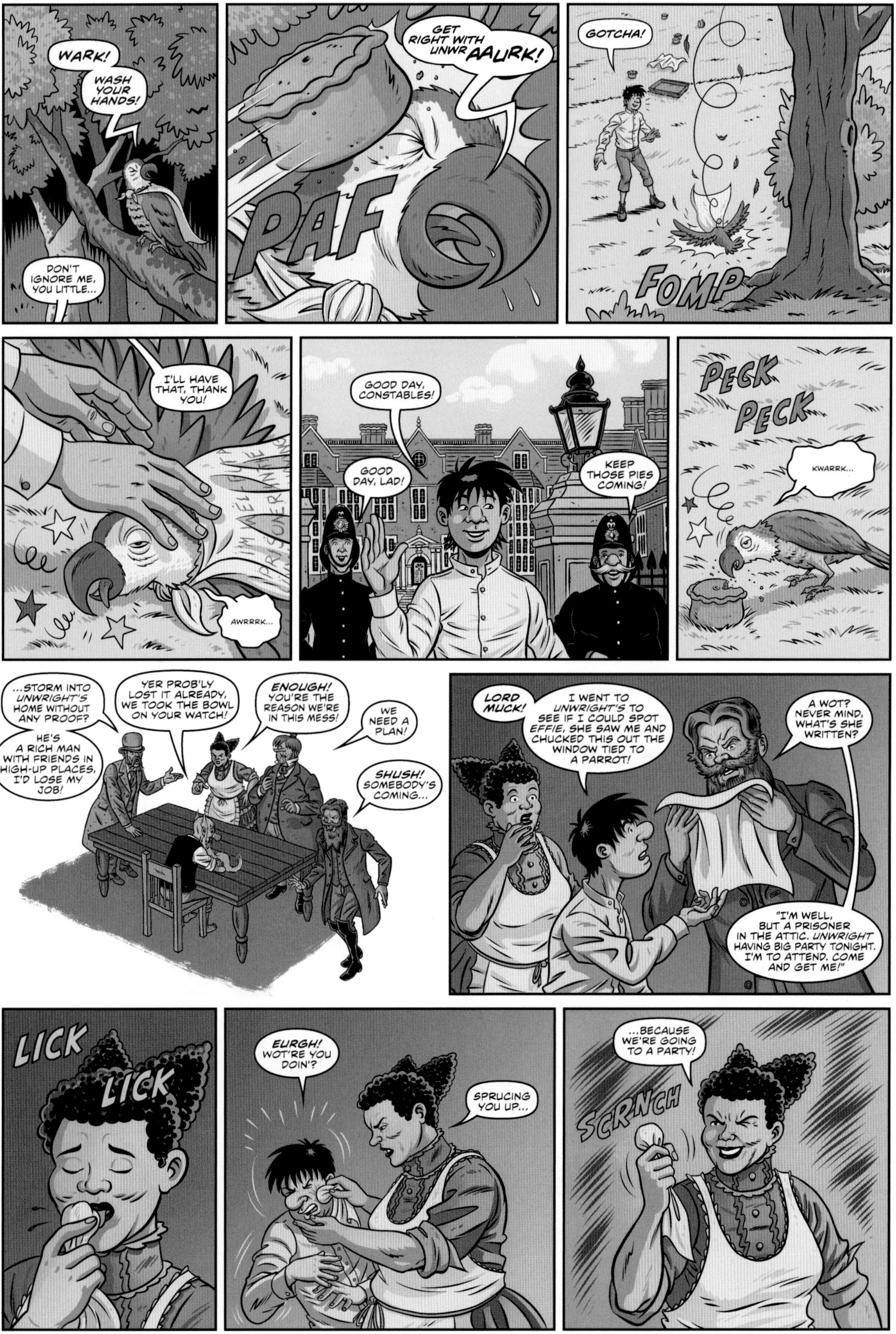

WARK!
WASH YOUR HANDS!
DON'T IGNORE ME, YOU LITTLE...
GET RIGHT WITH UNWRAAURK!
PAF
GOTCHA!
FOMP
I'LL HAVE THAT, THANK YOU!
AWRRRK...
GOOD DAY, CONSTABLES!
GOOD DAY, LAD!
KEEP THOSE PIES COMING!
PECK PECK
KWARRK...
...STORM INTO UNWRIGHT'S HOME WITHOUT ANY PROOF?
HE'S A RICH MAN WITH FRIENDS IN HIGH-UP PLACES, I'D LOSE MY JOB!
YER PROB'LY LOST IT ALREADY, WE TOOK THE BOWL ON YOUR WATCH!
ENOUGH! YOU'RE THE REASON WE'RE IN THIS MESS!
WE NEED A PLAN!
SHUSH! SOMEBODY'S COMING...
LORD MUCK!
I WENT TO UNWRIGHT'S TO SEE IF I COULD SPOT EFFIE, SHE SAW ME AND CHUCKED THIS OUT THE WINDOW TIED TO A PARROT!
A WOT? NEVER MIND, WHAT'S SHE WRITTEN?
"I'M WELL, BUT A PRISONER IN THE ATTIC. UNWRIGHT HAVING BIG PARTY TONIGHT. I'M TO ATTEND. COME AND GET ME!"
LICK LICK
EURGH! WOT'RE YOU DOIN'?
SPRUCING YOU UP...
...BECAUSE WE'RE GOING TO A PARTY!
SCRNCH

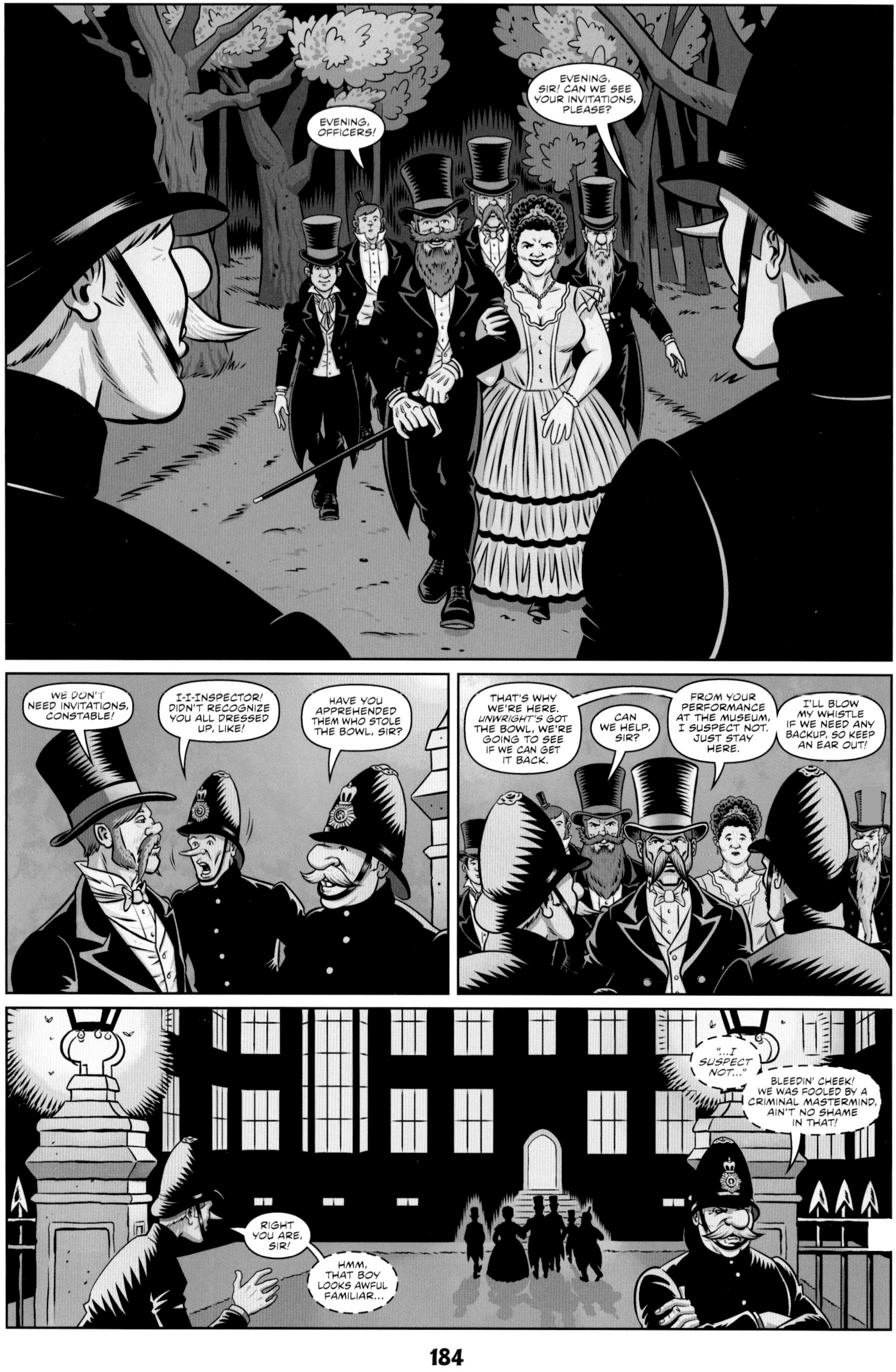

EVENING, OFFICERS!
EVENING, SIR! CAN WE SEE YOUR INVITATIONS, PLEASE?
WE DON'T NEED INVITATIONS, CONSTABLE!
I-I-INSPECTOR! DIDN'T RECOGNIZE YOU ALL DRESSED UP, LIKE!
HAVE YOU APPREHENDED THEM WHO STOLE THE BOWL, SIR?
THAT'S WHY WE'RE HERE. *UNWRIGHT'S* GOT THE BOWL, WE'RE GOING TO SEE IF WE CAN GET IT BACK.
CAN WE HELP, SIR?
FROM YOUR PERFORMANCE AT THE MUSEUM, I SUSPECT NOT. JUST STAY HERE.
I'LL BLOW MY WHISTLE IF WE NEED ANY BACKUP, SO KEEP AN EAR OUT!
RIGHT YOU ARE, SIR!
HMM, THAT BOY LOOKS AWFUL FAMILIAR...
"...I SUSPECT NOT..."
BLEEDIN' CHEEK! WE WAS FOOLED BY A CRIMINAL MASTERMIND, AIN'T NO SHAME IN THAT!

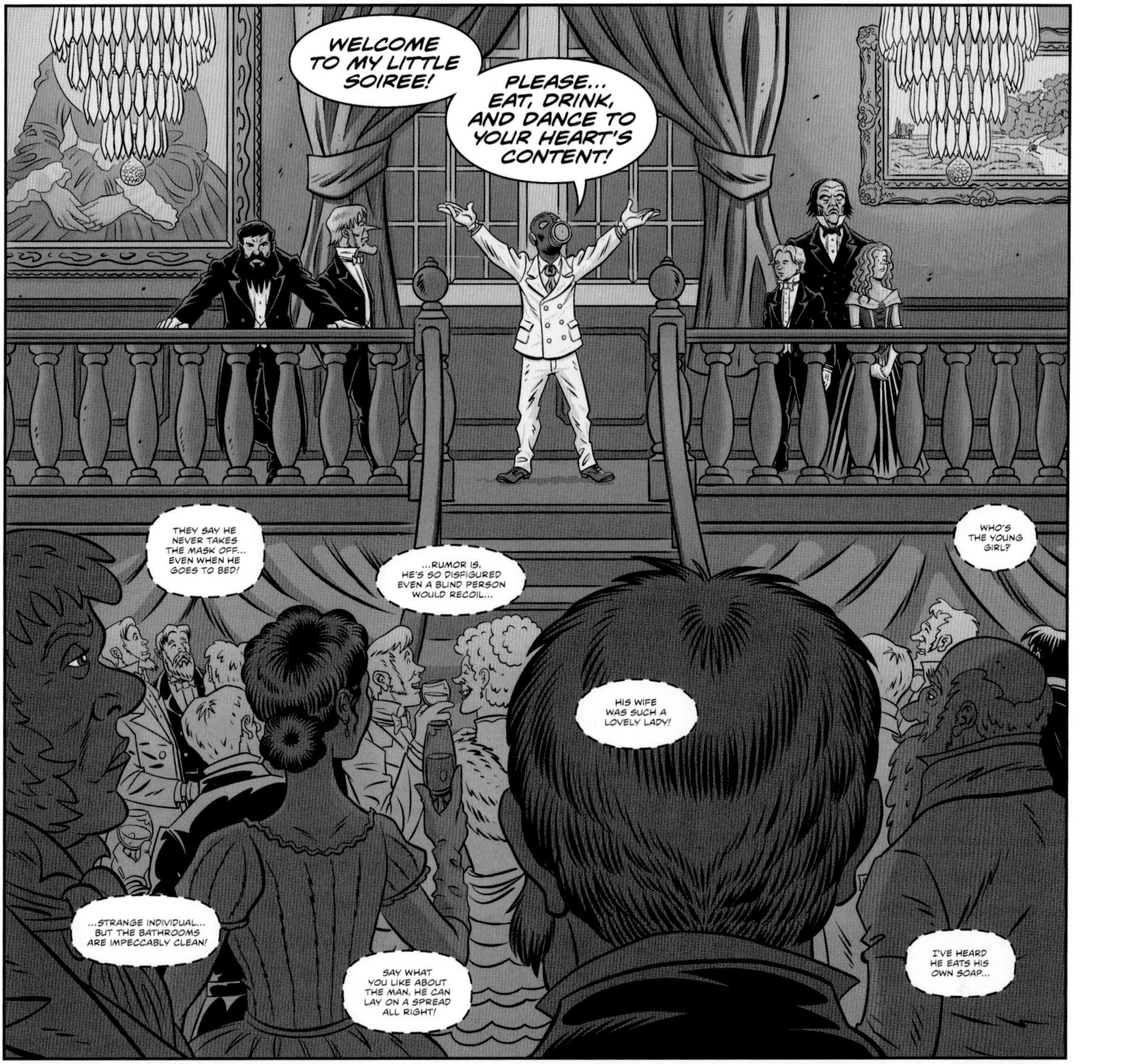
WELCOME TO MY LITTLE SOIREE!
PLEASE... EAT, DRINK, AND DANCE TO YOUR HEART'S CONTENT!
THEY SAY HE NEVER TAKES THE MASK OFF... EVEN WHEN HE GOES TO BED!
...RUMOR IS, HE'S SO DISFIGURED EVEN A BLIND PERSON WOULD RECOIL...
WHO'S THE YOUNG GIRL?
HIS WIFE WAS SUCH A LOVELY LADY!
...STRANGE INDIVIDUAL... BUT THE BATHROOMS ARE IMPECCABLY CLEAN!
SAY WHAT YOU LIKE ABOUT THE MAN, HE CAN LAY ON A SPREAD ALL RIGHT!
I'VE HEARD HE EATS HIS OWN SOAP...

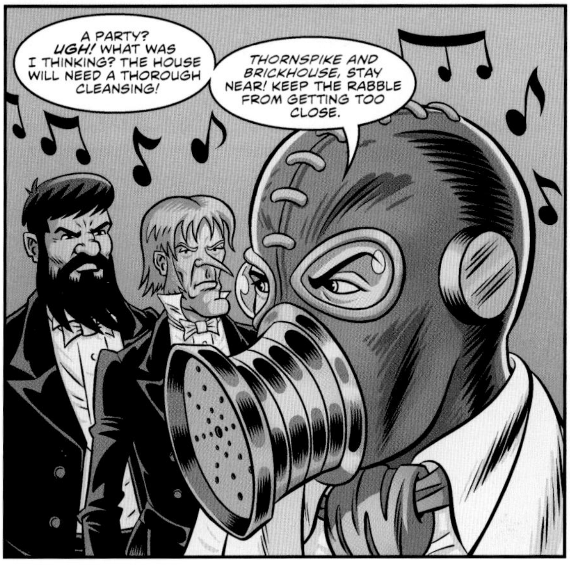
A PARTY? UGH! WHAT WAS I THINKING? THE HOUSE WILL NEED A THOROUGH CLEANSING!
THORNSPIKE AND BRICKHOUSE, STAY NEAR! KEEP THE RABBLE FROM GETTING TOO CLOSE.

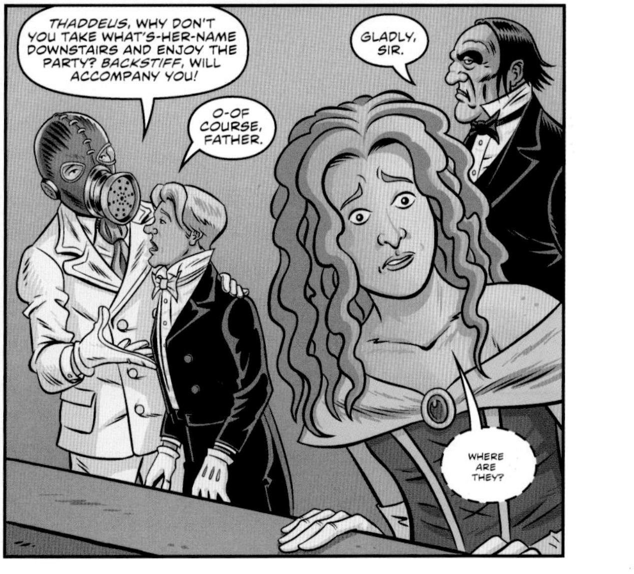
THADDEUS, WHY DON'T YOU TAKE WHAT'S-HER-NAME DOWNSTAIRS AND ENJOY THE PARTY? BACKSTIFF, WILL ACCOMPANY YOU!
GLADLY, SIR.
O-OF COURSE, FATHER.
WHERE ARE THEY?

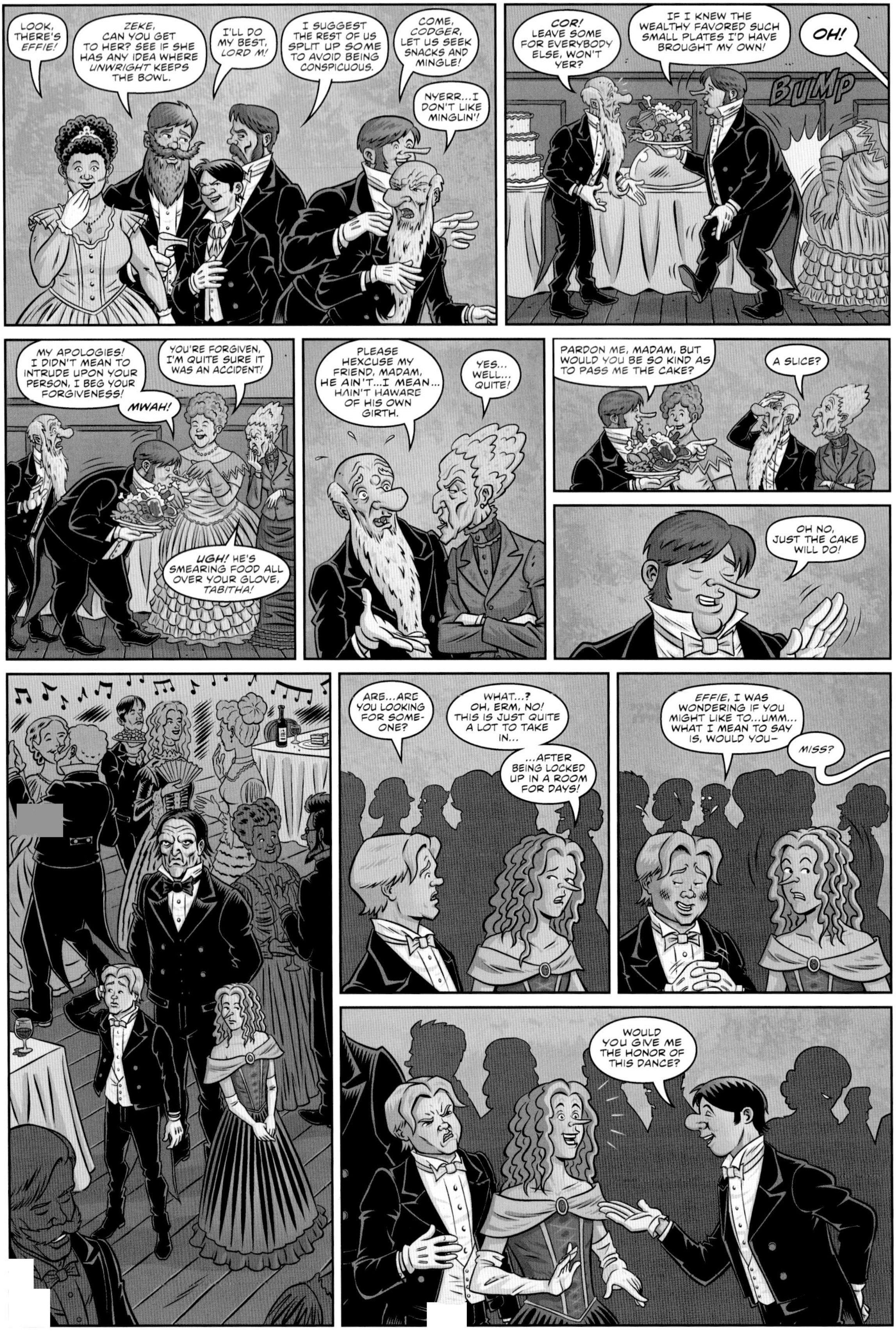
LOOK, THERE'S EFFIE!
ZEKE, CAN YOU GET TO HER? SEE IF SHE HAS ANY IDEA WHERE UNWRIGHT KEEPS THE BOWL.
I'LL DO MY BEST, LORD M!
I SUGGEST THE REST OF US SPLIT UP SOME TO AVOID BEING CONSPICUOUS.
COME, CODGER, LET US SEEK SNACKS AND MINGLE!
NYERR...I DON'T LIKE MINGLIN'!
COR! LEAVE SOME FOR EVERYBODY ELSE, WON'T YER?
IF I KNEW THE WEALTHY FAVORED SUCH SMALL PLATES I'D HAVE BROUGHT MY OWN!
BUMP
OH!
MY APOLOGIES! I DIDN'T MEAN TO INTRUDE UPON YOUR PERSON, I BEG YOUR FORGIVENESS!
MWAH!
YOU'RE FORGIVEN, I'M QUITE SURE IT WAS AN ACCIDENT!
UGH! HE'S SMEARING FOOD ALL OVER YOUR GLOVE, TABITHA!
PLEASE HEXCUSE MY FRIEND, MADAM, HE AIN'T...I MEAN... HAIN'T HAWARE OF HIS OWN GIRTH.
YES... WELL... QUITE!
PARDON ME, MADAM, BUT WOULD YOU BE SO KIND AS TO PASS ME THE CAKE?
A SLICE?
OH NO, JUST THE CAKE WILL DO!
ARE...ARE YOU LOOKING FOR SOME-ONE?
WHAT...? OH, ERM, NO! THIS IS JUST QUITE A LOT TO TAKE IN...
...AFTER BEING LOCKED UP IN A ROOM FOR DAYS!
EFFIE, I WAS WONDERING IF YOU MIGHT LIKE TO...UMM... WHAT I MEAN TO SAY IS, WOULD YOU–
MISS?
WOULD YOU GIVE ME THE HONOR OF THIS DANCE?

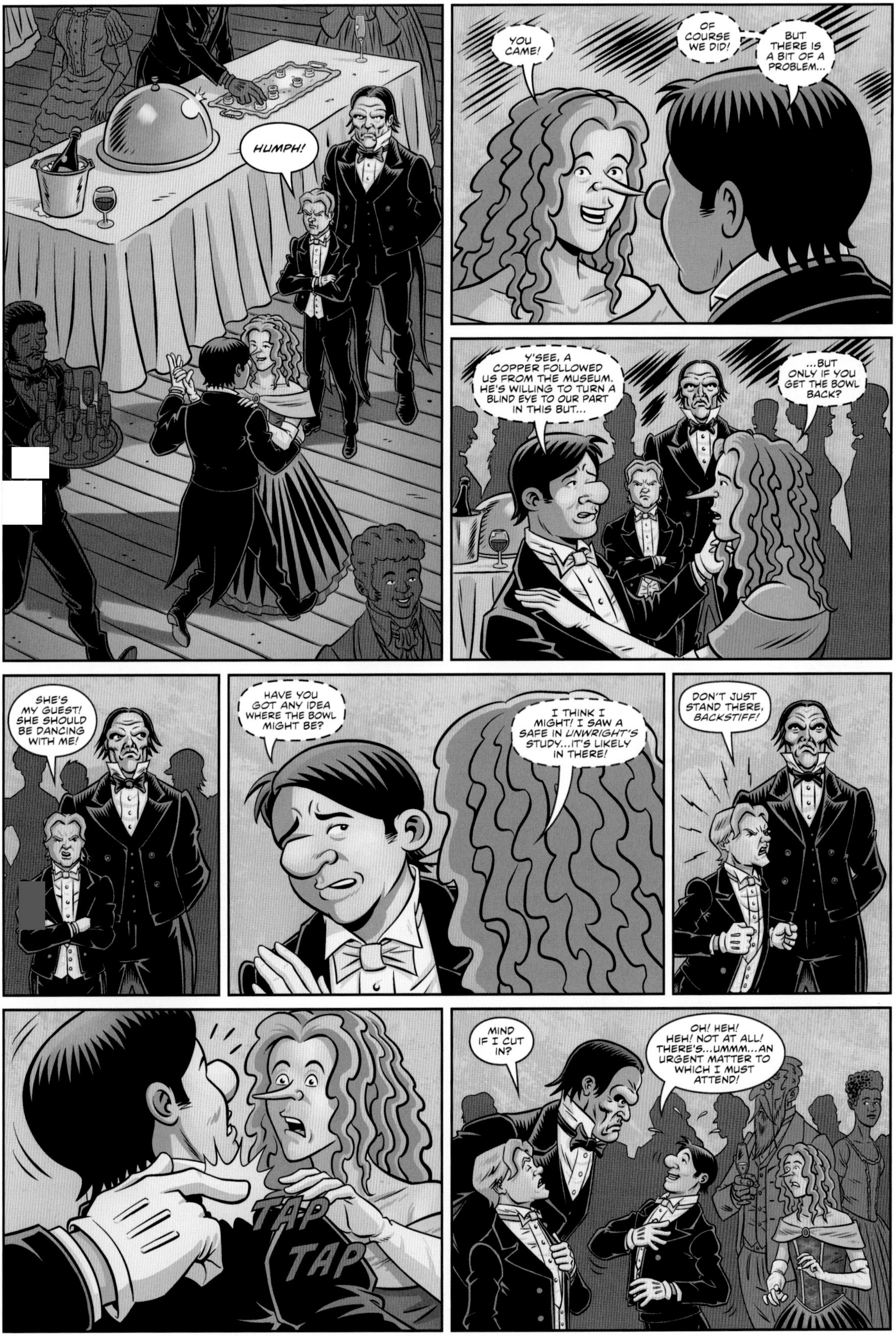
HUMPH!
YOU CAME!
OF COURSE WE DID!
BUT THERE IS A BIT OF A PROBLEM...
Y'SEE, A COPPER FOLLOWED US FROM THE MUSEUM. HE'S WILLING TO TURN A BLIND EYE TO OUR PART IN THIS BUT...
...BUT ONLY IF YOU GET THE BOWL BACK?
SHE'S MY GUEST! SHE SHOULD BE DANCING WITH ME!
HAVE YOU GOT ANY IDEA WHERE THE BOWL MIGHT BE?
I THINK I MIGHT! I SAW A SAFE IN UNWRIGHT'S STUDY...IT'S LIKELY IN THERE!
DON'T JUST STAND THERE, BACKSTIFF!
TAP TAP
MIND IF I CUT IN?
OH! HEH! HEH! NOT AT ALL! THERE'S...UMMM...AN URGENT MATTER TO WHICH I MUST ATTEND!

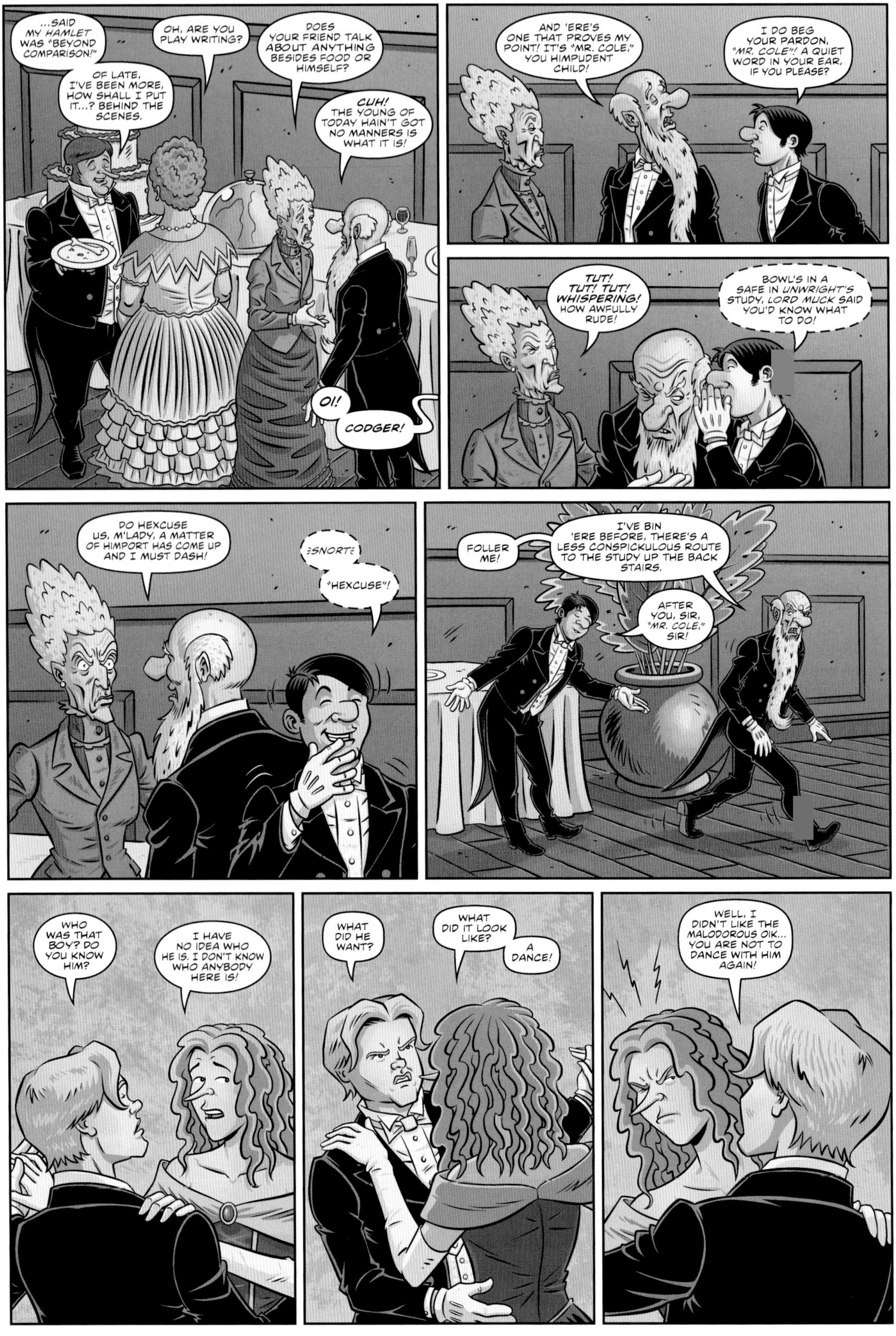
...SAID MY HAMLET WAS "BEYOND COMPARISON!"
OH, ARE YOU PLAY WRITING?
OF LATE, I'VE BEEN MORE, HOW SHALL I PUT IT...? BEHIND THE SCENES.
DOES YOUR FRIEND TALK ABOUT ANYTHING BESIDES FOOD OR HIMSELF?
CUH! THE YOUNG OF TODAY HAIN'T GOT NO MANNERS IS WHAT IT IS!
OI!
CODGER!
AND 'ERE'S ONE THAT PROVES MY POINT! IT'S "MR. COLE," YOU HIMPUDENT CHILD!
I DO BEG YOUR PARDON, "MR. COLE"! A QUIET WORD IN YOUR EAR, IF YOU PLEASE?
TUT! TUT! TUT! WHISPERING! HOW AWFULLY RUDE!
BOWL'S IN A SAFE IN UNWRIGHT'S STUDY, LORD MUCK SAID YOU'D KNOW WHAT TO DO!
DO HEXCUSE US, M'LADY, A MATTER OF HIMPORT HAS COME UP AND I MUST DASH!
SNORT
"HEXCUSE"!
FOLLER ME!
I'VE BIN 'ERE BEFORE, THERE'S A LESS CONSPICKULOUS ROUTE TO THE STUDY UP THE BACK STAIRS.
AFTER YOU, SIR, "MR. COLE," SIR!
WHO WAS THAT BOY? DO YOU KNOW HIM?
I HAVE NO IDEA WHO HE IS. I DON'T KNOW WHO ANYBODY HERE IS!
WHAT DID HE WANT?
WHAT DID IT LOOK LIKE?
A DANCE!
WELL, I DIDN'T LIKE THE MALODOROUS OIK... YOU ARE NOT TO DANCE WITH HIM AGAIN!

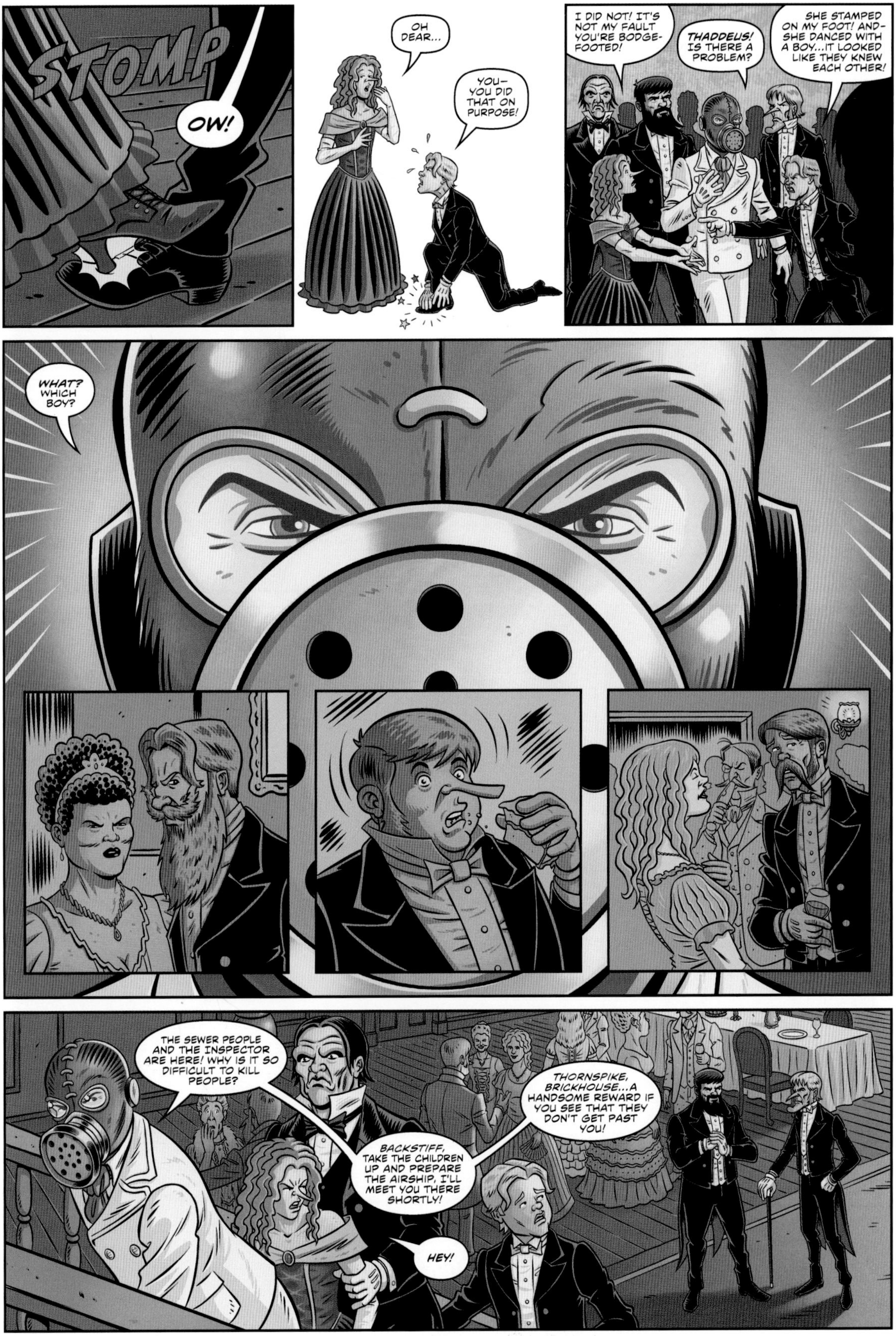
STOMP
OW!
OH DEAR...
YOU— YOU DID THAT ON PURPOSE!
I DID NOT! IT'S NOT MY FAULT YOU'RE BODGE-FOOTED!
THADDEUS! IS THERE A PROBLEM?
SHE STAMPED ON MY FOOT! AND– SHE DANCED WITH A BOY...IT LOOKED LIKE THEY KNEW EACH OTHER!
WHAT? WHICH BOY?
THE SEWER PEOPLE AND THE INSPECTOR ARE HERE! WHY IS IT SO DIFFICULT TO KILL PEOPLE?
THORNSPIKE, BRICKHOUSE...A HANDSOME REWARD IF YOU SEE THAT THEY DON'T GET PAST YOU!
BACKSTIFF, TAKE THE CHILDREN UP AND PREPARE THE AIRSHIP, I'LL MEET YOU THERE SHORTLY!
HEY!

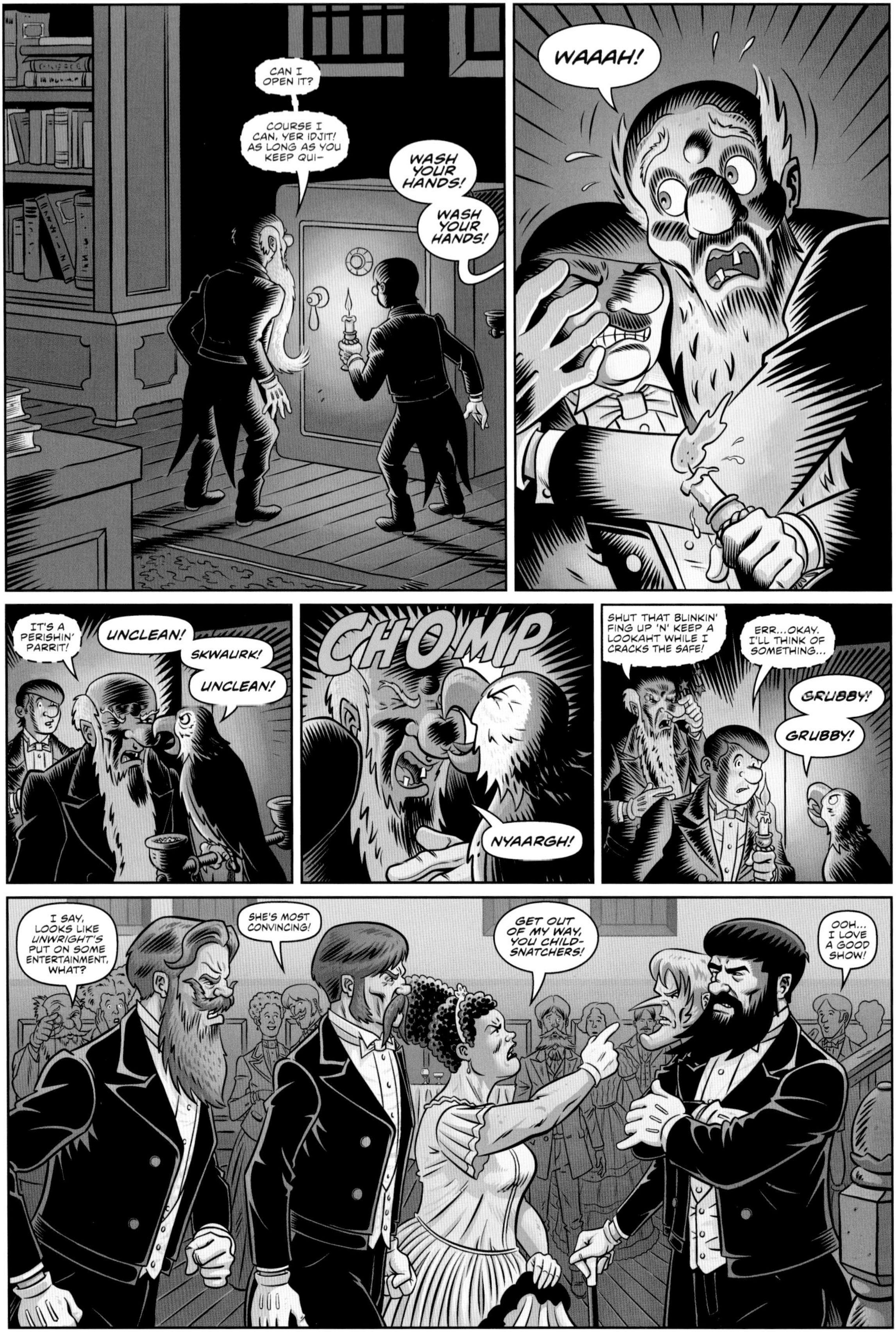

CAN I OPEN IT?
COURSE I CAN, YER IDJIT! AS LONG AS YOU KEEP QUI–
WASH YOUR HANDS!
WASH YOUR HANDS!
WAAAH!
IT'S A PERISHIN' PARRIT!
UNCLEAN!
SKWAURK!
UNCLEAN!
CHOMP
NYAARGH!
SHUT THAT BLINKIN' FING UP 'N' KEEP A LOOKAHT WHILE I CRACKS THE SAFE!
ERR...OKAY. I'LL THINK OF SOMETHING...
GRUBBY!
GRUBBY!
I SAY, LOOKS LIKE UNWRIGHT'S PUT ON SOME ENTERTAINMENT, WHAT?
SHE'S MOST CONVINCING!
GET OUT OF MY WAY, YOU CHILD-SNATCHERS!
OOH... I LOVE A GOOD SHOW!

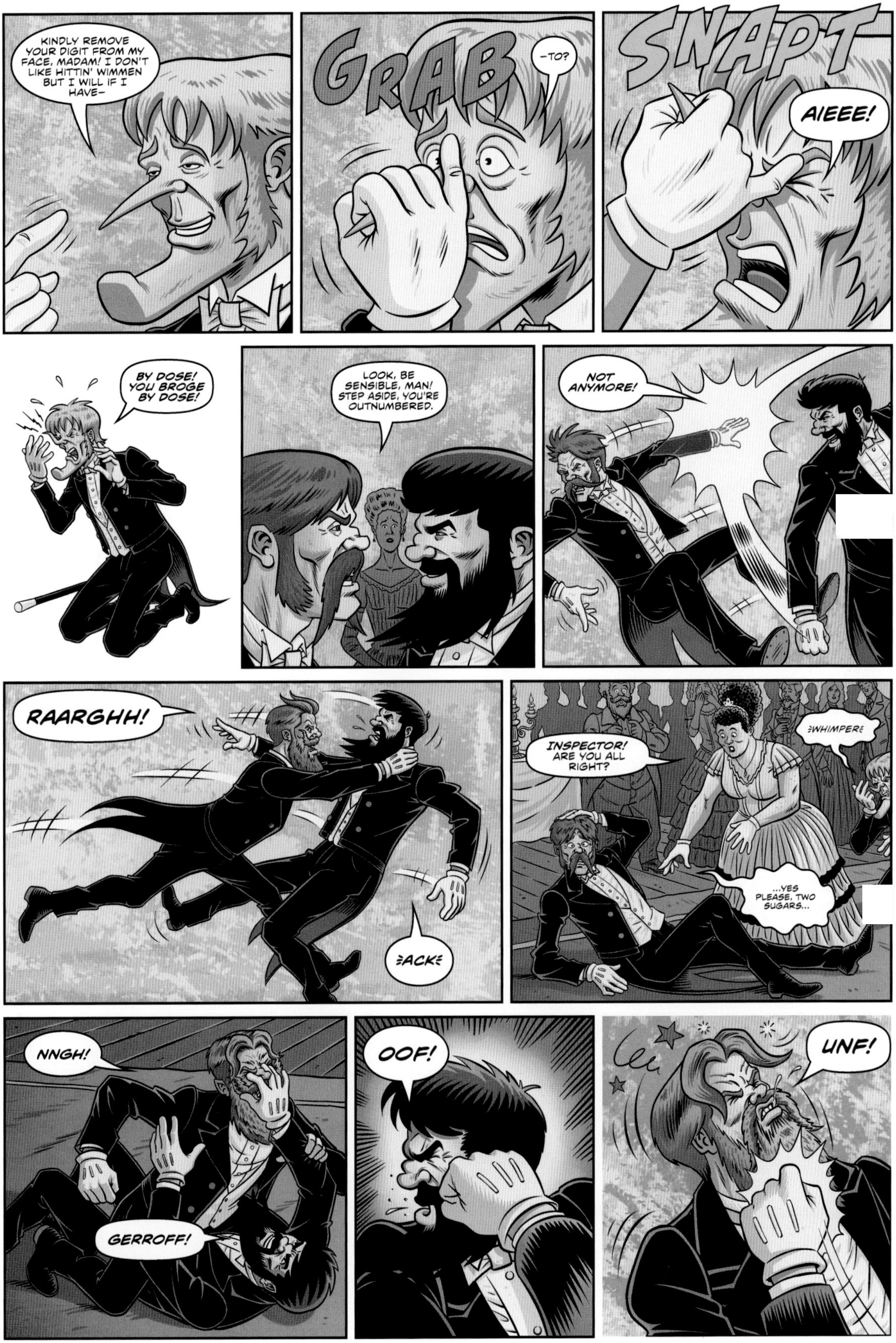
KINDLY REMOVE YOUR DIGIT FROM MY FACE, MADAM! I DON'T LIKE HITTIN' WIMMEN BUT I WILL IF I HAVE–
GRAB
–TO?
SNAPT
AIEEE!
BY DOSE! YOU BROGE BY DOSE!
LOOK, BE SENSIBLE, MAN! STEP ASIDE, YOU'RE OUTNUMBERED.
NOT ANYMORE!
RAARGHH!
ACK
INSPECTOR! ARE YOU ALL RIGHT?
WHIMPER
...YES PLEASE, TWO SUGARS...
NNGH!
GERROFF!
OOF!
UNF!

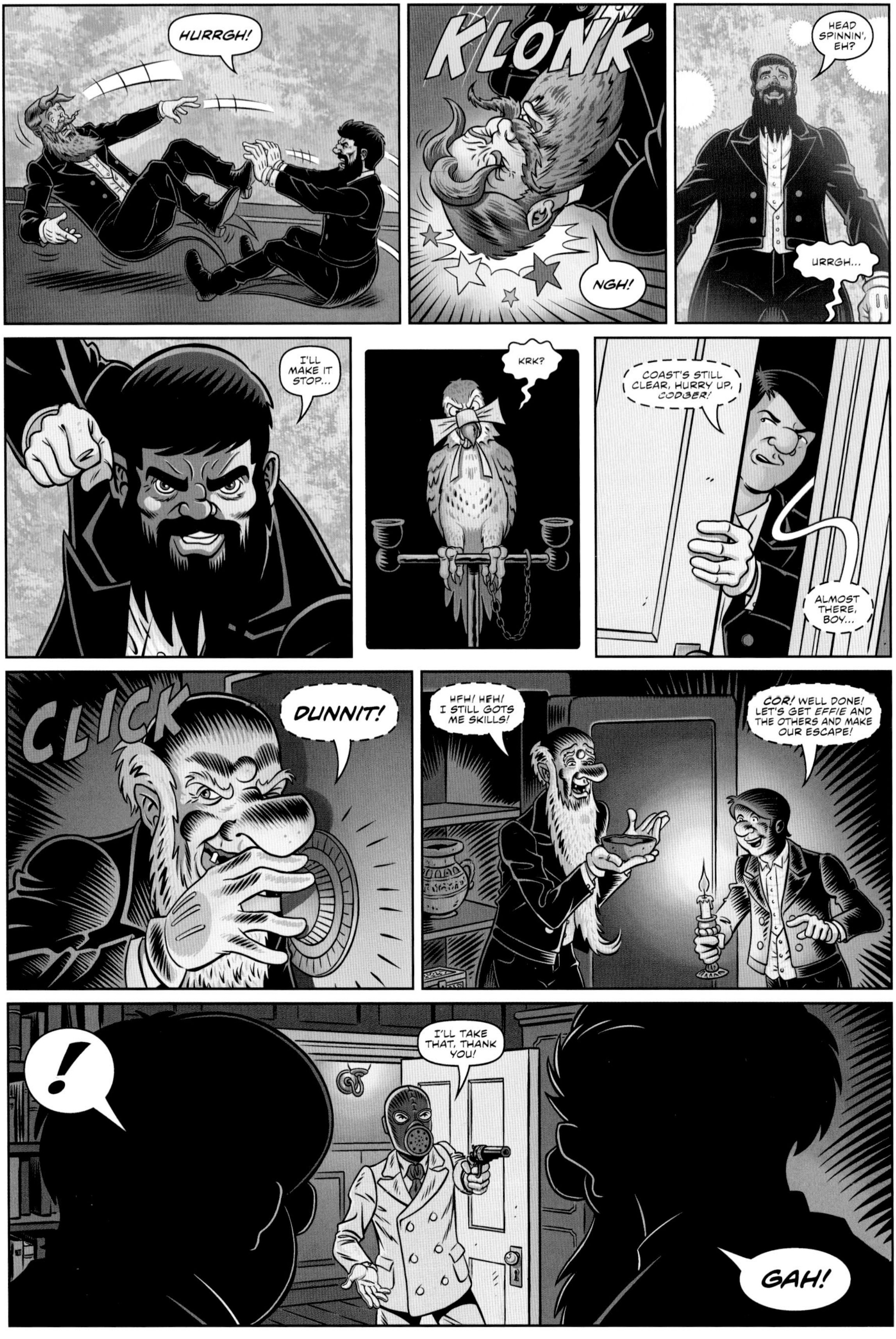
HURRGH!
KLONK
NGH!
HEAD SPINNIN', EH?
URRGH...
I'LL MAKE IT STOP...
KRK?
COAST'S STILL CLEAR, HURRY UP, CODGER!
ALMOST THERE, BOY...
CLICK
DUNNIT!
HEH! HEH! I STILL GOTS ME SKILLS!
COR! WELL DONE! LET'S GET EFFIE AND THE OTHERS AND MAKE OUR ESCAPE!
!
I'LL TAKE THAT, THANK YOU!
GAH!

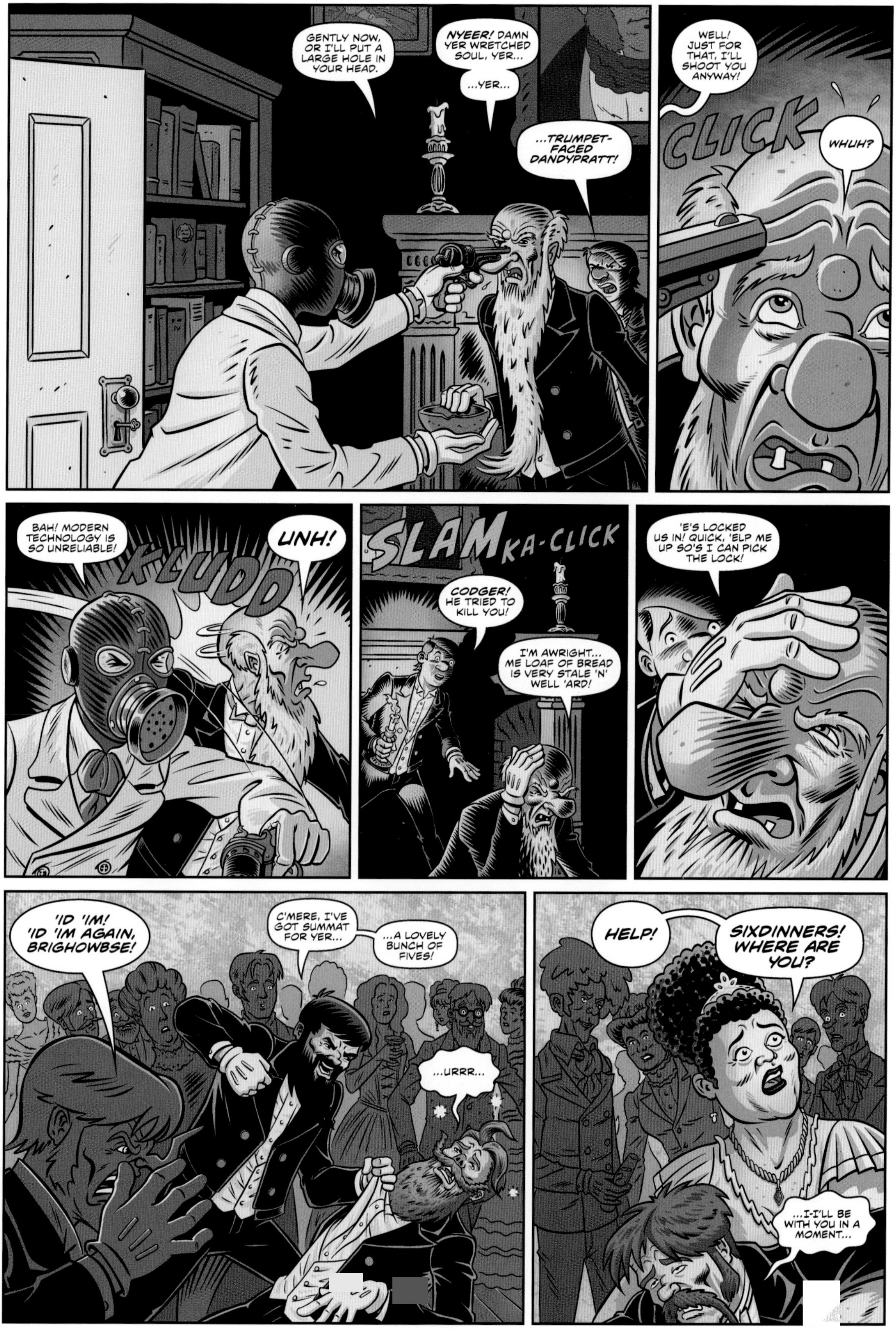
GENTLY NOW, OR I'LL PUT A LARGE HOLE IN YOUR HEAD.
NYEER! DAMN YER WRETCHED SOUL, YER...
...YER...
...TRUMPET-FACED DANDYPRATT!
WELL! JUST FOR THAT, I'LL SHOOT YOU ANYWAY!
CLICK
WHUH?
BAH! MODERN TECHNOLOGY IS SO UNRELIABLE!
KLUDD
UNH!
SLAM
KA-CLICK
CODGER! HE TRIED TO KILL YOU!
I'M AWRIGHT... ME LOAF OF BREAD IS VERY STALE 'N' WELL 'ARD!
'E'S LOCKED US IN! QUICK, 'ELP ME UP SO'S I CAN PICK THE LOCK!
'ID 'IM! 'ID 'IM AGAIN, BRIGHOWBSE!
C'MERE, I'VE GOT SUMMAT FOR YER...
...A LOVELY BUNCH OF FIVES!
...URRR...
HELP!
SIXDINNERS! WHERE ARE YOU?
...I-I'LL BE WITH YOU IN A MOMENT...

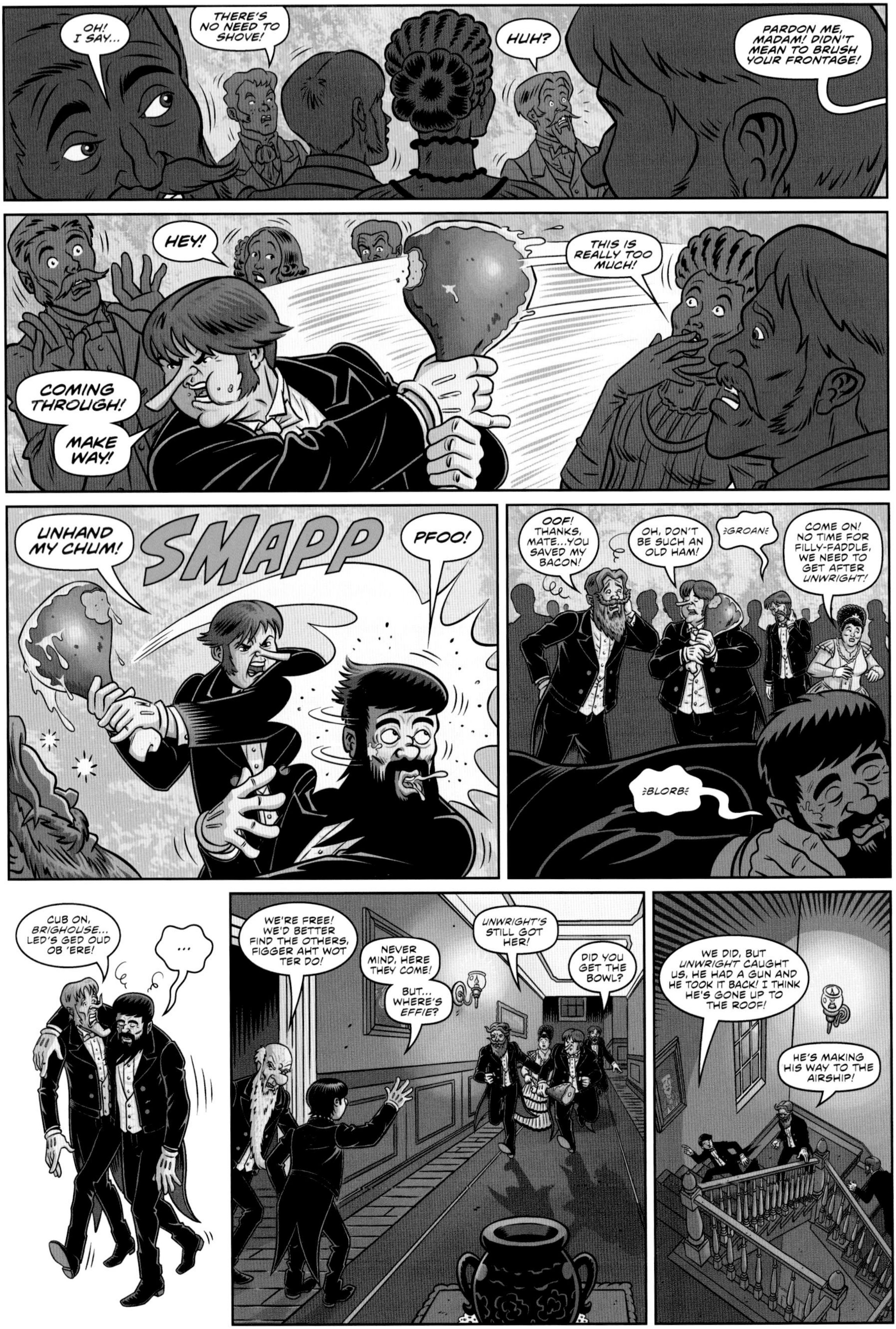
OH! I SAY...
THERE'S NO NEED TO SHOVE!
HUH?
PARDON ME, MADAM! DIDN'T MEAN TO BRUSH YOUR FRONTAGE!
HEY!
THIS IS REALLY TOO MUCH!
COMING THROUGH!
MAKE WAY!
UNHAND MY CHUM!
SMAPP
PFOO!
OOF! THANKS, MATE...YOU SAVED MY BACON!
OH, DON'T BE SUCH AN OLD HAM!
GROAN
COME ON! NO TIME FOR FILLY-FADDLE, WE NEED TO GET AFTER UNWRIGHT!
BLORB
CUB ON, BRIGHOUSE... LED'S GED OUD OB 'ERE!
...
WE'RE FREE! WE'D BETTER FIND THE OTHERS, FIGGER AHT WOT TER DO!
NEVER MIND, HERE THEY COME!
BUT... WHERE'S EFFIE?
UNWRIGHT'S STILL GOT HER!
DID YOU GET THE BOWL?
WE DID, BUT UNWRIGHT CAUGHT US, HE HAD A GUN AND HE TOOK IT BACK! I THINK HE'S GONE UP TO THE ROOF!
HE'S MAKING HIS WAY TO THE AIRSHIP!

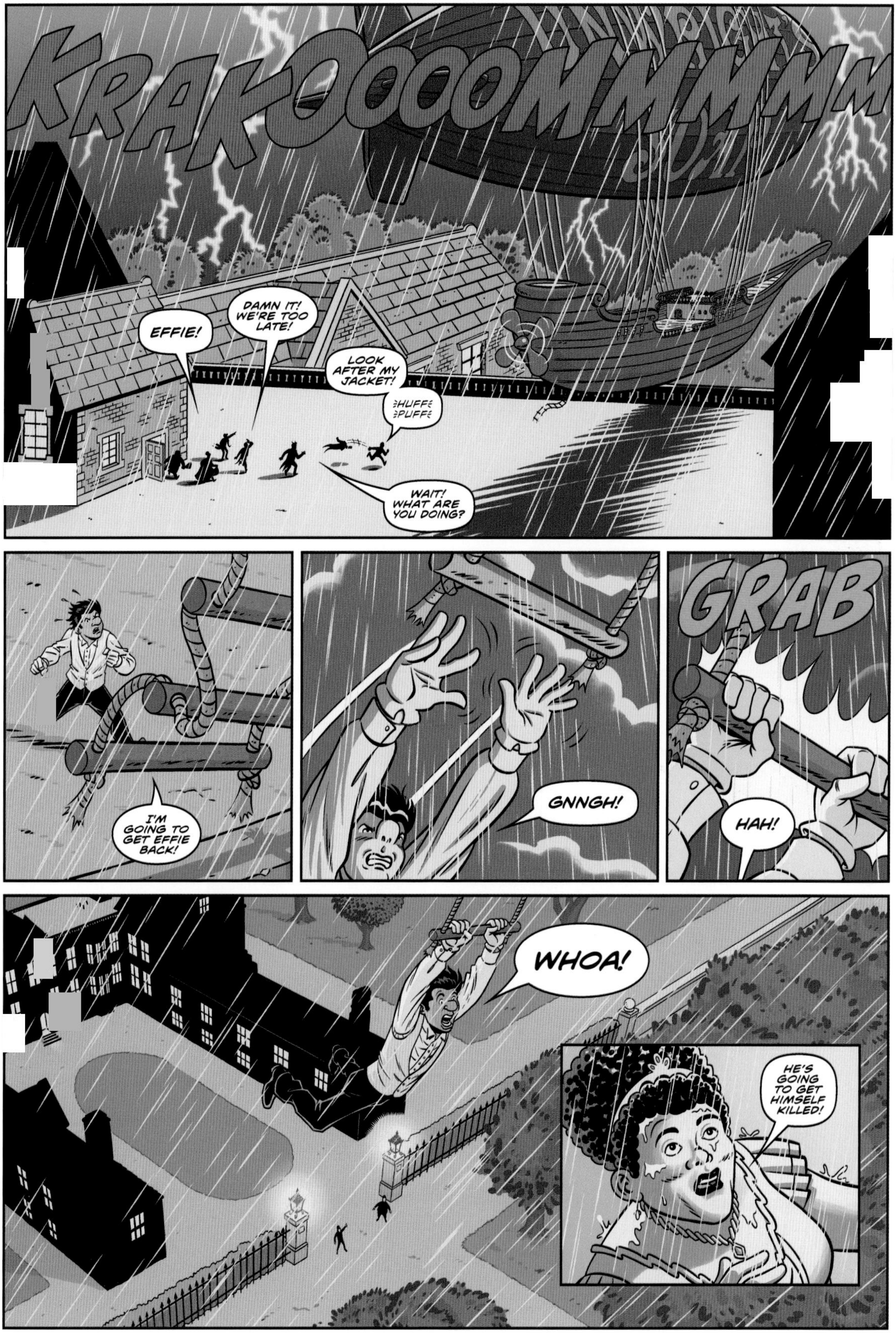
KRAKOOOOMMMMMM
EFFIE!
DAMN IT! WE'RE TOO LATE!
LOOK AFTER MY JACKET!
HUFF PUFF
WAIT! WHAT ARE YOU DOING?
I'M GOING TO GET EFFIE BACK!
GNNGH!
GRAB
HAH!
WHOA!
HE'S GOING TO GET HIMSELF KILLED!

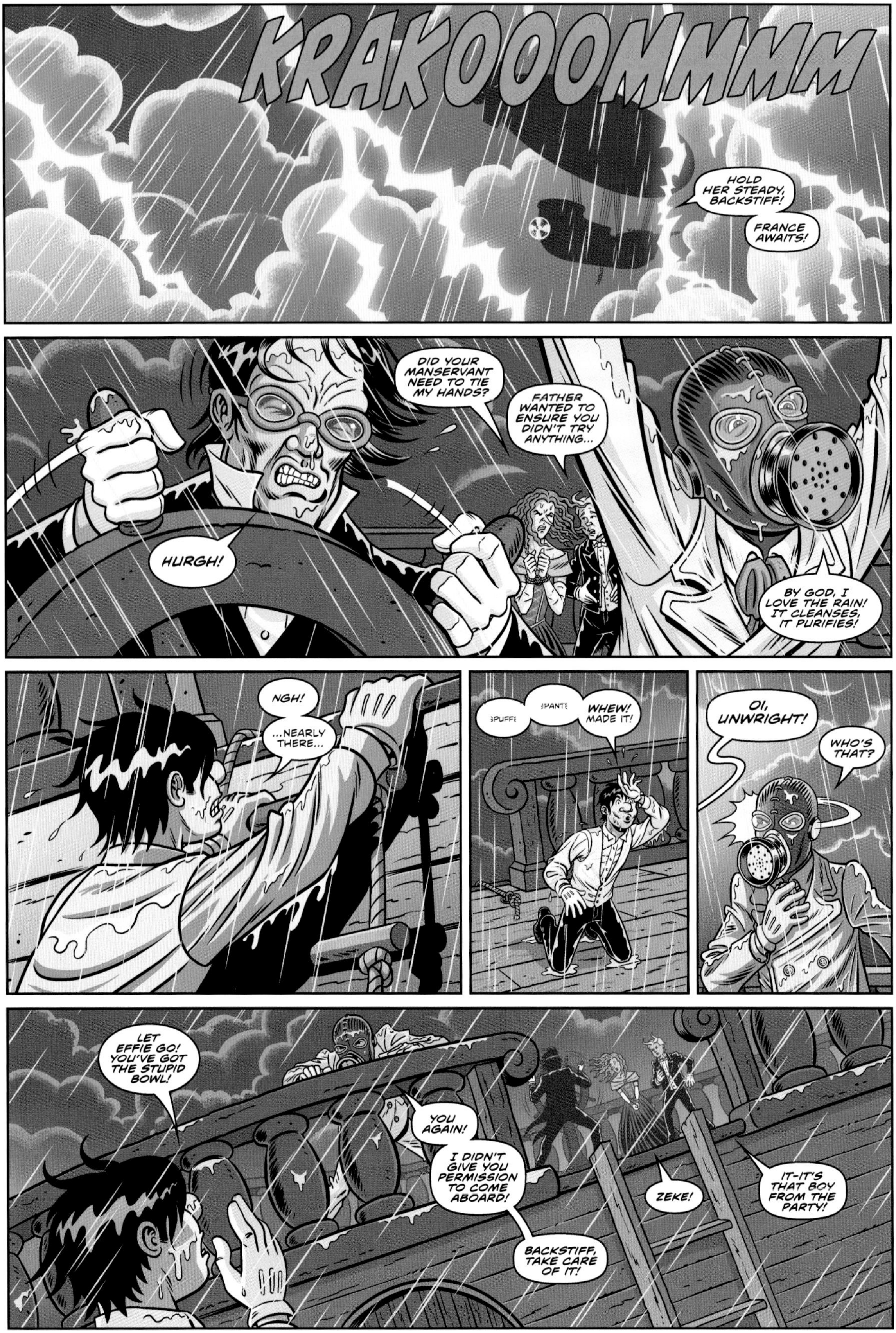
KRAKOOOMMMMM
HOLD HER STEADY, BACKSTIFF!
FRANCE AWAITS!
DID YOUR MANSERVANT NEED TO TIE MY HANDS?
FATHER WANTED TO ENSURE YOU DIDN'T TRY ANYTHING...
HURGH!
BY GOD, I LOVE THE RAIN! IT CLEANSES, IT PURIFIES!
NGH!
...NEARLY THERE...
PUFF
PANT
WHEW! MADE IT!
OI, UNWRIGHT!
WHO'S THAT?
LET EFFIE GO! YOU'VE GOT THE STUPID BOWL!
YOU AGAIN!
I DIDN'T GIVE YOU PERMISSION TO COME ABOARD!
BACKSTIFF, TAKE CARE OF IT!
ZEKE!
IT-IT'S THAT BOY FROM THE PARTY!

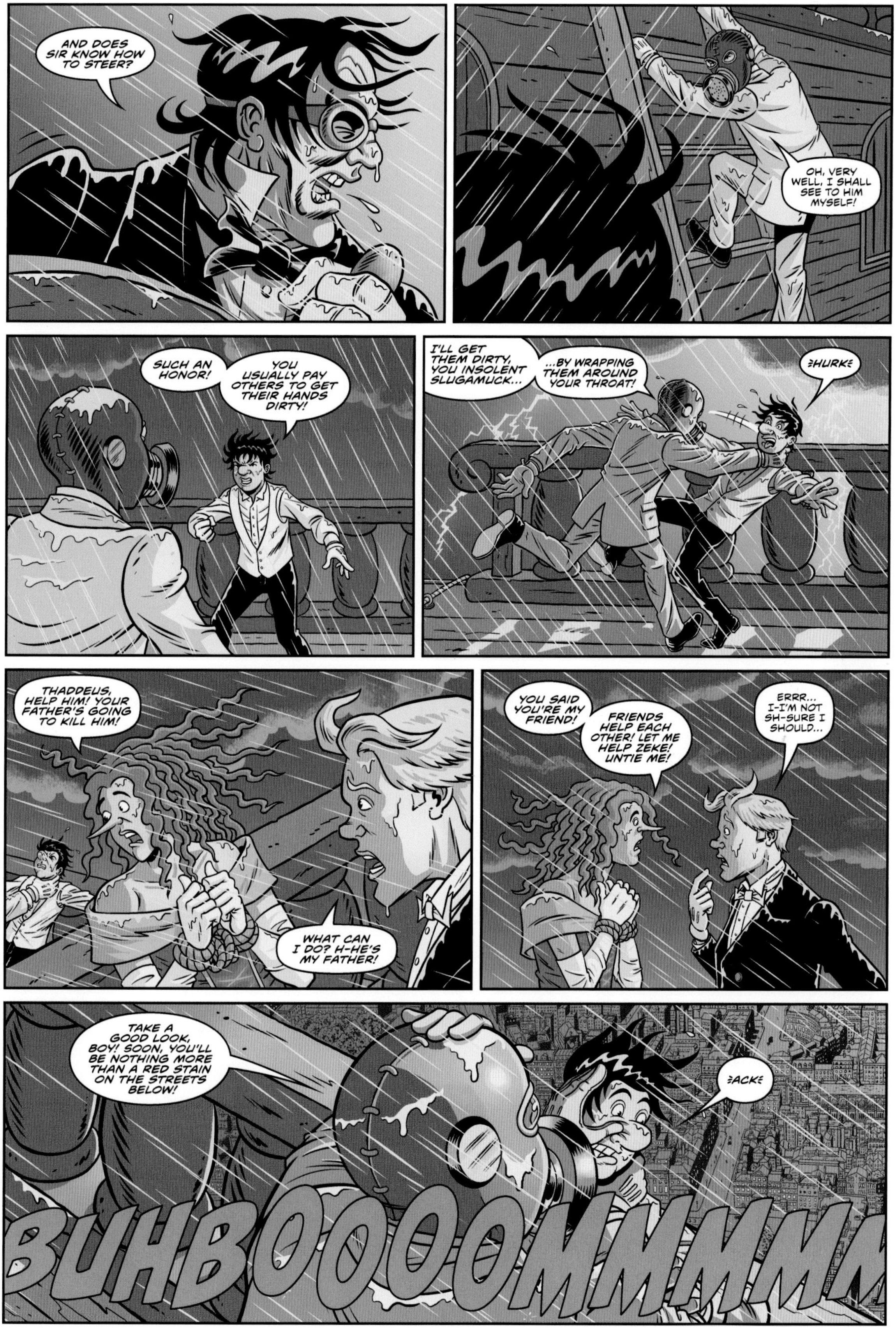
AND DOES SIR KNOW HOW TO STEER?
OH, VERY WELL, I SHALL SEE TO HIM MYSELF!
SUCH AN HONOR!
YOU USUALLY PAY OTHERS TO GET THEIR HANDS DIRTY!
I'LL GET THEM DIRTY, YOU INSOLENT SLUGAMUCK...
...BY WRAPPING THEM AROUND YOUR THROAT!
HURK
THADDEUS, HELP HIM! YOUR FATHER'S GOING TO KILL HIM!
WHAT CAN I DO? H-HE'S MY FATHER!
YOU SAID YOU'RE MY FRIEND!
FRIENDS HELP EACH OTHER! LET ME HELP ZEKE! UNTIE ME!
ERRR... I-I'M NOT SH-SURE I SHOULD...
TAKE A GOOD LOOK, BOY! SOON, YOU'LL BE NOTHING MORE THAN A RED STAIN ON THE STREETS BELOW!
ACK
BUHBOOOOOMMMMM

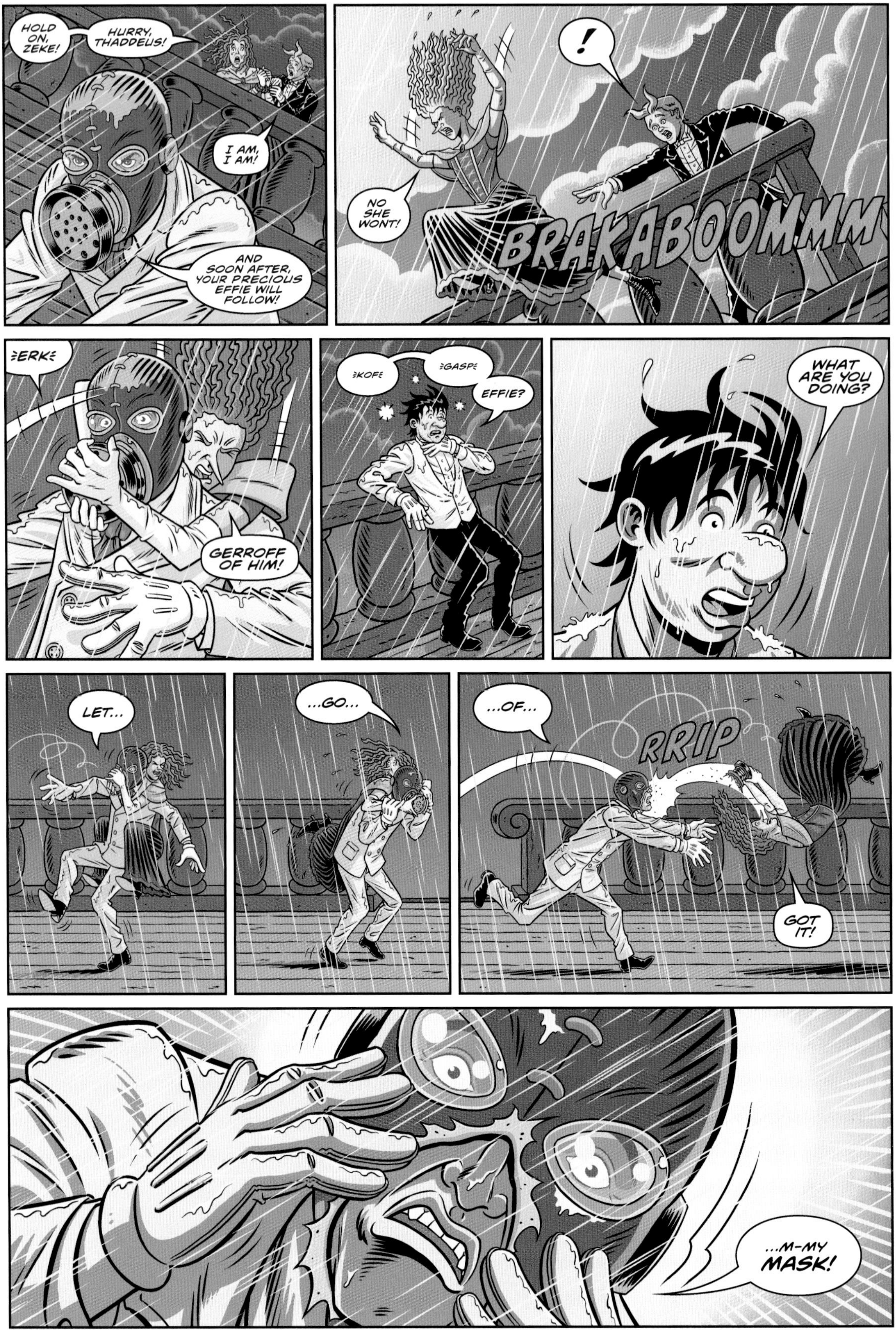
HOLD ON, ZEKE!
HURRY, THADDEUS!
I AM, I AM!
AND SOON AFTER, YOUR PRECIOUS EFFIE WILL FOLLOW!
!
NO SHE WONT!
BRAKABOOMMM
ERK
GERROFF OF HIM!
KOF
GASP
EFFIE?
WHAT ARE YOU DOING?
LET...
...GO...
...OF...
RRIP
GOT IT!
...M-MY MASK!

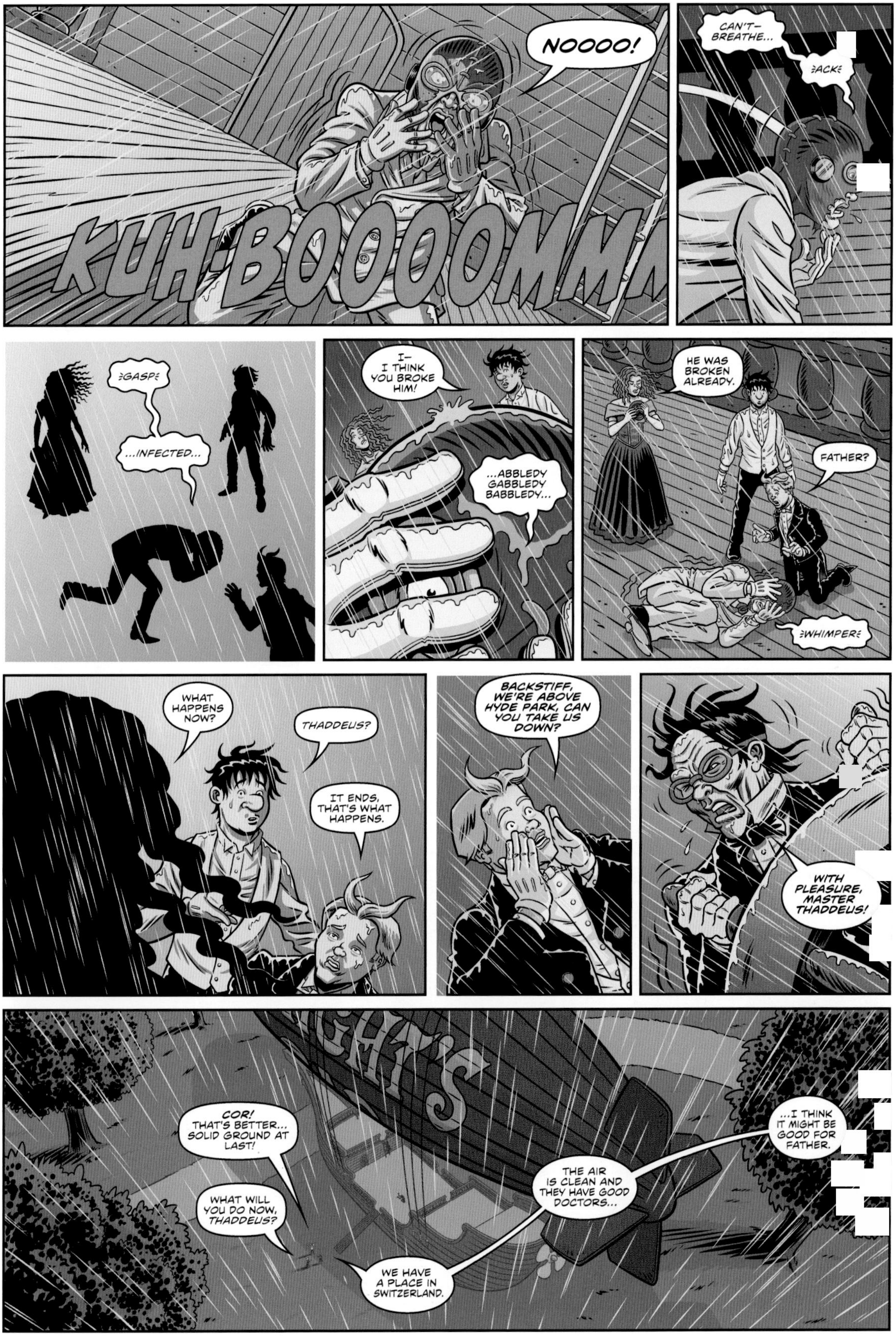
NOOOO!
KUH-BOOOOMM
CAN'T-BREATHE...
ACK
GASP
...INFECTED...
I— I THINK YOU BROKE HIM!
...ABBLEDY GABBLEDY BABBLEDY...
HE WAS BROKEN ALREADY.
FATHER?
WHIMPER
WHAT HAPPENS NOW?
THADDEUS?
IT ENDS, THAT'S WHAT HAPPENS.
BACKSTIFF, WE'RE ABOVE HYDE PARK, CAN YOU TAKE US DOWN?
WITH PLEASURE, MASTER THADDEUS!
COR! THAT'S BETTER... SOLID GROUND AT LAST!
WHAT WILL YOU DO NOW, THADDEUS?
WE HAVE A PLACE IN SWITZERLAND.
THE AIR IS CLEAN AND THEY HAVE GOOD DOCTORS...
...I THINK IT MIGHT BE GOOD FOR FATHER.

I'M DEEPLY SORRY FOR ALL THE TROUBLE YOU'VE HAD. PLEASE TAKE THIS CURSED BOWL AND RETURN IT TO THE APPROPRIATE AUTHORITIES.

OOH! THIS'LL PUT A SMILE ON THE INSPECTOR'S MUG!

AND KEEP THE OTHERS OUT OF PRISON!

FAREWELL, THADDEUS!

THANK YOU FOR HELPING US. I KNOW IT MUST'VE BEEN DIFFICULT.

ERR...YES ...WELL....UM... THE LEAST I COULD DO...

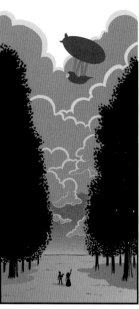

COME ON! YOUR MOTHER AND FATHER WILL BE GOING OUT OF THEIR MINDS!

DO YOU THINK WE'LL EVER SEE THADDEUS AGAIN?

WOT? YOU MISSING YOUR BOYFRIEND ALREADY?

HAH, HAH—

OW!

BIFF

SHUT UP!

≡SIGH≡ IT'S GOING TO BE A LONG WALK BACK.

WELL... AT LEAST THE RAIN'S STOPPED!

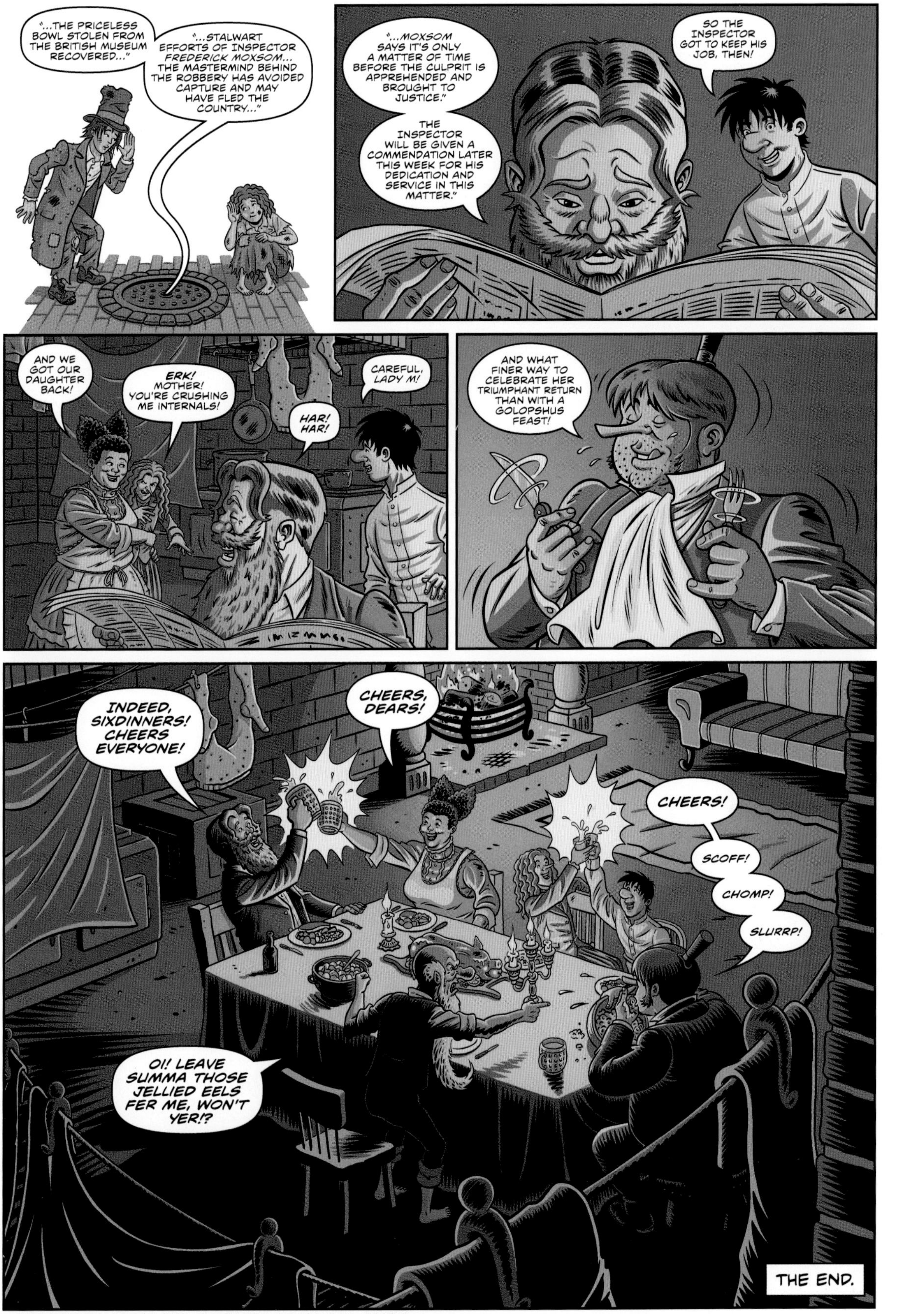
"...THE PRICELESS BOWL STOLEN FROM THE BRITISH MUSEUM RECOVERED..."
"...STALWART EFFORTS OF INSPECTOR FREDERICK MOXSOM... THE MASTERMIND BEHIND THE ROBBERY HAS AVOIDED CAPTURE AND MAY HAVE FLED THE COUNTRY..."
"...MOXSOM SAYS IT'S ONLY A MATTER OF TIME BEFORE THE CULPRIT IS APPREHENDED AND BROUGHT TO JUSTICE."
THE INSPECTOR WILL BE GIVEN A COMMENDATION LATER THIS WEEK FOR HIS DEDICATION AND SERVICE IN THIS MATTER."
SO THE INSPECTOR GOT TO KEEP HIS JOB, THEN!
AND WE GOT OUR DAUGHTER BACK!
ERK! MOTHER! YOU'RE CRUSHING ME INTERNALS!
HAR! HAR!
CAREFUL, LADY M!
AND WHAT FINER WAY TO CELEBRATE HER TRIUMPHANT RETURN THAN WITH A GOLOPSHUS FEAST!
INDEED, SIXDINNERS! CHEERS EVERYONE!
CHEERS, DEARS!
CHEERS!
SCOFF!
CHOMP!
SLURRP!
OI! LEAVE SUMMA THOSE JELLIED EELS FER ME, WON'T YER!?
THE END.

DEDICATED TO *SARAH* AND IN MEMORY OF MY MUM, *ISABEL*.

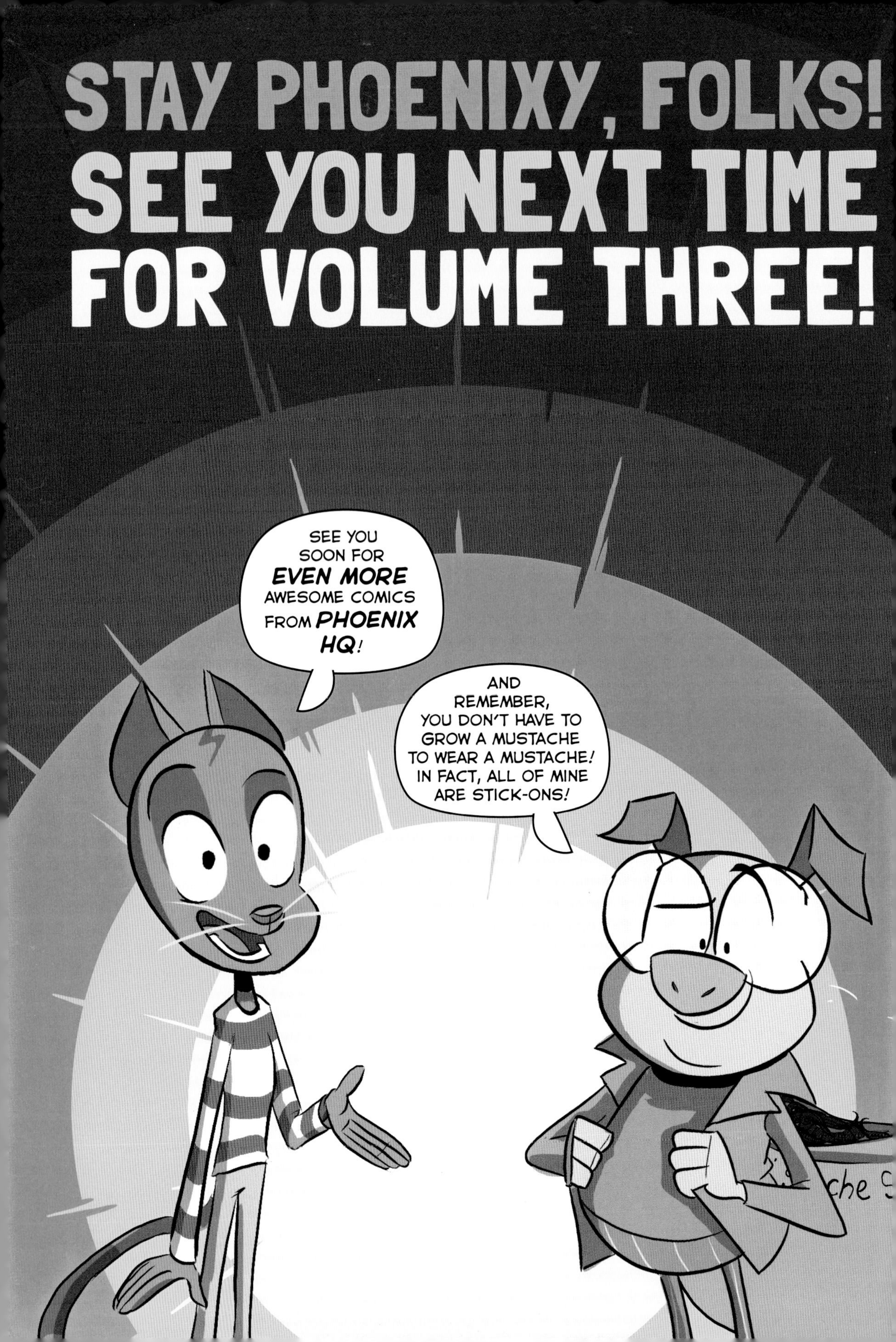
STAY PHOENIXY, FOLKS!
SEE YOU NEXT TIME FOR VOLUME THREE!
SEE YOU SOON FOR EVEN MORE AWESOME COMICS FROM PHOENIX HQ!
AND REMEMBER, YOU DON'T HAVE TO GROW A MUSTACHE TO WEAR A MUSTACHE! IN FACT, ALL OF MINE ARE STICK-ONS!

Squid Bits!

They're tentacool!

EVERY DELICIOUS BOX OF **SQUID BITS** **INCLUDES** ALL THIS AND MORE...

☆ ☆ Spot the Difference! ☆ ☆

What am I meant to do with these?!

Hot bread!

Happy Birthday!

Can you spot 6 differences between these 2 pictures? Look carefully!

In the OLDEN DAYS...

Achoo!

Very few things were in color.

Yo!

Boogers!

I keep my favorite smells in jars. This guy is pickled eggs.

The Reign of the Snowman

I am ALIVE! My evil reign can finally begin!

I will build a snowman army to crush the WORLD!

Um, maybe a small army and a few ice torpedoes?

A handful of snowballs, maybe?

Sniff

Ooh, don't you dare!

The Rather Odd Alphabet

b is for boorish babirusa

BURP!

Guff!

ptoo!

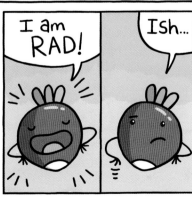

I am RAD!

Ish...

by Jess Bradley

WHO MADE THESE

FAZ CHOUDHURY

has been an illustrator and comic book creator for over 25 years. He's worked for various clients, including Panini, Dennis Publishing, Eaglemoss, Scholastic, and The Phoenix. He has also been known to make facial hair pieces for TV, film, and theater.

JESS BRADLEY

is an illustrator and designer of cute, colorful, and quirky characters. Her clients include The Phoenix, Capstone Publishing, Igloo Books, Genki Gear, UK Greetings, and Carlton Books. She enjoys drawing, video games, and drinking too much tea.

JAMIE SMART

has created colorful comics that have delighted children for over 20 years in the pages of publications such as *The Dandy*, *The Beano*, *The Phoenix*, and many more. He also creates children's books, including books for his ongoing multimedia project *Find Chaffy*.

All the comics in this book originally appeared in the pages of THE PHOENIX comic, a weekly paper magazine published by a small a team in Oxford, England. Additional illustrations by Lee Robinson.

AWESOME COMICS?

BENEDICT AND DOMINIKA TOMCZYK-BOWEN

are a cartooning couple from London. Ben is an animator who has worked with CBeebies, Aardman, Nickelodeon, Disney, and others. Dom is a professional wig maker and painter, with a flair for coloring cartoons. By combining their powers they create brilliant comics like *Daniel Crisp*!

JAMES TURNER

is a cartoonist, mathematician, and programmer from London, and his comic, *Star Cat*, won the Best Young People's Comic in the British Comic Awards. When not drawing comics, James enjoys board games, cooking, and making explosion noises with his mouth.

NEILL CAMERON

is the creator of a vast array of books, including *The Pirates of Pangaea* (with Daniel Hartwell), *Tamsin and the Deep* (with Kate Brown), and *How to Make Awesome Comics*. Neill also hosts workshops across the United Kingdom and is an advocate for children's literacy and creativity.

To find out more about THE PHOENIX comic, and maybe start reading it every week, visit our website: www.thephoenixcomic.co.uk

THIS BOOK WAS BROUGHT TO YOU BY

Squid Bits!

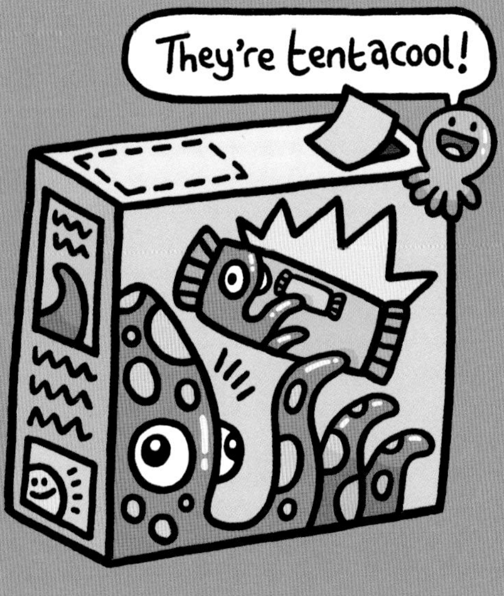
They're tentacool!